JONAS looked down into her face and his bright hazel eyes held her gaze. "Anita," he said. "Anita, we must…"

"Don't say anything more." She raised her face to his as he leaned down to kiss her with a swift, terrible hunger. As the feel and scent of him overcame her, she felt the core of herself turn to fire.

When his mouth released hers, Anita was still too overwhelmed to say a word. Her arms were tight around him when she heard him say, "You're afraid of me."

There was no coldness on his face, only tenderness and excitement, and she realized that his powerful emotions were affecting the way he spoke.

"Oh, no. No. Not afraid of you." The feeling was so overwhelming, so foreign, she didn't know how to express it. "Of this," she said finally in a shaken voice.

"This?" he questioned softly, and kissed her again.

Fawcett Gold Medal Books
by Vivian Lord:

☐ ONCE MORE THE SUN   14460 $3.50

☐ TRAITOR IN MY ARMS   14130 $2.95

☐ THE VOYAGERS   14358 $2.75

Buy them at your local bookstore or use this handy coupon for ordering.

COLUMBIA BOOK SERVICE, CBS Inc.
32275 Mally Road, P.O. Box FB, Madison Heights, MI 48071

Please send me the books I have checked above. Orders for less than 5 books must include 75¢ for the first book and 25¢ for each additional book to cover postage and handling. Orders for 5 books or more postage is FREE. Send check or money order only. Allow 3–4 weeks for delivery.

Cost $_____	Name _____
Sales tax*_____	Address _____
Postage_____	City _____
Total $_____	State_____ Zip _____

The government requires us to collect sales tax in all states except AK, DE, MT, NH and OR.
Prices and availability subject to change without notice.   **8999**

ONCE MORE THE SUN

a novel by

Vivian Lord

FAWCETT GOLD MEDAL • NEW YORK

ACKNOWLEDGMENTS

With thanks to Bob Strother and William Albert Anderson for their help and technical advice.

ONCE MORE THE SUN

Published by Fawcett Gold Medal Books, CBS Educational and Professional Publishing, a division of CBS Inc.

ISBN: 0-449-14460-7

Printed in the United States of America

First Fawcett Gold Medal printing: April 1982

10 9 8 7 6 5 4 3 2 1

Part I

FOUNDATION

Chapter 1

A DOZEN NARROW pleasure boats, gliding on the light-bordered lake, moved among inverted towers, great domed shapes and slender monuments reflected in the rippling night water. Most of the gondolas had several occupants: women scarved and shawled against the sharp air, because a chilly spring haze still clung to May, and men in bowler hats standing fore and aft to pole the boats along.

Of all the people on the lake, only one seemed to belong to the city of temples and palazzos surrounding them. And she was the one admiring it least. Something in her manner suggested she was used to a special place, that she would not be willingly found among the crowds lining the esplanades around the canal. The others were suited to their place and time; this woman's dress and hair might have originated in ancient Greece or next year's Paris. She occupied a swan-prowed boat with only two other passengers—an elegant young man serving as their gondolier and a correct older woman sitting stiffly opposite. As the man poled their gondola into the path of bright electric lights, the three could be seen quite clearly by the people on the esplanade.

The younger woman's hair, so black the light made paths of silver on it, was drawn up in a glistening chignon; the soft hair around her face was feathered short and made a petaled frame for her striking features. She wore no wrap, indifferent to the cool air; her pleated chiffon dress was like that of an actress in a classical drama. It was one of the new "artistic" dresses worn by more daring women in 1893. Crossed ribbons of phosphorescent blue, like a dragonfly's wings, formed a modest V at the throat and outlined her firm young breasts in an emphatic way. The dress flared away from under her breasts, and when she moved her arms or body, she moved in a graceful billowing. She shone in the misty night with no other ornament than her dress and hair. But the feature that was most dazzling was the woman's eyes: under black winged brows and set off by long, sooty lashes, the eyes were a startling bright blue, blue as fire or an Italian lake under noon sun. The expression in them was wary at the moment and her eyes had the look of someone who hid strong feelings habitually under a calm exterior. She did not say much to her companions but gazed absently around the artificial canal.

When the gondola drew near the esplanade, the young woman looked idly at the people standing at the top of the stairs. Then she noticed, a little apart from the others, two young men about her own age. One looked very much like Harry Brand, her escort. But the other was totally different: he was tall and lean and carelessly dressed, and his mane of light-brown hair fell over one of his brows. He was staring out over the water, and the electric lamps revealed direct, piercing eyes. Suddenly he focused on the swan-prowed boat and stared into the dazzling blue eyes of the young woman. Involuntarily she shivered.

"I told you that outlandish dress wasn't warm enough." The crisp voice of the older woman broke in on the younger woman's reflections.

"Shall we go in, Miss Byrne?" their escort asked, raising his voice to make himself heard over the plashing water, the murmur of voices on the landing and the music from the Midway farther on.

Charlotte Byrne said decisively, "Not yet, Harry. I'm certainly warm enough. It's time my niece learned some common sense, through experience." She glanced with reproach at Anita Byrne's unconventional dress, and drew her own wrap snugly about herself. Charlotte was a handsome, austere woman in her forties, and her tight, constricting dress with its high neckline and wide cuffs, her small, precise hat of moderate plumes, were perfectly suited to her meticulous looks. "*Are* you too cool, Anita?" she inquired then, as if a little ashamed of her fractious comment a moment before. "If so, then we shall go in."

"I am not cold at all," Anita said in a low, husky voice that was surprising in such a slender, fragile-looking woman. She was still studying the man on the esplanade.

"Good," Miss Byrne said crisply. "I wouldn't have missed

9

this for the world, particularly after Roderick forbade us to attend the opening. He and his colleagues did a splendid job."

Anita's father, Roderick Byrne, was one of the team of architects who had designed and built the "White City" for Chicago's Columbian Exposition of 1893, which had opened today. The Exposition was one of the most significant events of the century: important figures in the arts, sciences and social studies gathered to trade ideas in a series of congresses.

"What a pity," Anita's aunt said, "that we had to miss the President, and the duke and duchess. Don't you think it was absolutely wicked of my brother to forbid us to come?"

"Not at all, Miss Byrne. I'm afraid I agree with him," Harry answered in his careful speech. "Why, there were six hundred and twenty thousand people here, I heard. They actually hit each other with umbrellas and lunch boxes to get near the President. The troops had to be called in, and a lot of ladies fainted. You couldn't even hear the speeches."

"Well, I suppose you're right, my dear boy," Miss Byrne admitted with regret. "In any case," she added, "you're very kind to escort us, when there are so many livelier distractions for young men on the Midway."

Harry's ears turned red: the Byrnes were very plainspoken. He knew she was referring to the shocking dance of Little Egypt and like entertainments that rubbed shoulders with the more sedate exhibits—the Women's Building, and great works of art from all over the world.

The famous Frederick Law Olmsted had designed the Exposition grounds; tens of thousands of people were able to move about freely at the same time. But the architecture, a mélange of Venice and Rome, Athens and Vienna, was the most controversial aspect of the Exposition. Some laughed at the pretentious White City with its classical buildings; the exteriors of these temporary structures were a mixture of plaster and straw.

"It's a monstrosity," Anita said abruptly. When her aunt reacted with a horrified look, Anita added, "Well, it is, Aunt Charlotte. This is the architecture of the East, an imitation of the past. These buildings are tombs for dead civilizations."

"I hope you haven't said such things to your father," Charlotte commented; her neat lips shut in a tight line after she spoke. Harry Brand, their gondolier, neither turned nor said a word, but his stance expressed his deep embarrassment to hear Anita criticize the work of her father, one of the most prominent architects in Chicago.

10

"I suppose you learned these things from those...plumbers at that dreadful school," said Charlotte Byrne. She was trembling with indignation and also from the knowledge that she should not have scolded Anita before an outsider.

Anita could not help laughing at the reference to the Massachusetts Institute of Technology. To Charlotte Byrne, whose brother Roderick had graduated from Paris's noted Beaux-Arts, M.I.T. was a mere trade school that had nothing to do with beauty or style. Roderick Byrne had explained patiently to his sister that this was not the case, but she could not be convinced. She insisted that Anita should have gone to the Beaux-Arts, for then she could have "gotten some decent clothes, too."

There were only two young women in America thus far who had graduated from M.I.T.—Anita and Marion Mahoney. Miss Mahoney was now working for a Chicago architect and typically had been relegated to designing furnishings and ornamental detail. Anita's indulgent father, who had thought her desire to go to M.I.T. was a passing whim, was astonished when she stuck to the course and graduated.

The hard part, Anita thought, comes soon, when I tell him I want to go to work. But now she smiled at her aunt, and said, "Of course I haven't. But the critics are right. This is not America; it's not Chicago."

Harry Brand stopped his poling and let the swan-prowed boat rest a moment near the esplanade. He turned carefully and asked Anita, in a respectful manner, "What do you consider 'American,' Miss Anita? The so-called Prairie School?"

Anita looked at him. Harry always seemed so correct. His costly clothes were perfect, and he wore them with the careless air of someone accustomed to the finest. To him a house would be a place to eat and sleep, to entertain impressively among gilt and marble. An office would be a room containing law books and shelves, a desk and chair. It was part of his courteous pursuit of her, Anita knew, that made him listen to her opinions.

She answered, "No, not really. Maybe that school is indicative of the prairie. But for an international event like this, I can see a kind of building that doesn't really belong to any one country—a building of the future. A style that would express the fantasy that all cities are, the triumph of man over nature." Anita stopped short. She knew that she sounded preachy and confused. More than that, she felt she

11

was revealing her deepest feelings to two people unlikely to understand.

Harry laughed and said, "That's too deep for me. But then I'm not artistic." His reply was half apologetic, half smug. He was proud of his rational attorney's mind.

"Artistic! I should hope not," Charlotte Byrne said indignantly. "These artistic young men have such untidy hair. And their *cravats*"—she made a face—"no more than gypsy bandannas, flying about everywhere."

Anita grinned. She glanced again at the young man on the esplanade.

He certainly looked "artistic" enough, with his soft, flowing tie, his casual low collar and shabby corduroy jacket that seemed the worse for wear. He was extraordinarily good-looking, and Anita approved of him. Yet there was something in his direct and piercing stare that made her quite uncomfortable. She wondered if her aunt's voice had carried over the narrow water between the gondola and stairs.

Charlotte followed Anita's look, and said casually, "I think we'd better go in after all, Harry." To her niece she added, "We have a busy day tomorrow, you know. The final fitting for the duchess's dress, a hundred things."

Anita nodded. It was like her aunt to refer to Anita's dress for the Duchess of Veragua's reception as if it were the duchess's own. The Duke and Duchess of Veragua would be entertained all over Chicago; tomorrow night it was Mrs. Potter Palmer's turn. The titled pair were not the only royal visitors expected for the Exposition: Her Royal Highness the Infanta Eulalia of Spain and the Archduke Ferdinand, heir to the Austro-Hungarian throne, would be among them. Anita was not thrilled at the prospect. She had gone to affairs of state before, and she knew the Personage presented would stare through her with glazed, people-sated eyes, not Anita's idea of communication. But her mother and aunt were beside themselves with anticipation.

Harry poled their boat toward the esplanade. The crowd had thinned.

At the esplanade Anita took Harry's arm and, with her aunt on Harry's other side, walked lightly up the stairway. She did not look again at the young man with the wild mane of hair, although they passed close to him. Yet she could feel that he was still staring at her, and had not moved from his former place.

* * *

"Jonas." Charles Seton spoke a bit sharply, because his companion had not answered to the sound of his own name. Jonas Mark was staring after the beautiful young woman just going over the bridge with her companions.

"Yes?" Jonas Mark's reply was absent. He stood for a time looking after the three people departing, then he turned back to Charles Seton. Jonas's deep, soft voice made the single word sound polysyllabic; his speech still held a lazy trace of the South. But there was nothing soft or lazy in his face or manner: already, at twenty-three, he had fine lines around his eyes and between his brows from squinting at the sun, and his tanned cheeks were scored with the creases of sincere but infrequent smiling. He looked as tough and resilient as a young tree; Charles Seton knew, from long acquaintance, that under his easy manner Jonas Mark was not an easy man.

"Let's go down to the Midway," Charley said. "You've criticized this scene enough." He grinned. Charley was as unlike Jonas as any man could be. He was faultlessly dressed, with a dapper cut to his well-tailored suit. His dark hair was center-parted and sleekly brushed; his large brown eyes and rather sensual mouth were those of a susceptible and pleasure-loving man. "I'd rather see Little Egypt than take this postman's holiday." He gestured toward the great dome of the central building on the canal.

"I've seen Little Egypt," Jonas answered indifferently. "There's not much to it."

"Not much to it," Charley repeated. "What's the matter with you, Jonas? You had eyes enough for the beauty with the black hair."

Jonas did not answer. Charley said, "She looked like a goddess, right out of the Grecian temple over there."

"Not that sham temple, Charley." Jonas's deep voice was contemptuous.

"We had a hand in it, my friend."

"I'm trying to forget." Jonas and Charley were senior draftsmen with the conservative firm of Higsbee and Waite. They had been assigned to assist in the design of the sprawling Agricultural Building at the Exposition, which Jonas damned as a prairie palazzo with an unknown Greek father, topped by an eighteenth-century capitol dome.

Suddenly Jonas smiled, and the wide, infectious smile lit his hard, lean face. "Can you imagine what Gaudí could have done with this? He'd draw it all together in a union of fantasy. It could look like the playground it is, and not like a demented

13

college designed by fifty different incompetents from everywhere."

Gaudí again. Charley sighed. He and Jonas were always at odds in the matter of architecture; he supposed their warm friendship was based on their very differences. Charley had not even known who this fellow Gaudí was until Jonas had told him. Charley was a graduate of the Beaux-Arts, and to him nothing was more beautiful than the lines of classical architecture. Jonas, on the other hand, had a vision of architecture akin to the unlivable work of that Spanish eccentric who was almost unknown outside his own country. And for good reason, Charles Seton judged. The fellow's stuff was childlike, almost hallucinatory; it looked as if it had been squeezed out of a tube by a drunken pastry cook. Yet Jonas, who fumed when Charley made such remarks, was convinced this weird style could not only be adapted to but was expressive of the cities of the future.

"You're always working, Jonas," Charley said. "You're working now, when we're supposed to be relaxing. Is it worth it?"

"Of course." The answer, in Jonas's soft Southeastern drawl, which persisted in spite of a decade of Northern living, was matter-of-fact. It was a foregone conclusion, Charley thought, that Jonas was committed to the hard way in everything.

Casual as he looked, Charley reflected, Jonas never let his hair down. Not in his ideas, or apparently in his life. Several times Charley had suggested a night out—on him—at the elegant Everleigh Club, where the prices began at fifty dollars and the young ladies were rigidly schooled in etiquette. But Jonas always declined. He said he had "had enough of that on the road," but privately Charley thought Jonas was a secret romantic. And in any case, Jonas was always doing his own work at home, leaving himself little time for distractions.

"I think I'll stroll down to the Midway. I saw some dazzlers by the Ferris wheel. Are you coming?"

"No thanks, Charley. I'll be heading home soon. See you tomorrow at the office."

"You're impossible, my friend." Charley smiled and struck Jonas lightly on his hard-muscled upper arm. "See you tomorrow."

"Goodnight." Jonas spoke without turning.

The Exposition was about to close, and the crowds were

beginning to leave. But Jonas continued to stand on the esplanade above the artificial canal, thinking of what Charley had said about always working.

A sharp wind had risen to whip the incongruous banners flying over the Grecian temple opposite. In the lake water's plash, the rushing of fountains, Jonas Mark could almost hear the sea, and his mind journeyed back in time to his beginnings...to a life as different from Charles Seton's as anyone could imagine.

Jonas's father, William Mark, had grown up in the bitter sun of the Texas Panhandle; when Jonas was a child it seemed to him his father had absorbed its lonely hardness into his very skin. Though he did not love the man, he grudgingly admired his father. Jonas did not learn his father's story firsthand, because William Mark was a silent, angry man. Instead, his sad, more expressive mother, who had been a schoolmistress when she was younger, told him of their early life.

William was born in 1848, when the Republic of Texas was only four years old. He was too young to be conscripted into the Confederate Army during the Civil War, but William fought another kind of battle, scratching out a living with his brothers in Texas. Their mother and father had been killed by Indians; the boys were tough, independent and wild. Because they asked no help of anyone, they had their neighbors' respect, and the authorities were unwilling to go after them when it was rumored the Mark boys had acquired their herd in less than honest ways.

When William was nineteen he fell in love with Melissa Richardson, daughter of the biggest landowner in the area, and she with him. Boldly William Mark approached her father: he intended, he said, to make a lot of money, and he could take care of Melissa very well. Richardson was outraged and ridiculed William Mark for his temerity. He warned William that if he came within ten yards of Melissa, he would be shot. William was furious but determined to have what he most desired. He followed Melissa into town one day and pleaded with her to run away with him. She refused, admitting she was afraid of her father, afraid of the uncertain life that would face them. William begged and stormed, but she was immovable. In the days that followed he risked his life to seek her out at the ranch, until a friendly hand told him they had sent her east, to school.

In a grieving rage, William Mark resolved to leave Texas and go east. He would make a pile and then he would find Melissa. He had once seen a picture of a place in Florida, where horses ran by the sunlit sea. His brother George said it was the Florida Panhandle, famous as cattle country. The naive William decided it was the place for him; it was east, and so it couldn't be too far from where Melissa was.

He asked his brothers George and Robert, both younger than he, to go with him. George balked, but the youngest, Robert, was enthusiastic.

"I'd sure like to go," the young Robert said. "All we need is a stake. Where do we get it?"

"Where we got the others," William said, grinning. "This time from the biggest ranch in these parts." At his brothers' bewildered looks, William laughed and went on, "We're going to 'borrow' a hundred head from Richardson, and drive them east. We'll pick up more along the way."

"You're crazy." George shook his head. "Richardson's got about a thousand men."

"Not on the southwest quarter," William said. "They can't watch everything."

"You're crazy," George repeated.

"No, he ain't," Robert declared. "We can do it. I'm with you, Will." He turned to George. "What about you? Are you staying or going?"

George deliberated for a long, painful moment. Then he answered quietly, "Going, I guess. Louise will have to go, too."

"Louise." William frowned. In his preoccupation he had not thought of the quiet young schoolmistress of Galveston who was betrothed to George. The two planned to marry soon. "Louise? We can't take a woman."

"I can't go without her, Will. And I'm not staying here alone to run this spread, small as it is. Besides, what kind of life would we have, when my brothers robbed the Richardsons? They'd hang me and leave Louise a widow anyhow."

"He's right, William," Robert said.

"All right." William was reluctant but resigned. And so the Marks began to plan. William insisted, with George's agreement, that Louise could not go with them on the first leg of the hard, dangerous journey. They would pool their resources and send for her from Galveston; she would journey by boat to New Orleans and they would meet her there. By

16

then, they reckoned, the trail would be cooler, making it safe to travel with a woman.

In addition, William declared, taking a woman meant a wagon, and that would slow them down. They would have to ride hard to get out of Texas alive.

Overpowering the Richardson waddies guarding the small portion of the great spread, the Mark boys rode off in the night, herding a hundred head of stolen cattle. They drove the cattle across Texas, picking up mavericks and robbing smaller owners on the way. When they reached the border of Louisiana they had acquired five hundred head of cattle.

They met Louise in New Orleans; no one in the metropolitan city, renewing itself quickly after the war, knew or cared who the brothers were or how they had come by their stock. The Marks sold some of the unbranded cattle to buy a wagon and a wedding dress and ring for Louise.

The journey resumed more slowly. The Marks still figured the best way to get the cattle to Florida was to drive them across the land; the railroads had not yet come to the state, and it would cost a lot to ship them by boat. Besides, Richardson might even know somebody on the boats; he seemed to know everybody in the southern part of the country. It wasn't that a hundred head of cattle meant anything to Richardson, William said; it was the idea of being robbed by the Marks, one of whom had had the nerve to love his daughter. In Texas a man could die for rustling one maverick off another man's land.

The Marks drove the herd across Mississippi's lower border, and on through Alabama, close by Mobile, always staying near the water, because that was the quickest way to get to Florida. George and Louise, it was decided, would be married when they reached their journey's end.

But when they reached Pensacola, the jealous George accused William of paying too much attention to Louise. Actually it was the other way around; Louise had always been secretly in love with William, and had agreed to marry George only because she felt there was no hope for her with the elder brother. The brothers exchanged hot words and, before anyone could stop them, they drew their guns. They fired at each other, and George was killed.

Louise's horror was mingled with guilty relief that it was William who survived. And though he had murdered his own brother, Louise loved William with the same unswerving passion as before.

17

Aghast at what he had done, William helped Robert bury George in the sandy Florida ground. The three went on to settle in the Florida Panhandle, east of Pensacola near the Gulf of Mexico. William filed a homesteader's claim and was granted land. He and Robert built a house to accommodate the three of them. William married Louise; but he married her without passion or love, still thinking of Melissa. At least he could take care of Louise, he thought, to make up to his dead brother.

The brothers found that driving the cattle to its destination had been one thing, but sheltering the herd was another. It made sense to sell most of them; having stolen cattle was dangerous, anyway. Some of them were branded. The brothers found a buyer and with the proceeds of the sale bought dairy cows to start a dairy farm. William and Louise had four children in quick succession: a boy who died at birth; Jonas, born in 1870; and two younger children, a boy and girl.

Disease struck the dairy herd in 1873, and William faced disaster. Laboriously he built up his herd again, but he was never to reach the goal of his dreams—to be rich and find Melissa. He had ruined his life by killing George and becoming obligated to Louise. He had little love for the children, because they were hers and not the lost Melissa's; he did come to love his land, however, with a deep love. When the railroads began to move in and buy up acreage, William stubbornly refused the companies' first offers. Later, need, and the law of eminent domain, forced William to sell out at a bankrupting price. He was left with only enough land to keep up a very small farm. It was a narrow, grim and loveless place.

But when it was time for Jonas to go to school, he found a wider world. In the day school at Pensacola, the schoolmaster was impressed with Jonas's eagerness and his quick mind. His mother had already taught him to read—in secret, because William thought it was a "waste of time"—and Jonas was more advanced than his fellow students. In his school book he saw for the first time the venerable fortresses and castlelike houses of the city of St. Augustine, across the state from Pensacola on the ocean, which he had never seen.

The buildings were beautiful, nothing like the crude buildings Jonas had helped his father and his uncle build on the farm. When he went home from school the first evening he told them all about the buildings in the book; his mother and uncle were interested but William was scornful about Jonas's

18

"big ideas." He said, "This house is good enough for me and it ought to be good enough for you."

Secretly Jonas resolved he would someday live in a house like the houses in the book. As time went on the school became the center of Jonas's life and he began to long to get away.

He dreaded the summers: summer meant work on the farm, milking cows, pitching hay, cleaning the barns, gathering and storing fodder to feed the cows. There was more: a vegetable garden, a chicken run and citrus trees. There was always new drilling to be done, to keep the wells and drainage ditches running, and maintenance of the milking stable and outbuildings. They had a windmill that used a horsepowered pump to connect well water to the house. That was an innovation for 1878 and one of which William was very proud.

Five years went by too quickly, and Jonas was thirteen; he had reached the end of school. William said it was time for Jonas to "put aside all that nonsense" and take his place on the farm.

"I want to be a carpenter," Jonas said stubbornly. He was always happiest building something; the sound of a saw was like music to Jonas, and he loved to inhale the clean, pungent scent of wood. He had spent the happiest summer hours of his life the year before, when he had helped boys on a neighboring farm build a tree house. William would never let Jonas build one at home; it was a waste of wood, he said. But Jonas would sneak away to the neighbors' tree house, and climb the Spanish laurel with its spreading limbs. He would sit in the tree house and look out over the vast expanse of sandy plain; a few pines remained. In the distance beyond the plain was the shadow of the gloomy cypress swamp.

Jonas wished for a sight of the sea, imagining tall waves hollowed out like green magic caverns or curving houses. And he wondered if he could build a house shaped like a wave of the sea. He figured he could, but not with any wood he knew, and not here, on this sandy plain. Somewhere else, he decided, maybe in a big city by the ocean. Someday he would build something like that. And he knew he would have to leave to do it.

When he was fourteen, Jonas decided to go. He was afraid: he had no money at all. But late one night he wrote a brief letter to his mother, packed his few clothes and a couple of books in a croker sack he had taken from the barn and hidden in his room.

He stole down to the kitchen and wrapped up some food

19

to take along. His heart was beating so hard it sounded like a drum. He almost feared the sound would wake up his father. But no one stirred in the sad, silent house. Jonas left and started walking toward Pensacola. He would stay awhile with his uncle, if he would have him. Then he would go north. It was late morning before Jonas got to the Gulf and heard its calm waves lapping against the shore. Footsore and exhausted, Jonas staggered into his uncle's house.

The plash of fountains came to the older Jonas's ears, and it was a while before he realized it was the sound of fountains, not the Gulf of Mexico, the past had been so vivid in his mind. He shook his head and turned up his jacket collar. The night was getting chillier, and he was almost the last one left at the Exposition. He walked up the stairs and across the bridge, reaching the main entrance gate just as they were locking it for the night.

As he made his way across the hushed Chicago streets, Jonas thought of the years that intervened between his escape and this spring night—hard years, as backbreaking in their way as the work on the farm had been. Study that had reddened his eyes and made his head ache; the constant temporary jobs to keep himself alive that made his muscles always sore.

And yet he wouldn't have traded any of it: every blister, every drop of sweat was precious to him now because it had all brought him nearer to his old dream, the dream that he would fulfill, no matter what.

Chapter 2

"BERTHA, YOU GROW MORE beautiful every day." Roderick Byrne fervently kissed Mrs. Potter Palmer's hand. The renowned hostess was sumptuous in pale-blue satin, and wore one of her famous "dog collars" that was reputed to hold more than two thousand pearls and contained seven huge diamonds. Her pink and white skin was utterly unlined; the brilliant lights from the chandeliers ignited her wonderful golden hair.

Roderick gave a quick glance at the reception line, relieved that his wife was out of earshot. He turned reluctantly from the glamorous Bertha Palmer to his host and asked in a jovial way, "What are you doing downstairs, Potter?" The dry-goods prince frequently excused himself from these stately occasions, on the grounds that he was not a society man. He preferred to spend the time alone in a tower of the Potter castle, at the races, or with business cronies planning a richer Chicago. He and Roderick had often been in one another's company when there was a meeting on city planning. "Did this captivating lady persuade you?" Roderick asked Palmer, with a smile for Bertha.

"She has a way of doing that," Potter Palmer admitted.

"You've done a whale of a job at the Exposition, Bertha," Roderick said. "We must talk more about it later on. Right now I'm holding up the line." Roderick smiled broadly and moved on, excusing himself to the person behind him, a young man with sleek black hair and bright brown eyes, a sensual, merry look about his mouth.

Roderick noticed that he was not the only cause of delay: just ahead of Anita, who immediately preceded Roderick, he saw his wife, Margaret, fluttering before the Duke and Duchess of Veragua. Margaret was dressed in the full panoply of elaborate evening wear; her thin gray-blond hair was arranged in a stiff pompadour. With her gown of embroidered silk she too wore a dog-collar choker glistening with amethysts and diamonds, though more modest than Bertha Palmer's. The wide choker emphasized her haggard face and made her look older than thirty-eight. Margaret was making an elaborate curtsy. The titled couple seemed half-gratified, half-amazed at this Old World gesture in the democratic city of Chicago.

Roderick looked at his daughter, admiring the simple line of her white evening gown and the single strand of pearls about her neck. He and his daughter exchanged glances, and Roderick caught a mischievous look in Anita's bright blue eyes.

When Anita reached the duke and duchess, she smiled and nodded. Roderick saw the pretty duchess look through and beyond Anita with dark, weary eyes. She had probably seen more faces in the last few days, Roderick thought, than she had in a year in Spain.

When the duke offered Anita his hand, Roderick heard Anita say warmly, "I am honored to meet a countryman of Antonio Gaudí."

For a split second the duke looked as if he had not heard what she had said; an absent, polite smile lingered on his mouth. Then he comprehended. He broke out into very informal laughter. "*Magnífico,*" he commented. "I shall tell my friends their architect is famous even in Chicago, of America."

All along the line people were staring at Anita and the duke, wondering what had caused his laughter.

"America is a wonderful country, señorita, where the young ladies speak their minds."

And why not? Roderick Byrne thought, bowing to the duchess and duke. His daugher was as good as, if not better than, any titled lady Bertha Palmer could produce.

The young man behind Roderick, the one with the bright brown eyes, had heard the exchange, too. Charles Seton resolved to dance with the impudent young goddess—the very one they had seen last night on the lake—if it was the last thing he ever did.

It was a good while before he could get near Anita. She danced with her father and several young men, and after the

22

duke had danced with his wife and hostess, he danced twice with Anita Byrne.

As Charles Seton watched Anita waltz, from the sidelines, his father and Roderick Byrne came to stand beside him. Edward Seton was tall, thin and imposing; he looked more like a diplomat than a merchant, even if a merchant on a grand scale, as a partner of the famous firm of Carson Pirie Scott and Company.

"Since you're neglecting the ladies, Charley, by not dancing, I'd like to present Roderick Byrne." Edward Seton's pride in this acquaintance was as obvious as his pride in his son. "You two gentlemen should have a lot to discuss."

"Mr. Byrne." Charley was clearly impressed. "This is an honor, sir." He had seen Byrne a few times before—once when he had driven his employer to the planning dinner that preceded the building of the Exposition. But as he was only a junior architect in an obscure firm, Charley doubted that he had been noticed by the prestigious Byrne.

Now, however, the great Byrne was looking at him with friendly approval. "You've been remiss, Edward, not to introduce us before." They all knew that this was only a social nicety; the Byrnes moved in a far more exalted circle than the Setons, in spite of the latter's money. Nevertheless, Charley and his father were gratified by the attention.

"You must meet my daughter, Charles." Roderick nodded in the direction of the black-haired beauty dancing with the Duke of Veragua.

So that's who she was! Charley cursed himself for his own stupidity. He should have known. He remembered the family group in the reception line. Yet the girl was so unique he could not associate her with a local family; if she had sprung from the sea, like the Botticelli Venus, he would not have been surprised.

He said eagerly, "I would be delighted, sir."

The music stopped, and the duke bowed to the beautiful girl in white and led her to the place where her father stood with the Setons.

"There's no time like the present," Roderick said genially. Taking his daughter's hand, he drew her into their circle, after a careless and democratic nod to the duke.

"Anita, may I present my friend Edward Seton, and his son, Charles. Miss Anita Byrne, my daughter."

Roderick's pride in her loveliness was greater than Edward's in his son. Roderick sounded as if he were presenting a queen.

With reason, Charley thought, acknowledging the introduction. He took a quick, excited breath.

"Charles works for Higsbee and Waite," Roderick said. Charley thought that Anita Byrne was looking at him with greater interest.

He asked her with so much haste that it bordered on discourtesy, "Will you dance, Miss Byrne?"

Anita looked at him an instant and nodded. Charles Seton, for the first time in his poised and successful life, felt as awkward as a schoolboy. He put his hand on Anita's supple waist and glided her out onto the floor.

"You were wonderful," he blurted. Then he regretted his brashness. He was usually suave with women, both the society belles he met at Chicago affairs and the factory girls and women of pleasure who occupied his more casual hours.

"Wonderful?" Anita repeated. "What do you mean, Mr. Seton?"

"When you were talking to the duke. Few young ladies would have had the—"

"Nerve?" She grinned.

"You seem at ease among the nobility, as well you should be. Beauty like yours makes you anyone's equal." Charley felt his confidence return: that was better, more like himself. But he was disconcerted when she answered.

"Don't you think everyone is equal? Surely you are an American, Mr. Seton."

Then Charley realized that in spite of her sharp tone, she was teasing him, because she was smiling and there was a twinkle in her eyes. The look, and her next comment fascinated him; they were the last thing he had expected. Talking with her was like sparring: it was highly stimulating.

"I wouldn't have taken you for such a . . . royalist, Mr. Seton"—he smiled at her synonym for "snob"—"from the looks of your friend last night, on the esplanade."

So she remembered me, Charley thought with pleasure. "Jonas Mark, you mean," he said casually.

"So that is his name," she said. "Mr. Mark looked like something of a rebel."

"Oh, he is," Charley agreed. "You and he have something in common, Miss Byrne. Jonas also admires Gaudí." Charley thought what a strange effect this young woman had on him; first she had made him stammer like a schoolboy, now he

24

was talking to her as easily as if they had known each other for years. She was the most fascinating woman he had ever met in his life.

He looked down into her face. There was a new brightness in her vivid eyes.

"That is an unusual taste," she said dreamily.

"I beg your pardon?"

"Your friend Mr. Mark's interest in Gaudí," she replied.

"Yes. It is certainly not mine." He noticed her change of expression and he said quickly, "I'd much rather hear about you, Miss Byrne. No doubt you made the Tour? I'd like to know your opinion of European architecture."

"There are imitations enough in America, Mr. Seton. As for Europe, I danced with several dukes and counts, and even a prince. The dukes and counts wanted my father to renovate their castles—as a father-in-law, not for a commission."

Charley laughed. The impudent goddess had a tongue as rough as sandstone. She did not make the slightest effort to charm him, and girls usually did. Yet Charley was becoming more interested in her by the moment. He was determined not to show her how much she set him off balance.

Suddenly the most important thing in Charley's life was to impress Anita Byrne. "I suppose you've learned a good deal about architecture from your father."

"From him, and M.I.T." Charley could not help showing his surprise.

She smiled at his look, and he knew she was taking a mischievous pleasure in telling him that.

"You are a graduate?" he asked. When she nodded, he said deliberately, "Well, why not? Women are advancing more and more. After all, the Women's Building was designed by a woman. And our hostess"—he nodded at Bertha Palmer—"is in the forefront of such things, even if she is a bit of a dilettante."

Something flashed in Anita's wonderful eyes, and she smiled at him. "That's very astute," she said.

"Ungallant," he admitted, "but true."

Charley's grasp tightened a little on Anita's slender waist; he felt as if he had gained some ground.

But then she surprised him again, asking abruptly, "What did your friend Mr. Mark think of the Exposition?"

Charley was embarrassed. Roderick Byrne had been one of the guiding geniuses of the design; Charley could hardly tell the man's daughter about Jonas's remarks.

25

"What did you think of it?" he countered.

"Very little," she said frankly.

The waltz had ended, and Charley saw a tall, precise-looking fellow come forward to claim Anita for the next dance. It was a member of Charley's athletic club, Harry Brand, the lawyer.

"Hello, Charley." Brand greeted him in a friendly way.

"Harry." Charley nodded; his voice was cold. He relinquished the goddess of M.I.T. to Harry Brand.

"Will you join me in the library, Anita? Or are you too sleepy?" Margaret and Charlotte had gone upstairs; Roderick stood at the library door, waiting for his daughter.

"I'd love to," she said. "I'm not sleepy at all."

"I believe you. You look as fresh as when we started. Youth is wonderful."

There was a wistful note in Roderick's deep voice.

"Why, Father. Surely *you're* not feeling old!" Anita spoke lightly as Roderick held open the heavy door, gesturing for her to enter.

"A little," he admitted. He walked to a Chippendale cabinet near one of the leaded windows, opened the cabinet door and took out a decanter and two fine crystal stems. "Will you have a sherry?"

"Yes, thank you." Anita sat down in an alcove where a leaded bay window looked out on the vast terrace and English garden, only half-visible now in the golden light from the window. "It is absurd for you to feel old, Father. You never will be to me." She took the proffered glass of wine and set it on the small, intricately carved table at her elbow.

Roderick took a sip of his sherry and made an appreciative face. "Wonderful stuff," he commented, smiling at Anita. He crossed the Kirman carpet and sat down in a chair opposite her, saying, "I don't know what I'd do without you, my dear. I realized tonight, seeing you bewitch everyone, how the years have passed. It doesn't seem a week ago that you were building that little doll house."

The doll house! It had been so long since she had even thought of it. She turned her sherry glass absently in her fingers, remembering the occasion.

When she was only ten years old she had learned from a friendly carpenter employed by Roderick's firm how to build a house.

"What was his name, Father? The carpenter?"

26

Roderick considered for a minute, then said, "Roberts. Alfred Roberts. He was a good man."

"Yes, yes. Now I remember." Mr. Roberts had patiently shown Anita the pattern of braces and beams, supports and studs.

"I want it round," she had said of the house, "round and high. How do I do that?" Roberts showed her the proper way to frame.

With determination Anita finished the house herself. It was like no other that she or the carpenter had ever seen. Under the craftsman's watchful eye, she tried to saw peculiar shapes from the wood with a small handsaw.

"You need a coping saw for that." He found her one. She took up the coping saw and cut out curving forms and awkwardly nailed them to the roof.

"What are these?" Roberts asked gently.

"The snow," she answered seriously, not sure what she meant except that she had a vision of hills of snow, an impossible house, all curves and flowing, not sprawling and heavy, square-towered, like the house she lived in with her father, mother and aunt.

The finished doll house was a crude but interesting effort. Roberts said kindly, "Maybe you'll build a big house someday."

She recalled that her father had come into the workshop at that point, and when she saw the amusement in his eyes, she was a little hurt. But he complimented her on her work, saying, "You're a very smart girl to do all that yourself." Then he laughed a little, and added, "It doesn't do for little girls to be so smart, does it, Roberts?"

The quiet carpenter grinned, and answered, "No, sir, I guess not. A little girl as pretty as Anita doesn't have to be smart."

Roderick nodded and stroked his daughter's black hair. "When you grow up and marry, Anita, I'll build you the most beautiful house you've ever seen."

"Maybe I'll build my own," she had said with great seriousness. The memory came back to Anita now.

"You were quite the little carpenter," Roderick Byrne said. She heard the same indulgence in his voice that she remembered from that afternoon a decade ago.

Abruptly, she said, "Father, I'm going to work Monday."

Startled, he repeated, "Work?"

"For Higsbee and Waite."

He raised his brows, the empty wineglass held absently in his hand.

"Well," he commented at last, with a loud expulsion of breath expressing his surprise. "I don't know why I am surprised, though I am. Somehow I had had the vain hope that your degree was simply a way of proving yourself...proving that you could do it. That has always been your way, you know." He looked at her.

She was silent. He was right, of course. All through her life, whenever she was told that something was impossible, it had become vital to prove that it was possible, for her.

Roderick went on, "I see I was wrong, and I underestimated you. For that I apologize."

She was somewhat taken aback at this unexpected reaction on his part, but she waited for him to continue.

"I realize," he said, "that the young ladies of today are all very independent. You are not what the ladies were when I was young. Well, well. So you have been employed by Higsbee and Waite." He could not disguise his hurt, or the faint contempt when he said the firm's name. "It is hardly the most prestigious firm in Chicago."

She could not help laughing at the way he said it. She reached out and took his hand. "Of course not. But it is the only firm that would hire me."

"What?" He looked shocked. "Do you mean you've applied all over town and my colleagues never told me?"

"They didn't know who I was. If they asked I told them I was not related to the Chicago Byrnes." She added, "They wouldn't have recognized me, anyway, in the clothes I was wearing. I borrowed Cora's things."

"Cora's. Good God." Cora was Anita's maid. "Whom did you see?"

"The lot. Adler and Sullivan, Holabird and Root, Jenney." He shook his head. "And not Byrne Associates."

"No." She met his eyes levelly. "I couldn't do that, Father. I've got to make it on my own." She did not add that the designs produced by her father's firm were, among those of all Chicago architects, least to her liking. "I don't want a sinecure," she went on in a quiet, serious way. "I must be accepted on my own merits by people who have no interest in me at all, aside from my competence."

"It would be difficult for any man," Roderick commented, "to have no interest in you at all, Anita." She was surprised at this frank statement, but she didn't comment. One of the

28

architects who had interviewed her, in fact, had reacted to her application in a way that did not please her at all. She had left his office at once, fuming with anger.

Some of her thoughts must have shown in her face, because Roderick pursued, "I see you have encountered some of the ways of the business world. I don't like to think of your being...unprotected in that atmosphere. There are other things to consider, Anita. First of all, you are not in any financial need of employment."

"But I can hardly be taking the bread out of another woman's mouth," she put in quickly. "How many other women have a degree like mine?"

"All right, all right, you've made your point." Roderick sounded annoyed. "But this...course is going to upset your aunt and mother a great deal, you know. It's time you began thinking of...a life for yourself. Of marrying some good young fellow. What about that Harry Brand or the Seton fellow you met tonight? I like the looks of young Seton."

"Charles Seton. Good heavens, Father." Her disinterest was plain.

"What's wrong with him?" Roderick demanded. "He's a fine-looking boy, and his family is well fixed. I'm surprised that you're not aware of these things, my dear. It's high time. Why, you might even marry an architect. You'd be a great help to him, with your background," Roderick concluded a little weakly.

"Come, Father, how could I 'help' a husband—by redesigning his houses?" she asked ironically.

Roderick Byrne was vexed by her quick answers. Suddenly he felt like a fool. He had never been able to control Anita, or to deny her anything. But this was the supreme joke, he thought bitterly. His city master plan had been judged the greatest in America; the richest men in Chicago had turned over to him the planning and building of their fabulous houses. Yet he had no control over one impudent young twenty-year-old who happened to be his daughter. To make matters worse, he could not even hold a financial rein over her; a separate inheritance from her maternal grandmother left her quite free to come or go, as she wished. The situation confounded him.

"I need not remind you that this course will cause any number of difficulties. Your aunt and mother have an elaborate summer planned. And when the truth comes out at

Higsbee and Waite who you are, it may prove very embarrassing for me."

"I'm sorry about that, Father," she answered sincerely. "Perhaps I should go somewhere else, to another city."

"No," he protested sharply.

"I have often thought of going to Spain."

"To Spain! Good heavens. Surely you are not thinking of apprenticing yourself to that queer fellow, Grandi?"

"Gaudí, Father."

"Gaudí, whatever. Well, my dear," he said with satisfaction, "that alone shows me how naive you are, how desperately you need supervision. Do you think a Spaniard, with the Spaniard's attitude toward women, would dream of such a thing?" His voice had risen.

Anita's voice rose to meet it. "I'm sure not," she answered bitterly, "if the duke is any example. He laughed at me when I told him where I'd been to school."

"A sensible fellow, that," Roderick retorted. He was completely out of temper. "I really don't know how I am going to tell your mother."

"Tell me what?" Roderick and Anita turned, startled, to see Margaret Byrne standing in the middle of the Kirman carpet. Her thin hair, escaping from a huge puffed nightcap, cruelly exaggerated the thinness of her long neck and the haggard lines of her peevish face. She looked at them with baleful, faded eyes. Margaret Byrne was wildly jealous of her daughter, jealous of the frequent interludes in the library when Anita talked with her father of incomprehensible and boring things in which Margaret had no part.

"Tell me what?" she repeated sharply, coming toward them, trailing her elaborate dressing gown.

"That I am going to work, Mother," Anita said bluntly. "For Higsbee and Waite, as an apprentice, on Monday."

"Oh, my God," Margaret Byrne said, and sat down so suddenly in one of the high-backed brocaded chairs that it jarred her head. Involuntarily she had bitten her lip, and the lip began to bleed. She started to cry. "The disgrace of it will kill me, Roderick." Margaret sobbed. "Why can't you do anything with your daughter? And we had planned the most beautiful summer. You must stop her, Roderick." Margaret's thin, wailing voice was hysterical. "I shall be ill."

Roderick went to his wife in a vain attempt to soothe her.

By that time the voices had attracted Charlotte, who entered the library asking, "What is all this commotion?"

"Anita wants to kill me," Margaret cried out.

"Now, now, Margaret." Roderick looked pained.

"You aren't ill, Mother." Anita spoke in a cold, level voice. "You just want us to think you are."

As Roderick Byrne led his sobbing wife away, Charlotte, who was standing next to Anita, said, "You are very wise, my dear girl. But I think you may find you're too wise for your own good."

Chapter 3

THE SPRING CHILL THAT had marked the Exposition opening was gone. Monday morning Jonas felt the warmth of the strengthening sun; his slanted drawing table was placed between two large windows. He straightened his long, muscular body on the high stool and, putting his large T square down, loosened his collar and rolled up his shirtsleeves.

Before he resumed working, Jonas glanced at Charles Seton, who was working intently at the next table. They had barely exchanged two words since last Friday; during the Saturday half-day, Jonas recalled, Charley had not been his usual talkative self. He had been preoccupied and tense, saying no more to Jonas than "Good morning" and nothing to anyone else beyond the occasional orders to a clerk to stretch him a board or bring in some ink. Moreover, Charley, who was always a careful worker despite his casual air, had spoiled two sets of plans and had not bothered to redo them, though the draftsmen were under pressure to have the set finished by Monday noon for the blueprinters.

Well, Charley was making up for it now, Jonas reflected. He had not raised his head from his board since they had come in this morning. Jonas was ahead of schedule and could afford to work at a more comfortable pace. He wondered what had happened to Charley after they had left work Saturday afternoon. Charley had not mentioned his weekend plans, and he always had before.

Jonas moved his stool a little to escape the rays of the hot sun and went to work again on the plans for the firm's half of the Provident Building. Higsbee and Waite was sharing architectural duties with Byrne Associates in the construction of the sixteen-story office building, a common practice in the year 1893 in fast-growing Chicago. The Higsbee and Waite half followed the Byrne half's design but Higsbee chose to build its half with a steel frame, an innovation that was greeted with skepticism by those who were used to the load-bearing wall.

Jonas thoroughly approved of the steel frame; it was fire-proof and its thin exterior walls increased interior space. It made enlarging easier and faster. The design of the Provident Building was what Jonas disliked—another square cage that meant nothing, expressed nothing. And the decorative cornice added by Higsbee set it all out of kilter: the cornice sat squarely on the roof like a railroad car, squat and meaningless, as out of place as a wart on a smooth hand.

Nevertheless he worked on with steady care, and before he knew it, it was time to call to the clerk, "Stretch me a board, would you, Willie?" Jonas straightened up again from the table and carefully placed the finished board with the others he had accumulated since eight o'clock.

As he waited for the new board, Jonas rolled up his sleeves another few inches and unbuttoned another button of his shirtfront. He happened to be lounging on his stool, his long legs bent and the heels of his shoes secured to the rungs, when George Waite entered the room.

Waite was a fierce-looking, heavy man of middle age, with a walrus mustache and the spiky brows that sat like hairy eaves over his sharp eyes. The brows and the mustache gave his face a perpetually enraged expression. Actually Waite was a good-natured man, except in the matter of slow and slipshod work. He was the engineering genius of the firm; the man who won the contracts was Alan Higsbee. Like the genial socialite Roderick Byrne, Higsbee made a specialty of selling and design. Waite was the structural expert, the master builder.

Now he looked at the scene before him with some surprise. There was the workhorse Jonas lounging while the easy-mannered Charles was so intent he did not even look up when Waite came in.

"Well," Waite said in his deep, rough voice, and Jonas was puzzled. Usually Waite did not mince his words. He was something of a martinet in the question of dress as well. Jonas hastily buttoned his shirtfront and was about to roll his sleeves down again when the heavy, carefully dressed partner stood aside and held the door for a woman to enter.

Astonished, Jonas Mark saw that it was the beautiful girl

from the esplanade. At first he could see nothing but her eyes. He was so struck by their intensity that it was impossible to move for a moment from his nonchalant pose on the stool. He felt off-balance, as if he had just received a sharp, quick blow to the center of his body.

Suddenly he regained his senses and stepped to the floor, rapidly rolling his shirtsleeves down, buttoning the cuffs.

"Good morning," he said calmly to Waite and the woman.

"Miss Byrne!" Jonas was startled to hear Charley Seton's voice, so suddenly. Glancing aside, he saw that Charley was on his feet, buttoning his jacket. There was an expression of amazement and delight on his handsome face.

"Mr. Seton." The woman's voice was husky and low. Jonas realized that they knew one another. And he wondered why that was such an unwelcome piece of information. By now he had had time to observe the woman wholly. Somehow she was not like the goddess on the lake. Jonas recognized dimly it must have something to do with her clothes; she was dressed more conventionally today.

"You know each other, then?" Waite asked, and Charley answered proudly, "I have that honor."

Jonas took in the loveliness of her face and form, slender and yet curving, as Waite said, "I'd like you to meet your new associate, Miss Anita Byrne."

The partner looked from one man to the other, with a face of mischievous amusement that was uncommon to him. Only one other architect in Chicago had employed a woman, and Waite was quite aware of the effect of his announcement.

"Miss Byrne, this is Jonas Mark."

Anita Byrne held out her hand, and Jonas took it; the long fingers felt soft and warm in his palm. His gaze locked again with hers, and he found that he was still holding her small hand in his far beyond the conventional moment of release. He was strangely gratified that she did not withdraw her hand at once, and also very surprised. "Miss Byrne," he said after a drawn-out little silence; his voice sounded peculiar to him.

"Miss Byrne is an M.I.T. graduate, Jonas." Hearing Charley say that, Jonas noticed two things. Anita Byrne's manner was a little less relaxed. And Charley's air of pride deserted him. He looked chagrined.

It was all so awkward suddenly that Jonas felt obliged to say something. "Well, that's...fine." It was certainly not a

34

brilliant remark, but Anita Byrne smiled at him as if she appreciated his effort at sociability.

"Yes," Waite remarked genially. "The ladies are certainly forging ahead these days, what with Miss Hayden designing the Women's Building, and all," he said. "But I see you're way ahead of me, Charley," Waite added, with an interested and puzzled look at Seton. It was clear that the fierce-looking partner was wondering how Charles had come by the knowledge.

Waite turned to Anita. "You've been in Chicago only a short time, didn't you say, Miss Byrne?"

Charley looked bewildered, and Jonas saw Anita Byrne's white skin flush faintly.

Anita's color deepened. With a little frown, she answered, "It was absurd of me to try to keep the truth from you, Mr. Waite. Roderick Byrne is my father."

Jonas was more dismayed than ever: she was the daughter of Roderick Byrne, one of the prime movers of the Exposition, creator of the buildings Jonas most detested.

"Well!" Waite smiled. "I take off my hat to you, my dear. This confirms my high opinion of you, that you are in no way eager to trade on your name. Well, well. Roderick's daughter. May I ask what he thinks of all this?"

Anita hesitated. Then she replied with tact, "He is like all fathers, Mr. Waite. He has quite another life planned for me." She added, "It was remiss of me not to remember that Mr. Seton works for you. And we met Friday night at...at a friend's house."

"At Mrs. Potter Palmer's," Charley said, and once again Jonas noticed a disapproving look on Anita Byrne's lovely face. Good, he thought; she finds Charley's claim to splendor tasteless before people barred from it.

George Waite gave Charley a rather annoyed look. Then, apparently realizing the conversation had become too personal, he said, "Miss Byrne will be assigned, first, to helping with the Provident drawings. We'll give you that table," he said to her, gesturing to a drawing board set up on the other side of Seton's. "We're a little behindhand with these, Miss Byrne, so perhaps you'll begin right away."

"Certainly." Her tone was businesslike. "Whatever there is to be done." She removed her hat and slipped the small string-handle of her purse off her wrist. Eagerly Charles Seton said, "Let me." But she only smiled in a cool way and went to the hooks above her drawing board, hanging up first the pouch, then the hat.

"Jonas, I'll leave the rest to you." Waite nodded and left the room.

"I believe I have the greater load at the moment," Charley said quickly. "Jonas has been so industrious that he is far ahead."

Anita stood calmly waiting to be given the assignment. It was clear to Jonas that Charles Seton was determined to be the one she worked with; he himself felt easier now that they were on the familiar ground of work. Charley's efforts seemed a little pathetic. If she sticks, he thought, there won't be much time for such maneuvers; the drafting rooms of Higsbee and Waite were always flooded with drawings to be done.

Charley explained their operation to Anita, and when she was seated on her own stool, he fluttered around her with offers of a better board, fresher ink and other items. She thanked him civilly, Jonas noticed, but discouraged any further conversation. At once she set to work and said nothing again to either of them until the clock showed noon.

The clerk was already at the door, waiting to take the drawings to the blueprinters. Anita picked up her drawings and came with them to Jonas Mark. "Would you look these over, please," she asked, "before they're sent out?"

He nodded, more than a little disturbed by her nearness. She wore a scent of some delicious flower and had a silky cleanness that made Jonas think of the lovely white flesh below the stiff-sleeved blouse. Glancing over the drawings, he was astonished at their expertness and perfection, even as he realized his very astonishment was a kind of condescension toward a woman employee. And a graduate of M.I.T. would hardly be incompetent. With a swift, practiced eye he ran over the drawings again.

"These are excellent," he told her.

"Thank you," she said, looking at him closely.

Jonas met her glance and for a long, unmeasured instant he almost forgot where they were, nearly failed to remember that the clerk was waiting. With an effort he pulled in his wandering thoughts and repeated, "Yes, very good."

Then he rose and helped Charley and the clerk bundle the drawings to take away.

Charley adjusted his cravat, saying quickly to Anita Byrne, "It's time for some luncheon. Will you join me?"

Jonas, who hated the word "luncheon," felt his gorge rise.

He turned away from them and walked to the window, rolling down his shirtsleeves. He was disproportionately glad to hear her answer.

"No, thank you very much. I have some shopping to do."

Jonas turned from the window in time to see Charley leaving the room with a rather defeated air.

"How long do you generally take?" Anita asked Jonas.

"Not long," he replied, and he smiled. "But generally it's an hour."

"Thanks." She took down her small hat and set it perfectly on her head without benefit of a glass, then she retrieved her purse and went out.

Jonas sat down at his drawing board and looked out the window at the busy panorama of Chicago, massive, industrious and anonymous below the bright noon sun. He admired everything about Anita Byrne—her reticence and beauty, her quiet competence and pride. But of all women she was the one who would be the most dangerous: to love a woman like that would be a total thing. And there was no room in his hardworking life for anything like that.

Jonas had no appetite for lunch. He had the miserable feeling of being idle and restless at once. Walking aimlessly around the city, he found that his long-legged stride had carried him farther than he had intended, and he was on the very street of his boardinghouse.

When he passed, he raised his hand in greeting to his landlady, Mrs. Coppin, who was sweeping the outside stairs. "Why, Mr. Mark!" she called out in surprise. She rarely saw him at this hour. "You're not sick, are you?"

"Oh, no," he reassured her, smiling. "Just walking. I didn't mean to come this far."

"Well, I'm glad you did." She set her broom at an angle on the stairs and gestured him into the house. "You have a letter. All the way from Spain."

Spain. Jonas had written to Antoni Gaudí, in care of the Escuela Superior de Arquitectura, in Barcelona, from which Gaudí had graduated years before, in the hope that it would reach him. He had written to the master builder in his own language; not fluently, because Spanish was a tongue Jonas had only picked up in his travels and had not pursued as a scholar—and now there was an answer.

Jonas found a nearby park and sat down, examining the

37

envelope, postponing with pleasurable anxiety the discovery of what it contained. Then he ripped it open.

It was headed Astorga and dated several weeks earlier.

"Esteemed Young Colleague," it began. Jonas read that twice, with delight, wondering how Gaudí had known he was young. Fool, he said to himself, of course: he had mentioned the date of his graduation from M.I.T.

He read on: "I am at this time engaged in building the Palacio Episcopal of Astorga, and my labors are so intense and consuming that only the urgency of your request moved me to answer your letter. I am all too aware of the honor you pay me by your kind judgment of my efforts and I wish you well in your endeavors.

"But I must say at once that your idea of serving as my apprentice is too unusual and impractical to be entertained. I am certain that the employment of an American assistant would not only violate the traditions of my people but would also be out of the question financially. I cannot imagine your acceptance of the remuneration customary in my nation, when the great country of America offers rewards so large.

"I am touched, my young colleague, by your strong desire to work with me, and again I express my gratitude for your admiration, obviously the criticism of a knowledgeable young man. But I cannot urge you too strongly to study the character and people of your own land, to develop an art which is consonant with that character, and not the character of Spain. You did not once mention the name of God; He is my guide and inspiration. I cannot but feel, therefore, that your nature is unsuited to the type of labor in which I engage, no matter how strong your kind admiration for my structures."

The letter ended with the highly formal, wordy close characteristic of the rest of the letter.

Jonas read the letter through again, translating it more easily the second time, then he folded it carefully, put it back in the envelope and slipped it in his breast pocket.

He rose and began to walk slowly out of the park toward the office of Higsbee and Waite. Jonas went over in his mind the years that had gone into the building of his dream, the years that had led up to the letter from Antoni Gaudí. He could hardly believe that it had been only nine years since the night he had crept from his parents' house, walking all the way to Pensacola, where he had arrived exhausted at his Uncle Robert's house.

* * *

Responding to Jonas's timid knock, his Uncle Robert had opened the door, holding a gun. When he saw who it was, he put down the gun, dragged the exhausted boy into the house and gave him something to eat. Jonas was so tired he could hardly talk; when his Aunt Helene joined them in the kitchen, she insisted Jonas go to sleep before he tell them anything. She tucked him in bed with her oldest boy, Aaron, and Jonas slept through until the next evening.

It was suppertime, and once again his aunt and uncle made him eat before he explained his presence. After supper his Uncle Robert took him out to the porch. They sat down in the swing and his uncle said gently, "All right, boy. Now let's talk about why you ran off."

Jonas took a deep breath. This time he wanted it to come out right, wanted desperately to make his uncle understand.

He said simply, "I want to build houses."

Robert didn't say anything, but Jonas glanced at him and saw a smile crease his uncle's face; he felt the older man's pleasure.

At last Robert answered, "So you want to be a carpenter do you? What are you thinking of, going into the trade with me?"

"Not exactly. Well, I mean I'd sure like to work with you. I really would, for a while. But I want to go to school—up north—and learn to build houses. Be an architect, I mean."

"I see. I take it Will doesn't think much of that idea." Robert's voice was gentle, but there was a dryness in his tone that did not escape Jonas's sensitive ear.

"No. Well...I didn't tell him all of it, about wanting to go to school and all that. Just that I want to build. He said he needs me on the farm."

"I see. That may be, Jonas. But you see, a man has to do what *he* wants to do, or life is no good at all. That's what I think." Robert grinned at Jonas. "That's why I took off from the farm a couple of years ago, and took up carpentering. And married your aunt."

Jonas felt embarrassed. His father had complained about Robert's marrying a "foreigner"; his Aunt Helene's people were from the bayous of Louisiana. Robert had told Jonas that Helene was part French, part Spanish and maybe part Indian.

"I love her," Jonas said loyally, and Robert squeezed the boy's shoulder with a strong, callused hand. "Do you think I could work with you awhile? There's a lot I need to learn.

39

I wouldn't have to be paid." He swallowed. "And I wouldn't take up any room. You could just put a blanket on the floor. I don't care."

Robert cleared his throat, and when he spoke again his voice was choked-sounding, as if it were hard for him to talk. "I'd like that, Jonas. But if you work for me, you'll be paid the going rate. And you won't have to sleep on any floor. We can do better than that."

"Then I can stay here?" Jonas asked eagerly.

Robert laughed. "Not so fast. You're only—what, now? Fourteen?" Jonas nodded. "Your pa'll have something to say about it, you know. That's the law, Jonas."

"I know." Jonas put his head in his hands. His uncle patted him on the back.

"Cheer up now, boy. I'll talk to Will. I have a feeling he might know where you ran off to, and he'll be here pretty soon. Don't know why he's taking so long," Robert added. "Louise must be fit to be tied. I know I wouldn't..." he stopped abruptly, embarrassed to be criticizing his brother before Will's son.

"Tell you what," he said cheerfully. "If Will's not here early in the morning, you come out with me tomorrow. I have an extra job on a shrimp boat right now—do about everything, repair the nets, keep up the boat. Caulking, like that. You can help me. I'll pay you for the day, anyway."

"Thank you. I sure do thank you." Jonas was afraid he might cry, and he was horrified at the thought. He was already a man. What would his uncle think of him? He cleared his throat loudly, as Robert had done, and repeated more calmly. "That's mighty nice."

His uncle seemed as uneasy as Jonas. He shrugged off the thanks and said gruffly, "Forget it. Say, you want to take a walk down by the water, see the boats? I'll show you the one we're on tomorrow. Then you'd better get some more sleep. We get up at five o'clock in the morning."

Jonas smiled. "Same time as the farm. But this is sure different from that."

Robert got up from the swing. "Damn right, kid. This sure is nothing like the farm. Come on, let's go."

The next evening, when Jonas and Robert returned to the small house from their work, Jonas was tired but exhilarated. The shrimp-boat work was hard, and the hours had been long, but Jonas, accustomed to the backbreaking work of the farm, had looked on it as almost a vacation. He loved the smell and sound of the Gulf, and the wavy feeling of the shrimp boat under his feet. And he had money in his pocket for the day's work, something he had never had before.

Helene greeted them smiling, but there was a worried look in her dark eyes that made Robert say, "What's the matter, honey? Did something happen? Was Will here today?"

"Your brother came late this morning, a long time after you all went out on the boat," Helene said to Robert.

He frowned. "Was he...all right to you? Talk to you all right?" Robert gave Jonas an uneasy glance, hating to have to ask this question in front of him.

"Oh, sure," Helene said cheerfully. Jonas felt she was lying, for his sake and for Robert's.

"All right." Robert sounded uncertain. Then he asked, "What did Will say about Jonas? You had to tell him, I know that."

"Yes, I had to tell him. He said...he said that he didn't have time to run around looking for Jonas, that Louise had sent him." Her voice was scornful, and sad. She turned to Jonas, saying gently, "I'm not going to lie to you, *cher*. I think you have a right to know what your father said."

Jonas felt his mouth tremble but he held his head up and answered, "Sure. And I thank you for that."

"Go on," Robert prompted.

"Well, he said if we didn't send Jonas back, he'd...he'd have the law on you, Robert."

"God almighty, he's the coldest-hearted bas—feller I've ever known in all my days." Robert sounded very angry.

"Now, Robert, calm down, *cher*." Jonas noticed that his aunt pronounced his uncle's name "Roe-bair." He liked that. He also noticed that his uncle quieted down when she touched his hand. It was strange to be thinking things like that, because Jonas's head was whirling. He would have to leave again; he would have to go on. He couldn't get Robert and Helene in trouble.

"I'll leave tomorrow," he said in a quiet voice, proud of the steadiness of it.

"You going back?" Robert asked.

"No. I'm going on. I'm going to work my way north. You taught me a lot before; I can be a carpenter's helper. Heck, I can do a lot of things." Jonas forced a smile.

His aunt and uncle were silent. Then Robert said, "Well, I have to hand it to you, boy. If that's what you want to do, do it. I'll tell Will you ran off. But I tell you this: I've got a

41

little money, and you take it. You're going to need it. And you let us hear from you, you hear?"

"Thanks. Thank you for everything. Maybe I'd better go tonight." He got up from the steps.

"Not tonight," Helene protested. "In the morning. Go early, when Robert goes to the boat."

Jonas hesitated. "All right." Uneasy, he noticed that his aunt was crying. He left the two together and went into the house.

It wasn't so bad the next morning, not as bad as the last time he had taken off. This time he had some real money, which he solemnly resolved to pay back as soon as he possibly could, and some really good food Helene had prepared. He also had a strong canvas bag; in it were some extra items of clothing that Robert had given him. They fit pretty well, because Jonas was extraordinarily tall and strongly built for his age.

Robert had told him he might do better working his way north by boat; Jonas's uncle had many friends, and one of them knew of a boat that fished down around the Keys. Maybe from there, Robert said, Jonas could get on a boat going north.

Robert's friend gave Jonas a note to the captain, and the boat took him on. Jonas got his first sight of the Atlantic, immeasurably bigger and wilder than the blue Gulf. After a time he was able to get work on a passenger steamer that went all the way from Jacksonville to Savannah, Georgia, and to Charleston, South Carolina. Jonas was dazzled by the ruined but beautiful houses in the port city of Charleston; he had never dreamed anything could be like that. Finally in that port he managed to get on a steamer that went to New York.

Though he was only fifteen years old when the steamer pulled into the mighty harbor of the biggest city he had ever seen in all his life, Jonas could pass for eighteen. He was tall enough, and the work he had done had developed his body far beyond the strength of other boys his age. He was tough and proud, proud to have come so far, on his own, to have survived at all. By now Jonas knew where he wanted to go, exactly, and how much more work and money it would take. For the last year, he had read and listened hungrily, until he found out what he wanted so desperately to know.

There was a school called the Massachusetts Institute of Technology, up in Boston. And he was going there. He would have to go to another kind of school first; an engineer on the last boat had told him that. And he would have to get the money to pay the Institute. But he would; he was resolved on that. Somehow.

"I *beg* your pardon." The indignant woman's voice broke in on Jonas Mark's reflections. His memories had been so vivid he had imagined himself in the year 1885 in the port of New York. And he was actually standing on a crowded street in Chicago eight years later. He stammered an apology to the young woman with whom he had collided and went hastily into the office building.

Even the presence of Anita Byrne, during that warm and busy afternoon, made little impression on Jonas. He was still wrapped up in the letter from Antoni Gaudí, and in the grinding battle he had fought to reach his present place.

Chapter 4

ONLY FIVE DAYS AFTER the great Columbian Exposition opened the stock market plunged. The nation panicked. But Chicago, bolstered by the prosperity brought in from Exposition visitors, did not immediately feel the effects.

"Yes, sir, Chicago's all right," Roderick Byrne said that evening in the Everleigh Club. "Phil Armour and Marshall Field have guaranteed all the Illinois Trust deposits personally—and they're the two richest men in Chicago."

Roderick, who had told Margaret he would be detained downtown on important business, was relaxing with his cronies in the Everleigh's famous Gold Room. The room was refinished yearly in gold leaf and polished every day.

The club was the showplace of Chicago's Levee area, a section of town somewhat careless of its morals, featuring gambling houses, barrelhouse saloons, and more than two hundred brothels. The Everleigh, however, was a refined house under the direction of two upper-class Kentuckians, Ada and Minna Everleigh, who had failed in their ambitions to go on the stage. No one knew the Everleighs' real name; Everleigh was a pseudonym born of their grandmother's letters, which always ended "Everly yours," and of Minna's liking for the poems of Sir Walter Raleigh.

The club's patrons were always genteelly entertained and were customarily rich; the fees began at fifty dollars, an unheard-of amount in other establishments.

"I agree with you, Roderick," said Nathaniel Moore. "It will pass, it will pass. The railroads will still run." Nat Moore, the son of a Rock Island Railroad executive, was a frequent visitor and lavish host at the Everleigh. "Here, have some more Moët." Moore poured a glass of champagne for Roderick Byrne.

Miss Minna entered the Gold Room at that point, casting an eagle eye over the sumptuous dining table. She was dressed sedately and, Roderick thought with amusement, acted very much like Margaret. He wondered what his wife would make of that. But Roderick was well aware that under her coy and fluttering exterior, Miss Minna was a sharp woman. She said now to the men, "Are you gentlemen comfortable? Is everything all right?"

"Excellent, Miss Minna," Nat Moore said, and there was a polite murmur from the others.

"I hope you'll all enjoy yourselves and not talk about this horrible panic." Miss Minna fluttered her pale lashes roguishly at her patrons. "I hear they're killing themselves left and right in the East. I sure am glad Chicago's so sound."

"Sound as a dollar," Roderick commented, and laughed. "Good as the gold on these walls."

"Will you gentlemen be going upstairs later on?" Miss Minna inquired.

"Oh, yes. Yes, indeed." Roderick's dark eyes gleamed, and he took another sip of his champagne.

"Well, now, that's splendid. Enjoy yourselves, you all." With a switch of her elaborate brocade gown, Miss Minna left the Gold Room.

One of their companions set down his glass and stubbed out his cigar. "Think I'll go on up now. How about you, Jake?"

"Sure." The two rose from the table. "See you later, Nat. Roderick."

"Soon, boys, soon." Roderick nodded to the two departing men.

"How about it, Roderick?" Nat Moore asked. "Shall we go up, too? I hear the girls have a new one, from New York, a little dazzler."

"That right? I'm looking forward to it." Roderick's reply was a little absent; he lit a thin panatela, his dark eyes squinting in its fragrant smoke. He drew on it slowly, then said in a hesitant way, "Something I'd like to talk about first, though. Can't really relax with it on my mind."

"What's that?"

"Well," Roderick began sheepishly, "it's not quite the thing to talk about in a place like this. But what the hell. Say, let's go in the music room a moment, shall we? I'd rather hear another kind of racket." He laughed and gestured with a

45

backward nod of the head at the nearby table. The diners' uproar was increasing, and it was hard to make oneself heard. Even in the genteel Everleigh the patrons sometimes got a little out of hand.

"Sure." Nat got up and pushed back the intricate damask chair. The men strolled down the hall into the music room, where a small quartet of violin, piano, harp and cello was playing softly. At the moment there was no one else in the room but Roderick and Nat.

"Ah, good." Roderick made a sound of satisfaction and indicated one of the deep, cut-velvet sofas at the other end of the elaborate Persian parlor. Their heels struck polished marble, then their footsteps sank to silence on a soft-piled Persian carpet.

Roderick sat down on the luxurious sofa conveniently near a small octagonal table. On its inlaid surface was a large, curiously shaped ashtray of heavy brass.

"The girls do us well," he commented. Now that he was about to broach the subject, he felt a little nervous. "As I said, Nat, this isn't the place to talk about my daughter...."

"Your daughter?" Nat Moore said encouragingly, stretching out his legs in an easy manner, contemplating the toes of his well-shined shoes.

"Yes. She's got it into her head that she's going to have a 'job.' She ought to be thinking of getting married, Nat."

Roderick's companion sighed. "I have a niece who talks like that. These girls nowadays are getting above themselves, Roderick. Riding bicycles in those ugly thingamajigs...what do they call them now...bloomers? Ugh." He made a face. "Enough to drive us here. *These* girls act like ladies, right enough. Don't that beat all, Roderick? When sporting women are more like ladies than ladies." Nat chuckled.

Roderick was dismayed; he had apparently struck a nerve in Nat Moore, hit upon a topic that would carry Nat off into a general discussion omitting the specific problem of Anita. Maybe he could give some good advice, though. After all, there was his niece....

"See much of your niece, Nat?" he asked.

"I should say so," Nat Moore replied with emphasis. "Ought to; my sister's always after me to talk to her like a Dutch uncle, whether I'm Dutch or not." He laughed at his weak joke, then added more seriously. "Between you and me and the gatepost, Roderick, my brother-in-law's not up to much."

"What's the problem there?"

"Drinks," Nat said briefly.

"Oh. Well." After an instant, Roderick pursued, "What do you say to your niece, Nat?"

"Usual thing—woman's proper place, and all that."

"Oh, that's the wrong tack altogether," Roderick declared. "Whenever I say anything like that, Anita looks at me like I'm a dinosaur. I tell you, Nat, these women are getting out of hand."

"You're right, you never said a truer word. A lot of it around here, anyway, is that Bertha Palmer's fault."

"Bertha? What do you mean, Nat?" Roderick was taken aback.

"Well, look at her, Roderick. Beautiful woman—splendid. Rich, married and highly respectable. Yet she's not content with all that; has to take over the Women's Building at the Exposition, stick her nose into all kinds of things. Encourages the others." Suddenly Nat Moore laughed and hit his knee. "She told 'em off yesterday, didn't she? Did you hear about that?"

"Sure." At the Exposition, the Women's Building had been the scene for tears and hysteria. A group on the board had protested Mrs. Potter Palmer's leadership on the grounds that they had not been given the chance to meet the Duchess of Veragua, Lady Aberdeen and other titled guests. Sharp words had been exchanged, and Mrs. Palmer, in an injured rebuttal, had told the assembly that she thought they had banded together as women "for something fine," and had chided the women for "pulling hair over an introduction to a duchess." This emotional appeal had set off a storm of weeping among the delegates, and one lady from Louisiana declared that she would bow to Mrs. Palmer "as our American queen."

"Yes, Bertha won, all right," Roderick commented, but his smile was absent again, halfhearted. "Yes, sir, she's a beauty. Don't know why old Potter spends so much time up in that tower of his. I wouldn't."

"Maybe he's beyond it," Nat suggested. "But we're not, my boy, we're not. What are we sitting here for? Anita'll be all right. So will Gertrude. Tempus is fugitting. Let's go upstairs."

Roderick agreed. He followed Nat across the music room; the soft notes of the harp struck against his nerves, titillating him. The harp was like a woman's fingers, stroking. Maybe his discussion with Nat had been futile, but what the devil.

47

As Miss Minna said, they were here to enjoy themselves, after all. And Roderick tried to put the difficult matter of Anita out of his head.

Ever since the night Anita had seen Jonas on the esplanade, he had piqued her interest. But in the weeks that followed her joining Higsbee and Waite, Anita's interest in Jonas the man waned; she grew to admire Jonas the worker.

Besides, she was too wrapped up in her own tasks to take much notice of those around her. She had resolved to give Charles Seton no encouragement: he could quickly become a nuisance. And Jonas Mark was reticent to the point of incivility. He barely acknowledged her routine greetings in the mornings and evenings; she had come to feel he absolutely disliked her. She had an irritated sense that to him she was a frivolous society girl who had taken the job for a lark and would drop it at any moment.

At times, as she worked, Anita silently raged against Jonas and all men: did they imagine her four years at M.I.T. had also been a lark?

Because he was chief draftsman at Higsbee, it was tacitly understood that Jonas would give Anita her assignments. Avoiding her eyes, and careful never to brush her hand, Jonas loaded Anita with endless routine tasks, many of which amounted to sheer drudgery. She executed them with her usual degree of excellence, and Jonas Mark was not stingy in his praise of her performance.

The eager Charley continued to be attentive; he frequently offered to help Anita with many of the copying tasks she found so distasteful, but which she did without a murmur.

She was polite and cool in declining Charley's help and worked on during the warm days with mingled feelings of frustration and accomplishment. Anita had come to know that in these first vital months the main thing was to endure.

To escape any appearance of frivolity, she made almost a fetish of plain dress. Always fresh, cool and neat in spite of the burgeoning heat of June, Anita appeared daily in pastel shirtwaist blouses and dark skirts. The only difference in her attire was the substitution of a broad-brimmed leghorn for the small gray hat of spring.

Sometimes she thought Jonas Mark was studying her intently out of the corner of his eye, but if she happened to glance his way, he was always intent on his board.

The financial panic of May had extended into a frenzied

period of sell-off and decline; some of the railroads had gone bankrupt, and several European banks began selling their American stocks and bonds. But Chicago, still prospering from the Exposition, continued to build, and new commissions poured into the office of Higsbee and Waite.

Anita's habits had changed so drastically that her mother and aunt were distressed. Her job had made it impossible for her to attend the series of luncheons and teas planned for her, and more often than not she refused to attend evening functions because she was "too tired." To keep peace with her mother, Anita had gone to a ball or two on weekends; she always encountered Harry Brand and Charles Seton at one house or another, but was indifferently friendly to both. She knew it was a thorn in Charley's flesh that she danced with him at various balls but during the day kept him at a distance, refusing to lunch with him unless Jonas went or, for that matter, spend much time with him alone at all.

The reticence of Jonas Mark was becoming a challenge to her, but the challenge of work was greater still; she was more than ever determined that nothing was going to stand in her way, not all the weeping and nagging of her mother, or the gentle hints of her father and aunt about "easing up for the summer."

It was the Byrne family's custom to maintain only a skeleton staff at the mansion during the hot months of July and August and for Margaret and Charlotte to stay at their summer home in Lake Forest. Roderick generally stayed at a club in town and joined the women on the weekends.

One evening near the end of June, Margaret said at dinner, "It's time to go to the country, Anita. Have you told Cora what to pack for you?"

Anita held on to her temper with difficulty. After a moment, she answered quietly. "I am not going to the country, Mother, and you know I'm not. I'm employed at Higsbee and Waite."

"Are you a factory girl or a maid?" Margaret shrieked. "Of course you are coming. You've done this nonsensical thing long enough."

"Margaret..." Roderick began, and Charlotte Byrne looked uneasy.

"You are coming with us!" Margaret cried. "You are coming, or you can get out of this house, Anita Byrne!"

"I will be delighted to get out of this house." Anita's reply was calm, but the anger in her voice was apparent. She turned to Roderick. "As soon as you arrange it at the bank, Father, I will take my money and find a place of my own."

Margaret gasped. She began to fan herself with her long chiffon handkerchief. "I am going to faint," she declared in a loud wail that had no weakness in it. "I am going to die of an attack. An unmarried girl, living alone! You've got to stop her, Roderick—Charlotte—" Margaret implored her husband and sister-in-law with outstretched hands—"before I expire of the shock."

"Now, Margaret," Roderick said wearily.

"It is your choice, Mother," Anita said, her tone as calm as before. "I will stay here this summer, and keep on at my employment, or I will find a place of my own."

"I can't bear it!" Margaret's sparse lashes fluttered and she rolled her eyes upward as if she were having a fit. Then she fell sideways from her chair, in an expert fashion, onto the deep-piled carpet.

"Oh, dear," said Charlotte, with a pained expression.

Roderick gathered up his fallen wife in a practiced way and bore her limp body from the dining room and up the stairs to her boudoir. The doctor was summoned. Margaret declared herself too weak to go to the country, and the pilgrimage therefore did not take place until the middle of July.

Meanwhile Anita won her point, or rather Margaret won a compromise: Anita said she would stay on at the mansion for the time being. Charlotte was silent on the matter, and Roderick, to escape the whole situation, spent more and more time at his office and on evening business downtown. The associates and employees of Roderick Byrne felt the weight of his increasing tyranny. To atone for his powerless position at home, he began to be overbearing at the office.

The heat of July oppressed the city, sizzling up from the cedar-block and cobblestone pavements, and the noise of the streets seemed more incessant than ever, with street-level railroad tracks and cable cars offering a constant clang of locomotive bells. Anita moved through the heat and noise with a determined coolness. Charles Seton remarked more than once on her air of freshness in the midst of the thick heat.

On one particular afternoon in July, when even the conscientious Jonas had been late getting back to work from the natatorium at Jackson and Michigan where he swam, Charles looked at Anita and said, "You look just like a flower."

Anita did not answer, but her small Gioconda smile encouraged Charley. There was something about her, he thought, that was more vulnerable than usual, something soft and infinitely appealing.

"Yes, ma'am, you surely do." Jonas's soft drawling interjection surprised Anita; he was usually so silent and rarely entered into the personal banter between Charley and herself. "These are the good new days, all right," Jonas went on, smiling. "I never thought I'd live to see the day...when I'd hear such things in the drafting room."

Charley laughed, and Anita grinned at Jonas's expression. But she glanced at his eyes, and she thought she saw a gleam in them, something sharper and more urgent unexpressed in his casual words. She turned back to her drawing board and resumed her drawing.

For a little while they all worked in companionable silence. But soon Anita felt her concentration drift; she had never heard Jonas sound so easy and relaxed, so human. Her hand slipped. Her T square went a millimeter off and she found to her dismay that her drawing was spoiled.

She made a faint sound of annoyance, and Jonas Mark looked up from his board.

She looked up, too, at the same moment, and they stared into each other's eyes. Anita felt languorous and confused. For the first time in her experience she was responding in a direct and simple way to a man, with a response uncomplicated by her usual censors of feeling—those silent judges who warned that men meant marriage, curtailment of freedom; that the soft feelings could entrap her, divert her from her goal.

The feeling she had now was too strong for reason: she just felt the power of Jonas's eyes, and noticed the wiry strength of him, the scent of sun and wind he always had about him, and she gloried in the feeling. But then the feeling was gone as quickly as it had come, and she said calmly, "It's nothing much. I'm afraid I've spoiled this drawing. I'll do it again."

Jonas glanced at her keenly and, she thought, with approval for her matter-of-fact manner. He said, in a gentler voice than usual, "Let me have a look." He got up and came over to her table.

"Oh, that's not much. That's a very slight defect. I think I can fix it. I'll show you...may I?"

He was too close for Anita to feel easy, but it would seem not only rude but downright prudish to draw away. So she sat very still, and nodded, dismayed to feel an increase of warmth around her ears. That brief strange feeling she had had before was returning.

"Here," Jonas said, "I'll take it to my board." She got up and followed, this time leaning near him as he demonstrated his method of correction. "I'll wager you learned that from Ferguson," she said with impulsive warmth. "For some reason I always had trouble doing it."

"Ferguson's still at M.I.T., then?" Jonas asked. "He was one of my favorite professors."

"And mine," she replied, thinking, We also have another idol in common. She wanted to bring up the subject of Gaudí, but did not know how. Instead she said, when he handed her the drawing, "Thank you. That was very kind."

She could feel Charley's stare and, hoping that her cheeks had not changed color, went back to her board and started working again intently.

The hot afternoon went slowly on and the three worked mostly in silence, broken by an occasional groan from Charley, who asked them, himself, and heaven why they were slaving and not enjoying themselves at the races or the shore. Jonas smiled amiably at Charley's comments, retorting that they would not get paid at the races, but rather the reverse. More than once Anita looked up from her board to study Jonas's profile, and his hard, tanned arms exposed to the biceps in the rolled-up shirtsleeves.

At five, Charley gave a loud sigh of relief and slowly began to put away his tools. Anita finished soon after and went to get her carryall and broad-brimmed hat from the hook on the wall next to Jonas's. Jonas tidied up his board and rolled down his sleeves, sauntering to the wall hook to take down his worn lightweight suit jacket.

"May I?" He reached up and detached the strap of Anita's carryall from the hook, handing it to her.

She thanked him and, putting the carryall over her arm, put on her hat. He shook his jacket out, trying to shake away its creases, and a letter fell from the breast pocket into Anita's bag. She retrieved it and handed it to him, but not before she had seen the Spanish stamp and the return address af Astorga.

She remembered the duke's saying that Gaudí was working on the Episcopal Palace at Astorga. She felt a sudden wild impulse and did a very uncharacteristic thing: she had

52

a deep distaste for intrusion of any kind, yet she asked Jonas, "You have friends in Astorga?"

He looked at her for a moment, then answered quietly, "Not exactly." Then as if he realized he might have been rude, he added in haste, "This is from Antoni Gaudí."

"Gaudí!" she repeated softly.

"You know about Gaudí?" Jonas asked in a tone of amazement. "Why, I thought"—he smiled slightly—"I was the only one in Chicago who did. Who likes him, that is."

"Know about him?" she repeated warmly. "I admire his work more than any architect's in the world."

Jonas stared at her with a half-smile of surprise and pleasure on his dark, weathered face. He looks so young, she thought, when he smiles. His whole face lights up, and he's a different man.

"I...am quite surprised," he began hesitantly, and she laughed.

"May I escort you to your carriage, Miss Byrne?" She turned, startled. She had totally forgotten Charley's presence.

"No," she said quickly. Then she amended. "No, thank you, Charles. I...I am meeting my aunt, and we will dine in town." She stood with her hat in her hands for a long moment.

Charley, sensing his dismissal, nodded. "Very well. I'm sorry. Goodnight, then. Jonas." His farewell to Jonas was curt and cold. He walked out of the room.

"Well," Jonas said uncertainly. "May I...shall we walk downstairs together?"

"Yes." Instinctively Anita waited until she heard Charley's footsteps growing fainter on the stairs. She moved more slowly than was her custom, setting her straw hat with care on her head and taking down her handbag from its hook. For some strange reason she felt that her movements were almost labored, like a swimmer's in the heaviness of water.

Jonas, too, moved with unaccustomed leisure. He put on his jacket and adjusted it precisely; usually he threw it on anyway. She preceded him through the door and down the stairs. When they were in the confusion of the hot street, she said calmly, "My carriage is over there."

She indicated a small closed carriage, neat and shining, a few doors down the street. A gray-haired coachman in uniform sat smartly at the reins.

"But you told..." Jonas began, confused. Then his changeable eyes reflected the smile before it reached his firm mouth, and he said, "I see. Charley doesn't take a 'No,' does he?"

Anita smiled. "No, he doesn't. I'd rather lie than hurt feelings." She hesitated, then asked, "May I drop you somewhere?"

The simple, friendly question had a strange effect. Jonas's smile faded and he looked uneasy and embarrassed. She wondered why and wished she had not asked the question.

He looked down into her eyes and then said slowly, "Well, I generally walk to my boardinghouse. But...that's mighty nice of you. Yes, I'd appreciate it. And then...we can talk."

Anita decided he was not comfortable with women, and reflected how different he was from Charley.

"Good," she said casually. "Come along, then." Her manner, which had no coquetry at all, seemed to reassure Jonas Mark. His face cleared and he followed her to the carriage.

"Hello, Joseph."

"Good evening, Miss Anita." The coachman jumped down from his perch and opened the door for them.

When they were settled inside, Anita turned to Jonas and said, "Would you give him your address?"

Awkwardly Jonas leaned forward and called out the street to Joseph. He was obviously not used to giving orders to servants, and Anita, whose knowledge of the city was wide, was surprised at the shabbiness of the address. Jonas's position at Higsbee was surely well-paid; why, then, did he live in such a place?

But as they started off, she put the matter from her mind and asked him, without preamble, "You know Antoni Gaudí?"

"Only by letter," he answered briefly, and glanced at her with a puzzled expression. She knew that her sudden change of manner, after the rather formal courtesies of the office, had taken him aback. She was a little taken aback herself; she felt like a different woman. And it had happened so quickly that even her long-cultivated poise was shaken by its suddenness.

"I beg your pardon," she said softly. "I know you must think this strange. I am being rude and inquisitive. But you see, I've never met anyone else who even knew much about Gaudí, much less corresponded with him."

Jonas shifted in the seat, his long legs moving about as he tried to find a place for them in the narrow, padded interior. He is like something wild, she thought, like some beautiful wild animal in a pen.

"Oh, no!" he protested. "It's not in you to be rude." He seemed to have trouble finding the right words. Then he went on slowly, "I'm just...amazed that you feel the way I do. I can't get over that." He smiled. "It's wonderful. I never had a chance to talk about Gaudí to somebody who *likes* him. Most people don't understand what he's trying to do."

He told her about his first discovery of Gaudí's work—in an obscure magazine a foreign traveler had left behind in the M.I.T. library. With quiet, perceptive questions she gradually drew him out, and soon he was telling her about his own life.

She was touched and saddened by the grinding hardness of it; without a single complaint he still conveyed to her the mental poverty of his father's house, the backbreaking work he had done since he was eleven years old.

But he stopped talking abruptly, and said in a chagrined way, "I'm sorry. I'm talking too much, Miss Byrne. I don't think I've talked this much since...well, ever." He smiled broadly, and the smile, which lit his grim face and made him look young and wistful, touched Anita's emotions in a way she had never experienced.

The carriage was slowing. "Well," Jonas said, his awkwardness returning, "this is where I live."

She waited expectantly for him to linger; young men always did. Or to suggest that they drive on and dine together. It was the kind of thing that always happened to Anita Byrne. But he said, "Thank you very much, Miss Byrne. I...I enjoyed our talk. I'll see you tomorrow." And he opened the door and got down. Without looking back, he walked into his shabby boardinghouse and disappeared.

Nonplussed, Anita sat for a moment staring after him. She realized Joseph was speaking to her.

"Will you be going home now, Miss Anita?"

"Yes, Joseph. I am going home."

The carriage began the long ride to the mansion in Oak Park. Jonas Mark was like no other man Anita had ever met, and she had met a good many at school and in her parents' active circle.

At one moment he responded to her warmly, at another he would shut himself off from her in an incomprehensible way. Yet all the while she had known that their minds were related, that something had blossomed between them.

55

Chapter 5

THE NEXT MORNING JONAS was early; he had spent a restless night thinking of Anita Byrne. His eyes were gritty from lack of sleep. He blinked in the oppressive light of the warm room and made a determined effort to concentrate on the work before him. The famous "Chicago window" invented by local architects—a broad expanse of glass with a large fixed center pane and removable sashes on either side—usually made work more pleasant. The new-style windows let in enough light and air to compensate for poor electric lighting and the hot sun's blaze on stone and concrete.

But this morning even Jonas, who was impervious to heat, felt the weight of hot brightness on his neck and shoulders. He shifted on his stool. Sweat broke out on his back. He put aside his T square and thought, I acted like a fool last night. He should have offered her dinner, taken her somewhere. But there was never enough money for that. Every dollar he could save was another nail in what he was building—something for his mother, and Spain.

Jonas cursed and picked up his pencil. "Dammit to hell," he said.

He heard someone come in. It was Charley Seton.

"Damn what to hell?" Charley asked, with a smile.

It irritated Jonas to see his friend's dapper clothes; he himself felt as if he had been working on a chaingang for ten hours. Charley was dressed in a faultlessly tailored suit of pale gray with a maroon silk cravat, tied in a perfect knot. He sported a fresh white carnation in his buttonhole.

"What's the occasion?" Jonas drawled.

"A whole new day." Charley grinned.

Jonas grunted and bent over his board.

"I don't see what you have to cuss about, chum." Charley hung his jacket with care on a hanger.

"What does that mean?" Jonas did not look up as Charley sat down at his board.

"If I'd been in your spot last night, I'd be singing this morning." When Jonas did not answer, Charley added, "I saw you and Anita Byrne, getting in her carriage."

Jonas looked up to see a challenging gleam in Charley's large brown eyes.

"She was nice enough to drive me home. What business is it of yours?"

"Oh, come now, Jonas," Charley said good-naturedly. "Beautiful women are always my business." Then he repeated, "Drove you *home*? Well, well. You didn't make any more headway than I have." He laughed. "You crazy fool, I'd give a million dollars for a chance like that, and you muffed it. That's a turnabout: a beautiful woman takes you for a buggy ride, and *you* get out?"

It was the kind of joking thing that Charley always said, but this morning Jonas reacted as he never had before. He slammed his T square down on his board. "Cut it out, Charley," he said with dangerous softness.

But Charley was still in his teasing mood. "What's the matter with you? Are you studying for the monastery?"

Jonas got slowly to his feet, pushing back his stool. "We'll see what's the matter. Why don't we step out in the hall?"

Charley stared at him, amazed. "Oh, look here, Jonas."

Suddenly Jonas felt more like a fool than ever; the good-natured Charley was hesitating not out of fear, but because it was all a tempest in a teapot. Charley's no lightweight, Jonas thought. He had taken boxing prizes at school and his apparent indolence was deceptive. He had fifteen pounds on Jonas and was just as fast on his feet. He could take me, Jonas judged, in spite of my experience. And there had been plenty of that—climbing and hauling, brawls on the road, on the streets and docks.

Jonas's anger evaporated and he knew how foolish it all was. "Charley, I'm sorry I..." he began.

Anita Byrne came into the room. Both men, suddenly embarrassed, muttered a greeting and returned to their tables.

Anita's manner had completely changed from last night: she was very courteous, but cool, and paid strict attention to her work.

Jonas concluded, She thinks I'm a boor. Or maybe he had

told her too much, maybe she thought he was a cracker. Then he was shamed by the thought. She had been nice, interested in his family. But he said to himself, It's just as well. I can't afford a woman like Anita Byrne.

He had to get to Spain, no matter what. He was going to apprentice himself to Antoni Gaudí if he had to work for nothing and do manual labor elsewhere. He knew this was the only way to penetrate the secret of Gaudí's genius, to learn his sense of flowing space.

Anita Byrne was a woman to share a life with; Jonas had known that the first time he saw her, observing her uniqueness, her pride and grace, her look of stern intelligence, brightened and dazzled with wit. But he had also seen that she was born to a sheltered place, one that he could not offer.

For the next several weeks they all slipped back into their former ways—three busy people, polite but comfortable with each other in the familiar atmosphere. Charley made his usual jokes and Jonas and Anita answered him in kind. But the closeness of that one evening seemed to have gone for good.

As the long summer wore on, the offices of Higsbee and Waite continued to be flooded with work and problems to solve. The firm that Roderick Byrne dismissed as "hardly the most prestigious in Chicago" was nevertheless valued for its solid production and Waite's structural genius.

The technological revolution in Chicago's architecture was a response to the shortcomings in the city's site. It was ideally located as a trade center, but it was built on an impossible swamp. Many feared the large buildings would sink into the ground; the building methods of the East were not feasible in the moist, sandy clay of Chicago. Foundations needed special ingenuity; George Waite and Jonas Mark had that ingenuity.

In one building they devised a foundation of concrete, steel beams and heavy wooden timbers interwoven to create a huge platform on which the structure literally floated, held up by the soil and water pressure in the ground.

A theater under construction that summer by Higsbee and Waite was to be supported on 770 wooden piles. But now it had been discovered that driving the piles would cause vibrations that would upset the delicate printing presses of the newspaper building next door. To avoid the vibrations the contractors were digging shafts deep into the ground and filling them with concrete.

Jonas, who was working closely with Waite on the structural problems of the theater, soon found that so much of his time was taken up by that aspect that he was getting a backlog of drawings and minor designs. Waite agreed that Jonas would have to delegate a good deal of the design work. Charley was the logical person to take over. But one afternoon when Jonas glanced at Anita's drawing board while she was out and saw the sketches she had been doing on her own, he decided to discuss the matter with Higsbee.

Anita's designs were the most imaginative Jonas had seen in a long time. She had done the drawing in color and it featured unusual forms of enameled terra-cotta. The design had drama and grace. A glance told Jonas it was highly workable. He knew that Byrne Associates had been the first to use terra-cotta exclusively on streetside facades, but at the Provident Building they had used an enameled variety on all sides. This design of Anita's was far in advance of the others.

Though the drawing was highly original it recalled something of Gaudí and his novel use of rich earth-colored rubble bound with brightly painted *azulejos,* or tiles, the start of a renaissance of ceramic art all along the eastern seaboard of Spain. The feeling in Anita's creation touched Jonas deeply. He felt more than ever the kinship of their minds.

Higsbee agreed that Anita should be permitted to submit trial designs. In a carefully businesslike way Jonas took the matter up with Anita.

She tried hard not to show how delighted she was, and the effort touched him. He could not help feeling the same friendly warmth that had grown between them on that special evening. Anita smiled and said, "Thank you. I'll try to justify your choice."

Jonas said, "I'm sure you will." He stood at her board a moment longer, and they looked into each other's eyes. Suddenly he could think of nothing else to say and abruptly walked back to his drawing board.

Something impelled him to look up again, and when he did, he met her fiery blue glance for a long instant. This time she was the first to look away, and Jonas imagined there was a faint new color in her white face.

But he was not a man used to imagining things, not about people. He usually imagined the designs of buildings; that was all. Jonas felt moisture break out on his upper lip. Wiping it away, he thought, I'll be glad to get out on the site. This situation was getting to him in a way he had never foreseen.

On the building site the next morning, Jonas felt more at ease, more at home, in the hot sun. He breathed in gratefully the scent of wood and dust and steel, the wet odor of the swampy soil where they dug. This is more like it, he thought. This was what he was used to, after all. Most of his life had been spent out of doors, using every muscle, working with his arms and legs and hands.

He might have been one of the workmen, walking around the pitted site on his long, lean legs, his head protected from the sun in a battered hat, his rough clothes stained with dirt and sweat. The men liked Jonas Mark, because they had learned he could do anything they could, and better. On one job an extension ladder was too short to reach a certain spot, so Jonas had told a workman to rig a beam for him to ride. The man had protested it was dangerous; if the beam should cant too much with Jonas on it, he would slide off. But Jonas had insisted and they carried out the operation, with Jonas straddling the end of the beam precariously as he set the needed piece in place and nailed it in firmly.

Ever since then they had considered him one of them. Even so they knew that Jonas was a little more, a man with visions they did not possess.

On that hot afternoon in July, Jonas moved about in his rough shoes, checking the concrete-pouring around the piles. It was a Saturday afternoon, and some of the men were already looking ahead to Saturday night, and Sunday off. Here and there Jonas saw a man drinking beer. It was a practice strictly forbidden by Higsbee and Waite, but Jonas took an easier view of the matter, remembering the men he had worked with in his boyhood. There were some who could drink a good deal and still drive a nail straight and true.

We're not driving nails here, he thought. He glanced at the titanic wooden piles that would be driven into the soil: some looked as big around as redwood trees. The man who ran the crane, a hard-drinking, casual giant named Tom Hogan, looked a little the worse for wear, in Jonas's opinion.

He strolled over toward the crane and raised his hand in a friendly greeting. "How's it going, Tom?"

"Fine," Hogan smiled. "Jus' fine."

Observing Hogan's reddened eyes and unsteady manner, Jonas retorted, "You don't look it, Tom. Are you all right?"

"Course I'mallright," Hogan ran his words together in a disconcerting fashion. He began to operate the crane, raising a huge treelike pile high into the air, preparatory to driving it into the deep-dug hole.

Jonas thought the shaft was leaning a little too much to one side, but he made no further comment. But he was uneasy: the guy line didn't look right. He shaded his eyes with his long hand and looked up at the slowly descending pile.

Suddenly, he realized—too late—it was going to fall.

"Lillian Russell must be quite an inducement to bring you in from the country," Anita said to her aunt. "The weather is so oppressive."

"My dear, I wouldn't miss her for the world. Everyone is talking about her, and wondering if she is as beautiful as her pictures," Charlotte explained. "Besides, we might even get a glimpse of that Brady man—that is, if he can stay away from food long enough to go to a matinee."

The famous Lillian Russell was in Chicago for a sixteen-week engagement at the Columbia Theater. She was a former native, christened Helen Louise Leonard. Her most faithful admirer, Diamond Jim Brady, had followed Miss Russell from New York. He was dividing his time between the theater, the Fine Arts Palace at the Exposition and the restaurants where he could get his favorite treat, sweet corn.

"He looks as if there's no shortage of corn," Anita commented absently. In his newspaper pictures, Brady's bulk was as obvious as his diamonds. But Anita's comment had been automatic; she had been thinking of Jonas Mark. He would be on the site this afternoon. It was only three blocks away. Suddenly she knew she had to see him, if only for a moment.

Anita called to the coachman, "Joseph, turn down this street, would you? Take us down three blocks."

"This isn't the way to the Columbia," Charlotte protested.

"I know, Aunt. But there's plenty of time. There's something I want to see."

"What is it?" Charlotte was annoyed. "I'd like to get out of this heat, my dear. It's ninety degrees, at least."

"It's the site of the new Steiner Theater." At her aunt's sniff of displeasure, Anita prepared herself for the usual attack.

"A Higsbee building, Roderick says," Charlotte began. "He calls them the 'warehouse specialists.' They *do* build an extraordinary number of warehouses, don't they? Really, my dear, I don't know why you couldn't have joined your father's firm, if you had to pursue this outlandish idea of employment."

Ignoring the reference to her joining Byrne Associates, Anita replied, "Yes, Higsbee builds a lot of warehouses. Someone has to. They do a good job on them, too. They blend quite well with their surroundings. But Higsbee is hardly a specialist in that. The new theater will be quite impressive. Some of my own designs will go on the facade and in the interior."

"Well!" Charlotte was silent for a moment, then she commented, "I suppose Roderick had a hand in that; I assume he's guiding you."

"No, he's not. He knows nothing about it. We haven't discussed it at all." Anita's tone was indignant.

Charlotte grew serious, and asked quietly, "You and your father are not discussing much of anything these days, I gather?"

"Enough," Anita said curtly. As a matter of fact, she and her father hardly saw one another. Most evenings she returned to dine alone in the half-closed mansion; her father was presumably spending a great deal of time downtown. Anita had gone to the country with him on only one weekend.

But now, to allay her aunt's anxiety, she added in a gentler voice, "Everything is fine, Aunt Charlotte."

"Really?" Charlotte's skepticism was plain. "I think you ought to . . ."

"Here, Joseph," Anita called out, cutting in on her aunt's stricture. "Stop here."

"I fail to see the fascination of all this," Charlotte Byrne said in a bored voice as she looked out at the construction site.

Anita answered, "I'm interested in the building's progress. They are having difficulty with the foundation."

"I thought it was the design you're working on," Charlotte retorted, and Anita realized once more how shrewd her aunt was.

"It is, but naturally I must see the building as a whole."

"Well, I must say, my dear, I can't see why a lady would be interested in this . . . plumbing," Charlotte concluded with distaste. "Interior decoration and design are one thing—why, even that poor Mahoney girl, who's plain as a pikestaff, does suitable tasks. But to think of a beauty like you, in connection with this—this scrabbling in the dirt—is grotesque."

As always Anita was forced to laugh at her aunt's ideas;

she had to admit the site was not a place of beauty yet. It was a chaos of heavy machines, mud and massive piles, sweating workmen in rough and filthy clothes shouting at each other.

Then Anita caught sight of Jonas, and she turned her head away from Charlotte, so her aunt could not see her expression. Anita knew her face had changed; she could feel it. For a moment it seemed that Jonas had noticed the carriage; he was transfixed, staring in their direction. Then he looked up suddenly at a slowly descending pile.

Anita could see that something had gone wrong: it seemed to her that the guy line supporting the shaft around the pile was pulling loose from its mooring. She was aware of the tremendous tension of the line, enough to pull out the tiepins.

She heard a shout from one of the men, and saw it happen, very quickly: the descending pile fell too soon from its shaft and landed with a monstrous, roaring impact on the ground, pinning two of the workmen beneath it. Jonas had not been hit. But with a thudding heart Anita saw the cable flail like a whip through the air, hitting Jonas Mark and the man beside him, knocking them both to the ground.

"Good God!" Charlotte cried out. "What's happened?"

"I can't explain it to you now," Anita said in a choked voice, opening the carriage door.

"Where are you going?" her aunt shrieked. "You're not going out there!"

Anita called back over her shoulder, "Go on without me, Aunt Charlotte."

"Anita! Anita! Come back here at once!" Charlotte struggled out of the carriage. Joseph, the coachman, had jumped down from his perch and was staring after Anita's running figure. She had already reached the edge of the site.

Charlotte said, "We'll wait, Joseph," as calmly as she could.

She sat down again on the edge of the carriage seat to find an escape from the beating sun. She watched Anita rush to the edge of the site.

Charlotte saw a burly man, apparently someone in charge, gesturing Anita emphatically away. But Anita was not deterred and said something to the man, and his manner changed at once. He removed his hat. With a more courteous manner he pointed to a place where Anita could stand. Then Charlotte saw a tall lean young man, one of those hit by the cable, rise to his knees and shake his head.

Unsteadily he got to his feet: he saw Anita and stopped still. They stared at each other, oblivious to everyone. If they were friends, Charlotte thought, no one would guess it; they continued to stare, unsmiling, without greeting or gesture, almost like mortal enemies. Charlotte Byrne had never seen an encounter like that before. There was something so strange and…uncivilized, she reflected, in the way they looked at each other that Charlotte's uneasiness grew.

While Anita continued to stand there in the blazing sun, staring, as if she were hypnotized, Charlotte drew her skirts into the carriage and closed the door herself before Joseph could reach it.

"Drive on, Joseph," she said sharply. "Don't leave her standing in the sun. Are you quite awake?"

The coachman's resentful posture, as he drove to meet Anita, reminded Charlotte Byrne that she had been unjust and fractious, but her discomfort was great. She glanced at the site again and noticed that the tall young man was quite unharmed; already he was helping attend to the injured men. With great haste, Charlotte observed; perhaps he was trying to make up for his inattention a while before, when he and Anita stood looking at each other so oddly. How beautiful they had been, she thought unwillingly; something in them both was very touching. She had felt that once seeing panthers in a cage at the zoo.

You're maundering, Charlotte Byrne, she said to herself, and assumed a stern face for the benefit of Anita. They had caught up to Anita now, and Joseph was already jumping down to open the door for her and help her into the carriage.

"What is going on?" Charlotte demanded, when Anita had taken the opposite seat. The older woman stared at the girl: her face was quite pale, paler than usual, and her bright blue eyes blazed in the white face. The eyes had a closed expression that Charlotte knew well: her niece was up to something when she looked like that.

Anita answered in a cool, impatient voice, "The man who was nearly injured is the senior draftsman at Higsbee."

"That does not justify your running out like that."

"It was a human thing to do, Aunt Charlotte." Some color was returning to her white face, but now her tone was angry.

Charlotte felt a little ashamed of her own lack of concern, yet she knew her first instinct had been the right one. That young man was more to Anita than a human being in trouble.

She also knew from Anita's expression that she dare not question her now, so Charlotte kept her silence.

Now they could hear the big bell of the horse-drawn ambulance approaching; it passed their carriage, speeding to the site.

Jonas watched the carriage leave, and shook his head again to clear it. The cable had only glanced his shoulder; he was more stunned by seeing Anita Byrne standing on the hot, dusty rise in her thin, floating dress. And pleased by her obvious concern.

Then he was aware of a dull pain in his arm and shoulder; the cable must have hit harder than he had thought. And he was conscious that around him men were hurt, that there was work to do. He forced himself into action.

John Clancy, the burly foreman, asked him anxiously, "Are you all right, Mr. Mark? That was quite a knock you took. I, er, saw you shaking your head. Did you get it there?"

"No, I'm all right, John. Let's see about these men. Hogan's bad, I'm afraid. And Spinetti got the full force of the cable. He might have a broken shoulder."

The falling pile had knocked Hogan from the cab of the pile driver; he lay unconscious in the rubble. "Don't move him. Don't move any of them," Jonas ordered, and instinctively the men obeyed.

The ambulance had arrived; tensely the workmen watched the horses pick their way across the roiled and swampy ground. Two men jumped out of the wagon and took out a stretcher.

"He's the worst, I think." Jonas indicated Hogan. One of the white-coated men nodded and knelt by the prone body, running his hands in a practiced way over Hogan's unconscious form. He gestured to the wagon, and two other men came quickly to the spot. With great care they lifted Hogan onto the stretcher and carried him to the ambulance.

"Poor bastard," Clancy said, watching the men slide Hogan in. "He shouldn't have been allowed to work in his state. I feel like it's my fault. He could have killed a dozen men. I guess we were lucky, at that. Hogan's not so lucky."

Jonas shook his head. "No, he's not. I hope he hasn't killed himself." He turned to survey the squat Italian who was still sitting on the ground. One of the white-coated men was feeling Spinetti's shoulder and asking him questions. The attendant helped Spinetti to rise. As they passed Jonas, he called out, "How's it going, Fred?"

"Hurts like hell, Mr. Mark," the man answered tightly. "But I came out better than Tom. They gotta look me over."

"Good luck, Fred." Jonas smiled. Two other workmen followed Spinetti and the attendant to the wagon. "We gotta go too, Clancy," one of them called to the foreman.

"Right, Bill. We'll be right along."

Jonas and Clancy hailed a public carriage and followed the ambulance wagon.

"They'd better look you over too, Mr. Mark," Clancy said.

"I don't think so, John." Jonas's answer was so absent that the other man looked at him keenly.

"If you don't mind my saying so, you don't sound right."

Jonas thought, No wonder. First I get knocked down by a flying cable in ninety-degree heat, then I look up and there she is, standing there, staring at me. She must have come there to see me. The idea was so fantastic Jonas almost laughed out loud. "I'm fine," Jonas said to Clancy. But even as he said the words, a sharp pain shot through his upper back and shoulder, and the last word was choked out.

"I don't know." Clancy sounded skeptical. "I've seen men fall out from being hit like that; knocks the blood away from the brain or something, and you fall right out. I wish you'd let them look at you."

But Jonas hardly heard what the foreman was saying; he could not get the sight of Anita Byrne out of his mind.

Suddenly Clancy commented, "Funny that Miss Byrne happened to be there."

Jonas felt his face grow hot and kept looking out of the window, away from the big curious Irishman. The man had almost seemed to read his mind. "Yes," he said. "Yes, it was."

"Say, Mr. Mark, you don't think she—" Clancy stopped, and Jonas turned to look at him. His face was embarrassed, and there was a sheepish smile on his mouth.

"Don't think what, Clancy?"

"Well, it probably sounds crazy, but I wonder if she's in with the bosses. You know, these rich people stick together. Maybe checking up on things? Maybe she knows how easy we've been on Tom?"

Jonas hesitated, then he answered, "That is pretty unlikely, John. Miss Byrne is only a junior draftsman in the office. That's all she's got to do with anything. Her father didn't even know it when she came to work for us."

Clancy raised his heavy brows. "Well, I guess you know, Mr. Mark. All the same, it was funny, her being there today and all."

Jonas silently agreed. There was no reason for her to be on the site today. No reason except one. And he could not accept anything as unlikely as that. Why would she come to see him?

They had reached the hospital; in a daze Jonas got out and paid the driver of the public carriage. He followed Clancy into the medicinal-smelling chaos of the emergency wing. The thought of Anita's being there still haunted him. Mingled with the pain in his body were a vague amazement, an utter wonder.

Chapter 6

THE OPPRESSIVE HEAT had not abated on the Monday morning after the accident; at eight o'clock, it brooded over the city, bearing down on Anita almost as it had the previous Saturday afternoon.

She stepped down from the Byrne carriage and looked up at the windows of Higsbee and Waite. She felt a little giddy from the heat but even more from her state of mind. She had spent a lifetime fending off men's attentions. Now her whole self yearned toward one enigmatic man, a man who might not return her feelings at all. She was terribly confused. But of one thing at least she was sure: when she had seen the piling fall, the cable flail, her heart had nearly stopped.

Anita bade Joseph a calm good morning and went into the office building. She had dressed with particular care today in a thin shell-pink dress. It was slightly more elaborate than the usual plain shirtwaists and skirts she wore to Higsbee's, and she was a little shy of its splendor. Its floating sleeves were impractical for work at a drawing board, but Anita had found it irresistible. It was delicious-colored as an Italian ice and it cooled her just to look at it.

With a determined air Anita straightened her broad gray straw hat and went upstairs.

As usual Jonas was already at his board. But this morning he was alone: as soon as she came in he raised his head from his work. She was struck with the full power of his bright hazel eyes. There was none of the blank reticence in them she was used to; he made no attempt to hide his admiration.

"Good morning," he said in his deep, slow drawl. His smile revealed his dazzling white teeth, and she saw small lines deepen in his tanned cheeks and around his eyes when he smiled.

"Good morning." She stood in the doorway. "Are you all right?"

"Fine. A little sore."

"How are the others?" she asked as she went to hang up her hat and carryall.

"Hogan's in critical condition. Spinetti and the other two men are all right." She noticed that Jonas was still staring at her. Suddenly she felt quite self-conscious, an emotion utterly new to her. She sat down at her drawing board.

Jonas did not say anything else, but he got up from his stool and began to walk toward her.

Charley Seton came into the room. Jonas stopped where he was: Anita glanced at him. His eyes had changed; they looked blank and friendly as they always had before. He smiled at Charley. "Good morning."

"Good morning, all," Charley said cheerfully. "I heard there was some trouble on the site."

"Where'd you hear that?" Jonas asked in surprise.

"I ran into Alan Higsbee yesterday," Charley said with a pretense at casualness. Anita smiled. She had gotten used to Charley's hints that he moved in exalted circles; she knew it was to impress her, and it always made her a little sorry for him.

"Good *morning*," he said, and bowed to her with such ceremony she could not help laughing. "You dazzle me, madame, you are so beautiful today."

"Thank you kindly, sir," she said calmly.

"I hear you had quite a close call," Charley said to Jonas, taking off his immaculate jacket and hanging it up.

Anita said, "He certainly did. He was very fortunate not to be hurt."

Charley turned to her and smiled. "You spoke to Higsbee, too?"

"No," she said quietly. "I was there."

"You were *there*?" Charley's look of surprise was comical. "Good Lord, Jonas, I thought you'd assigned this lady to design, not construction."

Anita laughed. "I was just passing by."

She glanced at Jonas: it was the briefest of glances, but she saw something flare in his sharp eyes. It was almost as if they had touched each other without touching. She repressed a wild desire to actually touch him, and it seemed to

69

her for a moment that his whole lean body was yearning toward her. He sat tensely on his stool as if his long legs were about to propel him upright.

She looked at Jonas for a long moment, and his hard hands grasped the edges of his drawing board. The color of his eyes darkened. Across the slight distance between them Anita could feel the pull of his body and his hands.

She was so overtaken by her emotions that it was a shock to hear the heavy voice of George Waite.

As usual he barked out his orders as he entered the room. "Jonas, I want you to run out to the Adair house, stay there all day if need be. Adair and the contractor are at it again, and I want you to follow through. He's got to be satisfied. I'd go myself, but Alan's tied up with meetings, which leaves me to go to the site."

Jonas asked quietly, "Anything wrong with my report on that?"

"The report's fine; it's the site that's the problem," Waite returned dryly. "I'm going to look into things myself for a couple of days. I'll need you there tomorrow. But you'll take care of the Adair business today?"

"Sure. I'll leave as soon as I've approved these drawings."

"Fine." Waite left the room abruptly.

After a short silence, Jonas said to Anita, "I know it's a little irregular, but could you stop by the Adair house on your way home? I need to talk to you about the Provident designs, and there's no time now. Would you mind?"

"Of course not." Her tone was as careful as his, but when she answered, Anita saw a spark leap up again in his eyes, and her heart hammered in her throat. She felt the designs were an excuse.

"Good." Jonas went back to checking the designs on his desk and rose with them in his long, hard hands. "Would you send these to the blueprinters?" He handed them to Anita.

"Surely."

Jonas went to the hook for his jacket and said casually, "I'll see you about four, then. See you tomorrow, Charley."

Charley gave Jonas a curious look. "Tomorrow, Jonas."

For Anita the long hot day seemed endless. She kept hard at work, parrying Charley's usual invitation to lunch. A little before four, she rose and prepared to leave.

"Say, why don't I escort you, Anita?" Charley asked. "That's a rather deserted area, and..."

70

"No, thanks, Charley. Don't bother." She smiled at him. "I've phoned for my driver." His face fell.

Anita put on her hat, picked up the Provident designs and her carryall, and quickly left the room with a friendly wave to Charley.

As the Byrne carriage made its way out of the city, Anita could feel a certain cooling in the air; the whole languid afternoon had a green smell and the excited beat of her pulse echoed itself in the hoofbeats of the shining mare, the slight jolt of the carriage. She wondered what Jonas Mark was going to say to her.

When the carriage neared the site of the incomplete house she could feel her breath grow quick and shallow. She hoped Joseph had not noticed how nervous she was.

Even if he had he was far too well-trained to show it. Though he looked with dismay at the muddy ground, as if to protest that she would spoil her shoes, he only asked, "Shall I wait for you, miss?" as he handed her down.

"No, thank you, Joseph. Mr. Mark will take me home." Joseph nodded and drove away.

Anita started walking toward the shell of the house; there was no sound of hammering, no workman's call. She saw Jonas emerge from the sun-dappled wood.

His face lit up at the sight of her, and he hurried in her direction: all at once she knew with certainty why he had asked her to come here.

The woods were very quiet, his firm tread almost soundless on the moist soil. Suddenly there was the random call of a single bird and her heart overflowed with joy to see Jonas coming toward her, his face open and glad.

And for the first time she could see him in a place where he belonged, there among the tall green trees that hardly stirred in the hot, windless day. He might have been born of this sun and shadow, unfettered and wild. His sleeves were rolled up above his elbows, revealing the strong, tanned arms. He smiled broadly but did not speak.

When he reached her he took the portfolio of designs from her hands and put it on the ground.

He was not smiling now; his face was serious, almost grim, and she saw his mouth tremble. He took her hand and said, "Come."

He led her along a rough path into the deeper woods. They paused in a shadowy spot and once again she heard the plaintive cry of a single bird, a sound so piercing and so sweet that

71

she almost cried out to hear it. He looked down into her face, and his bright hazel eyes held her gaze for an indeterminate time.

"Anita," he said, "Anita, we must..."

"Don't say anything more." Her own voice sounded breathless, alien and hollow in her ears. She raised her face to his and he leaned down with a swift, terrible hunger to kiss her.

The hard feel of him, his musky scent, overcame her; she quivered over all her body and, swaying, fell against him, so close that she perceived the seeking hardness of his flesh and felt the core of herself turn to fire.

When his mouth released hers for an instant, Anita was still too overwhelmed to say a word. Her arms were tight around his waist. He leaned his head on her hair, and she heard him say, "You're afraid of me."

His voice sounded like a stranger's to her, hollow and cold, until she moved away a little and looked up. There was no coldness on his face, only tenderness and excitement, and she realized that his own powerful emotion must be affecting the way he spoke to her.

She managed to say, at last, "Oh, no. No. Not afraid of you." She knew then what she was afraid of—this overwhelming emotion that was so foreign to her, so new. "Of *this,*" she added in a shaken voice.

"This?" he questioned softly, and kissed her again.

When she had the breath to answer, she said, "Yes, that. Nothing like this has ever happened to me before."

He eased his grasp on her and looked down into her face. Suddenly his own expression was very tender, and he began to stroke her face with his hard hands. She shivered at the touch of them, and burrowed her face into his chest. Very gently, he kissed the top of her head.

"My dear," he said in a soft, easy voice. "Thank you for coming here. Thank you." His arms tightened about her again. "Oh, Anita, I have wanted to do that for a long time. When I saw you a little while ago, I wanted to hold you so much I just..." He broke off, loosening his grasp. He put his arm around her and said, "Come. Let's drive a while and talk...may we?"

"Yes," she said, "Yes, of course." She was grateful for his sensitive awareness of her confusion; he seemed to understand that she needed a while to draw back, to put a distance between herself and the wildness of those strange emotions.

"How do you feel?" he asked her with concern.

"Overwhelmed."

"I know. We'll talk."

"Yes," she answered breathlessly, looking up at his face, thinking, He has never looked so calm, so strong, to me before. And she thought with wonder, I love him. In dazzled silence she repeated to herself, I love him.

They had reached the carriage he had used to come to the site. Before he handed her into it, he tossed the portfolio onto the seat and took her once more into his arms.

"You know that I love you," he said, and his voice was gentle and calm and very certain.

"Yes," she answered. "Oh, yes." Somehow she could not yet say the words herself; he looked at her searchingly, and then leaned down from his great height to kiss her again, an urgent lingering kiss that made her feel even more shaken. She could not speak at all. He put his arms around her waist and lifted her into the carriage. As she sat down she tossed her broad-brimmed hat into the back seat with the portfolio and watched him leap into the driver's seat, admiring his lithe grace, the strength and competence with which he took the reins.

He murmured gently to the horse, and they drove away from the thickly wooded site to the road.

Without looking at her, he said, "When I saw you that first time on the esplanade, I thought for a minute you weren't real at all. You looked like the statue of a goddess. I see now how wrong I was." He glanced sidelong at her then, grinning. "I've never known a woman like you."

She was so touched by the earnestness in his voice that she could not speak at all, but she reached up and touched his face with a light, almost imperceptible touch.

He turned his head and kissed her hand. "I love you," she said. "I love you, Jonas."

Abruptly he reined in the horse. He turned to her, his eyes blazing with happiness. Now, it seemed, it was his turn to be silent. He did not answer her, but took her in his arms and kissed her for a long, breathless moment. Then he leaned back and expelled a loud, sighing breath. He put his head in his hands.

"What is it?" She reached out and touched him.

He dropped his hands and looked at her with a wondering expression. "I can't believe it," he said. "I just can't believe it." He kept staring at her. "You know, all this happened to me the first night I saw you."

"I knew it then, too. But the other day on the site when I thought you might be killed..." She said the last word brokenly, and he put his hand on her cheek.

Suddenly he began to laugh. "I feel half crazy. I don't know what we're doing, where we're going."

"It doesn't matter. Just drive. Let me be close to you."

He hugged her to him and called out, "All right, horse. Go."

She laughed, feeling giddy.

"You're right," he said. "It doesn't matter where we are as long as we're together."

They drove aimlessly and in perfect content until it was quite dark. Then Jonas said the horse needed rest, and they needed dinner, so he took her to a small restaurant frequented by students and working people. She had never been to such a place, but saw a couple of young men she had met once at a party—an intense and serious fellow named Dreiser, a newspaper reporter who wrote of crime and tenement miseries, and George Ade, whose "Stories of the Streets and the Town" appeared in the *Record*.

Jonas knew them, too, for he waved and nodded. Dreiser looked at Anita in surprise.

"He wonders what I'm doing here," she said to Jonas, amused.

"No, he wonders how I'm so lucky." She felt warm, elated by the look in Jonas's piercing eyes; that look seemed to shut them in a world of their own.

It was very late when Jonas drove Anita back to the Byrne Tudor mansion. He held her in his arms again as if he could not bear to let her go, kissing her repeatedly. At last they said goodnight, and she went in quietly, using her key to the broad front door. Everyone seemed to be asleep, but when she reached the bedroom floor, her father emerged from his room. His expression was worried and angry, and he said in a stern tone, "Do you know the hour?"

"Not exactly, Father. Why, has your watch stopped?"

"Don't take that tone with me, young lady." His face flushed with anger. "I've been worried sick about you. Why didn't you phone? Where have you been?" He stared suspiciously at her face. "You look...intoxicated."

"I'm sorry you were worried. I'm not 'intoxicated' at all, Father. I just had dinner with some friends, some writers I know, and then we went on to someone's house. That's all."

"Who are these friends, Anita?"

"I won't be cross-examined, Father. If I can't lead my own life, I'll move out."

Roderick Byrne was furious. But he said wearily, "Go to bed. We'll talk in the morning."

Anita went into her room and slammed the door. Her feeling of elation, of magical happiness, was marred by the irritating encounter. But as she prepared for bed, she looked at herself in the mirror: no wonder her father had thought her drunk. Her eyes were wide and blazing; they looked twice their usual size, and her cheeks were highly colored.

I love him, I love him, she thought with joy, as she drifted off to sleep. And he loves me. When we are together, we're in a world of our own. She was determined that their private world would not be intruded upon by her father and his world of money and status and common sense. Jonas must not meet him. Not yet, Anita decided. They must go on as they were, enchanted and undisturbed; at least, she resolved, for a little while more.

Anita and her father did not have their talk the next morning, nor for many mornings after. She managed to elude him at breakfast, because he usually went to the city earlier than she, and his business often kept him late. But when Anita's complaining mother and sharp-eyed aunt returned to the mansion in September, Anita was afraid her secret could not be kept much longer.

Her father apparently remembered her threat to move out of the house, for he no longer questioned her directly about her friends and activities. Charlotte Byrne was not so reticent, however. When Anita made some excuse about late work at her office, her aunt would make an ironic comment. "It's hard to picture Alan Higsbee as such a slave driver," she said once.

Charley Seton, Anita discovered, was worse. Charley studied her and Jonas covertly. Now and then he would make a joking remark, as if trying to catch them out.

But Anita met all this with smiling calm; for the first time in her life, she was totally happy. To see Jonas every day, and almost every night, to work with him at projects that stimulated them, was enough for the moment. He hinted several times that he should meet her father, but she was still hesitant; she told Jonas that she didn't want their bubble to burst.

"We have something stronger than that," he protested.

"I want us to face things together. I want to marry you." She could see his resolve in his eyes, feel it in the urgency of his mouth on hers.

But she was not ready yet. What they had was too precious for the intrusion of her father's world.

One night Jonas asked her, "Are you afraid to marry me? Afraid that I will interfere with your work? You ought to know me better than that."

"It might happen of itself," she said. "I might have a child, and then my life would change utterly."

They quarreled sharply, and did not speak at all for two whole days until Jonas, miserable, approached her. They were reconciled with passionate kisses and everything was right again, at least for the moment. Anita begged him to give her time, and he agreed.

The arguments with her family began anew; Anita threatened again to move out and the questioning and reproaches stopped. But she knew it was only a matter of days before it would all begin again.

"There's quite a nip in the air today," Roderick Byrne said to Charley Seton. "Ah, I see the ladies have made us a fire."

They were having lunch in the Copper Room of the Everleigh, which usually served only dinner. But Charles Seton and Roderick Byrne were valued clients.

"Yes," Charley said, "the fire is nice today." The orange flames cast a pleasant glow on the coppery walls, the fine crystal, silver and china of the elegant table. Charley took a sip of wine and smiled at Roderick.

"Good of you to meet me, my boy." Roderick noted with appreciation the faultless cut of Charley's clothes, his ruddy color and the smoothness of his well-barbered hair. "You're a fine young man, Charley. I think the world of you and your father."

"And we of you, sir." Charley took a substantial bite of filet mignon. "This is choice."

"Everything is at the Everleighs'," Roderick commented, and Charley laughed.

"How right you are." They ate their lunch in contented silence for a while, then Charley said, "Your cuisine is every bit as good, sir, if not better."

"Well, well, that's civil of you, boy. Enjoy having you out to the house. I'm sorry Anita's away so much." The smile died on his lips. "Young ladies are very intractable these days ... all

76

this women's rights nonsense, I suppose. Women all wound up in these 'artistic' things. Just last night she was rushing out to a...what is it?...poetry reading. Some fellow named Field."

"Gene Field?" Charley looked surprised. "But he's out of town. I mean—" He looked a little chagrined. "Looks like I've let some cat out of the bag."

Roderick studied the younger man. He had a feeling Charley's comment had not been as impromptu as it sounded. The young fellow had a funny look in his eyes. What in the devil did it mean?

"Charley, I think you're hiding something."

"What do you mean, sir?" Charley asked with an innocent air. There it was again, Roderick decided. This boy was a sly one.

"Come on, Charley. What's going on? You work with my daughter. Is she seeing some young man?"

Charley hesitated. Once again Roderick had the feeling that the young man was very eager to tell him something. "Well," Charley began slowly, "I don't like to tell tales out of school, sir. But I think Jonas Mark has...an interest in Anita."

"And what about Anita?" Roderick asked dryly. "Does she have an interest in him?"

"It looks that way," Charley said with gloom.

"Dammit, I knew something was in the wind!" Roderick got up from his high-backed chair and paced back and forth over the carpet of the private dining room. "Who is this Mark fellow, anyway? Where's he from...who are his people?"

Charley hesitated again. Then he replied carefully, "Well, sir, he's a talented fellow. Actually he's a friend of mine." Roderick grunted and sat down again. "But I don't think his people are..." Charley paused. "Er, they're farmers, or something. He comes from Florida."

"Farmers. My God," Roderick exploded. "What prospects has he? Anything?"

"No, sir. Not to my knowledge. As a matter of fact he's been saving money for a long time, living like a...peasant, to go to Spain. To work for an architect named Gaudí."

"Not that fellow again! Dear heaven. Mark's a fool. I've never been able to see anything in those monstrous ...confections of Grandi's, though Anita swears by him. Just like a woman." Irritably Roderick unwrapped a cigar and lit

77

it. He offered one to Charley, who took it, inclining his sleek head in thanks.

"Gaudí, sir," Charley corrected gently, lighting his own cigar. "Neither can I. I've said to Jonas time and again the man is more like a pastry cook than an architect."

Roderick's gloomy expression lightened into laughter. "Capital, my dear boy. We agree completely. A pastry cook!" Then with a return of his former gloom, Roderick said, "Jonas Mark. Good Lord. I'll tell you frankly, Charley, I had hopes you and Anita might get together. I like your style. You're a man of the world, and you've got a head on your shoulders. I'd like to have you in Byrne Associates."

"Thank you, sir. I appreciate that. I've had certain hopes, too... about your daughter."

"Well, don't give them up, boy. There couldn't be much to this fellow. Sorry, you say he's a friend of yours. But all's fair in love and war. And I don't think much of a man who sneaks around and doesn't present himself to me, as he should. That is, if he has the right intentions."

"I have to agree with that, Mr. Byrne."

Roderick looked at the boy again. There was no mistake about it, he thought. Charley looked like a cat that had been at cream. Roderick laughed. "I'll be damned if I don't think you've rigged this whole conversation, Charley. You're a slick article. I like that. I could use you in the firm."

"Why, Mr. Bryne, I don't know why you say that." Charley's bright brown eyes met Roderick's gleaming black ones with humor, and his smooth face looked triumphant.

After lunch Roderick suggested they make a day of it, since they had both been working hard. Roderick offered to "make it good" with Alan Higsbee, who was a friend of his. Charley accepted with pleasure, and the two men went upstairs to be entertained.

It was after five o'clock when they emerged from the Everleigh and proceeded down South Dearborn Street. Roderick exclaimed to Charley, "There's Anita."

At the end of the street he saw his daughter, walking hand in hand with a tall, raffish-looking young man. The young man had a wild mane of hair, like a lion's, and he looked tough and strong and confident. His head was uncovered.

The four were approaching each other, and there seemed no way to avoid a meeting. Roderick saw Anita raise her head in a belligerent fashion as she came toward them with the man; they continued to hold hands.

"Good evening, my dear," Roderick said to his daughter, removing his hat. Charley doffed his hat, saying, "Miss Anita, Jonas," with a significant smile.

"Good evening, Father," Anita replied calmly. "I'd like you to meet Jonas Mark, who works with us."

"Mr. Byrne." The fellow had a powerful grip, Roderick thought, and he certainly looked you straight in the eye.

The bastard had some nerve. "Mr. Mark, how do you do?" Roderick said coolly.

He noticed that his daughter took the fellow's hand again, unashamedly, openly.

"It's always nice to meet my daughter's friends," Roderick commented in a dry tone. "Why don't you come out to the house for dinner some night? Tomorrow night, for instance, if you're not engaged?"

"Thank you. I am not engaged. I'll be there, Mr. Byrne." The nerve of this nobody! Roderick thought. Cool as a cucumber.

"Fine," he said aloud. "About eight, then."

"Eight o'clock," Jonas repeated, meeting Roderick's look in a steady way.

"Well, good evening then, my dear," Roderick said to Anita. "Mr. Mark."

"Mr. Byrne. Charley." Jonas's farewell was curt and proper, like that of a man making an appointment to meet another man at seven paces at the next day's dawn.

Chapter 7

"WILL YOU JOIN ME in a brandy, Mr. Mark?"

"Thank you." Jonas accepted the glass, holding it in his hard, competent-looking hand, waiting for Roderick Byrne to drink his.

Roderick's irritation increased: the fellow had been waiting all the evening, waiting for this conversation, with an unruffled calm that was most annoying.

If Roderick had expected to succeed in making Jonas Mark uncomfortable he was sadly disappointed from the first. Roderick didn't know exactly what he *had* expected; it was certainly not this.

Perhaps he had expected Mark to be intimidated by the house and the occasion. But the fellow had walked in with dignity and poise, apparently indifferent to the fact that Roderick was wearing an evening jacket, that he himself was in a neat but shabby suit. At dinner the array of cutlery had not confounded him; he seemed indifferent to the fact that he used the wrong fork without fail. When he smiled, it seemed he was smiling at the array of forks and not because he was embarrassed to be using the wrong one.

When Charlotte Byrne said baldly to Jonas that he was an interesting man—delighting Anita, infuriating Roderick and horrifying the uneasy Margaret—Roderick began to feel he was also a dangerous one. And he began to plan what he would say to the fellow after dinner, when the women had left the room.

"What do you think of our custom of dismissing the women?" Roderick asked him suddenly.

"It's like one of those drawing-room comedies I saw once in New York," Jonas replied calmly.

"And of this house? I understand you're one of these modern fellows who scorns tradition."

"Not necessarily, Mr. Byrne. The house is a beautiful example of pure Tudor."

Even more annoyed, Roderick thought he read a certain irony in the fellow's answer.

Suddenly Jonas Mark said, "I don't want to be rude, sir, but I don't think you invited me here to discuss the house. Could we talk about Anita?"

The calm effrontery of Jonas Mark set Roderick off balance, but he managed to reply in a cool manner. "By all means, Mr. Mark. You and my daughter have apparently been seeing a lot of each other. Is that correct?"

"A great deal. To put it plainly, I'm in love with Anita and I want to marry her."

There was a brief silence, then Roderick said, "She has agreed."

"No, not yet."

"Well, you are frank at least. I must warn you, Mr. Mark, I don't think Anita *will* agree. She is willful and independent and is bent on having what they call a 'career,' I think."

"I want to marry her, sir, not enslave her. If she has her work I will be very pleased. We share the same ideals."

For the first time Roderick was encouraged; he had managed to make the fellow show some emotion. He started to say, "Yes, you share the same foolish admiration for this Gaudí." But he realized that Charley had told him that, that he was not supposed to know it.

"So you have ambitions of marrying my daughter."

"It is a hope, sir, not an ambition."

Nettled at being corrected, Roderick demanded, "What are your prospects?"

"Very good," Jonas answered simply. "I know that someday my work will be appreciated. As it stands now I have the prospect of a partnership at Higsbee & Waite."

"Higsbee and Waite," Roderick repeated with faint contempt.

"And I have a plan," Jonas said frankly, "of going to Spain to work with Antoni Gaudí."

Roderick repressed a snort of irritation and asked, "And you think my daughter would go with you?"

"I hope so, sir. I have reason to believe she will."

"She has said so?"

"No. But she has told me she loves me, Mr. Byrne."

Roderick studied the young man before him, unsettled by his piercing eyes, his calm assumption that he would get his own way.

"I'd like to have your approval, sir, for Anita's sake," Jonas Mark said in an open manner. "But I intend to marry her with or without it."

Roderick rose in a dismissive manner. "Then we know where we stand, Mr. Mark. You do not have my approval, and you never will. I have other plans for my daughter."

Jonas rose. "I see. That's too bad, sir. I think it's time for me to say goodnight to Anita."

And to Roderick's further annoyance, the calm young man turned on his heel and strode out of the massive dining room, not even waiting to be dismissed.

"What happened?" Anita asked Jonas when he came into the hall. She had heard the doors of the dining room open and close and hurried out from the music room.

"Where can we talk?" He looked down at her with a serious expression.

"In here." She indicated the music room. "My mother and aunt have gone upstairs."

He held open the door for her, and they went in. He stepped onto a deep Persian carpet, his glance taking in the molded plaster ceiling, gleaming Tudor panels and crystal chandeliers. There were grim portraits in gilded frames; one of the faces looked like Roderick Byrne's.

"Oh, my love," she said, pausing in the middle of the great room as he took her in his arms. "I love you so much."

He kissed her with a hungry, savage kiss, then said gently, "Sit down with me." He told her what her father had said.

"I knew it would be that way." Her voice was calm and bitter. "You see what I meant—the world is intruding on the world we had together."

"Had?" he asked with soft reproach. "Can anything really intrude on that, Anita?"

"No, no. Forgive me. It's just that..."

"It's just that we *have* been living in a dream," he said, taking her hand. "A beautiful one, one that cannot be destroyed, by anything. But we've got to face certain things: one thing is I can't go on forever, saying goodnight to you, being parted from you when I am aching to stay with you all night, sleep with you in the same bed...love you, hold you until the morning."

She leaned against him, feeling herself melt again to hear his urgent words. "I know," she answered, her voice muffled against him, "I know."

"I want to go away with you tonight," he said. "I want to marry you now. But there are things we must settle first. Can you leave this"—he indicated the splendor around them—"for the uncertain life I can offer you? Can you live with me in Spain, when I go there, and postpone your own work for a while?"

She looked up at him and answered slowly, "Yes."

"Are you sure? Are you really sure?"

She touched his face. "Surer than I've ever been of anything in all my life. Oh, yes, I admit my work is important to me. But even that can wait. I know I have to be with you, Jonas. Don't you know it has been an agony for *me*...these nights, when we have said goodnight, and that was the last thing on earth I wanted? When all I wanted in life was to cling to you, to stay with you? Oh, Jonas, the only time in all my life I've ever been happy has been this summer...since that afternoon."

Anita looked into his eyes, and he exclaimed in a low tone at the open love he saw in them.

"My darling, my darling," he said and kissed her again and again.

"Let's make this the last goodnight," he said then, and she smiled at the conspiratorial way he spoke. Elated, he said, "Let's get married Saturday."

"Yes, Jonas, yes. Saturday."

"Then this will be the last goodnight," he whispered.

Anita looked down at the circle of aquamarines on the fourth finger of her left hand, as they came out of the house of the justice of the peace. They got into the hired carriage.

"Where shall we go, Mrs. Mark?" he asked her, smiling.

He slapped the reins against the horse's neck. "Just tell me where; I am at your command."

She was exhilarated by his careless, easy air. It means nothing to him, either, where we are as long as we can be alone, she thought. "Turn left at the main road," she said, "and go through Oak Park. We're going a rather long way."

He only smiled and, gathering the reins in one strong hand, drew her close with his other hand.

They drove in silence through the autumn woods; as the great houses grew farther and farther apart, he broke the

83

silence: "You will be with me tonight, and all the nights to come from this night on."

Anita was touched to hear his voice tremble, and she answered solemnly, "Yes, Jonas. From this night on."

His arm tightened about her, and he drew the carriage to a halt. The dark was falling on the deserted road. She could barely see his face, but the light in his eyes was like a fire. With his free arm he drew her closer and bent to her to kiss her mouth and eyes and cheeks and hair.

He said her name over and over, as if he could find no other word, and she felt his big frame shaking with emotion.

"Are we almost there?" he asked her suddenly, and she heard the urgency in him.

"Yes, yes, my love," she answered, leaning against him. "We are almost there. See, there ahead? That small side road. Be sure to take that one, and not this, please."

The emphasis of her request made him stare down at her. "All right," he said, smiling. "What is this place?"

"It's a little cottage on our summer...place," she answered, hating the sound of "estate." There was already so much between them, in this way, so much that divided their worlds. She wanted to erase it, wanted almost to wish it from existence.

"There are servants at the big house, but the gatehouse will be unoccupied. It was a gamekeeper's place, but my mother and aunt are opposed to hunting, so no one ever lived there. I've used it myself, sometimes, so it should be habitable. There may even be some food," she added, laughing.

"It's not important," he assured her.

"Very tactful, and brave," she commented, and ran her hand down his muscular arm. She felt him tremble again, from her touch.

"Let's go," he whispered, and her pulse quickened to hear the renewed desiring in his simple, urgent words.

The road she indicated took them up a small wooded hill; over its rise, they saw the house.

"That's it," she said. "That's the cottage."

It was a well-built, two-story structure, and Jonas commented, "That 'cottage' is bigger than the house I grew up in."

She glanced at him anxiously, but there was no irony in his judgment, she saw. He was smiling at her in amusement. The house was dark.

"Doesn't seem to be anyone there," he said with jubilation.

Their eyes met, and she saw in his gaze the same anticipation that pounded in her body. We will be alone tonight, she thought, alone in this quiet place.

There was no view of the big house from the cottage, and for one wild moment she fancied that the cottage was their own house, that nothing would ever touch them here, nothing could sully the simple magic of the world they had made for each other.

"Come." She pulled at him excitedly as the carriage slowed and stopped. "Come, my love."

With an eagerness that even exceeded hers, Jonas jumped down and held up his arms. When she stepped down, he caught her close to his body and let her slide to the ground, her body pressed against him. She could feel again the renewal of his need, and her own flesh seemed to catch its fire.

Without caution and without haste, Jonas held her to him for an endless moment, kissing her at first with great gentleness, then with increasing savagery.

She was breathless when he let her go. With wild impatience, he secured the horse's reins to a tree, then turned to Anita and scooped her up in his arms.

"This is a very important ritual," he said, as he strode up the long brick walk to the cottage. "Will it be locked?" he asked with sudden practicality.

"I think not." She heard her own voice, choked and breathless in her ears.

They reached the door, and he grasped the knob and turned it. The door opened, and he carried her over the threshold into the dark, clean-smelling hall.

Still in darkness, he kissed her once more before he set her carefully down. Quickly she found a light and switched it on: they stood staring at each other, bright-eyed and smiling, almost hypnotized with the joy they had found.

She had never been this close to him. The feel of his hard body was a revelation. Exalted by his hardness, she ran her fingers up the length of his muscular arms and perceived again the trembling of his body.

He bent his head to hers again, and their parting lips clung to each other; now his hands explored the softness of her below the drifting fabric of her gown. Her cloak fell backward from her white raised arms and slipped to the floor. His mouth released hers for a moment and he turned his head, making a deep, groaning sound, to kiss the silken whiteness of the inner arm around his neck. The caress woke her to an even

85

more urgent trembling; a stronger heat, a flowing, swept her and she swayed inside his grasp.

Suddenly Jonas made a sound like a man in unendurable pain; he took off his coat and let it fall to the carpet. With urgent hands he led her toward the bedroom.

With quaking hands he started to unfasten the neck of her dress and kissed her neck and face, inhaling the odor of the strange white flower she always had about her skin and clothes. The smell of that peculiar flower seemed to fill him with even more urgent longing, for his hands were shaking so that he was confounded by the fastenings.

Anita stroked his fingers and undid the buttons of the dress. It fell away as lightly as petals, whispering on the carpet, revealing the whiteness of her skin above the lace-bordered garment underneath. He looked at her, and said in a wondering, low voice, "You are so white, Anita, you are so soft."

Very gently he urged her backward on the bed; with great delicacy and leisure, as if a world of time lay before them, he began to kiss her neck and shoulders and bare white arms.

Through half-closed lids, silvered by the candlefire, expectant and yet very calm, as if she were someone under a powerful opiate, Anita saw herself and Jonas divest themselves of their clothes.

The cool air of the room now touched her everywhere, and with a sensation of floating, dreaming, she looked at his tanned naked body, potent and lean. She gloried in the smooth and tawny skin, the beauty and the firmness of him as he came to her.

Then she could not tell any longer whose skin was whose, because there was a madness between them such as she had never dreamed, never hoped for or expected. She waited for the pain she knew would come, but it did not come. Instead there was only a heightened sensation, a flood of pleasure so whole it was almost unbearable; she cried out silently, This must be, always, this must never end.

At last she heard from Jonas one deep, rending gasp, and in their nearness she felt the sound with all her feelings, buoyed still on that unending wave of sensation. Her mind cried, This is the only world there is, the only meaning.

Again, she waited for something that did not come—this time, the end of that incessant joy. But the joy that raised them like two wild-winged birds that flew in unison did not ebb at all. Although they lay spent, close together, with slowing breaths, the feeling went on and on between them for a longer time than she could measure or comprehend.

Slowly she turned her head: they were lying side by side now and the candles had burned low. Her head was on Jonas's shoulder. In the dimness she saw that he lay with his eyes closed. She had never seen his face so peaceful and relaxed; some of the stern lines had been erased and he was smiling, a childlike smile, serene and open.

She thought, How wonderful it is. Nothing in my life was ever so all-absorbing, nothing has ever made all other things insignificant. Even her work had not let her lose herself in such an utter way.

She raised her hand—it felt limp, boneless—and stroked his naked chest. He murmured, and she felt the vibration of the sound under her fingers. He made the happy, lazy sound again and drew her close, pressing her face against his chest. She inhaled the scent of him with enormous delight; his body had the delicious aroma of new-planed wood or sunlight on April grass.

He still held her, closer and closer, with such a strong grip that it hurt. But that no longer mattered. For now, already, long before the final ebb of the last great wave of pleasure, another longing rose to take its place, and they were once more together, as if their bodies had never been separate, all the hours of their lives.

When Roderick Byrne inquired about Anita, Margaret said vaguely that she was spending the weekend with friends. Roderick and Charlotte exchanged a glance; he felt cold with apprehension.

Anita did not return on Sunday night. On Monday morning Roderick went to the law offices of Drake and Sheldon. He was not kept waiting. When Roderick was announced, Patrick Sheldon came out of his office with his hand extended.

"Roderick! It's good to see you. What can I do for you?" When the attorney saw his client's grim face, he fell silent. Then he said, "Let's go in my office."

He closed the door softly and gestured to a large chair opposite his shining Hepplewhite desk.

Sheldon asked soberly, "What is it? Something's happened."

"Something has happened." Roderick felt the cold apprehension creep over him again. He leaned his head into his hands. Sheldon waited, silent.

Then Roderick removed his hands and looked at Sheldon. "Pat, my daughter's ruined herself."

"What?" Sheldon stared at his client and friend with shocked eyes. "What do you mean, 'ruined herself'?"

"She's run off with a fortune-hunting scoundrel. At least that's what I fear."

Sheldon shook his head slowly. Then, steepling his hands, he asked calmly, "Who's the man?"

"Fellow name of Jonas Mark. Works for Alan Higsbee."

"Mark! But Roderick..."

"You know him, Pat? What do you know about him? Tell me!" Roderick's words tumbled out.

Sheldon held up his hand. "Wait a minute, Roderick. Yes, I know about him. A cousin of mine—you know Howard Adair—is having Higsbee do his house. Couldn't afford you." He smiled slightly. "Howard's had something to do with this Mark boy. He says he's a fine fellow."

"Fine fellow, God almighty!" Roderick slammed his fist down on Sheldon's desk. "He's stolen my daughter and you call him a fine fellow!" To his horror, Roderick heard his own voice grow unsteady.

"Hold on, Roderick." Sheldon's voice was placating. "I'm only telling you what Howard said. Why don't you tell me exactly what's happened?" He leaned back in his chair.

Haltingly Roderick told him of Jonas's visit to the house and of Anita's disappearance.

"But have you tried to trace her?" Sheldon insisted. "Have you called her friends? Did you check the office this morning? I know you told me she works with Higsbee."

"Ashamed to," Roderick admitted. "I didn't want the word to get around. Anyway, what good would it do to call the office? That wouldn't tell me where she's been this weekend."

"True," Sheldon admitted. "But what is it, exactly, that you want of me, Roderick?"

"Well, first of all"—Roderick drew a document from his breast pocket—"I want to see what you can do about this, just in case."

Sheldon took the paper that his friend offered him and scanned it rapidly. Finishing his perusal, Sheldon tapped the document with his long finger. "Roderick, I'm sorry to tell you that I don't think there's any way you can stop this. Is she twenty now?"

"Yes, but twenty-one's the legal age, isn't it?"

"In the usual cases, yes. But this specifies that she comes

into the funds on her twentieth birthday. As it is, some attorney's been remiss. I recall her birthday is sometime in the spring."

"Yes, March." Roderick nodded miserably.

"Then she's entitled to it now." Sheldon looked at his friend. "Listen, Roderick, as for Mark's being a fortune hunter—well, there's no evidence. He has a good name in town. He's never pursued much of anybody, according to Howard, much less fortunes."

Roderick was silent. If anyone knew what was going on in Chicago, it would be Pat Sheldon. His wife, Una, was known locally as "Western Una," a pun on Western Union; she was a mine of information. Even now Roderick was painfully aware of the information he had given Sheldon. Roderick said uneasily, "Pat, I know I don't have to say it, but I will anyway. Not a word of this to Una...please?"

"You've known me for twenty years," Sheldon said, smiling. "Don't you know me by now?"

"I'm sorry, Pat. I'm not...myself today." Roderick put his head in his hands again.

Sheldon got up from his desk and came to his friend. He clapped him on the shoulder, saying, "Cheer up. It may not be as bad as you think. I know Anita. She's smart as a whip. She wouldn't do anything foolish. Meanwhile, why don't you give Carson a ring?"

Carson and Braun handled all the matters pertaining to the estate of Roderick's mother-in-law, who had left her fortune to Anita.

"Wouldn't that be...a violation of confidentiality, all that?"

"You never know. Anita's still a woman, and a young one, and you carry a lot of weight in this town. Emmett Carson's quite a misogynist, a martinet at home, Una tells me." Sheldon grinned.

For the first time Roderick felt a glimmer of hope. He laughed. "Your wife is a very useful woman, Pat."

"So I am told. Use my phone."

When Roderick had spoken to Carson and hung up, he said to Sheldon, "She was there the first thing this morning. The whole thing's already in motion. Not a shining reflection on Jonas Mark, if that's who she's with."

"I must admit it doesn't look good," Sheldon commented. "Maybe you're right about him, Roderick."

"I know I am." Roderick rose abruptly and left the office.

Jonas walked into the drafting room. George Waite was already there. The heavyset partner looked like a thundercloud; Jonas glanced at Charley Seton. Charley's face gave away nothing, but Jonas thought his dark eyes had a gleam of triumph.

"Come into my office, Jonas," Waite growled.

Without removing his jacket or speaking to Charley, Jonas nodded and followed the partner from the drafting room.

"Sit down," Waite said gruffly when they were inside his office. He closed the door carefully and went around his desk to sit down facing Jonas.

"I don't know how to say this, Jonas, except to say it," Waite began in his curt fashion. "I'm obliged to let you go. And I'm mad as hell about it."

Jonas did not answer, expecting the partner to go on.

"What have you done with Anita Byrne?" Waite demanded abruptly.

Jonas smiled his one-sided smile. "I married her, George. On Saturday afternoon."

Waite was silent a moment, staring at Jonas. Then he said, "Congratulations. Is that why she's not here this morning?"

"No. She had an urgent matter to attend to; she'll be here later. Why am I being fired?"

Waite's sharp eyes gleamed under his grizzled brows. He seemed amused by Jonas's directness, so like his own. "Because of Roderick Byrne, of course."

"I didn't know Byrne was a partner in Higsbee and Waite."

"Byrne has never had anything to do with Higsbee and Waite; you know that. Heaven forbid. But he's on the board of directors of the Provident Mutual Insurance Company, and several other companies. The Provident commission was a part of his bounty, a crumb thrown to us because his cake was already too big to eat," Waite said dryly.

"And Roderick Byrne owns a lot of stock in enterprises we're working on. He's also connected with two banks that control our loans. He and Alan arranged all this without my knowledge—apparently in about thirty minutes this morning," Waite added bitterly. "I just walked out of Alan's office in a rage before you came in."

Jonas nodded.

"Well," Waite said, "Byrne gave us a pretty alternative:

fire you or lose the Provident Building, five other commissions and our standing at the banks."

"I see." Jonas looked at the bitter Waite, and added, "Don't look like that, George. I don't see what else you could do."

"Goddammit, Jonas, this was never my idea."

"I know that, George. It's all right." Jonas got up and went to the door. "When does my dismissal take effect?"

"At the end of the week. Look, Jonas, I'm going to . . . make it worth your while. Alan . . . we talked about it, and there'll be a substantial amount set aside for you when you leave. I saw to that. And remember, Jonas, there are other firms here."

"You know better than that, George. Byrne's got Chicago tied up. You mean there are other places."

Chagrined, Waite did not answer. Jonas's statement was all too true.

"I'm sorry, Jonas. I sure hate to lose you."

"Never mind, George. I know that." Jonas left the office.

Spain, he thought, was closer than they had reckoned.

Chapter 8

THE STREETS OF BARCELONA were full of people. Carriages drawn by proud horses, filled with handsome men and women, drove up and down the Rambla, the city's chief promenade, or through the Paseo de Gracia, the Central Park of Barcelona. The women wore lace mantillas over their heads; the only hats and bonnets were worn by foreigners and travelers.

Anita Mark was glad for the shade provided by her broad-brimmed hat as she walked down the Rambla with Jonas; even on the tree-lined thoroughfare the autumn air was very warm and dry. But there were all sorts of delights for the eye: flowers were everywhere, and there seemed to be dozens of pretty children; a band of gypsies played guitars and mandolins. An aged beggar bowed to Anita and Jonas, saying ceremoniously, "Señor, señora." Anita handed him a coin.

When they passed on, she said, "It seemed a pity not to reward such politeness," and Jonas smiled, looking down at her with admiration. As always she was fragrant and cool, dressed in pale, drifting blue, in sharp contrast to the hot, gay colors warn by the Spanish women around them.

The whole town seemed to be in the streets; unlike most other towns in Spain, women thronged the walkways, adding to the constant clatter with their vivacious conversation. They were like exotic birds, yet to Jonas most of them seemed garish and shrill compared to Anita. But he liked the city, and was strangely touched by the little mules that pulled the tram cars; the beasts were clipped in curious patterns.

"Look there," he said to Anita, indicating the patient mules.

She nodded with appreciation, her smile tinged with pity

for the straining animals. "They work so hard," she commented softly. Jonas nodded, bemused by the Spanish temperament that had devised the baroque, with its splendor and tension, its contradiction and drama, the same strange Catalonian temperament that drove Antoni Gaudí.

Jonas's pulse beat quickened, thinking of Gaudí and their imminent visit to the Güell estate, where the park was open to the public. This would be his first actual sight of the master's work.

Anita glanced at him and said, "I believe you're thinking of Gaudí."

He was gratified and amazed, as he had been during these first brief weeks of their marriage, when they had grown so close that such things had happened many times. One would be thinking of something, and the other would immediately feel the thought.

"Yes." He put his arm around her waist and drew her close to him, so that their steps matched as they moved together down the crowded Rambla.

Beyond the market, at the foot of the Rambla, they could see the Muralla del Mar, a spacious promenade formed by a seawall that overlooked the harbor, and the towering masts of many vessels.

"Shall we go in there awhile?" Jonas asked, gesturing toward a side street that had many handsome cafés.

Anita nodded, and they turned from the Rambla and entered a small mirror-lined saloon.

"People don't sit at cafés on the sidewalk here, as they do in Paris," Anita commented.

"It's just as well. Paris isn't as hot, is it?" They sat at a small round table by the window, and Jonas ordered a cool drink. They were surrounded by men drinking wine, reading their journals and talking politics. Everywhere the noise of talk was increased by the clatter of hundreds of dominos on the marble tables; through the open door the sound mingled with the cries of itinerant vendors and the city's roar.

As Jonas and Anita sat gazing out the window, a voice broke into their reflections: in accented English, the voice said, "Surely it is Señorita Byrne."

They turned together in surprise. A lean, noble-looking Spaniard, dressed in fashionable clothes, stood by their table.

"Señora Mark," Jonas said, rising to meet the stranger.

"Jonas," Anita said calmly, "this is the Duke of Veragua. Your grace, my husband, Jonas Mark."

93

The duke shook Jonas's hand and bowed. "You are a gentleman of the greatest fortune," he said. Then he turned to Anita and bowed again, his small dark eyes taking in every detail of her, her exceedingly white skin in the shadow of the creamy leghorn hat, the vivid eyes and pink mouth, his gaze sweeping downward to her pale, foamy sleeves falling back from the delicate arms. He took her hand and kissed it.

Jonas watched them curiously. The duke released Anita's hand and said, "I had the pleasure of dancing with your wife in Chicago at Mrs. Potter Palmer's. But then she was the beautiful Miss Byrne, you see." He smiled, and his rather sharp, small teeth lit up his swarthy face below the full black mustache. "I did not know then that you were betrothed."

"Will you sit down?" Jonas's inquiry was civil but cool.

"With the greatest pleasure," the duke said, "if I do not intrude."

Anita made a polite murmuring sound, but Jonas could only manage a grunt. Anita looked at him, and feeling chagrined, tried to atone for his rudeness with a half-smile, but he could not warm up to the fellow. He disliked the duke's smooth, unruffled looks—the damn fellow didn't seem to feel the heat at all—and his soft, manicured hands aroused Jonas's distaste. Obviously he had never done a day's work in his life.

What bothered Jonas most was the way the duke was looking at Anita. He even resented the fact that the man had danced with her and he himself never had.

The duke raised his hand in an almost imperceptible gesture—something Jonas had not yet mastered—and a waiter rushed to their table, bowing, calling the duke "your grace." Jonas felt another unpleasant twinge of jealousy.

The Spaniard gave his order with an arrogance that only seemed to increase the waiter's look of respect, then he turned to Anita and asked in a softened tone, "You and your husband are traveling for pleasure in our beautiful country? You make the . . . honeymoon, is it?"

Deliberately Anita waited for Jonas to answer, and he felt a warm wave of love and gratitude. Her manner seemed to say, "I wish my husband to speak for us."

Jonas tried to force friendliness into his own reply. "Yes, that, of course. But we have come to meet Antoni Gaudí, in Astorga."

The waiter had brought the duke's drink. He ignored it and turned again to Anita. "My friend Gaudí! I remember you questioned me about him at Mrs. Palmer's in Chicago, Miss... Mrs. Mark."

"Yes." Anita smiled. "Both my husband and I are great admirers of Master Gaudí."

"How fortunate, then, that he is even now here in Barcelona. Apparently you did not know that the Bishop of Astorga died, and that therefore work on the Episcopal Palace has been abandoned for the moment. Antoni is working again in Barcelona on the Teresan School."

"No, we did not know," Jonas said shortly, and saw that Anita was studying him again.

"But you must let me take you to the Güells' palace!" the duke insisted. "Have you met them yet, Miss... Mrs. Mark?"

Jonas felt doubly annoyed: this was the second time that Veragua had started to call Anita "Miss Byrne"; and his question to her, alone, implied that her husband was not a likely guest of the rich Güells. Jonas glanced at his wife. He was gratified to see that she had caught the implication, too, and was angered by it. There was a dangerous glint in her vivid blue eyes as she replied coolly, "My husband and I know no one in Barcelona, your grace. We're planning to go to the Güell park, with the sightseers. Master Gaudí has expressed his admiration for my husband's own work; that is the basis of our seeking him out."

The duke seemed a little taken aback, but he said, "How nice that you have been accorded such an honor, sir." He smiled at Jonas. "The master's approval is not lightly given, as I am sure you are aware."

"I am," Jonas said briefly.

"Then it will be a double pleasure to invite you both to the Güell palace this afternoon. I happen to be going there myself."

"I'm sorry that your lovely wife is not here," Anita said. Jonas realized why she had said it, and once again he was amused by her subtlety. He thought he saw a slight withdrawal in the duke's manner, an uneasy flick of the dark eye.

"The duchess goes to the mountains until the late autumn," the duke replied, rallying. "I am in Barcelona on business of my estate."

Anita only smiled but made no answer.

Once again the duke said, "Will you accompany me this afternoon?" He still addressed Anita, and again, with that reproachful air, she turned to Jonas. He almost laughed aloud at the duke's manner of repressed annoyance.

"Would you like to, dear?" Jonas asked Anita. "It's mighty nice of the duke to ask us. Why don't we?"

"By all means," Anita said.

Jonas grinned. "We're both looking forward to seeing the master's work, your grace. It'll be exciting to see it in all its dimensions, at last, not just a picture in a magazine." Anita's manner to the duke had fully restored Jonas's good humor, and now he was eager to go.

"Then by all means, let us leave at once. My carriage is just outside." The duke moved forward to assist Anita, but Jonas had already pulled out her chair. The nobleman tossed a number of gold coins on the table, and again Jonas was too swift for him, saying, "Thank you, sir, but I have already settled the bill."

The duke looked into his eyes for an instant: the dark eyes and the hazel ones locked in a challenging stare. Then the duke gestured for Jonas to precede him from the restaurant; Jonas had a peculiar feeling that there had been more to the small incident than met the eye. He puzzled about the matter during their drive through the city, but soon his natural curiosity and good nature overcame his unpleasant thoughts and he looked about him with interest as the carriage passed down the Calle de la Platería.

The duke explained that the silversmiths lived there and made quaint silver ornaments and earrings of antique form for the peasant women. "Señora Mark, of course, prefers gold, I am sure," the duke commented. "And yet her wonderful whiteness recalls silver, does it not, señor?" He included Jonas in his question, but the latter could not help reading an impudence in the remark.

"And if one loves old and curious treasures," the duke went on to Anita, "one can sometimes find great prizes here in the work of former times."

Again Jonas was sure that there was another meaning in the duke's words, as if he were praising his own superior civilization and ancient lineage.

The streets in the older part of the town were narrow, winding and dull, but they opened into squares and revealed some interesting buildings.

When they passed through the square of the Constitutio, the duke pointed out two palaces. One, a fine Gothic hall of the fourteenth century, was called the Casa Consistorial; councils were held there. The other, said the Duke, was the Casa de la Disputación, and had a beautiful staircase leading to the Chapel of St. George, which he would enjoy showing to the Marks.

Jonas only half-listened to the duke's conversation; he was staring ahead, waiting for his first sight of the Palacio Güell. He knew it was situated just off the Rambla de Capuchinos, and he believed they were on that Rambla. When he asked Veragua, the duke confirmed that they were.

Jonas turned to Anita and saw in her vivid eyes an excitement equal to his own; this was a sight they had waited for, and for a very long time. He smiled at her, and when she returned his smile, taking his hand, he felt a deep satisfaction.

The carriage turned from the Rambla onto the shady side of a narrow street, and Jonas could see, midway in the block, the pale roofs of the six-story palacio, with its oddly shaped chimneys, some like the hats of a witch, others like clusters of fantastic fruit, gleaming in the sun. He leaned eagerly out of the carriage and stared. The carriage drew up before the entranceway, with its double parabolic arches; the curling ironwork of the doors contained the initials E and G for Eusebio Güell.

At the bottom of the doors were coiled serpents; there was an air of Moorish mystery to the deep shadowed interior glimpsed through the grilles. Already Jonas felt the enchantment of Gaudí's creation; this was another world, the world where he and Anita belonged, together.

Once again he glanced at his beautiful wife, and she met his eyes with understanding. She seemed as cool and poised, as marked with perfection, as ever, but a slight smile curved her mouth and her fiery blue eyes were lit with excitement.

The duke's smart coachman descended and pulled at a bell below the intricate center sculpture between the two grilled arches. Almost at once they heard the sound of soft-booted feet; someone seen dimly within was opening one of the enormous arches so the carriage might pass through.

The coachman jumped back onto his box and guided the shining mare through the vaulted archway into a brick-paved vestibule, cool and dim, lit here and there with white globes of light. The carriage paused by a small flight of dismounting steps, and after the coachman had handed Anita down, Jonas followed.

The three went up the carpeted stone stairs set between columns of fluted marble, and Jonas was dazzled by the master's use of light. A bulging grille behind the steps allowed the entrance of natural light, which blended with the globes' illumination in such a magical way that one seemed to be in a strange country under water. The Spanish sunlight filtered through narrow windows set with grilles of beaded wood.

Jonas could feel Anita's excitement, although neither spoke a word. They reached a polished upper hall, and a stiff-faced servant ushered them into an immense chamber with a ceiling so high it gave the effect of a small cathedral. Here again the real and artificial lights gave Jonas the impression of an underwater palace, glimmering and diffuse. He was so intent on examining the vaulted arches of carved wood and the marble columns, standing like peculiar bare trees before an enormous bay window, that he did not realize they were being announced to someone in the room.

He heard the servant intone, "His grace, the Duke of Veragua; Señor and Señora Mark." Jonas was surprised to realize that the duke had given their names to the servant and he had not even heard.

"Señora Eusebia de Montenegro y Albéniz," the servant announced, gesturing toward a small, stately old woman sitting in a great chair just beyond them under an intricately carved panel of glowing, somber wood.

The servant stepped aside and took up his post among the oddly shaped marble columns.

"Madame." The duke gave an elaborate bow. Jonas bowed awkwardly; he had never bowed before in his life. His piercing eyes took in several things at once: the duke looked uneasy and annoyed, and the dignified old lady was regarding the duke with open dislike.

"Eusebio is not at home," she said coldly. "It has become my duty to receive you and your guests. Señor and Señora...Mark?" She pronounced their surname with difficulty, as if it had a new and interesting taste on her tongue. She gave both Jonas and Anita a penetrating stare.

"It is very kind of you to receive us, señora, in this wonderful house," Anita said with a naturalness that aroused her husband's admiration.

Apparently her manner greatly impressed the old lady, for she said with greater warmth, "Please. Sit here by me, my dear, and make yourself comfortable. I believe you are an American?" Señora Eusebia smiled at Anita and indicated a chair near hers. In the center of the arrangement of chairs was an elaborate tea table with a huge silver chased pot, fragile china and plates with cakes and fruit.

The servant moved forward to hand the guests their refreshments. Though Señora Eusebia and Anita were soon talking in a very friendly animated manner, discussing Paris, Jonas made no attempt to converse with the duke, who sat a little apart from the others, his dark eyes sullen, his gaze on Anita. It appeared that he was a little lost without his friend Eusebio.

Jonas calmly took a sip of the tea and, disliking the taste, set his cup and saucer down and stared about him at the wonderful room.

Suddenly Señora Eusebia laughed and said, "Mr. Mark ... Mr. Mark," using the American form for the first time.

Jonas turned to her and grinned. "I beg your pardon, señora. My interest in Master Gaudí's work is so great I guess I just ... drifted away."

"That is wonderful," the old woman said. "Veragua here is too big a fool to appreciate Antoni's genius." Glancing at the duke, Jonas saw him stiffen and for a moment felt a little sorry for him. "Your lovely wife," Señora Eusebia continued, "has told me of your work, and your intent. Surely Antoni cannot refuse you. If he were a woman, he would refuse you nothing."

Anita laughed, and Jonas felt his face grow hot.

"I am old enough to talk like this, you see," the old woman said matter-of-factly. "I will be eighty-five in November, and my husband was for me the greatest man who ever lived. When he died, he left me with an eye for exceptional men. And you, Mr. Mark, are one."

Jonas was touched. "Thank you," he said simply.

"Now," said Señora Eusebia, rising, "we have done with this nonsense of tea. I have a feeling you and your wife, Mr. Mark, came to see Antoni's work. I will show it to you."

The duke's face was like a thundercloud, but Jonas felt a rising elation. He liked the frank, rather acid old lady, and the thought of examining the house under her guidance delighted him.

Anita had also risen eagerly and was waiting with the expression of a happy child anticipating wonders to come.

"I have known Antoni for thirty years," said Señora Eusebia as she led them from the vaulted chamber. "Now that he has returned to Barcelona, Mr. Mark, I will effect an introduction."

"You are very good," Jonas said sincerely. He was even

more delighted that the introduction would come from the señora and not from the obnoxious duke.

"Come along," she said briskly. "We will start with the roof."

"The roof?" The duke's expression made the old woman smile.

"If you are not up to it, Veragua, you need not come."

Stung, the duke replied, "I was considering you, señora, and Señora Mark."

"I'm looking forward to it," Anita protested.

"You are all kindness, Veragua," the old lady said ironically, "but at my age all caution is absurd. Shall we go?"

Jonas and Anita followed Señora Eusebia up two flights of stairs, noticing the varied wonders of the palace—everywhere the constant magic of light and shadow, flowing shapes, wrought-iron decorations like great metal vines. In one particular spot, Jonas looked up and was almost struck speechless by the sight of Gaudí's three-dimensional version of what the Spaniards called an *artesonado* ceiling: wrought-iron leaves and tendrils, vines and flowers seemed to grow from the latticed ceiling in the profusion of a fantastic garden that had emerged not from earth but from a dream.

When at last they reached the roof, Gaudí's incredible chimneys loomed in the brilliant sun like fanciful hedges that had been sheared by a giant and humorous hand, not built of mere brick and stone. The tallest cupola shell was surmounted by a cross, with which Gaudí nearly always finished off his buildings.

Shading her small, faded eyes with a wrinkled hand, Señora Eusebia gave Jonas a searching stare. She said, "Antonio's faith is very strong. Do you have such faith, Mr. Mark?"

"Not a religious faith, señora," he answered frankly. "My faith is in myself, and in my work and love."

She looked at him for a moment before she answered, "That is good. Yes, that is good. I like that. Now, I am weary, I admit. Come down, and before I bid you goodbye we will look at the rear of the palace. Then tomorrow perhaps you will invite me to go with you to the Teresan School to meet Antonio Gaudí."

Jonas felt so overwhelmed with happiness that he could not speak. Then he managed to say, "Of course. I am most grateful."

A little later they stood in the rear courtyard of the Palacio

Güell, gazing up at its simple, almost medieval facade. The unusual blinds and the variety of roof elements contrasted in a dramatic way with the simple rhythms of the window openings, stark yet full of grace. The titanic shuttered bay window of the room in which they had been received was ornamented by a huge enclosure that extended upward for three stories.

They escorted Señora Eusebia into the house. Holding out her frail hand to Jonas, she said, "Tomorrow, Mr. Mark. If you will call for me here at eleven."

"With the greatest pleasure," he answered. He did not bow but took her hand to his lips and kissed it.

The old lady kissed Anita on the cheek and nodded coolly to the Duke of Veragua.

Instead of waiting with the duke for his carriage, Anita and Jonas took their leave of him at the palace doors.

They thanked him for his kindness, explaining that they would walk back to their hotel. Anita said she wanted to see more of the city.

The duke received their thanks and their explanation with dismay; his dark eyes were fixed on Anita. Jonas knew that she was as eager as he for them to be alone together; it seemed difficult for her to be civil.

Finally they escaped. They walked slowly down the narrow, shaded street, in happy silence, the enchantment of Gaudí's palace still upon them.

Shortly after eleven the next morning Jonas Mark sat opposite Señora Eusebia in the Güell carriage on their way to the Teresan School. He was lightheaded from lack of sleep: he and Anita had talked far into the night, going over every detail of their astonishing visit and their tour of the Palacio Güell. Even several cups of the strong, bitter Spanish coffee had left Jonas in a state of half-drowsiness.

His feeling of unreality was accentuated by the sight of his companion. Señora Eusebia was dressed in shining black from head to foot, from the usual Barcelona mantilla to her glowing European shoes with their paste buckles that glittered in the shadow of her dark, rustling skirts. By her side she held a cane upright; the cane was ebony with a golden lion's head for a handle.

"You, too, were November-born, were you not?" The sudden question startled Jonas.

"Yes."

101

"Ah! I thought so," Señora Eusebia said with satisfaction. "We are two of a kind, Mr. Mark. We were born under similar, obdurate stars. The red star Antares rose at the time of our births, making both of us relentless and driven by passion." She caught the expression on his face.

"Oh, yes," she commented, "you laugh at such things, as most men do. As my husband did. You are also stubborn."

He laughed. "Yes," he admitted.

"I know. Yes, yes, the men laugh and the church frowns on such things, but they are true all the same. I knew what you were the moment I saw you. Your wife is another. What is her name—Anita? It is beautiful, that word, like a dance, an arabesque. And she is *hidalgo,* of a proud family."

"Yes. And I am not."

"You are an *hidalgo* of nature, Mr. Mark. And so stubborn that Antoni might as well hire you; if he does not, you will work for nothing. Am I right?"

Jonas stared at the remarkable old woman. "How did you know that?"

"I told you. Because I, too, am a Scorpion. But you do not want to hear of that; you want to hear of Antoni Gaudí."

Jonas nodded, amazed at her ability to read him.

"I have known Antoni since I was in my prime, and he was only a child. His father, like my husband's people, was only a coppersmith. His mother died when he was just a baby, and his brother and sister died young. Antoni has always been alone; he cares for his motherless niece—he designed the chapel furniture for her school in Tarragona some time ago—and for his father. They live here in Barcelona. When Antoni graduated from architectural school he was already well established. He was apprentice to some important builders in this city. In 1878, my cousin finally listened to my praises of him"—the old woman smiled—"after he had designed for the Paris Exposition. After that he did not leave Barcelona much. He did not have to."

She glanced at Jonas, who was listening avidly. She went on, "He is very active in the Catalan movement, as you may know, and sometimes he speaks only Catalan. Someone might have to translate for you." Her smile was mischievous. "Although your Spanish is excellent," she added politely.

"Thank you. I'd like to show you this." Jonas brought out the worn letter from Gaudí.

"Read it, please. My vanity does not allow spectacles in public."

Jonas laughed and read the letter to her aloud. She studied him, and said, "And you have come to Spain with so little encouragement? Well, I was right. You are a stubborn man."

Jonas replaced the letter in his pocket. "Yes, I am."

"Ah, there," said Señora Eusebia. "We approach the school. About six months remain until its completion. I have a great interest in these matters, you see."

Eagerly Jonas leaned forward for his first view of the Teresan School. The exterior was all but complete; the external walls were of rubble interlarded with brick and terra-cotta ornament. Its simple Gothic delicacy reminded him with a pang of Anita's Provident designs.

"My wife is an architect," he commented suddenly.

"Oh?" The old woman's voice was noncommittal. "We have no women architects in Spain, Mr. Mark."

"I know." Jonas was thinking about Anita's exclusion from this visit; of her generous acceptance of the fact. He felt a twinge of guilt that darkened his pleasure in the anticipated meeting. He felt Señora Eusebia's thoughtful stare.

But now they had reached the entrance of the school. The coachman was helping the old woman from the carriage. Jonas followed her to the entrance gate. It was in the age-old Spanish tradition of *rejas,* grillwork, but this grille was spiky like those of Léon, and Gaudí's unmistakable genius was everywhere; again Jonas received the impression of metal flowers and tendrils so live they actually grew.

They were admitted by an old nun, who greeted Señora Eusebia warmly and looked with curiosity at the tall American. As they moved through the light and shadow of the graceful parabolas, Jonas noticed with delight how simple and strong were the structural lines of the arches and piers.

They walked down an arcade, and Jonas interestedly watched the men at work with bricks. He was amazed to see that the piers being built to support the narrow arches had the thickness of only one brick.

"One brick," he said thoughtfully.

A small, thin man with thick, gray-touched hair and a luxuriant beard and mustache that completely covered his lower face appeared from behind the brick masons. He was solemn and intense, and his very black eyes glittered under heavy brows.

He stared at Jonas. Then he caught sight of Señora Eusebia. He came forward, holding out both his hands. "Elena, Elena Eusebia," he said. He bent to kiss both her cheeks.

103

"*Bienvenida*, Antoni," she replied, smiling. "Be so kind as not to speak Catalan today. This is Mr. Jonas Mark."

Gaudí looked up, unsmiling, at Jonas. "Mark," he repeated. "You are the one who wrote me from Chicago." Gaudí pronounced the name of the city strangely, with the accent on the first syllable.

"Yes. This is an honor and delight I have long awaited." Jonas bowed.

Gaudí still did not smile, but it seemed to Jonas that his expression had lightened a little. "You speak well, Mr. Mark. And you come under the auspices of a great lady. I had no idea you knew anyone in Barcelona. You did not mention that in your letter."

"I did not, Master Gaudí, until yesterday."

Gaudí's thick brows swooped upwards. "Yesterday?"

"I will leave you gentlemen now, to talk." Señora Eusebia smiled in her mischievous fashion. "I have business with the sisters." Slowly she tapped away down the long corridor of parabolic arches; the men watched her small black-clad figure diminish as she moved through the alternating patches of light and shadow toward the pool of light the sun made at the end of the aisle of arches.

Jonas again studied the pattern of arches. "We are doing this in metal now, in Chicago," he said to Gaudí, indicating the structure of the parabolas.

"Come, Mr. Mark, let us step aside a moment." Gaudí moved away from the men working around them and walked a little way with Jonas down the aisle of arches.

"You have come to work with me," Gaudí said, looking up into Jonas's face with a somber expression.

"Yes, Master Gaudí, that is my hope."

Gaudí studied the American and shook his head. "Elena Eusebia believed in my work, for a long, long time. She made possible a great deal of my good fortune. Now that she brings you here, her very presence says that she believes in you. I have seen the drawings that you sent me, Mr. Mark. You are gifted. But I told you that imitation is not greatness; you should stay in your country of America and develop a style of your own. Your America moves too fast"—for the first time Gaudí smiled—"and loves God too little to accept the work of Antoni Gaudí."

"I would consider it a privilege and honor to work with you," Jonas said, as if Gaudí had not spoken.

The little man looked at him again for a moment. Then

he said, sounding a little like Señora Eusebia, "Mr. Mark, you are a very stubborn man. If you work for me, the work will be hard and grinding, and the recompense, as I told you, will be small. Are you a bachelor?"

"No, I am married."

"Your wife is here?" Jonas nodded. "What does she think of your...quixotic enterprise?"

"She is..." Jonas started to say "an architect herself," but amended it to, "...a great admirer of yours, as well. She is fully in accord with my wish. And there is no immediate financial need. I have saved for years to come here."

"I see." Gaudí folded his arms close to his body and paced back and forth with his head bent. "Very well. Appear tomorrow, at seven in the morning."

Jonas's heartbeat quickened with excitement and thickened his voice as he answered, "Thank you. I will be here."

Gaudí nodded curtly and returned to the brick masons.

Jonas strode to the entranceway, where he found Señora Eusebia with a nun.

"I will be starting work tomorrow," he said bluntly. "How can I thank you?"

"I have done nothing," Señora Eusebia protested. "You can thank me by coming to see me, with your so beautiful wife. Now, are you ready to return?"

"I will walk, thank you, señora. I must walk...and think. Thank you." Jonas was almost shaking with impatience.

The old woman laughed and looked with approval at his eager face, his wild mane of hair and his vital, lean body.

"Go, go," she said. "You look like a wild horse waiting to run. Go, Jonas Mark."

He smiled at her and hurried out into the brilliant sun, knowing his long legs could carry him faster than any carriage back to the Cuatros Naciones to share the news with Anita.

Chapter 9

ON A CLOUDY DECEMBER morning, Anita Mark woke up with
an unusual feeling of languor. Jonas had been gone for hours.
She remembered dimly his goodbye kiss. It was her custom
when he got up to stay awake and take a siesta in the afternoon, but this morning her whole body felt heavy. She had
been almost unwilling to open her eyes.

She sat up in the bed and looked out the window of the
Cuatros Naciones. As always it was very mild for winter, a
mildness that she had not gotten used to, but the sky today
was overcast; the air had a brooding quality, full of imminent
rain. Anita's spirits rose: the brightness of the Spanish sun
had begun to unnerve her. At times, during the warm fall,
she had fairly ached for the crisp, cool air of Chicago, whipping in from the lake; the changing leaves, the fresh-smelling
snow.

Such things had never meant a great deal to Anita Byrne.
But now, looking at the gray Spanish sky, Anita Mark realized that her present life was full of such trivia—weather
and clothes, small enjoyments and the expense of time.

For the last two months, even if she had fallen under the
spell of Barcelona, had been in many ways the loneliest of
her life. Jonas was so engrossed in his work that there were
times when he looked at Anita with a blankness in his eyes
over the obsessive fire of his preoccupation. He was as tender
with her as ever, more passionate if anything, but he seemed
to have totally forgotten the fact that she was without employment, without direction.

If we only had a house, she reflected, even that would
occupy me. But it seemed more expedient to Jonas to go on
living in the hotel, for the time being, at least. He did not

like the idea of her having the responsibility of a house. In any case, he had begun to treat her like a beloved pet, or a child. As long as she was there to greet him in the evenings, beautiful and welcoming, it was all he required of life. Loving him more than ever, repressing her resentment, Anita accepted it all.

But the days were long: she regretted her solitary independence of days past. There were not many to whom she could even write letters, none to whom she could unburden herself. Their visits to Señora Eusebia and ultimately, when he returned, to Eusebio Güell, made her feel more shut out than ever from Jonas's days. Señora Eusebia patently believed that marriage to Jonas Mark, in itself, should suffice for any woman. She had shown little interest in Anita's talent.

The duke had gone away soon after their first visit to the Güell palace; Anita felt a vast relief, because she knew Jonas disliked him. But there had been moments in the months that followed when she would have welcomed even his company. Anita had gone once to Madrid to visit a Parisian dressmaker there, but she had missed Jonas so sorely that she made no other journeys without him.

So on this morning, she put down her feeling of depression to the usual causes; the slight dizziness she felt when she rose from the bed she ignored.

She dressed carefully in a new fall gown that she had bought in Madrid and prepared to go out. Going downstairs and out onto the Rambla, she decided to visit a sixteenth-century cathedral. Though the cathedral, deemed by artists and architects as a noble example of Gothic structure, was on her list of places to see, she had not visited it yet.

The cathedral was approached by an elevated flight of steps; as she climbed them, Anita looked up at the lofty bell towers, and the elaborate carving over the entrance representing the fight between a dragon and Vilardell, the legendary hero of Spain. She entered the interior; on this cloudy day the gloom was intense, darkening the stained-glass windows.

Suddenly Anita wished that she had not come; her Protestant temperament was oppressed by the high altar, and by the subterranean chapel below it containing the body of a saint. She saw women kneeling and praying at the head of the staircase that led down to the tomb of the saint. Their black-veiled heads and posture of submission reminded Anita of what she had become, in these few short months—a secondary person, an idler forced to seek out ways to pass the time.

Below the great organ hung a carving of a monstrous Saracen's head, with open mouth and long beard, and somehow the male head mocked Anita, looking smug and triumphant, the sex that ruled in Spain. To shake off her angry, gloomy thoughts, Anita walked on, looking for a more cheerful sight. Ahead, she saw one, a great round arch leading into the cloister. She found a large courtyard. Old orange trees, still full of golden fruit, and big trees of geraniums and giant shrubs flamed with color in the grayness. She heard the plash and murmur of fountains. One of the fountains was the figure of a knight. He rode a horse that spouted water from its nostrils and had a long curving jet of water instead of a tail.

Around the fountains were flocks of geese. They stretched out their long necks and hissed at Anita. At this small sign of unwelcome, which ordinarily would have amused her, Anita burst into tears. She sank down onto one of the benches, letting her tears fall freely.

"Señora." She looked up in surprise; she had not heard anyone enter the close. The Duke of Veragua stood before her, splendidly dressed in velvet, with his hat in his hand. There was a look of real concern on his smooth, swarthy face, and for the first time Anita almost felt affection for him.

"Señora," he repeated. He drew a dazzling handkerchief from his pocket and held it out to her with a smile. "What should such a beautiful lady have to weep about?"

She took the handkerchief from him and wiped her cheeks and eyes. "Thank you." She hesitated a moment, then said, "I was feeling...homesick, I think."

"Ah. May I?" The duke sat down beside her. "Homesick," he said softly. "That is too bad. Our beautiful country is shamed to make such a lovely woman sad. You have not found Barcelona amusing, then?"

"Amusing? No." Anita saw his dark eyes glitter, and she wondered what he was thinking. She began to regret the whole encounter. To distract him, she asked in a calmer voice, "Business has brought you again to Barcelona?"

"Not entirely." His voice was full of a heavy, hidden meaning. Uneasily Anita felt that he was about to become troublesome. She said quickly, making her words false and bright, "I am quite over my mood now, your grace. I really must go soon. I have a great many things to do."

"Oh?" His skepticism was plain. "But please, do not run away. Let me show you this beautiful building. I am sure, as an artist yourself, you will find it of great interest."

Anita hesitated. This was the first time in months that anyone had referred to her as anything but Jonas's wife, and it was a welcome reference. Taking advantage of her hesitation, the duke put on his hat and touched her elbow in a light, respectful manner. "Please," he said and smiled.

"Very well."

He looked so triumphant that once again she regretted being there with him. But it was too late now; to change her mind would only confirm him in his judgment of all women as capricious, harebrained creatures, and she was too proud for that.

"You must see the city from the bell tower," the duke insisted. She walked with him under the arch, returning the way she had come. He led her to a narrow flight of curving stairs, saying, "I will precede you, señora. I know the way, and the stairs are steep."

Anita nodded, giving him a cool smile, and followed him up the stairs. As they climbed, her legs felt heavy and her breath drew short. She was puzzled: nothing had ever affected her like this before. She had never been ill in her life, and this slight exertion was almost nothing. She climbed determinedly upward behind the duke until a path of light fell on the dimness of the stairs.

"Ah! We are here." He turned to offer her his hand. She did not take it, but came slowly up the two remaining steps. When she was standing in the tower, Anita felt another great wave of vertigo, this one too strong to withstand, and she had to sit down until it passed.

"Señora, what is it?" She was leaning against the arch of the open tower; he knelt down beside her and steadied her with his arm. "What is the matter?"

His concern was so real that she was grateful for his presence. His arm felt firm and strong. "I felt a little dizzy, that's all."

"Stay here for a moment, until you get your breath."

She nodded, glad to remain where she was, because she felt weak all over, in her arms and legs. After a little while she felt some of the strength return and said, "Let us go down now."

The duke helped her rise, saying, "Slowly, slowly now. I

will go first. Come down slowly after me. I am going to take you to Eusebia."

"It is happy news, señora. You are with child." The doctor, a man so stately and so old that he looked like an ambassador, smiled at Anita and patted her hand.

Embarrassed over the flurry, Anita lay back in the regal bed. Señora Eusebia approached from the other side of the room and sat down by the bed. She smiled her weary smile. "Don't worry, my dear. It was exactly so with me."

"I can't trouble you any longer," Anita said. She wanted desperately to be with Jonas; she wanted him to hold her in his arms.

"Nonsense, child. You must rest a little longer and then Veragua will take you back to your hotel."

From that dictum Anita knew there was no escape, as little as she wanted the duke's company. When she had rested the prescribed time and dressed, she thought of going directly to the Teresan School. But she could not go there with the duke; Jonas would never understand. So she asked Veragua to drive her back to the hotel.

At the entrance to the Cuatro Naciones, he said firmly, "You must not go in alone. I will accompany you to your rooms."

"No!" she said sharply. Then, with more civility and calm, she said, "Thank you, but it is entirely unnecessary."

Veragua seemed not to hear. He told the coachman to wait and, taking hold of Anita's arm, walked with her into the lobby.

A slight and proud-looking man with deepset eyes and gray-threaded beard rose from one of the sofas under a palm and walked rapidly toward them.

"Antoni!" the duke exclaimed, holding out his hand.

The slender man ignored the duke's hand and said calmly to Anita, "You are Señora Mark." His powerful dark eyes rapidly scanned her face, and the sad-looking mouth below his thick mustache was unsmiling, tense.

"Yes."

"I am Antoni Gaudí," the quiet man said.

Gaudí! Anita could not help staring at him for an instant: here was Jonas's and her idol standing before her. She had never seen his picture, somehow had not connected Jonas's description with this stranger. Then at once she wondered

110

uneasily what he was doing there, asking for her. It was Jonas, something about Jonas.

"My husband," she said, and heard her voice shaking with fear. "It's my husband," she repeated, feeling her tears near the surface. "Something has happened."

"I fear so, señora," Gaudí answered, and he put out his hand to steady her arm. "He has been injured. He is now in the hospital. I will take you there."

"Yes, yes," she said breathlessly, forgetting Veragua, forgetting everything but Jonas. She stood there like a confused child, waiting to be led, not knowing what to do.

Gently Antoni Gaudí took her arm and said, "Come."

The duke intervened. "The Güell carriage is outside."

"Very well." Even in her terror Anita's quick mind noticed that Gaudí's reply was cold. But she was almost beyond thinking; there was only the terror, the sick fear, and she let Gaudí lead her, as if she were walking in her sleep, back to the carriage.

No one broke the silence; Anita was so preoccupied with thoughts of Jonas that it hardly seemed strange for her to be riding next to Antoni Gaudí, the man whose work had captivated her for so long. At last she recovered enough to ask him, "How was my husband hurt—I mean, what injuries were there?"

"His back was hurt, señora, in a fall." She looked at Gaudí; a half-smile touched his mobile mouth, and he added, "He was making a climb too dangerous for any of the other men."

"That is his way," she said. But then, in her daze, she realized fully the seriousness of what Gaudí had said. "His back," she repeated, and a colder terror than before swept over her whole body; she felt naked in a freezing wind of fear. "His back. That could mean..."

"Yes, señora. You are most intelligent. It could be very serious indeed. I will hold back nothing from you, for that would not be a kindness."

"No," she managed. "It would not at all." She wanted to scream, to cry out, but the stiffening of her pride upheld her. Gaudí looked at her with respect, and compassion.

"Let us trust in God," he said simply. Anita thought grimly, I would trust a great deal more in an excellent doctor, a proper hospital.

The place they were approaching seemed nothing more than an old, crumbling convent; it was a neglected structure surmounted by a cross, with thick-barred gates; over the gates

111

hung an iron bell. It looked dark and dirty, and Anita was horrified.

Noticing her glance, Gaudí said, "This is the infirmary kept by the sisters. When your husband is better, he should go to Madrid, where there are more...adequate facilities." He paused, then asked delicately, "Are there...means for such a journey?"

"Means!" she blurted. Then she replied, "Yes, yes, of course." Her indifference seemed to surprise Gaudí. But there was no time for that now; he was handing her down, and soon they had been admitted through the gloomy gates and were following a small Sister of Mercy, in her winglike coif, down the dim hall toward Jonas's room.

The room was hardly brighter than the corridor, and Anita saw candles at the head and foot of his bed. It was a scene so like a scene of death that she covered her mouth with her hand so that she would not cry out and disturb Jonas.

He lay with closed eyes; his ruddy face was pale, and his mane of hair disordered. The Sister of Mercy offered her a chair, whispering as Anita sat down, "They have given him something for the...*dolor*"—she seemed to have lost the word "pain," although she had been speaking English. "He will sleep for a long time."

"I will wait here," Anita whispered. The nun nodded and withdrew. Gaudí and the duke stood by the door, speaking in low tones. Then they left the room.

Suddenly the mournful word *dolor* echoed itself to Anita; she remembered that the word meant both "pain" and "grief." Her own grief was too strong to bear, and she burst into weeping, leaning forward to lay her head next to Jonas's on the pillow. How long she stayed there weeping, she did not know, but at some point in the endless interval, she felt him stir, and heard him say, "Anita."

She raised her head and dried her face with her hands. Her relief was enormous, her heart was hammering at the sight of his familiar eyes, open now, staring at her hungrily. His arms reached out for her and she went into them; he held her with surprising strength, kissing her face and hair. She clung to him, then leaned back to look at his face.

He seemed overjoyed to see her, but in his changeable eyes, that were usually so direct and bright, there was a faint look of shame, and of fear.

"Anita," he said weakly, "I took a damned-fool chance. I
112

had no right." She could see that the short sentence had tired him.

"Please," she said. "Not now, my love."

He shook his head stubbornly. "I had no right." He raised his hand and put it over his eyes, turning his face away. Horrified, she saw that he was crying; the silent tears rolled down his cheeks, more awful than any sound of crying. Anita knew what it cost him for her to see him like that, so she took his arm and held it tightly.

"I can't..." he began, but his words were choked in his throat. He cleared his throat awkwardly and said again, "I can't... move my legs. I can't move my legs, Anita."

The bald, simple statement struck Anita like a blow to the breast. She almost reeled, thinking, Dear God, not him, not Jonas. He was too active, too self-reliant to bear such a thing.

But she made her voice as calm as she could, and said quietly, "My dear, that is just now, today. You'll be all right, I swear it. When you're stronger, we'll go to Madrid, where there is a better hospital. From there, we can go anywhere we have to. Don't you know that? It'll be all right, Jonas. I love you. I love you so much."

His face brightened at that, and he gave her a slight, drowsy smile. In no time he was asleep. She rose softly and went to the door. Just outside she saw Gaudí and Veragua, a few paces away, talking with the Sister of Mercy and an imposing man of middle age she took for a doctor.

He was, for at once Gaudí came forward and introduced him. "Come," Gaudí said to Anita, "you look so weary and pale, señora. Come just along the corridor and sit down with us a moment. The doctor wishes to speak with you."

After hesitating, Anita nodded and said, "Very well. But I must be near when he awakes."

The doctor said, "He may not wake for some time, señora. You must not overtire yourself. Now please, come with us for just a moment."

Anita felt dizzy with exhaustion. Vaguely she noticed that Veragua had disappeared, and only Gaudí and the nun remained when the doctor beckoned her into an anteroom a few doors away.

"Are you all right?" he asked with concern. She nodded, sinking into a chair.

The doctor sat down opposite and said, without preamble, "Your husband's condition is serious. In his fall, as far as I

113

can determine, some vertebrae were displaced. You comprehend 'vertebrae,' señora?" he asked a little uncertainly.

"Too well," she answered curtly, feeling her throat close up with pain. He stared at her curiously.

Then he went on, "It is possible that he may never regain the use of his lower limbs. There is now paralysis in his lower body." Anita closed her eyes and bowed her head. Then she steadied herself and looked up again.

"He needs more specialized care than is available in Barcelona. Señor Gaudí tells me that you have the means for such treatment. I would advise that he be taken to Madrid tomorrow or the next day. Initially."

"Initially?" she cried.

"I will be frank with you, señora. Better care would be available in Germany, England... or America. Spain is not in the forefront of medicine," he concluded bitterly.

"Whatever it takes," she said impatiently. "Will you make the arrangements?"

"I will, señora, at once."

"Thank you." He assisted her to rise. "May I stay here?" she asked.

"I would not advise it," he answered, "but it will be as you wish."

In the corridor she saw Gaudí waiting patiently.

"Señor Gaudí," she said, going forward to hold out her hand, "I am most grateful to you. You have been so kind."

"I feel responsible, señora." His sensitive face was full of pain.

Anita did not reply, but she reassured Gaudí with a slight pressure of her hand on his supporting arm. Her mind was whirling with anxious thoughts; she could think of nothing but Jonas and his care, unable to find anything to say to the small man at her side.

They were walking slowly toward an open archway that led to the convent's garden, and soon were outdoors. The fruit trees and the holy statues were ghostly in the falling twilight.

"Sit down, señora," Gaudí said, urging Anita onto a bench. "You look ill."

"I am well enough," she answered, but now she felt overwhelmed with apprehension.

"Your husband loves you devotedly," Gaudí said. "Whenever he has spoken of you, there is a... light upon him. I have become very attached to that young man in these weeks." Gaudí smiled his sad smile. "I of course have never been

114

blessed with a son. Jonas is a gifted man, a unique one. He was working with me on my funicular polygons..."

"Yes, yes, he told me about that," she interjected.

"I know you understand these matters," Gaudí said. "Your husband told me that you even worked together in the city of Chicago." She noticed that again he emphasized the first syllable of "Chicago," making it sound almost Spanish.

She nodded. "Yes."

"His understanding of load and thrust, as determined by my little models—they are string and wire—approaches that of a genius. Did he tell you I said that?"

"No." Anita smiled.

"But you, señora. You have given up your work to be his wife?"

"For the time being, yes."

"He is a very fortunate man, Jonas Mark. He is going to need your help very much now. He is a proud and difficult man. But I do not have to tell you that. I see in your eyes a great intelligence and understanding."

"I will do anything... anything to help him, Señor Gaudí."

"I think you will." Gaudí looked toward the archway. "But here is one of the good sisters; no doubt your quarters are ready. You should go to them soon. You look very pale."

"Not yet," Anita said. "I must see Jonas first. Goodbye for now, Señor Gaudí. Perhaps we will meet again before Jonas and I go to Madrid." She rose and held out her hand.

"I hope so. One moment, señora, before you go in. I have told your Jonas Mark that ultimately he must return to the country of his birth and find his own way. My way cannot be his; his gift is his own. Help him do that."

Anita looked at Gaudí, impressed by the kindness and sincerity in his noble face. "I will," she said softly. "Yes, I will."

Then she followed the nun into the convent, leaving Antoni Gaudí standing among the statues and orange trees in the darkened garden. She realized it had not even occurred to her to talk with him about his magnificent creations: Jonas was all that was in her mind.

Anita had found on her previous journey that Madrid was a little Paris, with the same sort of active life in the streets, brilliant shop windows, and handsome carriages driving around the Retiro every afternoon, just as people did in the Allée des Acacias in the Bois. And the crowds on the Prado

115

in the afternoons were much like those on the Champs Elysées. The French language was almost as common as Spanish, which reassured Anita, who was much more proficient in that language.

A month had elapsed since the day of Jonas's accident; they were staying in the Hotel de Paris, the best in Madrid. But even that, Anita thought, was none too good: there were five long staircases in the hotel and no elevator. Consequently she and Jonas had gotten a suite on the first floor. The lower rooms were noisy and ill ventilated, but it was impossible to occupy a higher floor with Jonas in a wheelchair. The rooms were well furnished, but the all-pervading odor of stale tobacco and the abundance of insect life made them very uncomfortable for the thin-skinned Anita.

This afternoon a deluge of rain had come; outside an icy blast of wind was howling from the surrounding Guadarrama mountains. Anita was standing at the window, watching the natives wrap themselves closely in their fur-lined brown cloaks and pull their sombreros about their ears. The usual assembly of loafers and beggars on the Puerta del Sol had disappeared; the great fountain in the center of the square, which on sunny days threw its sparkling jets high in the air, was silent. The scene was desolate. Over the rain Anita could hear the Guadarrama wind, like a messenger of death. She shivered.

"What is it? Are you cold?"

Anita turned from the window. Jonas had been asleep, but now he was wide awake, his piercing gaze on her. The corners of his mouth drooped downward; it had a perpetually sad look that tore at her heart.

She smiled and walked toward the bed. "No, my darling. It's just the wind."

"It sounds like it's saying 'gone,'" he commented softly. "The way my strength has gone. The way our lives have gone," he concluded.

"Jonas, Jonas. Don't talk like that. Soon we'll go to England; you know what the doctors say. All you need is some rest here awhile, and then..."

"Anita, sit down." He sounded so serious and stern that she obeyed at once. Ordinarily she would have made some joking comment about his imperious manner. But now there was a look in his eyes, a desperate, lost look, that checked her impudent reply.

She put out her hand and stroked his face, but he drew

116

away and said, "Listen to me, my dear. I can't talk when you do that."

"I don't want you to talk," she retorted, and the echo of her old flirtatious fire was in the words.

"What else am I good for?" he asked savagely.

"It doesn't have to be like this, Jonas. I don't care what any doctor says. You are suffering and you won't let me do anything to help."

"What the hell can anyone do?" he demanded. "I'm a cripple. I'm not a man, Anita, not any more."

"That's not true. You can still do your work—you still have your genius and your gift. You know that. You draw with your hands."

"I'm not talking about my work."

"I know." She stroked his face gently, then her hands caressed his neck and his hard, bare chest, where the shirt had fallen away.

"What are you doing?"

"Loving you," she said.

"Anita, stop it. What good can it do? Why are you doing this?"

"To show you that doctors are fools. And that love is the strongest medicine ever known. Let me love you, my darling. Let me."

He was staring at her, puzzled. But when she slid the filmy wrapper from her body, his eyes fired at the sight of her whiteness in the dim room with its drawn curtains and one lamp burning in a far corner. He cried out when she lay beside him, closing his eyes.

He lay with closed eyes, smiling, caressing her loosened hair with his hand as she undid his clothes and took them from his body.

She looked up and saw tears emerging from his tight-closed eyes. "Don't, my love," she whispered. "Don't. You'll see."

He did not move, then, and the terrible faith in his expression was so touching that she nearly cried out. She stifled the sound and raised her body, lying very close to him, kissing him deeply, with their bodies so closely mingled that the act was in itself a great kiss that strangely filled her with desire and satisfied her at once. She had never felt such a burning and exaltation.

With a slow, sinuous, dancelike motion of herself, Anita let her body caress his bare body, again and again; like a

117

miracle she felt the faintest stirring of his desire, and he cried out in amazement and triumph.

"My love, my love," she murmured, sliding down his passive body slowly, feeling with delight the far, faint trembling of him, until she lay on him again, caressing, touching, kissing, and hearing him cry out, "Oh, God, I felt, I felt, Anita."

She went on and on with the stubborn, rhythmic drawing of the strange caress, stroking his belly and legs, reaching upward to his chest, stroking the hardness of his arms and then again the passive lower limbs, feeling the absolute wonder of his awakening and pounding desire, never relenting, never slackening in her obdurate, steady and demanding kiss, drawing him, drawing him to the fulfillment of his drumming need; she could feel his awakening, the rise of wanting and the anonymous demand of his heated flesh; continuing, continuing, knowing that now his need had captured and freed him at once, that his fear had dissolved, that for him there was only the fiery demand and the pounding climax.

Something deep and hot in her joined in his ecstatic release; Jonas gave a great, moaning cry and she lay on him, weeping, tasting the salt of the sea.

He cried out again and said her name, like a talisman; she listened to his slackening breath, and the inchoate words that issued from him as he tangled his fingers in her hair and then, with his strong arms, lifted her upward and drew her to him in the hollow of his shoulder.

"I worship you, I worship you," he whispered, kneading her trembling arm with his long-fingered hand. She kissed his chest and burrowed into the hard hollow below his arm.

"I felt, Anita," he said. "I *felt,* I felt."

At last she found her voice. "I knew you would. I knew, Jonas. There is always a way, when there is love."

"You must love me," he said wonderingly. "If I never knew before, I know it now. You don't know what...you've done."

"Yes, yes, I do know. This has brought us back to ourselves. We will never lose each other again."

"No, no. Not ever. This won't stop us, Anita...this thing that happened to me. I'll be all right again; I know it. I know it."

She raised her head and studied his face in the lamplight. There was a look on it she had not seen in all these weeks, a look she had been praying for, an expression of triumph and hope.

Soon, she could tell him about the child.

Chapter 10

MANY PASSENGERS NOTICED the handsome young man and woman occupying deck chairs on the Cunarder *Lucania* on that mild day in February. But no one could understand the constant look of watchfulness on the beautiful young woman's face, nor the look of grimness on the man's. To all appearances, the couple had every reason to be happy: they were obviously people of means, because the woman was wrapped in a sable cloak against the cold. They were young and beautiful and seemed to be in splendid health.

But on closer observation, the man's posture in the chair was strange. He moved his upper body with ease, but his legs were slack and still under their blanket. Instead of paying close attention to the beautiful woman at his side, the young man stared into the middle distance as if he were looking at something no one else could see, beyond the expanse of the gray Atlantic. And his chair had wheels.

Jonas Mark was thinking, How can I tell her? How can I tell her that we can't go on with this any longer? He kept hearing the words of the great English doctor. "I'm very sorry, I can hold out little hope. But there is a very good man in New York...."

And after New York, Jonas reflected with bitterness, where then? Anita would never give up, he knew that, and they would go on and on; to Saratoga, to "take the waters," back to Europe. With horror he even pictured her kneeling before a shrine at Lourdes, among all the hanging crutches, and he felt sick at his stomach.

"How are you feeling?" He heard her clear voice raised to make herself heard over the rising wind and turned to smile at her.

"Fine," he lied, keeping the stiffened smile on his face, loving her so much that it was an ache.

"It's not a long journey," she said, still in that horribly bright, raised tone that distorted her low, husky voice. "Only five and a half days." Jonas looked into Anita's eyes and saw the desperation and pleading in them.

"Yes, that's right. It'll be good to get back." His mouth was brassy with the bitterness of the additional lie. He thought of the hot, bright days in Spain, and the balmy nights in the Cuatros Naciones, when he and Anita had lain in each other's arms. The days with Gaudí. The nights with her, when he had been a man.

For days after their first passionate encounter in the Madrid hotel, Jonas had been buoyed by a new joy, a fresh determination. He was awed by the depth and power of Anita's love, powerless to tell her in words what she had done for him with that unfamiliar, miraculous caress. The awkwardness of his own body had made it hard for him to respond in kind; he had tried again and again but had given up, feeling like a fumbling schoolboy. Then she ... gently and insistently she had made love to him again.

Jonas was torn between delight and a nagging sensation of guilt and impotence: somehow he was not playing the man. He could not help thinking it, although nothing on earth could have induced him to tell her so. Only an ingrate and fool would have done that. Besides, he resolved, it will eventually be all right. If the center of his body lived, then his legs would, too.

Still there had been times, when he lay awake during the long nights, that Jonas fell back into despair. He thought with an ache of his days of physical power and the brief, strange dream of his work with Gaudí. The black knowledge that he was not a man now would steal over Jonas. He wondered uneasily if he could ever give Anita a child.

He remembered bitterly how much hope they had pinned on the English doctor. They would go through it again in New York, and all on her money.

He glanced at Anita's perfect profile, half hidden in the folds of her sable hat. The Spanish sun, for all her care, had given Anita's white skin a rosy glow; he studied her shapely nose, the incredibly long black lashes and the pink lips. Her mouth was no longer relaxed and smiling; it always had a small tightness now, as if she were trying to keep from crying.

She felt his look and turned, smiling. Her fire-blue eyes

had lost the openness he knew. He wondered if she was keeping something from him, and he felt an angry ache.

"What is it?" Her voice was gentle now in the falling wind, and concerned. He marveled that she always knew when there was something wrong with him.

"Nothing. I was just thinking how beautiful you are. And that you should be walking around the deck, not sitting here with me. You're a very good sailor."

She reached out her gloved hand and took his. "I don't want to be away from you."

The greatness of her love filled him with a deep joy even as it shamed him. I don't think I can go on, he thought, the rest of our lives, taking and taking and never giving. He wished he could say that to her, but he could not, any more then she could tell him what she was keeping dark. He wondered again what it was, longing to ask her. There had been a time, he realized with pain, when they told each other everything.

"Aren't you cold?" he asked.

"Not at all." Her voice had that false brightness again.

"Why don't you take a turn around the deck?" he urged her.

"Come with me," she said.

He had a sudden picture of her wheeling him, slowly, walking slow to keep back with him, when her usual pace was brisk as a young pony's. "No, you go ahead," he said in a level tone. "I want to read a little more of this." He indicated his book. "Maybe I'll catch up with you."

She looked at him uncertainly, but rose from her chair. She bent and kissed him. "I love you," she said in a low voice, "I love you so much."

Watching her move away, Jonas noticed other men's glances following her graceful figure and he thought, She feels better watching me, and yet she is going now, because I told her to. He stared at Anita until she was out of sight.

Then he saw a familiar figure, following in her direction. It was the Duke of Veragua.

Jonas's tenderness dissolved into a blinding anger: the man had seen Anita and was going after her. And here he was in a wheelchair, helpless as an old, invalid woman. He wanted desperately to be able to walk again, to stride after the bastard, pull him around and knock him flat to the deck, or over the rail. And all he could do was rage and wonder, wonder what the smooth bastard would say when he reached her.

121

Jonas clenched his hands into impotent fists; the sweat broke out on his face, turning cold at once in the rising winter wind. He had stood a lot in his time, and laughed at it; he couldn't take this. Well, he didn't have to: he could go after them. He would not sit here any longer and feel his guts being ripped out. Jonas raised his chair from the reclining position and undid the safety catch. Soon the silent rubber wheels of his chair were in motion.

Anita Mark paid no attention to the footfalls behind her, engrossed in the management of her heavy cloak, whipped by the growing wind, obsessed with the thought of the secret she was keeping from Jonas. She had decided that it was still not the time to tell him about the baby; it was enough for them both to concentrate on his getting well. She was afraid of what the news would do to him: he would not welcome the idea of another responsibility now.

Strange as it seemed, Jonas Mark was the kind of man who still felt responsible for her, even if now she was actually responsible for him. There was so much, she thought sadly, that they could not say to each other. Somehow it had been that way ever since they were in Madrid.

The wind seemed freezing: she must go back to Jonas and get him back to the suite. But that would hurt his pride, she thought. And the stewards she had tipped so handsomely, without Jonas's knowledge, would keep an eye on him. Better to let him stay.

Anita caught sight of a handy shelter from the wind: the opulent ship's library, with its open fire and seats of bright blue velvet, invited her. She entered, glancing at the walls of carved mahogany and Ambona panels with writing tables and chairs arranged alongside. There were heavy-looking books behind the glass doors of the bookcases. Anita thought what a far cry it was from the "few good books" which Charles Dickens had found kept under lock and key on the *Britannia*. For the first time in days she smiled broadly, examining the ponderous-looking tomes.

There were only two other people in the library at the moment, a peaceful-looking old man who did not even look up when she entered and a young woman writing a letter.

"This solemn place amuses you, señora?"

Anita turned quickly, startled, recalling that a little while before she had felt a slight draft of icy air. But she had not heard anyone approach on the deep-piled Persian carpets. It was the Duke of Veragua.

122

She knew she had not hidden her dismay, because he said softly, "You do not look very happy to see me."

"I'm not," she said bluntly. She was determined not to continue the charade of politeness, when the man was the last person on earth she wanted to see. "What brings you here?"

"Come, come, señora. Let us sit down for a moment." He indicated one of the double rows of velvet seats; each bank of wide chairs, three to a side, was attached to mahogany columns extending to the frescoed ceiling. Anita glanced at the other occupants of the library; the fashionable young woman had glanced up from her letter and was looking at the duke with interest and approval; the old man frowned at them over his book. There was another quick drift of cold air, but whoever had entered was hidden in an alcove.

Anita was unwilling to talk to Veragua, but even more unwilling to cause a scene which might be talked about, which might even reach Jonas's ears. Resigned, she tossed her cloak on one of the seats and sat down. Veragua sat down next to her; she was delighted that the construction of the chairs prevented any intimacy. Each seat had a broad curving arm that effectively separated a sitter from his neighbor.

But the chair arms did not deter Veragua. He reached suddenly over the arms of his seat and grasped her hand, kissing it fervently. *"You* bring me to America, señora."

"You must be insane," she said, wrenching her hand from his, getting up from the banquette of blue velvet.

He rose at once and stood very close to her, staring down into her eyes. "No, my dear, I have never been more sane. I have seen your husband, and what he has become. How long do you think a woman like you can endure it?" He held her by the arms to keep her from running away, continuing to stare down into her eyes, whispering urgently, "A blind man could see the fire in you, my dear Anita. I have, always, since the first time I danced with you in the barbaric city of Chicago. And I will dance with you again."

She looked at him with angry eyes, helpless in his tight grasp.

"I had not meant to blurt all this out, like a savage." He smiled. "But the sight of you has almost made me lose my senses, Anita."

"Let me go," she demanded coldly. "Let me go, and do not let me see your face again on this voyage."

The young letter-writer was looking at them with consternation. Chagrined, Veragua released Anita's arms. She picked up her cloak.

"Allow me to help you," he said, trying to take the cloak from her.

"Leave me alone." Hastily she put on her cloak of heavy fur and rushed from the library back to the windy deck.

The encounter had shaken her more than she cared to admit: she hated the man, and yet when he had touched her, something in her, something that she had believed could be aroused only by Jonas, had responded. But that could not be; the time of deprivation had left her momentarily weak and vulnerable. Jonas was the only man she had ever wanted, ever would want. She was sharply disappointed when she returned to their place on deck and saw that he was gone.

She hurried back to their suite. He was still in his chair and had not removed his overcoat.

"Hello, darling." She went to him and took his head between her hands. "Did you just come in?"

She thought he had an odd expression and his smile was a little stiff when he answered. "Yes. How was your walk?"

He seemed to be looking at her strangely, and she hoped that the encounter with Veragua did not show in her face, her manner. "Lonely," she said.

Jonas raised his brows. "Really?"

She bent over and kissed his mouth with quick, fervent kisses.

"My love, my love." He leaned against her for an instant, and she felt a tension, a withdrawal in the body that she knew so well. But she kept on stroking his face with her hands.

"I'm always lonely without you now," she said softly. "Don't you know that?"

She turned up his face so he would look at her. His eyes had the same lost, peculiar expression she had seen in them when she came in. "I want you," she said baldly.

Suddenly his eyes lost the blank look; they were gleaming. He reached up to draw her face down to his and kissed her with long, hungry kisses.

The touch of his mouth aroused her to a wild, savage yearning: never before had she felt, even for him, a desire so urgent, of such awesome power. She closed her eyes and realized that her fingers, of their own volition, were unfastening her clothes and his, that she was urging him with her touches and, with almost formless sounds, downward, downward,

124

from the prison of his chair, and then they were lying together on the deep-piled carpet of the sitting room.

And somehow then she knew how to guide him, how to fix his body and hers in that new and unknown posture so he might love her freely as she was loving him. There seemed to be no end to her caress; she was beyond time, beyond all consciousness, knowing she would never grow weary of this caress of him; steady and obdurate, she went on and on, feeling with delight his returning, a thousandfold, the joy of that caress.

With a dazzled wonder Anita found herself able in that frenzied interval to give the rhythmic, unvarying caress even while she rode the waves of pleasure eddied from his mouth; she opened like a blossom in the sun and in their dancing motions flew the arched dolphins of the sea round them, the innermost of flesh resounding as her body drummed in a breaking of light. She heard the cry of strangers in herself and him; the deepest shuddering began to burn within her flowing core, crying out again she rode the widening pools of broken light, blinded, selfless, blank and wild on that excruciating edge of joy. With his deep-toned answer came the savor of the salty sea again.

They lay unable to speak or move for an undetermined time; she could feel the aftermath of his delight in the tender stroke of his fingers on her head. But sensitively in a moment Anita read a withdrawing and uncertainty in him. She raised her head and looked at him; in the dim lamplight she saw that his eyes were closed. His mouth, instead of smiling, was set, and his momentary happiness had fled.

"Leave me a moment, darling," he said in a flat, quiet voice. At once she realized that he faced the humiliation of being helped into his clothes, being supported into his chair.

"But, my dear..." she began.

"Please. Please, Anita, just a moment."

"Yes, Jonas. Yes, darling." And gathering up her clothes, feeling suddenly shy and exposed, Anita held a petticoat around her and went into the bedroom.

The door was ajar, and she listened with pain to the struggle of his body; she could imagine him straining to cover himself, then heave himself upward by his strong arms into the chair. She felt like crying, and there was a bitter taste in her mouth. All their pleasure seemed like nothing, after all.

Anita shook off the gloomy thought and with determina-

125

tion freshened herself in the bathroom and then put on the most becoming dress she could find. Slowly and with care she brushed and dressed her shining length of black hair. After she had finished, and put a simple pair of aquamarine eardrops into her ears, she examined herself in the glass, feeling a return of good spirits.

She was astonished to hear him whistle from the sitting room. "May I come in?" she called, and when he answered yes, she opened the bedroom door and entered.

Jonas was sitting in his chair, neatly attired, his cravat in order. "As soon as I brush my hair, let's go to dinner," he said calmly.

She looked at him for a moment, puzzled; his tone was that of a courteous stranger, and his bright eyes had a shut expression.

"Fine." She made herself smile. He wheeled himself into the bedroom and soon returned, his mane of hair smoothed down. He was still smiling that awful courteous smile that chilled her heart.

But she forced herself to keep calm, to assume the same cool manner as his. She opened the door and wheeled him onto the deck toward the first-class dining room. The wind was very calm, and there was an eerie quality to the night.

Both Jonas and Anita had smiled in secret over the opulence of the dining room, maintained in the "modified Italian style" by a heavy coffered ceiling in white and gold, supported by Ionic columns. The Spanish mahogany walls were richly carved with pilasters and other devices, and there were broken pediments and clocks over all the sideboards.

They both preferred cozier quarters, and generally they dined in their suite. But tonight for some reason Jonas had opted for the enormous room, which sat 430 people. The old tradition of the long dining table, which Anita detested, had not entirely been abandoned, even in 1894, on the *Lucania*. But instead of one table there were at least four with numerous small side tables set in alcoves separated by heavy carved screens and mirrors.

Assuming that Jonas would prefer the privacy of one of those, Anita wheeled his chair toward an alcove. To her surprise, he said, "Let's join the party tonight." His eyes looked so bright he seemed almost drunk.

Trying to hide her astonishment, Anita answered easily, "All right. Why not?"

She wheeled him to one of the long tables, and a steward

126

quickly helped Jonas into one of the armchairs, upholstered in red-figured frieze velvet. The armchairs were bolted to the floor and could not be moved. The chairs swiveled, and were turned away from the tables so that the passengers could sit down comfortably before rotating themselves to face the table.

Suddenly the bright lights and the numerous palms, the elaborate settings on the snowy cloths, seemed horribly oppressive to Anita, mocking the intimacy of the scene in their stateroom such a little while before.

She stared at Jonas, who was matter-of-factly studying the menu, unable to believe that he was the same man who had just made love to her with such a closeness and abandon, in an act that was even more intimate than the ordinary act of love.

Horrified, she saw the Duke of Veragua approach them, smiling. Even worse, Jonas did not look annoyed, as he always had before, but was smiling back at the duke and greeting him warmly. She wondered how she would endure the hour that lay before them.

It was very late before Anita fell into an uneasy sleep. The encounter with Veragua in the dining room had been even more uncomfortable than she had expected. Jonas had continued to act like a jovial stranger, and the duke's veiled compliments to Anita had barely seemed to touch Jonas at all. He drank a great deal and appeared not to notice the ironic quality of Veragua's inquiries about his health.

Yet all the time below the civilized exterior and the apparent indifference Anita sensed in Jonas a painful savage anger, a terrible despair. When the endless dinner finally came to an end, she looked forward with eagerness to their being alone. But Jonas had agreed to the duke's suggestion that they all attend a concert together in one of the luxurious saloons, so Anita had to endure further discomfort. Jonas drank a great deal: by the time they arrived at their suite, he was almost overcome with sleep.

He rang for a steward to help him get to bed, rather than allowing Anita to do so. Pained and anxious, she lay awake beside him for at least an hour; he was deep in sleep. She thought she heard him stirring some time in the dark hours, but by then she was too exhausted to wake.

Now, however, something brought her sharply awake. She heard men shouting belowdecks and sat up in bed, her heart pounding. She reached over to touch Jonas: the bed was empty. Jonas was gone.

Frantically Anita got out of bed and slipped into a concealing wrapper. He was in neither the bathroom—the door was ajar—nor the sitting room, and his chair was gone. So frightened that her knees felt weak, she was overcome with a swift, stabbing nausea. Where was he? What had he done?

Now she recalled the awful brightness of his eyes, the distance in them, the uncharacteristic behavior at dinner. She swayed and caught hold of the elaborate molding by the door.

The men's shouting was louder now, and she thought she heard one call out, "Man overboard! Man overboard!"

Her terror was so great that she thought she would lose consciousness. But now, of all times, she must keep her head. She fastened the wrapper more securely about her, ran into the bedroom and found slippers, and rushed through the sitting room, flinging open the door that led to the deck. Leaving it ajar, she ran to the rail. A wave of dizziness took her again, and she was sure she was going to fall into the water. But she gripped the rail with such frantic urgency that her fingers ached, and peered downward.

She could see little, so she ran down the stairs to the deck below. The great blinding light that she could see only partially from the upper deck was revealed now as torches fanning the choppy water. The previous calm of the sea and wind had gone: a smart breeze was whipping the deck, and the waves looked stormy and sinister. Seamen were lowering a lifeboat to the water, and there was a flurry of activity below.

The searching light's beams revealed nothing.

"Dear God," she said aloud, "dear God. Don't let it be Jonas. Don't let it be."

She was so overcome with fear that she did not know what to do now, how to proceed. To make herself heard over the screaming winches and the shouting men was impossible. Anita leaned a moment against the rail, trying to still the trembling of her body. She was shaking so that she could not summon herself to walk. At last the shuddering abated and she made her way back up the stairs, slowly as an old woman, clinging to the rail.

When she finally returned to their suite, Jonas was still not there. Frantically she reached for the bell and leaned her body against it. In moments a worried-looking steward came in.

128

"Mrs. Mark!" He stared at her in consternation.

She caught sight of herself in a mirror; she looked like a madwoman, with staring eyes, disordered hair. But nothing like that mattered now, when Jonas could be sinking in the dark water around them.

"My husband!" she screamed at the steward. "He's missing!"

The small, slender boy stood there staring at her.

"Please," she cried out, "please! Find out who it is...do something!" She had never known such terror or such pain; her throat ached as if something hard and big were lodged in it, as if someone had thrust a stake into her flesh. The pain was so all-encompassing she had to force her words out; she felt cold all over, and shook uncontrollably. My God, I am going to break in two, she thought wildly.

The frightened boy stammered, "You...you just lie down, Mrs. Mark. I'll...get somebody."

He rushed out, slamming the door in his excitement.

Anita felt weaker and colder, yet she could not bear to sit down. She sobbed, walking back and forth like a wounded animal. The terrible pain in her throat was spreading to her chest; every breath seemed to hurt, but she could not stop the wild sobbing. A steady knock sounded at the door. "Come in." Again she forced the words out, choking. The burly captain stood on the threshold, grasping the knob. He looked at her with compassion, his sad eyes taking in her wild and disheveled appearance. Behind him stood another man.

"Mrs. Mark," the captain said slowly, "this is Dr. Monroe, the ship's physician. Please sit down."

"No," she protested, but she was swaying now on her feet. "No," she repeated. "Whatever it is, tell me. Tell me now and do not keep me waiting."

The doctor moved toward her and grasped her by the arm. He pushed her gently toward a chair and with his hands on her shoulders forced her to sit down. Then he stood beside her, still with his hand on her shoulder.

"Mrs. Mark," the captain said in a low voice, "I have some very tragic news."

"For God's sake, what is it?" she heard herself screaming again in a voice she hardly knew.

"We fear your husband has drowned."

"No," she said, shaking her head. "No, that is not so. It's not so. No."

129

The doctor took her wrist between his fingers. "Mrs. Mark," he said, "you must lie down. Now. You must."

She began to laugh, wild, hysterical laughter that was not her own. Some madwoman was laughing. "Hold her," she heard the doctor mutter, and the captain was holding her down in the chair. The doctor opened his bag and took something out, and in a moment Anita felt something bite into her arm, like the bite of a huge bee. Almost at once she felt her arms and lips growing numb; the room floated about her. The men's faces were distorted and their voices came from very far away.

Weeping and weeping, with convulsive sobs that racked her frame, Anita knew they were raising her from the chair and walking her toward the bedroom and the bed. Her feet were sinking into clouds, and the pain in her throat was going away, going, going. She was so tired, so very tired; she was nodding. That was the last thing she remembered.

Anita did not leave her stateroom once during the rest of the voyage. When the meals ordered for her by the ship's doctor arrived three times each day, she would go through the motions of eating, but the trays were carried away with dishes almost full.

She had no visitors except the doctor, who came each afternoon to give her a cursory examination. Once he asked who would meet her in New York, saying that she should not land alone, to endure the ordeal of customs and finding a hotel. She answered him with such total indifference that it aroused his anxiety; her state approached the catatonic.

The Duke of Veragua sent daily messages and gifts of flowers. She was too weary even to wonder how they had been procured, or at what expense and difficulty, from the ship's store of fresh flowers. She refused to see him, but each day the flowers and the messages continued to arrive.

At last, the day before the landing in New York, Anita got up. She went to the dressing table and looked in the mirror; the sight was so strange, and her legs so weak from lying in bed, that she sat down abruptly to stare at herself.

The face in the mirror looked like that of a much older woman; she did not recognize it as her own. With the same terrible apathy that had possessed her since Jonas had drowned, Anita noticed that her skin looked rough and muddy and her hair was without sheen, disheveled and lifeless.

Suddenly she remembered the things Jonas had said about

her eyes and lips and hair, about the whiteness of her satiny skin. In the soft Spanish nights, they had lain together by an open window listening to the watery trill of the guitars, to someone singing the tragic and melodious songs of Spain. The music had not seemed tragic then, she thought with a fresh sensation of pain. Then it had been sensuous, arousing; together they had seen life spreading out before them, like the long, sunlit aisles of an endless garden.

And he, whose speech was always stumbling and plain, had been almost lyrical, saying her hair looked like the night water by moonlight, that her mouth was like a flower.

Looking at the haggard stranger now in the mirror of the lonely room, Anita remembered it all with an agonizing clarity; she started to cry. She had not been able to cry for days, but the sudden tears melted the knot of coldness in her, the hard thing in her throat, and she cried and cried.

She thought, Our lives were just beginning. Now mine is over. Without Jonas it was emptiness and cold, nothing else. Life was a burden to be carried, not a shining time to be lived.

Rising, she prepared to go back to bed. A soft knocking made her pause. "Please leave me alone," she called out hoarsely. But the knock went on.

Anita was too listless to argue. She went slowly to the door and opened it. The French maid assigned to her stood there patiently with a tentative smile.

"Madame will need me to attend her," the woman said, her sharp black eyes making a rapid inventory of Anita's wasted looks. "Before the landing tomorrow," the maid added. "May I come in, madame?" she persisted.

"I suppose so. Come in, then."

Anita submitted to the woman's washing, brushing and dressing of her hair, to her application of creams, of hot and cold cloths to the face. It took less energy to submit than to resist, she found. Patiently the woman wrapped ice in a cloth and rubbed it below Anita's eyes again and again. When Anita looked obediently into the mirror, some of the puffiness was gone. She saw traces of the face she had always seen before, but there were still deep lines, like sharp parentheses, slashed downward from the corners of her mouth.

An awful coldness, deeper than before, possessed her. She thought, I will never be able to smile again; my face is like a death mask and it doesn't matter. But the woman had worked so hard, was so kind, that Anita rallied and said, "Thank you," managing the ghost of a smile that was more

131

like a rapid wince. She gave the maid a handsome tip, stemming her voluble thanks, desperate to be alone.

She went back to bed. It was better now, because she felt nothing at all but exhaustion. Sleep came at last, erasing thought for a short time. But the dreams came all too soon: she dreamed of Jonas standing at a great distance from her. They were separated by a span of water that was the sea and at the same time the lake before the esplanade at the Exposition. He was beckoning to her and smiling. She felt, in the dream, a feverish longing to reach him, to touch him, to be in his arms, and she began to move in the slow and agonizing leisure of dream-movements toward her husband.

Then she was sinking into the water, and it was soothing, delicious, sinking with him. He had his arms around her and they were going down together.

Anita woke up with great abruptness, feeling the pain return, the huge hard thing form again in her tight throat. This time, in the lonely night, she could not cry, but lay racked with grief, fearing once again that her body would break before the hurt lessened. Helpless and defeated, all she could do was cry out again and again, in that awful croaking voice, "Oh, God, oh, God."

She slept a little again, without dreaming but with miserable restlessness. Early the next morning, she got up trembling and exhausted. Her body felt ill and weak, but at least the pain was manageable; she felt nothing at all now. It would be possible to move like an automaton through the necessary hours before the landing.

There was one bad moment, when the attendants came to pack their possessions. Through a tiny chink in her languid armor the pain needled in once more: she watched the steward putting Jonas's things into a small trunk. There was the disreputable corduroy jacket she had seen him wear so many times, a garment he clung to despite her joking references to it. The jacket was deeply wrinkled at the elbows with the long impress of his bending arms, and on one of the pockets was a large burn hole from his cigarette. One of the lapels lay flat, the other forward; it looked like an animal with one flopping ear.

The sight of the jacket was too much for Anita; she left the room while they finished packing.

She was standing on the deck huddled into her sable cloak when the Duke of Veragua approached. She was so cold inside now it felt like impacted ice, and she was able to greet him calmly.

"Señora," he said, bowing, "I have taken a great liberty."

She felt no curiosity or surprise. She simply waited for him to explain.

"I cabled your father in Chicago."

"Very well," she answered in a dead voice. "Thank you."

"You will let me escort you from the ship?"

"Very well," she said again. How could it matter? she thought. Nothing could matter much any more. She just wanted to get it over with so she could be alone, and not have to talk to anyone at all.

When the ship drew into New York, she stood with the duke at the rail. Looking down, she caught sight of her father, Roderick Byrne.

He thinks I am Anita Byrne again, she reflected, that life will be the same again in Chicago. The duke thinks so, too. But they are wrong, both of them. I will always be Anita Mark until the day when death relieves me of these goings and these comings, when I am with Jonas again.

PART II

RENEWAL

Chapter 11

CHARLES SETON TAPPED at the door of his wife's dressing room, a sanctum where, lately, he was not easily admitted. But tonight something had given him courage, perhaps the brandy he had drunk to fortify himself against the dinner at the Fanes'.

He heard Anita say, "Come in," and opened the door. Catching sight of her face in the brightly lit mirror, he was surprised to see an expression there he hadn't seen for years—since the days of Higsbee and Waite. She had looked at Jonas Mark with that expression. Her mouth had an unusual softness, her cheeks a high color. She hastily shut the top drawer of her dressing table and met his look in the mirror. The fire of her vivid blue eyes went out. He wondered what she had been looking at in the dresser drawer.

"Hello, Charley," she said, and he felt the old sadness that never left him; she spoke to him as if he were a child, or a large, bumbling dog, with affection, and impatience. Just for a moment there, the wonderful look in her eyes.... Despite himself Charley could never withstand her vivid beauty. He stared at her gleaming, high-dressed hair, the flawless skin, the long, intricate earrings of sapphire that emphasized the color of her eyes.

"I was just wondering if you're ready."

"Not quite, as you see," she said in that patient voice that was worse than snapping. His gaze wandered down from her smooth, powdered face to her white neck and the full, pale breasts exposed by the filmy negligee.

He stepped forward and put his hands on her creamy shoulders, caressing her upper arms, his fingers sliding down until they almost touched her breasts.

Perversely, he wished she would withdraw from him, show some emotion. Hate was akin to attraction. But she was so indifferent that she made no move at all. She touched her coiffure and said, "I see you're not ready yet, anyhow."

"What do you mean?" he asked, stung. He leaned over and checked his reflection: his black hair was smooth and perfectly cut, his cravat in faultless alignment.

"You're drunk." Her reply was matter-of-fact, also without emotion. "I won't go to the Fanes' with you when you're like that."

She got up abruptly and, brushing past him, went into her room and shut the door.

Charley never followed her when she was in that mood. He went to her bedroom when she sent for him; he had been hurt too often, going on his own. And even that had been infrequent these last few months.

In any case as soon as she was dressed Anita would go to Iris's room. She always did before they went out together. And Charles Seton admitted to himself how much he hated the child. She had the very eyes of Jonas Mark.

Charley sighed and went through the door of his own bedroom. Yes, he hated this house, which Anita had designed herself; he hated the child and he hated his goddam life. But one thing still kept him there: Anita and his right to her bed, infrequent as it had become. That should be enough for any man, Charley thought. The desirous sweat broke out on his fresh-bathed body under the immaculate clothes. If she locked him out tonight...

He walked unsteadily to the cabinet by his bed and opened one of its carved doors. He wasn't used to drinking like this, but tonight he really needed it to blunt the pain. He took out a brandy decanter and poured a little of the liquor into a glass. Looking at the level of the brandy, he added some more. Then he carefully took off his evening jacket and hung it over the back of a chair.

"Just one," he said to himself, "to take the edge off." He drained the brandy and poured another half-glass. Then he lay down, fighting off the soft escape of sleep. If he fell asleep Anita would leave without him, for certain. He didn't want to be alone tonight.

Drowsily he let his eyes close for a minute. He went over it again in his mind, as he had a hundred times before. What had he done wrong? It hadn't been this bad four years ago

137

when she had finally said she would marry him. Floating between wakefulness and sleep, Charley remembered.

For three years after Anita Mark returned from Spain, Charles Seton had not let a day go by without some attention to her. By then, Charley was a junior partner in Byrne Associates, and often invited to the Tudor house. He caught no glimpse of Anita during that early spring of 1894, for she never appeared when he arrived. Roderick Byrne told Charley worriedly that she was almost becoming a recluse. But obdurately Charley continued sending her notes and small, respectable gifts of candy and flowers.

On her birthday he gave her a jeweled watch that aroused the protests of her mother and aunt; such a gift was highly improper, they said, unless a couple intended to marry. Charley replied that he intended to marry Anita, if she would have him, no matter how long he had to wait. That mollified the Byrne women, and Roderick consented to deliver the gift to Anita. She never wore the watch. At her mother's prodding, however, Anita sent a thank-you note.

Anita's confinement was approaching, and the whole situation, Margaret Byrne complained to her husband, was "most indelicate." Roderick retorted, "Indelicate be damned," declaring that Charles Seton was the very man he would choose for his daughter. Because she secretly concurred, Margaret Byrne continued to deliver Charley's gifts and messages to her daughter.

A daughter was born to Anita in July 1894; she was named Iris. The baby was fragile and pale, blue-veined and beautiful as the flower she was named for. She was so like Anita in features and temperament, even as an infant, that Roderick Byrne adored her. What disturbed him and his wife—and Charles Seton, when he was permitted a glance at the baby—was that the child had Jonas Mark's eyes, direct, unfeminine and piercing, of a changeable hazel color; she also had Jonas's thatch of golden-brown hair.

Charley had his first visit with Anita when he came to see her after the baby's birth: she was even more beautiful than he remembered or imagined. But in some ways she was an utter stranger to him; the old Anita Byrne had been cool, though indifferently friendly, but there had been a hidden, slumbering fire. Anita Mark looked frozen. The only time there was any warmth at all in her was when she held the baby.

A month or two after the baby's birth, Anita appeared quite suddenly one day at the offices of Byrne Associates. Roderick announced, beaming, that she was being made a junior partner.

Charley was overjoyed: now there was no way she could avoid him. However, his joy was short-lived. Though they worked in close proximity, it brought him no nearer. Anita had erected a wall between herself and the world, and in particular Charles Seton. Now that she was out of the house and had escaped the dictums of Margaret Byrne, Anita discouraged Charley's gifts, and her attitude toward him was like that of the old days at Higsbee's—friendly, distant.

But privately Roderick advised Charley not to despair; Anita was seeing no other young men, and Charley must not give up.

Obdurately Charley continued to pursue her; her beauty maddened him now. She was no longer the untouched goddess, but a woman who had known love. And the intuitive Charley, whose sixth sense was almost feminine, discerned a new quality in her that made him desire her more than ever. What had been a slumbering intensity, a passion for love, now seemed to be a leashed sensuality. He was determined that if she could never love him, he could make her want him. And he bent every effort in that direction.

Bustling Chicago in the Naughty Nineties was becoming ever more squalid and corrupt. Several civic organizations had pushed for the creation of a master plan for the city; Byrne Associates was in the forefront. Soon Roderick Byrne was to undertake a reorganization plan for Baltimore. Comprehensive plans for other cities, of course, would follow. Anita worked closely with her father on these plans; she appeared oblivious to everything but her work. But there were moments when Charley sensed a growing restlessness in her, an awareness that the world was changing around them, and women with it. The styles and manners that had seemed so daring in 1893 were no longer so: Charles Dana Gibson's lovely and captivating Gibson girl was very like Anita.

That splendid creature of ink and paper appealed to women because she typified what most of them yearned for—beauty, self-assurance, freedom from the old subservience of woman to man, while retaining the power to win a man or scorn him as whim or occasion dictated. Anita was all that, and more; she would be the heiress of the great Byrne empire. She was a woman who did not depend on anyone, a woman who might confer her gifts, like the queen bee.

The change in women reflected itself in Chicago, as everywhere across America. A new sophistication was being born. Evelyn Clayton, a young Chicago widow, who had married a Russian envoy, a prince of Imperial Russia, announced she was taking up cigarettes. The prince "loved to see a woman smoking," the new princess claimed.

Anita, who was a friend of Mrs. Clayton's, had been smoking for two years.

One evening in the early spring of 1896, Charley noticed an especial nervousness in Anita, an almost vulnerable look. Something urged him to approach her; he asked her to dine, an appointment she had always refused before. But on that evening, to Charley's astonishment, she accepted.

In the carriage after dinner, when he was driving her home, she suggested that they visit his bachelor apartment. Flabbergasted, Charley took her there. She made it clear that she would allow him to make love to her: this longed-for consummation left him feeling utterly enslaved by her. Anita was as cool to him as ever, after that, indicating that the incident gave him no rights to her at all. Whenever the evening was repeated, it was she who made the first move.

He felt he no longer knew this independent creature who took her pleasure so matter-of-factly. Even the sophisticated Charley was shocked at some of the things Anita suggested; he performed them, however, with zest, for he could deny her nothing.

Charley begged her to marry him, again and again. She told him lightly that she was not ready. But that autumn, her father had a stroke, and Roderick begged Anita to marry Charles Seton so he might "die in peace." Finally, she consented. Anita and Charles were married in December 1896, two months after Roderick's death.

Until the winter of 1899, Charley had sometimes been almost happy; it was enough, at first, to live with Anita, to have her bear his name. He enjoyed the envious looks of other men and gloried in his right to touch her, be near her. His lovemaking, at least, always seemed to bring her pleasure, even if afterward she appeared to drift away in the privacy of her mind to a place he could not enter. But Charley told himself she would come to love him, if he waited long enough and was patient.

He had believed that until the last winter. One night near Christmas they were preparing to go out together to a holiday party. As always, Anita went to Iris's room to tell her good-night before they left. Charley did not intrude on those leave-takings, but on that snowy night, for some reason, a jealous ache in him impelled him to follow Anita.

He stole down the corridor and stood outside the open door of Iris's room. Ashamed of himself but unable to resist, Charley listened.

He heard Iris's sleepy murmur, then Anita's low, husky voice.

"Yes, my darling, Uncle Charley and I are going out."

"Mother?"

"What, darling?" Charley's shameful jealousy deepened at the tenderness in Anita's question, a tenderness that he never heard when he and Anita were alone.

"Why is he my uncle? Other girls have a daddy."

There was a brief silence and then the whispering sound of rustling bedclothes, the swish of silk which seemed to indicate an embrace. "I told you before, my love," Anita's voice sounded again, and it was soft but full of pain. Charley clenched his fists, leaning against the wall. "Your daddy . . . died," Anita went on. There was another short silence, and Charley wished he could see her face. She sounded as if she were fighting off tears.

"I wish my daddy hadn't died." The small voice was wistful.

"So do I, Iris." This time the agony in his wife's voice was all too plain to Charley Seton.

"Is that why you look . . . sad sometimes, Mother?"

"Yes." Again there was the sound of rustling cloth, and Anita's words appeared muffled. "Oh, yes. You see, I'll never love anyone again like that . . . except you."

"Don't you love Uncle Charley, Mother?"

"Well, yes, Iris. But it's not the same thing, you see. I've tried. I've really tried." Now Anita sounded as if she were speaking more to herself than to the child. Charley felt a sudden jolt of pain; he had experienced that many years ago, at college, in a boxing match. His opponent had given him a sudden punch on the side of his head. This hurt was just like that—brutal, quick, from nowhere.

"Why did you try, Mother?"

"Someday you'll understand, darling. You must go to sleep now. All right? And I'll see you in the morning."

Charley did not wait to hear more; he retreated down the carpeted corridor, and when Anita joined him he had himself in control.

141

Their marriage, he thought darkly, was more like the relationship of a princess and a favored courtier. Anita Byrne Seton was now the head of Byrne Associates, and Charley for all practical purposes was her employee. And her gigolo, he concluded with helpless anger. In bed, she used him, all the while imagining he was Jonas. Yes, his greatest rival was a dead man. And the child who looked at him coldly from a dead man's eyes.

What I have become, Charley told himself, is her little pet dog. And now even that might be threatened. Charley struggled to get up, to clear the fumes of brandy from his head. But it was no use. It was so much easier, he thought, so much less painful, just to sleep.

Chicago had become famous for its "business block"; all important buildings in the city were commercial structures. Byrne Associates still had the monopoly in commercial buildings. But an eccentric young architect named Frank Lloyd Wright had gone into the business of building residences. One of the most outstanding was the Fane house in Springfield, to which the Setons were invited that night for dinner.

Anita considered Wright's buildings stark and unappealing, but she liked the Fanes and enjoyed their company. Entering the long, flat-roofed building, she passed through a small, forbidding archway set in a wall of long bricks. And suddenly she remembered the blooming grills of Gaudí in the palace of the Güells, the day she had first passed through them with Jonas Mark.

It was a memory she had repressed for nearly seven years: all the thoughts of Jonas brought too much pain. And yet there was something in the night that had sent her mind wandering into the past; something so deep and with so much power that the cold in her was threatening to shatter, melting, melting.

Anita thought with anger, It took me too long to build those defenses; I cannot lose them now. It's this damned house, she decided. She was not an admirer of Wright, but she admitted that the man had genius, a genius that brought to her mind the gifts of Jonas Mark.

Suddenly, she knew she could not face the dinner, or her hosts. No matter how unmannerly it was, she would have to get away. She would phone them later, from somewhere. And Anita turned and hurried to her little voiturette parked nearby. Tonight was hers; Charley was snoring safely at home, she had left Iris sleeping like an angel in her pastel nursery. Tonight, Anita thought, I will face what I have not faced all these years—all that I have lost.

She drove out of the Fanes' manicured drive and onto the wooded road. When the house was out of sight, she removed the motoring veil from her smoothly-coifed hair. It didn't matter at all now what happened to her hair; she wanted to feel it blowing wildly in the wind.

She began to drive faster: the obliging breeze was playing havoc with her hair. She shook her head, feeling suddenly light and free, hearing the spatter of hairpins on the elegant leather and fainter on the carpeted floor of the voiturette. She almost felt like laughing; this was wonderful.

She gave the car its head, and the speed was marvelous, exhilarating: she felt the little car rocking from side to side and the spoked wheels vibrate and sing. If one were to choose a way to die, how pleasant this way would be! She increased her speed.

But she was approaching a crossroads; suddenly she thought of Iris. No, it wasn't time yet. There was still Iris, the last trace of Jonas Mark.

And Anita carefully slowed the car. She paused at the crossroads, still jubilant with her sensation of daring, a little breathless; she had come very near an accident. She wondered now which way to go. The thought of returning to the house was unbearable.

Then she realized fully where she was: she was on the old road to the Adair house, improved for the convenience of the new motorcars, different now. And yet the Adair house still stood at the end of this thoroughfare, the shell of a house where she had met Jonas on that summer afternoon so long ago. There was the wood where they had first kissed, in the sun and shadow, listening to the cry of the single bird.

She would drive there now: it was a foolish and quixotic thing to do, for a woman alone at night, but something was urging her, the thing that had urged her to take out Jonas's hidden picture in her dressing room and look at it. She had been putting it away when Charley had come in.

Charley. No, she would not think of him now; he was part of the superficial world she had adopted. There was no place for him here in the free spring wind, and the fragrant darkness.

Anita turned the voiturette with skill and drove down the

143

road toward the Adairs'. She would have to park the car a little way away and walk into the woods. It would never do, she thought with amusement, to be discovered by the respectable Adairs. Anita Byrne Seton, caught wandering in the woods alone at night, with her hair streaming down like a gypsy or a woman of the streets! This picture of herself aroused Anita's sense of humor; she bubbled inside with silent laughter.

She pulled the voiturette up to the side of the road, let it roll under the shelter of trees, stopped, and jumped down. The moonlight would aid her to find the spot. She made her way into the woods, looking for familiar landmarks—a lightning-blasted tree that she and Jonas had remarked upon, a certain clearing. Then there came to her the silvery note of a single night-bird.

The long-cultivated coldness in her breast began to dissolve with the poignant sound; she stopped in the clearing and felt the moisture gather in her eyes and the tears roll down her face.

A stealthy motion beyond her in the woods caught her attention, and she stiffened with cautious fear. It was probably some animal, she told herself uneasily. But the sound was growing louder now, and it sounded like something far bigger and heavier than a rabbit or bird: it sounded like a man.

She began to be afraid, and fervently wished that she had not come. Her fear was so great that it rooted her to the spot; she stood transfixed in a ribbon of moonlight, waiting for the man to approach. But as the crashing of the thicket became louder, Anita snapped to her senses and turned to run.

"Anita." The man had said her name: she paused in her flight, her heart beating wildly. "Anita," the man repeated, and she knew it was the voice of Jonas Mark.

She was afraid to turn and look: it had to be a hallucination. Jonas was dead. And yet ghosts did not appear as humans did, their footsteps making sound.

Slowly Anita turned and looked. Jonas was standing in the clearing, in the moonlight's path. His face was in shadow, but she could see the tawny, golden-brown mane of his hair, his raffish clothes, his leanness. He started toward her, and she was aware that his walk was hesitant, the walk of a man who was trying to disguise the limping of his leg..

She began to tremble all over, trembling so that she feared her legs could not support her shaking body.

144

"Anita. It's Jonas. Don't be afraid. Anita," he said again and was near her in three long uneven strides. He stood looking down at her, holding out his hands; now she could see his face. There were new lines there, deep planes of suffering and deprivation. The bright, piercing eyes were more wonderful than ever, but there was a new wisdom in them that she had never seen before.

Jonas Mark was alive and standing before her. She could not credit her senses, but kept staring at him without speech.

"Yes," he said, smiling, "I am alive." He moved closer and held out his arms. She rushed into them, and they closed around her tightly, holding her to his hard, lean body with such fierceness and hunger that she was aware of the straining of every muscle in his powerful frame.

He said no more, but she raised her face and he bent to kiss her, holding her ever closer, kissing her without ceasing until she felt her body warm and warm to a mighty burning.

But when he released her she cried out, "How could you have done it, Jonas? How could you go, leaving me with nothing, letting me think that you were dead?" She felt her passion melding into rage and pain. "Do you know what you have done to me?"

"Yes." His arms dropped from her, and they hung at his sides. His bright, changeable eyes shone with hurt and shame and despair. "Yes," he repeated, "I have given you back to the life you were meant for."

"Meant for?" She stepped back and said, "Look at me. Look at me, Jonas. Is this the woman meant for a life—a death—without you?"

He stared at her, from her wild, disheveled hair, shining in the moonlight, tangled with the long gemmed earrings in her ears; the disarray of her costly dress, with its train caught with barbs and twigs, its hem muddy and disreputable. He looked again at her face, and his gaze dropped to her white neck and the perfect shoulders exposed above the silk of the gown.

"Anita," he whispered, and came to her again, taking her in his arms. "What does it all matter, now? I am here, and we are together. I will tell you about all the years; about the times I longed for you so that I nearly broke in two, the times I swore I would leave you alone, thinking you were better off without me. I've kept up with everything, everything you've done and been. I know you have a child. Seton has given you a daughter, which I could never do."

145

"Jonas," she answered, sobbing against his chest, "Iris is your child. Ours, ours."

"My God." She felt his arms grow stiff about her, and he asked in an agonized voice, "Why didn't you tell me? Why? It would have meant everything, Anita. Everything."

"I know that, now." She could hardly speak for crying. But she forced the words out. "But then, I felt if I told you—after your accident—you'd look on it as another burden."

"My God, my God," he said again, and drew her closer. "My child. Our child."

She could feel him holding her closer and closer, and her wild sobbing ceased, feeling again the powerful nearness of his body, the heat of him pressing her, enfolding her.

"My love, my love," he said softly. "Sit down with me. Let me look at your face. It has been so long, Anita, so very long."

They sank together to the cool grass, and he turned her face into the path of pale white light. She stared into his eyes, the direct and piercing eyes that had always had such power over her, that even now were changing her into what she had been so long ago, when they had first met. Magically she knew that, at this moment, she was no longer the woman submerged in the ugliness of her captive life. She felt a quickening in her pulse, a flooding wave of fire over all her body.

As they looked at each other in the cool silence, broken only by the random rustle of some small animal, Jonas seemed to be possessing her with his stare. Her look began to drown in his, and to her amazement, the pain and the resentment, the anger and aloneness of the years started to fall away. She said breathlessly, "I love you more than ever in my life."

Once more he bent to kiss her mouth. He released her then, and, breathing hoarsely, he pulled her down onto the grass. He cried out something she could hardly understand, fumbling at his clothes to free himself of them. More gently his fingers worried at her gown, and she unfastened it, rising a little to let it fall away.

And there was a savage meeting when she felt they could never again be close enough; she realized with exaltation that his old powers were fully his again, for he was possessing her with a strength unknown to her, even in the first wild days and nights of their old love. She felt her tears break free, heard his outcry and knew her own incredible releasing, an overpowering joy she had thought never to feel again.

Jonas tasted her salty tears and planted quick, small

kisses on her nose and brow and chin, still holding her to his body's length. He ran his hard hand down her curving side, and she trembled with new pleasure at the rasping, callused touch.

They did not speak for a time, then he said, "I thank God for you, and this, Anita. Will you...will you let us be together?"

"Let us." She burrowed into his arms, and said tightly, "Promise, promise me, Jonas, swear. That we will never be apart again."

"I swear," he said solemnly. "I swear it. I couldn't go on without you, I couldn't stay away any longer. I had to come, I had to."

"And never again," she repeated, "never again will we be without each other."

"Never again, Anita."

She leaned back a little and looked up at him; his face had the look of stubborn determination she had always known and loved. She went back into his arms, thinking, If only we could keep this night forever.

After a long, peaceful silence, he said, "You can't go back to Charley now."

"There was never anything to go back to," she replied, and he drew her head to a more comfortable position on his bare shoulder. She inhaled the scent of his skin with the ancient hunger: he smelled, as he always had, of pine trees and the sea, that clean, pungent scent she had missed as much as anything about him. She told him so, and he hugged her to him.

But he persisted, "That's not an answer, darling. You're not going back to him, are you?"

"No. Not to *him*. But Iris is there, Jonas."

"Yes." After a moment of silence, he spoke again. "Your marriage is invalid now, you know," he said thoughtfully. "That is, if..." He stopped abruptly.

"If?"

"Let's talk about it later, after we go back to my hotel."

"Like this?" She laughed at the thought of her ruined dress and wild hair.

"No, not just like this," he retorted, looking down at their bare bodies, dappled with the shadows of the leaves. "We will find a way to smuggle you in." Her laughter rose higher at the idea of Anita Byrne Seton, prime mover of the Chicago Plan, stealing into his hotel.

147

"We still keep up the summer place," she said. "We can go there."

He kissed her. "Yes. It'll be the first night, all over again."

After a silent moment she said abruptly, "Tell me now. Tell me what happened that night on the ship."

"We should go. You'll be cold here."

"Not with you. Tell me now, while we're in this special place. I need to know."

"All right." Covering her with her long petticoat, he lit cigarettes and offered her one.

"How did you know I smoke?"

"I told you I've learned a lot about you." He smiled. "But let me tell you about that night on the ship."

She lay on his arm, smoking, listening.

"You see, my love, that night I wanted to die."

"Jonas." She turned and studied his profile, sharp and fine by the moon's dim glow. She touched his hair, and he responded, as always, to her lightest caress.

"Yes," he went on. "I had no faith in the doctor's 'man in New York.' I couldn't face the idea of being a drag on you, the rest of our days, of not carrying my weight...the idea of never being able to climb and run, to dance...never having ...anything like this again. I heard you and the duke that afternoon, in the ship library."

"The duke! But darling, he was never anything to me."

"I know that. But still, some of the things he said were true." Jonas put his fingers over her lips and smiled, saying, "Let me explain. The hardest thing in my life was saying goodbye to you on the ship that night. I was saying goodbye to everything...literally. You were asleep. I kissed you and wheeled that damned chair out on deck. I dragged myself out of the chair and got over the side; my arms were strong enough for that. But the second I hit the water I knew I'd made the biggest fool mistake I'd ever made: I wanted to live, all of a sudden I knew I didn't want to die. So I started swimming. My arms were strong enough for that, too." She lay silent, stroking his arm, listening intently.

"I saw the lights from the ship, heard the men...saw them throwing down the life preservers. They couldn't see me." His tone was ironic, almost amused.

"It was so cold in the water my tongue felt numb; I couldn't even form a word, much less cry out for help. The wind, the currents, kept carrying me farther and farther away. I don't know how long it was before I was picked up by some fish-

148

ermen off the English coast. My head took an awful knock somewhere—it was a very rocky shore—and for a while I didn't even know who I was."

Anita was still so intent on his story that she let her cigarette burn her fingers. Repressing a cry of pain, she put the cigarette out in the cool grass.

He had not even noticed, he was so deep in the past. He continued steadily, "The strangest thing about it was, one of my legs had feeling in it by the time the fishermen picked me up. How that came about, I'll never know. But there it is. After about eight months, the feeling came back to the other leg. I exercised them both constantly, day and night, without a letup. All I can figure is that something in the shock of the fall pushed some of the vertebrae back into place."

She stroked his face caressingly. "But how did you live? What did you do?"

"One of the fishermen took me in. You remember, I told you I worked on boats when I was a kid. I worked for them, as well as I could at the time. They took pity on me. They were very good people."

"And after that?"

"Afterward," he said, and she could feel him searching his memory. "Afterward. I went to work in England, once I got the use of my legs back...as a carpenter. And I saw in an American newspaper, from the East, that you had married Seton, and taken over Byrne Associates."

There was great pain in his voice; she caressed him softly but did not speak.

"I had planned to save up every penny and get on a ship and come back to you. But there I was, with almost nothing. And there you were, with everything."

"Everything!" She heard her own voice break. "Everything except my life...and hope and happiness. I was the one with nothing, Jonas. I have never known a moment's peace or happiness since you went away."

"I know that now, my darling. I know how wrong I was. Oh, Anita!" He held her close again. "It was a hell beyond description, being without you. Thinking I'd never see you again, never hold you, never..."

"Don't say any more, my beloved. Not now." She turned until they were facing each other, the flesh of their bodies clinging in one starved embrace. "Don't say any more right now."

His mouth found hers, and slowly, deeply, in a singing silence, they were once more together.

Chapter 12

THE MOON HAD SET and the sun was almost rising over the Byrne cottage, as Anita called the shining little house, before she and Jonas finished talking and fell into exhausted sleep.

During those hours he told her something of the intervening years, his anonymous employment, his restless wanderings that had taken him from England through France to Germany. In Germany, he told her, he had found the germ of the exciting Art Nouveau school of architecture, a school that not only recognized but fairly idolized Antoni Gaudí.

And in that country he had met architectural students and young practicing architects whose imagination leaped over the boundaries of convention; men whose ideas matched Jonas's and Anita's own.

"They've finally discovered," Jonas told her with excitement, "that cities have no race, no nationality, but are a universal symbol...a symbol of man's triumph over nature."

She told him that she had said the same thing years ago to her aunt and to Harry Brand in the gondola at the Exposition.

Now in the postered bed of the cottage, where they lay together, they felt a renewal of their long-ago closeness.

Waking the next morning, Jonas Mark reached out with closed eyes for Anita. The bed was empty but still warm with the impress of her slender body. He rolled over and opened his eyes; she was brushing her hair at the dresser across the room.

He watched her with a sense of joyful awe; even unaware of his scrutiny she was as poised and beautiful as a goddess, with dignity and grace in every gesture. Jonas marveled at her resilient vitality but even more at the power of their love.

Beautiful as she had been last night by the moonlight in the wood, his first sight of her revealed a lovely, frozen creature locked within herself. But the woman he was looking at this morning was soft-eyed, fresh as a very young girl. A smile lingered on her parted lips and her skin was faintly flushed.

"History repeats itself," he said softly. Anita put down her brush and turned on the stool, smiling at him. "We are in the same wonderful room," he continued, as she came toward him, "yet it is different now."

"How?" She sat down on the edge of the bed and touched his shoulder.

"You're more beautiful than ever, for one thing. And this time we are hiding out from Seton, instead of your father."

There was a shadow in his tone when he said the name; he could not bring himself to say "your husband." *He*, Jonas Mark, was her husband, and always would be.

"Perhaps the greatest difference," he said lightly, "is that now you're a very powerful lady. And all kinds of obligations await you today. I was the one who had them before. Now, my only prospects await me in Germany."

At her look of question, he nodded. "Yes, there was so much to tell I didn't get to that. I've been offered a partnership in Munich."

"I see." He watched the different expressions cross her face—gladness for him, succeeded by anxiety and confusion.

"And your work is here," he said, reading her mind. "But remember, as a partner I will be able to take you in, my darling. We could work together. It would not be like Spain."

She still did not answer; her confusion was plain.

"I'm sorry; it's too much at once, isn't it?"

She smiled and admitted, "Yes. And what about...Iris?"

"She will go with us, of course, everywhere. We're a family, Anita. We're going to be a family from now on."

"And Charley?"

"I'll deal with Charley," he said grimly. "But first, when am I going to see my daughter?"

"Today." Anita looked jubilant. Then her face darkened, and she said, "Not at the house, though. I know you don't want to go there. I'll bring her to you downtown. Shall I?"

"That will be wonderful. I can see in your eyes you have a thousand things to do...and so have I. Cables to send, things like that."

"To Germany."

He nodded and took her in his arms. "Oh, God, I don't

152

want to leave. Do you remember, Anita, the nights in that hotel in Spain...and the mornings when I never wanted to leave?"

"Yes, oh, yes. I remember everything, Jonas. I always have; I've never forgotten for a moment."

He was so quiet that she seemed to know he was thinking of Seton.

"Even then, especially then," she said softly, and once again he marveled at the closeness of their minds, their ability to read each other.

He felt his desire stirring, again, and he said lightly, "If you don't get out of this bed, we won't be going anywhere. Go, my darling, go now, and get yourself ready to face the world. And so will I."

She stared at him for a moment, then answered in the same vein, "If you insist. And we will see you at your hotel at four—your daughter and I."

The phrase buoyed him throughout their leave-taking and all through the busy day. At four, he thought, exulting, I will see them together—Anita and our child.

Jonas waited eagerly in the living room of his suite at the Palmer House for the arrival of his wife and child. He looked around: he had had flowers put in the vases, something he had not even noticed before. The hotel housekeeper had had to remind him that the vases were empty; the staff, she said, could be a little forgetful of a bachelor guest. He asked her what his expected guests should be served; all this was utterly new to him. The housekeeper smiled and said, "Leave it to me."

She had done well, he thought, examining the inviting array on the table before the sofa—a nice-looking coffee service, cakes and fruit; a small pitcher of milk for the little girl.

Jonas's excitement grew: when the clock on the mantel struck four, he was in a state of agitation. Only a moment later, he heard a soft knock on the door, and rushed across the room to open it.

Anita was standing there, looking more beautiful than ever, and she was holding by the hand a small, delicate girl, with hair and eyes exactly like his own.

Jonas drew in his breath and said awkwardly, "Hello...welcome. Come in."

The child was looking up at him solemnly, never taking her gaze from him, as she followed her mother into the room.

153

"Iris," Anita said quietly, "this is your father."

Jonas kept staring at the little girl; he could not quite take in the wonderful surprise of her face, a blend of his and Anita's. She had Anita's brief, straight nose and small, shapely mouth; the shape of her face and her slender gracefulness were also like his wife's. But the lion-colored wealth of hair and the direct, piercing eyes that changed from blue to green to hazel as she moved around the room in the changing light were exactly his.

"Come," he said, still awkwardly, "let me take your things." And he held out his hand for Anita's long, elegant afternoon coat of gray embroidered silk, admiring the tilted hat on her softly puffed hair. Then he leaned down to Iris and took her small coat.

"I'll take mine," she said independently, and marched off to the bedroom with her coat in her arms. Giving Anita a delighted, amused look, Jonas followed with the larger coat and carefully laid it on the bed beside Iris's. He took the child's hand, and was touched when she put it trustingly in his to be led back to the living room.

Anita was seated at the table, pouring coffee for herself and Jonas. She poured a glass of milk for Iris, who sat down beside her mother and took a cake from the plate on the table.

"Well." Jonas sat down in a chair near Anita, feeling an overwhelming happiness and a great unease at once. He did not know, now, what to say.

All at once Iris set down her glass and got up from the sofa. She went to Jonas and climbed onto his lap. The ice was broken: he put his arms around the small, fragile body and bent his face to her tawny hair, kissing the top of her head. She had the smell of milk and soap and fragrant silk. He was dismayed to feel his eyes grow wet; a tear dropped on Iris's small head.

"You are my daddy," the child said.

Anita got up from the sofa and came to stand beside Jonas's chair. He put his free arm around her; she bent to kiss his face.

Suddenly things were easier among them, and Iris began to chatter to Jonas, telling him of her puppy and her toys. To his amazement Jonas found himself telling her stories about children he had seen in his travels.

After a while, her head began to droop against his chest, and she fell quite abruptly asleep.

"She was up early," Anita said. "I'll take her in the bedroom."

"No, no, I'll carry her." Jonas rose with the child in his arms and went to the bedroom, carefully laying her on the bed.

When he returned Anita was standing by the window, studying the busy panorama of Chicago below them.

Jonas strode to her and, turning her around, took her close in his arms, kissing her hungrily. "I did not know what happiness was before. To see you both together ... to be with you both, this is something I never imagined."

She smiled and touched his face. "You see now that she could be no one's but yours."

"Yes. When I look in her eyes it's like looking in a small mirror; like seeing myself as a child in a way. God, Anita, it's the strangest, the most ... I can't express it. Next to you it's the best thing that ever happened to me." He gripped her hand tightly and kissed it.

"I know, Jonas." She went to the sofa and sat down again. "She'll sleep awhile, then I'll phone her governess. She'll take Iris ho—to the house."

"Anita, stay with me." Jonas went to the sofa and stood behind her, caressing the top of her head with his long hands; his fingers slid down to her neck and she turned her head so her mouth could touch his hand.

He shivered. "You don't know what that does to me. Anita. Please, stay with me for good. Tell Seton you're not coming back."

She reached up and took one of his big hands between both her own. "Jonas, sit down, darling." He obeyed. "Hold me," she said, "while we talk."

He held her close and she put her head on his chest, caressing his hard arm with her hand as she spoke. "I can't leave him like that, so suddenly." She felt him stiffen.

"Why are you so hesitant?" he asked gruffly. "What is it? Have you come to love him, Anita?"

She raised her head from his chest and looked into his eyes. "No, no! It's not that, Jonas. When I thought you were dead, when I consented to marry him, I didn't love him. And I never have. I even tried, but I couldn't, I couldn't. How could I, after you?"

He held her face in his hands and kissed her slowly and gently, then with greater urgency. "If you keep doing that, I'll never remember what I'm trying to say."

155

"That's what I have in mind."

"No, no, please," she said softly. She smiled and moved a little away from him. "I married Charley in apathy, almost despair," she continued. "And my father, when he was dying, begged me to. It didn't seem to matter then. I was so wrapped up in the business, and in Iris, and Charley was just there on the sidelines. Sometimes I'd forget he was there at all. Even now Charley is peripheral to my life."

"Being your husband is hardly being 'peripheral,'" Jonas remarked, and his face was hard and grim.

"You have nothing, nothing to be jealous of." She looked at him earnestly, and his grim look lightened a little. "But you see, there's Iris."

"She's our own child," he protested. "She belongs with us."

"I know that. But we've got to give her a little time to get used to all this. And there's the firm," she added.

"What is Charley's position?"

"He's a vice president. I think he expected to be made a full partner when my father died, but somehow I couldn't do that. I just felt he wasn't...the man to work with me," she continued, trying to gather her thoughts. "You know his ideas."

"I remember them vividly," Jonas said in an ironic tone. "You're right; if Charley had power equal to yours it could change the whole face of the business. I've been checking up on you, you see," he said, smiling, "since I came to town. The firm is doing excellent work."

She smiled back and took his hand. "Thank you. The board, as you might guess, insisted that I have all-male advisers. Even in this advanced year of 1900," she added dryly. "But when push comes to shove, I still manage to move them in a more progressive direction."

He grinned. "I'll bet you do."

"But the firm needs a man like you, Jonas," she said. "Is this German arrangement..."

"It's a great opportunity, Anita. I'd be working with Hubrist."

"Hubrist! He's a very exciting architect. No wonder you want the partnership. Now I understand completely."

"I knew you would." He leaned back on the sofa and urged her once more to put her head on his shoulder.

But she remained sitting a little apart from him, and said soberly, "And there's another thing, Jonas. I've been hesitant to tell you." He looked at her, concerned, and waited for her

156

to go on. "Charley's adopted Iris, you see. He's done everything he can to...make me love him. She calls him Uncle Charley, but the fact remains that he has legally adopted her. So you see there's a lot to straighten out before I can be with you for good."

"I see." The grim shadow had returned to Jonas's face. Then he managed a smile, and said, "Forgive me, Anita. I've come back from the grave...I've been away all these years, and now I'm asking you to undo it all in a day. I know I'm being a damned unreasonable fool. I'm sorry. It's just that I can't stand the thought of being away from you again, not even for one night."

"My darling, I know that, and I thank God for it." She caressed his arm, took one of his hands in hers and kissed it. "Don't you know I feel the same way?"

Suddenly she tilted her head, and listened. "Iris is waking up."

"I didn't hear a thing," he remarked in surprise.

"You don't have a mother's hearing," she said lightly. She rose, and added, "I'll call her governess. And then, when Iris is gone, we'll have no more talk of problems. I want this evening and this night with you, Jonas. I want to feel there's no one else in the world but us, not even Iris, for this little while."

"Wait." He stood up and held her close. Running his hard hands up and down the sides of her body, tracing the shape of her soft form, from her slender waist to her rounded hips, he kissed her. "Tonight there will be no one else in the world but you and me."

At the turn of the century the revolt against the old order in society extended to a rebellion against traditional forms in expression, and that rebellion showed itself in the city's architecture. Anita's greatest rival, Frank Lloyd Wright, was designing whole developments of his "prairie houses," a trend started by Anita and Byrne Associates. It was also a great source of satisfaction to Anita that one of Wright's colleagues had drafted a Byrne-type city plan based on one of her own. Anita had met the brilliant Wright on one or two social occasions and they had engaged in friendly debate over styles of architecture; Wright told Anita bluntly that her forms, inspired by Gaudí and certain Expressionists of Europe, "had no relevance to nature." She retorted that they were an improvement on nature.

157

Despite those comments and the continuing problem of selling a woman's ideas to a hidebound board of men, Anita Byrne Seton had stuck to her guns. Gradually and in almost imperceptible ways Chicago began to accept her designs, even praise them.

As more commerce animated the city and new kinds of merchandising were devised to sell new styles to the nation, Chicago's big department stores grew bigger. Anita found a strong new interest: the architecture of display. In that area, at least, the board of Byrne Associates was happy to give her *carte blanche*. After all, who was more knowledgeable about such frivolous matters than a woman? Anita played that advantage for all it was worth, and soon her display designs captured Chicago. The city's building technology, especially the metal frame, allowed her to turn the stores' ground-floor exterior walls into huge, stunning windows. The stores became Anita's exclusive concern, and she delighted in designing their facades and display areas. The workload increased to such an extent that she found it necessary to hire two young women assistants, Louisa Kerr and Helen Barrett, to help in the projects.

Charley Seton considered that area beneath his dignity, although he never said it in so many words to Anita. Nevertheless she was aware of how he felt.

As the spring moved into summer following Jonas Mark's return, Anita was especially glad that Charley had no interest in display design. It gave her greater freedom; she was able to explain her absences by saying she had to drop in to check on the progress being made at buildings using her store designs. It was a perfect excuse, she thought, to be away from the office more.

Jonas moved from the Palmer House to a less conspicuous hotel: the risk was too great there, he said, with half the elite of Chicago milling about. Anita saw him every day, at whatever hour could be arranged, but since the night in the Palmer House she had not spent a whole night with him again. One night had been hard enough to explain to Charley.

She remembered the exciting, secretive days and nights of their original courtship, seven years before. Instead of her family, Charley was the one she had to deceive, and each day that passed made her a little more uneasy. She wondered how much longer they could go on undetected.

And Jonas pressed her, more and more, to leave Charley, to go away with him. She knew Jonas could not put off Hubrist much longer. And yet, almost as she had done in 1893, Anita asked Jonas for a little more time. Like the world they had discovered then, their rediscovered world of 1900 seemed too precious to her to risk.

And this time, facing the future involved not just the postponement of a barely begun career but the dissolution of an empire she had built so painfully and with such struggle. This time there was Iris, and her custody. Still, Jonas kept up his urgent pleading; once or twice they had argued bitterly.

They were in the midst of one of those arguments on a bright day in June. Standing outside Jonas's hotel, Anita said, "I can't be with you today."

Jonas grasped her arm, demanding, "Why not?"

"I'm supposed to be at Carson's, right now."

"Well?"

"Charley's getting suspicious."

"But you said he never goes to the stores. What does that matter?" He tightened his hold on her arm, urging her toward the entrance of the hotel.

"I have a...funny feeling today," she protested. "It's the way he looked at me this morning in the office."

"Darling, please. Don't be fanciful."

"But, Jonas...look! There he is, right now." She nodded toward the massive facade of the department store, just across the street. Charley Seton was standing outside the store, peering at the ground-floor renovations. He turned abruptly and saw Jonas and Anita.

They stood stock-still, watching him come toward them across the busy street, dodging in and out of traffic. There was a wild expression in his bright brown eyes, contrasting in a grotesque way with his dapper clothes. It seemed that at any moment he would be hit by a passing vehicle, but somehow he made it to the curb. He kept coming toward them, still staring in that wild-eyed fashion.

"I welcome this," Jonas said in a low voice to Anita. "It's high time."

Charley was standing before them now; he seemed incapable of speech. He did not even look at Anita but studied Jonas as if he could not believe his eyes.

At last he said in a shaky voice, "You're alive. Goddammit, you're alive."

"Let's go upstairs, Charley," Jonas said in a quiet voice. "We've got to talk."

159

Without replying, like a man in a trance, Charley Seton followed Jonas and Anita into the hotel. He stood stiffly by while Jonas got his key. The three stepped into the elevator; they were the only people in the car.

But no one spoke until the elevator reached Jonas's floor. "Down there," Jonas said briefly, indicating a door at the end of the hall.

Charley, noticing that Anita had automatically started walking in that direction, said coldly, "I see you know where you're going, my dear."

Anita did not reply. Jonas took her arm. He glanced at her face: the softness was gone and he saw the look he had seen that night in the woods, two months ago—a face that was cold and contained, like a painted statue.

When they entered Jonas's suite, Charley stood by the door. He had not removed his hat.

"Do you want a drink?" Jonas asked him, with a note of compassion in his deep voice.

"No." Charley's eyes glinted with hatred. "No, my cuckolding friend."

Jonas said sharply, "She's my wife, Charley." He looked Seton in the eye, and the other man's look fell.

Jonas looked at Anita; she was white and shaken. "Sit down," he told her gently. Then he said to Charley, "Why don't you sit down, too?"

"I prefer to stand."

Anita sank down into a chair, but Charley continued to stand by the door. Jonas stood facing him.

"I know this isn't easy for you, Charley."

"You're damned right. But it's been easy enough for you—sleeping with my wife." Charley turned to Anita. "You didn't expect me to come to Carson's did you? No, you thought you'd have it easy, that you could go on wallowing in bed with this..."

"Stop it, Charley. I'm not going to tell you again. Don't talk to her like that."

"Jonas." Anita got up and came to stand beside him.

"It shouldn't have happened like this, Charley," Jonas went on more evenly. "But now that it has, we've got to talk about it."

"What is there to talk about?" Charley's angry eyes gleamed with naked hate.

"Charley." Anita moved out of the circle of Jonas's arm

and held out her hand to Charley. "We've got to talk about a divorce."

"I'll never give you a divorce."

"You're crazy," Jonas snapped. "You're crazy, Charley."

"Please." Anita put her hand on Charley's arm; he shook it off. "Please, Charley, can't you see it's over?"

"I'll never give you a divorce," he repeated doggedly.

"But I'm going to move out tonight, Charley. With Iris."

"Move out if you like, but you can't take Iris."

"What do you mean by that, Charley?" Jonas asked with dangerous softness. "Are you going to make trouble about our child?"

"She's my legally adopted daughter, Jonas." Charley's voice was no longer unsteady; it was hard and cold. It was clear that he was regaining his composure. "We'll see how far Anita will go—without Iris." Charley smiled a very unpleasant smile.

"What do you think you can do?"

"You'll see."

"Get out, Charley. Get out now," Jonas ordered. He walked toward the other man; Charley faced him unmoving. Anita cried out, "Stop it, please stop it, both of you."

"I'll see you in court." Charles Seton went out and slammed the door.

That encounter had taken place on Wednesday evening; late on Friday morning, Anita opened her eyes to a brilliant shaft of sunlight piercing the drawn drapes. She turned over; Jonas was beside her, sleeping.

"Darling, good morning," she said softly, putting her arms around his body, kissing the back of his head.

"Ummm." He made a drowsy sound of delight and turned over. His eyes were still closed, but he was smiling broadly. "Good morning," he said indistinctly. Then he opened his eyes wide, exclaiming, "Anita, Anita," and held her close, kissing her with several brief, swift kisses.

"Oh, my dear, it's so good to be home again," he said, "where we belong. No more goodnights...remember?"

"Of course I remember." She lay back on her pillow with a smile and looked up at the ceiling.

Jonas always moved so quickly, she thought. They had checked into a larger suite at the Palmer House on Wednesday evening, large enough for Iris and the governess, Katie Richardson. There had been no real need for Katie, because either Jonas or Anita was always available to Iris, but the child was used to Katie, Anita decided, and she did not want to force Iris into a totally new situation, with all familiar things gone. It must seem strange enough to her, Anita reflected, without her dog, and in a strange room.

There was a light tapping at the door, and Katie entered when Jonas called, "Come in."

"Good morning, Mrs. Seton." Katie flushed scarlet, and amended, "Miss Anita." It apparently seemed very strange to her not to call Anita Mrs. Seton.

"Good morning, Mr. Mark."

He acknowledged her greeting, and Anita asked, smiling, "What is it, Katie? Is Iris demanding breakfast with her father and mother?"

"Well, not yet, Mrs. . . . Miss Anita. There was a man at the door."

"It's probably breakfast, Katie. Would you mind letting him in?"

"Oh, he's been and gone, Miss Anita. He left these." For the first time Anita noticed the blue-covered documents in the nurse's hand; they seemed to contain many pages. "He said I had to take them," Katie added.

"Let's see them, Katie," Jonas said. She brought them to him and handed him all of them—three blue-covered packets. "Thanks."

The round-faced woman smiled uncertainly and went out.

Anita got up and came to Jonas's side of the bed. He was sitting on the edge of it now, examining the papers. Anita read with him.

"Well, well," he said in that tone she knew so well—a tone that boded rising anger. He was looking at the outsides of the folded documents.

"Summonses," he said. "Summonses, Anita, as I live and breathe. 'Seton versus Seton and Mark,' headed 'Illegal Abduction.' 'Seton versus Mark,' headed 'Alienation of Affections.' 'Seton versus Seton,' entitled 'Desertion.'"

"My God."

"He's leaving no stone unturned, as they say. Here, would you like to look at this one?" Jonas handed her the "Desertion" paper.

She scanned it rapidly, and then as Jonas handed her the other two, read through them. Charley was charging her and Jonas with illegally abducting his child, charging Anita with desertion and Jonas with alienation of affections.

"But this is ridiculous...absurd!" she cried.

"Yes, my darling, it is. We know that...and probably Charley's attorney knows that. But Charley doesn't."

"What do you mean, 'Charley's attorney knows that'?"

"Well, I don't think anyone's won an alienation of affections suit in the last fifty years. As to the desertion and abduction, that may be another matter. Charley's just so crazy-mad he's trying everything. The business will be next, Anita." He looked at her soberly.

"Do you think so?"

"I know so. Who's your attorney?"

She told him.

"Well, you'd better give me his number. We're supposed to appear to answer these charges within ten days. So let's get busy."

While Jonas was dialing, Anita got up and dressed, thinking, This is absurd. No judge will let Charley Seton have my child.

The conservative lawyer, Emmett Carson, who had known Anita since she was a child and acted for her in all financial matters, excused himself from involvement, saying that he was not "competent" to represent them. Jonas read between the lines; Carson was unwilling to involve his firm in such a distasteful proceeding. He recommended a "talented young man" named Marshall Ribner.

Anita was furious. "Then he can damned well be replaced as my financial adviser," she stormed to Jonas.

"Hold on, darling. I know it's maddening, but I also know Carson is the best in money matters. Let it ride, at least until after the hearing."

Reluctantly she consented.

She disliked Marshall Ribner on sight: his manner was slick, and his too-dapper clothes bordered on loudness. But he was also bright, quick and experienced, and it was these latter qualities that Jonas valued.

"He'll know how to sway the judge, I think," Jonas reassured Anita. Anita began to see the justice of Jonas's confidence when the wily Ribner instructed her in how to dress for the hearing.

"I want you to look very proper," he told Anita, "even dowdy. If that's possible for you," he added, eyeing her chic ensemble and vivid face.

"Why?" she asked him bluntly.

Ribner grinned. "We've got to play the grieving mother for all it's worth."

Anita repressed her annoyance. Did this idiot think she loved Iris less because she dressed well? But when Jonas touched her hand, soothingly, she merely answered, "Very well. I'll do anything I have to. I want my daughter."

"I know you do, Mrs. Seton," Ribner said, and this time he sounded sympathetic and friendly. Anita felt a little of her anxiety abate.

On the morning of the hearing, following Ribner's suggestion, she dressed in a quiet ensemble of navy blue; it had touches of white. Certainly it was the most dismal thing she had ever put on; she had shopped for it with great care. Setting her hat on her head at its usual tilt, she studied herself in the mirror. Then she straightened the hat until it rested at a prim and unbecoming angle.

"Very good," Jonas commented. "I hardly know you." She saw that his bright comment was forced; his smile was stiff and there were pain and apprehension in his eyes.

"It all seems so trivial...and ugly," she said to him, "to think of such nonsense when Iris is at stake. My heart is in my mouth right now."

"And so is mine, darling." He took her in his arms for a moment and kissed her cheek. "But it's all part of the game, part of the battle. And I've never known you to walk away from one yet."

His words heartened her. She straightened her shoulders and said, "You're right. And thank you. We'd better go; Ribner told us to be there at ten."

When she preceded Ribner and Jonas into the judge's chambers, her heart sank. The judge was already there, seated at the end of a table; across from him were Charley Seton and his counsel. The judge was Felix Linton. Ribner had told Anita and Jonas a name, but somehow in her anxiety Anita had not remembered it. Ribner said something about "getting the right judge"; apparently he had been unsuccessful. Anita remembered Linton vividly now: her aunt had pointed him out to her, years ago, at Bertha Palmer's. Charlotte Byrne had remarked that Felix Linton was a confirmed misogynist; his wife had run away with another man long before.

She glanced at Ribner. "Something's wrong here," he said to her and Jonas in a low voice. "We were supposed to get McClellan."

Aloud he said to Linton, "Good morning, your honor. Gentlemen." He nodded curtly at Charley Seton and his attorneys. "This is a surprise."

"I'm sure it is, counselor," Linton said gruffly. Anita knew at once that Linton disliked Ribner, for his deep-set eyes glittered with malicious amusement under the shaggy brows. "Judge McClellan was taken ill. I was summoned to replace him."

"I see," Ribner said calmly, and Anita felt he was stalling for time. "May I have a moment to confer with my clients?"

"Very well." Linton was irritable. "But be quick, counselor; we are late as it is."

Ribner raised his brows and consulted his watch. "I make it only two minutes before ten, sir," he said with great respect.

"Would you get on with it, Mr. Ribner?"

The attorney motioned to Jonas and Anita to come with him into the hall.

When they were alone, Ribner said frankly, "This is rotten luck, I have to tell you that. Linton is—"

"I know the story," Anita broke in.

"I'll ask for a postponement," Ribner said, "with your approval. We can't let Linton hear this matter."

"Do that." Jonas nodded.

"Yes," Anita added, "please."

They returned to the hearing chamber. When they were seated, Judge Linton growled, "May we proceed?"

"First, your honor, I respectfully request a postponement of this hearing...for ten days."

"On what grounds, Mr. Ribner?"

"On the grounds that such a request may routinely be granted at the discretion of the bench," Ribner said in a soft, mock-respectful tone.

The sharp Linton caught his irony and was angered by it. "The bench does not so choose, counselor. Request denied."

Anita heard the judge's pronouncement with a premonitory chill. But then she told herself, It has only begun. I can't give up before we've started. Jonas took her hand and held it. Linton's repressive stare had no effect upon him at all. He continued to grasp Anita's hand on the top of the long table.

"For the sake of expediency," Linton began coldly, "we shall hear all of the separate charges at this single hearing."

"I object, your honor." Ribner's voice was sharp and quick.

"On what grounds?"

"On the grounds that the three charges cannot be thoroughly examined in a single sitting."

"If we weary you and your clients, Mr. Ribner," Linton retorted, "you may always be excused."

Jonas made an involuntary motion of protest. Anita glanced at him, and his face was stiff with anger. The judge had given Ribner an evasive and improper answer, and they all knew it but were powerless to retaliate now.

"I could have him up on charges for that later," Ribner whispered to Jonas, "but it's no help to us now."

"Thank you, your honor," he said sarcastically to Linton. Suddenly Anita remembered something else about Linton— she had seen him on two or three occasions in close and friendly conversation with Charley's father. Her feeling of imminent doom deepened.

Contrary to Jonas's expectations, Linton treated with great solemnity the charge of alienation of affections, which was usually dismissed—even by lawyers in consultations with clients, before the charge ever reached a judge—and with even greater seriousness the charge of desertion.

No wonder, Anita reflected, recalling Linton's own history. He was hardly being impartial. But her anger and resentment were useless. I came here prepared to fight for my daughter, and the odds are all against us, she thought.

Jonas was looking at her; he seemed to read her despair in her face, for he leaned to her and whispered, "Don't give up. It's not over."

Shamed at her own negative feelings, Anita managed to smile.

But as she feared, Linton read the final charge, accusing her and Jonas of abducting Iris, in a thundering voice. The judge seemed to have been working up to this matter with an inappropriate relish.

He listened to the arguments of both counsel with a serious and impassive face. And once, for the first time that morning, he stared piercingly at Anita. She saw the contempt and disapproval in his eyes, and her flagging hopes died altogether.

Judge Linton stated, at the conclusion of arguments, "Mrs. Seton, you have acted irresponsibly and foolishly. You have committed a symbolic act with wider implications than the act itself—you have attacked, root and branch, the flourishing life that nurtures the stable community, the institution of the home. I have heard the arguments of the defendants' counsel and am ruling as follows: I find that Mrs. Anita Byrne Seton has deserted her home and husband, cohabiting in an unmarried state with another man. The fact that Mr. Mark was also Mrs. Seton's husband is irrelevant here; the statute of limitations decrees that the former marriage is dissolved. A fortunate circumstance," Linton added with gratuitous malice, "otherwise Mrs. Seton would be charged with the additional 'crime of bigamy."

At the word "crime," Ribner looked deeply indignant; desertion and alienation of affection were not, strictly speaking, crimes. But there was no way he could intervene in a judge's summation.

"I find," Linton continued grimly, "in Mr. Seton's behalf in the matter of the abduction of Iris Byrne Mark, legally known as Iris Seton. My ruling is this: if Mrs. Seton will return to Mr. Seton, and take her proper place in society and in her home, then all these matters will be dismissed, and there will be no further actions against Mr. Mark or Mrs. Seton."

Anita gave an involuntary cry: Linton did not even look at her, but again Jonas took her hand.

"How do you answer, Mr. Ribner?"

With a defeated air, Ribner whispered to Anita. She shook her head, feeling the tears form in her eyes. "Never," she said in a low voice.

"My client would find such a course impossible."

"Very well," Linton said solemnly. "I have no recourse but to award custody of Iris Byrne Mark, known as Iris Seton, to her legal father, Charles Seton, and his sister, Emily Seton."

Anita looked up through tear-dimmed eyes. Charley was triumphant: he rose at once and hurried from the chamber, followed more slowly by his counsel.

When Jonas and Anita returned to the Palmer House, they saw Charley shepherding Iris and Katie Richardson into a taxi-cab. "Mommy!" Iris called out, waving, "Uncle Charley and I are going home! Are you coming, too?"

Jonas cursed. Anita started after the departing taxi, but Jonas restrained her with a gentle hand.

Despite the discretion with which the hearing had been held, the newspapers of Chicago were on to the story all too soon. The city buzzed with the scandal: the well-known Anita Seton, envied for her beauty and success, had been brought low in a sordid triangle. It was not a week before the City Council revoked its agreement with Byrne Associates in regard to the Chicago Plan; three of the firm's largest commissions, after a court wrangle, were withdrawn and awarded to Higsbee and Waite.

Three members of Byrne Associates' board resigned; struggling to hold the floundering business together, the remaining members, prodded by Charley, "urged" Anita to sell out.

She received the news by telephone in the suite at the Palmer House. She replied calmly that she would give them an answer that afternoon.

Jonas was out; she faced the moment alone. She lay down wearily on the sofa and lit a cigarette, remembering the old splendor of Byrne Associates. True, she had never admired her father's productions; she remembered almost with affection the prolonged debates she had had with Roderick Byrne. After his death, she had worked hard and long to win a place for her ideas. Her name and position had been insufficient for victory: diehard Chicago did not look kindly on the revolutionary ideas of a woman, and such a young one at that. It had been a struggle, all the way, and she was weary of the struggle.

Worst of all, the firm had been her substitute for living. Why, then, cling to it now, in the face of this overwhelming opposition? She would let it go, just as she had let go of the notion of continuing the case by appeal.

"I will sell," she said to herself. And wondering, Anita realized she had a sense of freedom, with that decision, that she had not known since she and Jonas had gone to Spain.

Now, she thought exultantly, we can go to Germany.

With a decisive motion she ground out her cigarette and went to the phone. She told the board of her decision. Her attorneys were instructed to put the sale in motion.

She was still buoyed by her strange sense of lightness, of freedom, when Jonas came in.

"I'm selling the firm," she told him abruptly.

"Selling it," he repeated. She smiled at the amazement in his voice. "Well, well. I must say I didn't expect that." He came to her and took her in his arms, holding her for a long moment, kissing her hair.

"We will go to Germany now," he said, and the statement was a question. "Your passport's in order?"

"Yes," she said. "Oh, yes. I want so much to get away,

away from all this ugliness and anger. But Jonas, I cannot leave Iris...I can't give up the fight to get her back."

"We will take her with us," he said simply.

She leaned back and looked up at his face. "But...but how? Kidnap her from Charley?" She pronounced the word as if it were a word in a foreign tongue.

"Just that." She continued to stare at Jonas; the bright, piercing eyes were hard with determination. He was very calm. "I'll take care of it."

He sounded as if he were going on a casual errand that hardly merited discussion.

"I want to go with you," she said at last.

"No, darling. Better not. Just get your things packed and be ready to leave. I've had the tickets—three of them—for the last month."

"But Jonas, they'll...they'll be watching the ships ...they'll..."

"'They' won't be able to find us at all. We are not sailing directly to Germany; I have made other arrangements. All we need is Iris. I've been planning this for weeks, Anita. I'll get her tonight."

Anita could not believe it; it was all happening too fast. In a few weeks her whole life, even if it was a hated and superficial life she had only endured, had fallen about her ears.

But she was ready to take whatever came: this was a whole new life, and she would be with Jonas, and Iris. Nothing, she thought, had ever defeated Jonas Mark, and he would succeed in getting Iris. He would not fail. He had come back from the dead, and their love had been resurrected from the ashes. They would take Iris and go.

Suddenly Anita felt a wild exhilaration, a sense of daring and hope that had been sleeping all these years, ever since the night that Jonas had gone into the sea.

"Tonight," she said, and smiled up at him. "You will do it, Jonas."

His eyes gleamed brighter, hearing the note of confidence in her few simple words. "Now," he said, "draw me a plan of the house."

Iris Mark heard the soft footsteps in the corridor and wondered who it was. Katie was sleeping next door, and her Uncle Charley and Aunt Emily had gone out. She wished her mother would come. She sat up in her small bed, listening.

The footsteps had stopped outside the door.

The door opened very softly, and to Iris's delight, her daddy came in. She started to call out to him, but he smiled and put his finger over his lips. Iris obeyed.

He looked very tall over the bed; she had to turn her head far back to look up and really see him. He whispered, "I'm going to take you to see your mother, and then we're all going to take a trip together."

Iris clapped her small hands softly. It sounded like a lot of fun. Quickly she got out of bed and went to her bureau to get something to put on.

Her father's big hand stopped her; he gently touched her arm. "We'll have to put some things in a suitcase. Will you get them ... can you ... quickly now?"

She whispered, "Yes," enjoying the game very much.

She was proud that her mother had taught her how to choose her clothes and how to dress herself. She went to the little dressing room next to her room and put her clothes on. When she came back her father was at the closet, taking things out very quickly and putting them into the suitcase.

She was surprised at how fast he moved, and how light the big case seemed in his hands.

"Are you ready?" he whispered.

"Yes," she whispered back. She was glad she had thought to pick up her favorite doll.

"Now," he said in the same whispery voice, "we'll have to hurry. Come on."

Obediently she followed him out into the hall; she noticed he was walking on his tiptoes. It looked funny for a grown person. She always did it herself when she was up after she had been put to bed.

They went very quietly down the long stairs, and soon they were out of the house. Iris wondered how a grown-up person could move so quietly. Nobody had waked up at all, not even Katie, who had been right next door.

In a minute they were in her mother's little car. Iris remembered something and tugged at her father's sleeve.

"What is it?" he asked, smiling down at her as he started the car.

"My puppy, Pepper. I can't leave him."

Her father let go of the stick that started the car and hugged her. "We can't, my darling. There will be another puppy where we are going. But we can't take him along, you see."

170

Iris started to cry, but then she looked at her father's face. He looked so worried and sad that she didn't want him to see her cry, so she made herself stop.

"It's all right," she said, and smiled at her father.

Jonas explained to Anita that if anyone sought them out it would likely be in New York, so they would sail from Boston. They took a late train east from Chicago to Cleveland, from Cleveland to Buffalo, and on to Boston.

The days of their journey were anxious ones, with Anita and Iris spending most of the time in their double compartment. But when they came to Boston, Jonas and Anita felt they could breathe again. No one had discovered them yet.

On the following day, the three boarded the *Potsdam* for Hamburg.

Chapter 13

Scenting fresh scandal, the newspapers of Chicago were quick to publicize the mysterious disappearance of Iris Mark. Charles Seton stated flatly to reporters that his wife had kidnapped his ward. A human-interest writer made capital of the statement: in his view, no kidnapping had been committed. A bereft mother had taken her own child to her bosom.

"That's exactly right" was the verdict of most of Chicago, and the tide of public opinion, formerly in Charles Seton's favor, began to turn.

"Charley, that was most ill-advised," said John Sadler, Seton's chief attorney. He was pacing the carpet in Charles Seton's luxurious office.

"Ill-advised," Seton repeated angrily. "It's the truth. Sit down, John, you're wearing a hole in my Persian rug."

Sadler ignored him, continuing his angry promenade of the room. "The truth is not always the most discreet course," he said severely. "Particularly in a case like this. And now you want me to trace them. They could be anywhere in the world—do you have any idea what that could cost?"

"Damn the cost. They are laughing in my face somewhere, right now."

"Your wife has taken her own child, Charley."

"Who can prove it's not mine?"

Sadler paused and stared at Charles Seton. "You must be crazy."

"Am I, John? What if I make a move to retrieve my own child?"

"I want no part of this, Charley. You can take your business elsewhere."

"Fine, John. I will."

Sadler stormed out of the office, slamming the doors behind him.

When Charles Seton's new legal counsel approached old Patrick Sheldon, the Byrnes' chief attorney, who had been Anita's godfather at her baptism, Sheldon retorted crabbily that no legal action on earth could induce him to part with the information of his client's whereabouts; that was privileged information. If Charles Seton's attorneys could find a precedent for bringing such an action, he, Patrick Sheldon, would eat his law books, page by page.

The new counsel left Sheldon's suite of offices with his tail between his legs. An exhaustive search of precedents failed to unearth one in the tangle of international law. He was forced to report to his client that he was powerless. Charley dismissed the new attorney and decided to hire detectives.

The detective bureau advised Charley that such a search could consume a great deal of time and even more money. Rashly, Seton gave the bureau *carte blanche*.

What Sheldon knew and refused to disclose was very little; his client's funds were sent to a certain postal drop in London whose contacts were Europe-wide. The postal service had no interest in the probity of its clients; it only knew that the clients paid and paid handsomely. The service had offices everywhere; one was in Munich.

Hans Schmeling, employed as a clerk for that discreet service, had often dreamed of how much money he could make with the information he had garnered on his job. He read every scandal sheet he could find, and newspapers from all the major cities all over the world, including those of Chicago in the country of America.

The beautiful American woman who received mail in the name of Byrne—now that was an interesting case! Hans was convinced she was Anita Byrne Seton, of the Chicago Seton scandal. Hans would bet that Charles Seton would give a good deal to know her whereabouts; he had read about her taking the child. Furtively Hans scrutinized the American paper again; he had picked up a little of a lot of languages in the course of his work. They interested him. English was hard, but he didn't need to know much of it to understand that Charles Seton could be found at a place called Byrne Associates in Chicago, U.S.A. Hans decided to write a letter.

Otto Hubrist, cofounder and teacher at the Debshaus School in Munich, was an anomaly—a very practical man with the visions of an artist. He had welcomed Jonas Mark as a kindred spirit, for his own gifts as well as his apprenticeship to Antoni Gaudí.

Anita was almost as excited to meet Hubrist as she had been to encounter Gaudí. Jonas brought her to the office where he was to work with Hubrist.

She was startled at first at the great man's physical appearance: he was short and squat, with the ugliest face she had ever seen, low of brow, broad of feature. But the full lips below his thick mustache were kindly and mobile; the deepset gray eyes were blazing with intelligence and shrewdness. The eyes studied her with interest and approval.

"Gnädige Frau," Hubrist said, bowing. He led them around the place, showing them plaster models of his monumental tombs and buildings. The spiraling towers and solidly based domes, the aqueducts meandering like snakes and the capitals throwing out broad, flowing fronds suggested Hubrist's demand for what he called "deepened expression and an intensification of life."

The forms fairly sang to Anita's eyes, and she responded wholly to Hubrist's wild inspirations; he saw fairy-tale cities without nationality, of a beauty inconceivable to ordinary architects, a quality she had found so far only in the works of Gaudí and of Jonas Mark. Her expression, her respectful silences, told Hubrist what she felt.

"But let's go to a coffeehouse and get some refreshment," Hubrist said. The three went down the narrow street to a place frequented by the architectural students of the Debenshaus. Anita reflected that the countryside was exactly as she had pictured Germany—she had visited there only briefly before—a land of dark forests and soft rain, a setting from the Brothers Grimm. She understood very little German; Hubrist was considerately speaking in halting English. But she wondered how the German language had ever been considered harsh; here it sounded soft, almost sensuous, and the air was softer, too, than that of America, in the rain that had begun to fall.

Hubrist ordered beer for Jonas and himself, chocolate for Anita, and the three of them were soon in excited talk, about the new kinds of architecture in Germany, and about Antoni Gaudí.

Anita quickly discovered that Otto Hubrist was a man without illusions; like Jonas and herself, he had a skeptical cast to his thinking that contrasted sharply with the aesthetic

174

nature of his vision. He made short work of artists' clichés, and said that politics were absurd, a statement with which Anita fervently agreed.

"The Social Democrats," Hubrist said, "are more hostile to art than the bourgeois civil servants. The true artist shuns any organization or committee; private initiative is everything. You feel this, too, Jonas Mark, I think." Hubrist smiled. "And you, Frau Mark."

"Yes," she agreed at once, returning his infectious smile.

"Ah, there are not many of you from America," Hubrist continued. "This young Frank Wright...he is not bad...some of his buildings approach greatness. But he is too practical for me."

Anita laughed. "And Gaudí?"

"Now, there is an artist. Antoni Gaudí! *Gott*, what daring and imagination! They don't understand him. Now *you*, Jonas Mark, you do. Of course, you worked with the man. It was you yourself who pointed out what I was about to point out to you—remember?"

Jonas nodded.

"Yes," Hubrist turned to Anita. "Your so intelligent husband knows what so many do not—that Antoni Gaudí has moved farther away from traditional architecture than almost anyone has ever done. He also saw," he said to Jonas, "what others have failed to see...that Gaudí's 'Gothic without crutches'...without flying buttresses...takes care of the load-and-support problem with a building that follows the paths of force."

Jonas intervened, "And he relies on intuition for his statics. He works with an endless series of spontaneous decisions; he never knows what the building will look like until the last man lays down his tools."

"That seems unthinkable," Anita commented.

"It would be," Jonas said, "without the Catalan building trade. That's the highest level of craftsmanship I've ever seen. So far," he added to Hubrist, half-apologetically.

"It may *still* be the highest level you've ever seen." Hubrist laughed.

Anita was silent, dazzled and happy. To be sitting there with Jonas, listening to him and to Hubrist, had fired her again with the desire to create.

With that ability almost to read her mind, the ability that made her love him more than ever, Jonas said calmly to

175

Hubrist, "I must advise you that there is one important proviso to my becoming your partner."

Hubrist raised his brows. "And that is?"

"That my wife be included. I have written you already of her qualifications, and sent you examples of her work."

Anita looked at Jonas, surprised. She had no idea he had sent the samples; he must have gotten them from her office before they had left Chicago. She felt a new wave of love and gratitude.

Otto Hubrist hesitated, and she was apprehensive; perhaps he disliked "advanced" women. But he considered an instant and then said, "Very well. I am my own master, after all; and if this sets Munich on its ear...well, I have done so before, with enjoyment."

Anita laughed at his mischievous expression.

"Aside from the fact that your competence is established, Frau Mark, I *like* you." Hubrist held out his pudgy but strong-looking hand.

Anita shook it, replying, "I like you, too, Herr Hubrist."

"Then you had better show it by calling me Otto."

"I will do that, from now on."

She glanced, excited and uplifted, at Jonas. His face reflected the same pleasure she was feeling.

"Now," said Hubrist, rising and pushing back his chair, "I had better get going. I have a very important tomb to finish," he added with dark humor. "And you, Jonas Mark"— he gave the name a stately sound with his careful pronunciation—"when will I expect you and your wife at Hubristhaus? Or do you need another week to settle in?"

"Three weeks has been more than generous. I don't want to be idle any longer."

"Nor do I," said Anita.

"You do things quickly in America," Hubrist commented with admiration. "Very well. *Sehr gut. Morgen früh,* tomorrow morning."

"Morgen früh," Anita repeated.

Jonas and Anita watched him hurry away, then they took their more leisurely route back to the inn, where Iris was waiting with her new companion, a motherly woman who had come highly recommended by Hubrist's sister.

"Gut Nachmittag, Frau Mark, Herr Mark," the woman said warmly. Then with apparent pride in her smattering of English, she added, "The sun cômes once more, does it not?"

"Yes, Frau Benz, the sun comes, and it's nice to see." Anita smiled and embraced Iris. She was delighted with Frau Benz, delighted with Iris's quick adaptability. The child was used to Anita's being away during the day, but her matter-of-fact acceptance of the new country filled Anita with pride and astonished Jonas. They were still looking for a school for her.

Iris said now, *"Gut Nachmittag,* Frau Benz," and the woman reached out and patted her cheek.

"She is good," Frau Benz told Anita and Jonas. "Soon she speaks German, you see."

With Iris between them, Jonas and Anita walked to a nearby park. They sat down on a bench and watched her play with the other children. The language barrier, apparently, made little difference to the confident and worldly Iris.

Anita said softly, "The sun comes once more, does it not?" She had never been so happy or fulfilled as she was at that moment. It was noontime, and the park was filled with workers enjoying their hour of freedom. The soft, sunny air was mild and agreeable.

"The sun always will, Anita." Jonas took her hand.

Looking around, Anita enjoyed the peaceful scene. But suddenly there was a faintly jarring note: that furtive-looking, unpleasant little man she had seen somewhere before, on the streets of Munich.

"Jonas," she said slowly.

"Umm?" His reply was absent, lazy; his head was turned back and his eyes were half-closed against the sun.

"Do you see that man?" she said softly. Jonas turned in the direction of her cautious nod and answered, "Yes. What about him?"

"I know it may sound...foolish. But I've seen him so often since we came here. It's almost as if...he's following me. Do you think Charles could be sending a detective after us?"

"If he is," Jonas retorted, "this one is in excellent disguise. I've never seen such a pipsqueak detective." He looked after the man with amused distaste. But he sobered, and added, "You could be right. Let me know, darling, if you see him again."

"All right." A shadow had fallen over the day for Anita.

For the first time in so many years she had been feeling a perfect happiness—the adventure of living in a new country, the closeness of Jonas and Iris, the feeling that they were a tight, inseparable family at last. And the anticipation of working with Otto Hubrist and Jonas. She supposed her cup had been almost too full, for now just the sight of the furtive man had been enough to upset it.

Surely, she reflected, after all we have been through, there will be some security and peace here.

As he so often did, Jonas seemed to read her thoughts. "Don't worry. We're almost out of the woods, my darling. Even if Charles found us, I don't think he could do very much, at this distance. Nevertheless, I'm going to stay anonymous for a while."

"Anonymous?"

"In the work. Architecture is a small world."

She considered. "I see. But what will Hubrist say?"

Jonas took her hand again and held it tightly. "Hubrist," he said, "is a very good man who asks a minimum of questions. He'll wonder, but he won't say much at all."

"That's good." Anita's glance returned to Iris, romping with the children of Munich under the trees, throwing a red ball back and forth. She listened to Iris's laughter, resolved that nothing and no one would separate the three of them again. She looked at Jonas: his face was grim as he watched the furtive man depart.

Anita saw nothing of the furtive stranger for the next two weeks, and her feeling of joyful security returned. Every aspect of their lives was happier than she had ever imagined: they had found a small but pleasant house which she was busy furnishing. Her days were full and rewarding.

Each morning she delivered Iris to her school, and each afternoon, on an earlier schedule than Jonas at Hubrist's, went to get her. They would walk companionably together back to the nearby house. Now it was October, and the fall was beautiful, a time of vivid leaves and birdsong, more serene somehow than the brisk autumn that Anita was accustomed to in America.

Besides Frau Benz, Anita found that the house functioned well with only one other servant, one of Frau Benz's many nieces. Ilsa was rather dull but very pleasant, and Iris liked her.

Frau Benz was an accomplished cook, and Jonas was delighted with the meals she gave them. She indulged them often with her remarkable pastries, so light they almost melted on the tongue. And Frau Benz outdid herself when Otto Hubrist came to visit, which he often did.

Soon their small social circle widened to include several

young architects and students, with their lovers or wives. The sophisticated Anita, accustomed to the rather cynical ways of Chicago society, and living under the shadow of her ambiguous marriage herself, won the hearts of the radical younger people by her calm acceptance of their status.

In this year of 1900 there was emerging in Central Europe a condition of mutual tolerance between the leading classes of society and the avant-garde of architects and designers. The movement of Art Nouveau, which the Germans called Jugendstil, had attracted the country's most progressive architects. The German entries to the Paris international exhibition of that year included the names of Behrens, Endell, Kreis, Mohring, Paul, and of course Otto Hubrist. German science and architecture seemed to be marching side by side with German industry on the road to world dominion. The country's import and export quotas, some economists claimed, would in the next decade exceed those of England, France and even America.

In this blossoming period of expansion and prosperity, the firm of Otto Hubrist prospered. Already Hubrist had progressed far beyond Jugendstil; the cultured and rich men who could afford to commission splendid buildings looked to Hubrist as a highly practical man as well as a visionary artist.

The little German exercised the same magic over her creative mind that Gaudí had, but it was a thousand times more satisfying and more real to Anita, for she was in the center of it. Her days were filled with work and love, the nights with quiet times devoted sometimes to Iris and Jonas, other evenings bright with the stimulus of productive minds.

She lived in a state of almost dreamlike happiness, shadowed at random moments by the realization of how fragile their personal lives really were, with the threat of Charley's pursuit hanging over them.

But she put the matter out of her thoughts, as well as she could, until one terrible afternoon when she walked into the kitchen and found the giggling Ilsa giving tea to the furtive man from the park.

"Frau Mark," Ilsa said, chagrined. She had been instructed by Frau Benz never to entertain her friends in the Marks' house.

At that moment Iris came in to help herself to a piece of Frau Benz's cake and a glass of milk.

"This...this is Hans Schmeling, Frau Mark," Ilsa stammered. The odd little man who had so dismayed Anita stood

179

up at once with a polite bow, but Anita thought he had a peculiar look in his eyes, and that he stared rather long at Iris.

"Good afternoon," Anita said coldly. "When you have time, Ilsa," she added with soft irony, "Mr. Mark would like a pot of coffee." Jonas had come home early that afternoon, after having worked very late for three straight nights, and was lying down upstairs. "He is in the bedroom."

She turned and left the kitchen, holding Iris by the hand, leaving an appalled silence behind. A moment later she heard Ilsa and Hans Schmeling conversing in low voices.

She will have to go, Anita decided. Poor, silly Ilsa, who had been so good and kind to Iris and so willingly served all of them. She had been duped by this man Schmeling, and now he had invaded their very house. She was now convinced that he was in the hire of Charles Seton, that Charley knew where they were and soon would make a move to take Iris back.

She explained the situation to Jonas; he went down to the kitchen at once. She was thankful that he found Hans Schmeling gone. Jonas's face was like a thundercloud. With regret he agreed that Ilsa could not stay.

"We must somehow explain this to Frau Benz," Anita said.

"Don't worry," Jonas said. "Leave it to me."

She heard him ask Frau Benz that night, after dinner, to come into the study. She did not even ask what he had said, but Frau Benz emerged from the study with a calm and understanding face. She said to Anita, "That foolish girl will have to learn how to act, Frau Mark. I will see to it."

Hans Schmeling never appeared again in the neighborhood, and Ilsa was replaced with another niece. Anita was vastly relieved and once again submerged herself in the happy business of her life.

In November a letter came for Anita through the cautious postal service, a letter that was to change the course of all their lives. She held it out to Jonas, and he scanned it quickly. When he had finished, he looked up at her, his eyes full of triumphant joy. "We're free, Anita. At last, we're free. Now our lives can really begin."

They went into each other's arms, and Anita cried with relief. Now the divorce that Charley had denied them was no longer needed.

The letter was from Emily Seton, Charles's sister, a woman

who had never been an enemy of Anita's and who now, apparently, wanted to be her friend.

Charles Seton was dead, the letter said. He had died in an accident caused by his drinking—his sister had never minced words—and as his heir and executor, Emily was taking immediate steps to try to undo the harm her brother had done Anita and Iris. Charles Seton, Emily wrote, had had in possession certain letters from a Hans Schmeling of Munich, Germany. "And I want the whole dirty business," the forthright Emily wrote, "to be put to an end. I have communicated in no uncertain terms with Herr Schmeling and advised him that he will receive no further emoluments from the Setons; further, that if he persists in harassing you, I will personally seek his prosecution under the law."

Yes, Anita thought, now we are truly free. Now we can go on with the business of our lives. Jonas will no longer be "anonymous." And now that we can be remarried, I can tell him the other thing I have been keeping dark.

"There is something else, Jonas. Something very happy, and good."

She told him that she was expecting another child.

"A son, Anita, perhaps a son," he said, grinning, and holding her close. "Now there is nothing left to want, not any more."

"Just to be sure," as Jonas put it, they were remarried the following week in Berlin.

As the time of her confinement approached, Anita was not surprised to discover that her ambition was flagging, that she was becoming totally wrapped up in Jonas, in Iris and the expected child. Otto Hubrist and Frau Benz took all this very much for granted. Jonas was overjoyed.

By the time Jon Mark was born in May 1901, the name of Jonas Mark had been added to those of the other young and prodigious builders of Germany. The international exhibition scheduled for Turin in 1902 would feature two of his designs.

For the next few years Jonas's creativity was at its height: as the Jugendstil passed its peak and massive buildings with less and less ornamentation began to dominate the scene, there was a vogue for Egyptian architecture. On a trip with Anita and Iris, Jonas had been inspired by the titanic enclosure wall of the funerary district of King Zoser in Saqqara; square pillars and weighty corporeality dominated Jonas's designs in the years 1908 through 1910. The Temple of Horus in Upper Egypt served as the catalyst for several of his designs. And a journey to Granada, where he and Anita studied the twelfth-century stalactite vault in the Alhambra, fired him with the idea for the circular ceiling of a great theater in Berlin. An unusual pattern began to emerge in Jonas's work: in all of his designs, which resembled Hubrist's in that they transcended nationality of any kind, a unique quality could be seen, a thing that Hubrist said could only be called American.

A critic compared some of Jonas's massive Egyptian-inspired work to the giant silos of the American Midwest, his flowing forms to rugged mountains that recalled the Rockies. Sometimes reading these things Jonas felt a faint homesickness nag at him. Always, however, it had been quelled by his present content and the happiness of Anita and the children.

The Mark household was now quite cosmopolitan and bilingual; Anita and Iris had grown proficient in German, and when Jon began to speak, his first words were in that language. The change in all of them was so gradual that none of them realized what total expatriates they had become.

But all through the years of that decade, Jonas kept close tabs on American happenings, even if Anita did not. Jonas was uneasily aware that Germany and the United States were drifting toward enmity. While the peace of Europe continued to hold, imperial rivalries, protectionist trade practices and the escalating arms race had resulted in minor disputes as early as 1905. America under the irascible leadership of Teddy Roosevelt was generally in sympathy with Britain and France, less so with the imperialist Kaiser. But the problems of the wider world seemed distant to the Marks, absorbed in their own concerns.

In 1904, when Iris was ten years old, they discovered her extraordinary talent for music. By the time she was twelve, they were advised to send her to Berlin to study with one of the great teachers.

Because so much of Jonas's work had begun to take him to that great city, and Anita was delighted at the prospect of living again in a metropolis, the Marks moved to Berlin in 1906, saying an affectionate farewell to Hubrist and Munich, the scene of so many happy times. Frau Benz consented to make the move with them.

The world beyond Germany was shrinking, with the boom of communication and transport: by 1910 nearly a half million motor vehicles were registered in America alone; the radio, the telegraph, the phonograph were commonplace. Newsreels appeared the year before. And an unprecedented time of experimentation, in the world of art, had brought forth expressionism, cubism, futurism.

Architects were exploring new uses of steel structure: Gaudí completed his curvilinear Casa Milá in 1910; Frank Wright's streamlined Robie house had gone up. In Berlin, Jonas Mark began a fantasy cathedral. Seeing it take form, Hubrist said, "The student has surpassed the master."

Chapter 14

IN THE SUMMER OF 1912, Iris Mark celebrated her eighteenth birthday. And in the changing city of Berlin, where the tango was being danced, the works of Dr. Sigmund Freud were gaining attention, and women were beginning to enter the university, Iris met a man whose ties were all with the past.

There was no place in her future for men: it was already mapped out. She was going to have a career as a pianist, and a fine one. Jonas and Anita applauded her efforts, and shared her admiration for the splendors of Wagner and of Strauss, but they were a little disconcerted that Iris's enthusiasm for German music extended even to the Kaiser and his "toy soldiers." To Iris the soldiers were hardly real at all; they were characters from a magnificent opera.

And on one bright August morning, as Iris stood on the parade ground with her parents watching the Kaiser review the Hussars' most famous troop, the soldiers looked more romantic than ever. Cavalry General Friedrich von Helsing, commander of the Hussars, rode behind Germany's young princess at the head of the regiment while her father, the Kaiser, observed the splendid horsemen.

The general's son, Oberleutnant Rikard von Helsing, riding straight as a ramrod but easy in the saddle, was bored with the whole affair. They had mounted at half past nine and would ride until a quarter past three with only a twenty-minute rest. After that there would be a meal in the mess, with Princess Viktoria Luise as honored guest.

When the regiment had done its walking pace and was making the smart turn to start the gallop, Rik von Helsing's sharp blue eyes caught a glimpse of three interesting-looking people at the front of the watching crowd. Two of them at least were interesting, for they were women. His brother officers always teased Rik about his ability to watch women without seeming to do so; he could catalogue their charms with an astounding thoroughness while appearing not to move a millimeter from the strict attention position. Rik knew quite well he was at his best on horseback; there was rarely a woman who was not impressed by his face, with its dashing scar acquired in the dueling club, his lean, hard body upright as an arrow in the saddle.

The two women he had just seen were especially fascinating: they looked like foreigners, maybe Frenchwomen. Maybe not, Rik considered. Perhaps it was just the way they wore their clothes. A foreign observer had aroused the Berliners' ire by saying their young women had fresh skin and healthy forms, but no eye for style in clothes, and too often adopted "the stiff walk of the soldiers."

Rik von Helsing privately agreed, but these two women wore their clothes with an air of chic, and they were undeniably feminine. The older woman had jet-black hair and a daring look. But it was the younger one who attracted Rik the most.

She had the coloring of a young lioness; her hair was a luxuriant golden brown, and when he glanced at her again, Rik saw that her eyes were a wonderful tawny color, golden brown as her hair. She did not have the candy-box look of the girls his mother always pushed at him. He was bored with their white plumpness and the unvarying sweetness of their blue eyes and blond hair. This girl looked as if she had a temper.

Rik chanced a long look at her: to his delight, she stared back into his eyes. He could see she was excited by his look; her lips were parted and she seemed to be watching him rather than the princess and the Kaiser. All through the endless exercise he thought of her.

He was still thinking of her in the mess. After the princess had made her stiff little speech of thanks to the Kaiser for making her colonel-in-chief of the regiment, there was a general buzz of talk. Rik's friend Heinrich Brun said, glancing at the princess, who wore the regiment's peaked cap bearing the Death's Head emblem, "She's a sweet young lady, isn't she?"

Rik answered, "Sweet enough, but there's not much to her, is there?" After a moment, he added, "I saw something at the parade ground that would put her to shame."

185

"I don't know how you do it, my friend." Brun láughed softly. "You look just like your father's son and yet you're always eyeing all the women. And after a night like last night!" Brun was hollow-eyed; neither of the young men had slept more than three hours after an enormous amount of wine and an exhausting visit to some dancers. Rik's eyes were clear and his skin looked as if he had just come out of the gym.

Rik had heard that a good many times before. He was his father's son, but he was also proudly aware that that fact had little to do with his advance in the regiment; the general was harder on his son than on any other member of the troop. The others knew it and respected Rik for it. Rik von Helsing was also proud of the fact that they envied him for his success with women.

"Didn't you see them?" Rik asked Brun. "The foreigners with the tall man."

"Don't you know who they were?" Brun inquired with surprise. "That's Mark, the American architect, who's doing the Johannes church. Hubrist's pet."

"Who's Hubrist?"

Brun mocked, "You are a barbarian, Rik."

"That's what my aunt always says."

"She's right," Brun declared. "Hubrist is our best modern architect."

"Oh." Rik was uninterested. "Who were the women?"

"Mark's wife and daughter. Don't tell me you haven't heard about the wife. She—"

Brun's recital was interrupted by another toast. The meal was coming to an end, and it was time for the officers to come to attention for the exit of the princess. Rik was getting a headache, and was glad the damned thing was over. But Brun got away before he could find out what it was about Mark's wife that was so interesting. From the look in Brun's eyes, it must have been a scandal.

So that was Mark's daughter, Rik reflected, joining the parade of Hussars leaving the mess. An American. That's why she looked so different. Just like a little cat, with those eyes and that hair. Her earthy, sensual look was to haunt him for days.

Even at the theater or concert hall it was a common sight in 1912 to see German girls and women knitting stockings or doing crochet work, so ingrained were their domestic habits. It was quite an event in the life of a German woman to attend amusements outside the home, unless she was a member of the very privileged class.

Frau General von Helsing (née Krupp) was a formidable blend of both kinds of women: tonight to the recital hall she had brought along her crochet. After all, she was fond of saying, even the Kaiserin was known to do needlework in company. And the Kaiserin was an excellent example of German womanhood—with simple tastes in all directions, a good housewife, religious, modest, yet having many accomplishments.

Once, to Irmgard von Helsing's horror, her son Rik had said that the Kaiserin sounded like a boring old cow. General von Helsing had forthwith taken away Rik's allowance for a month and forbidden his attendance at the circus, his favorite treat. He had also whipped his son's bottom.

Tonight's attendance at the recital hall was much more serious than amusement; it was a family duty. The general's nephew was to perform on the pianoforte. When Rik protested about his evening being wasted, the general put his foot down.

"Your light-o'-love can use the rest," the general said with heavy humor. Rik was very annoyed; he had a long-standing engagement with the dancer Kiki Schmidt, and had been looking forward to it.

Frau General von Helsing, who had been in the hall, was not meant to hear her husband's coarse remark. "I turned quite pale," she reported later to her sister, Emma Krupp, who also brought her knitting to the performance.

As they settled into their seats in the concert hall, Friedrich von Helsing, trying to make his peace with Rik, remarked in gruff companionship, "It is a bore, my boy, but you'll learn that life's important events are usually boring. The Kaiserin is very interested in these matters herself. There she is, over there, with that sweet little princess." The general stood and bowed with great respect, receiving a polite bow from the princess in return. "Just as well," he added, smiling as he sat down again, "to be in good standing with the boss's wife."

Rik grinned when his father used the Americanism, one he had picked up from Colonel Theodore Roosevelt when that dignitary had visited the Kaiser in May. The general was proud of the term and used it as often as possible; the Americanism reminded Rik of the beautiful catlike girl at the parade, and he recalled her intense eyes.

187

"I hope," the general continued in his companionable way, "there won't be much of this 'modern' music. These young fellows will tell you it represents a ship in a storm; sounds to me like a catastrophe in the kitchen."

Rik laughed. That was one subject, aside from the Hussars, in which he thoroughly agreed with the general.

"So do I, Father. Give me some Strauss and Wagner, every time. That's music with meat on it; I like something I can whistle."

Frau General's sister said, "You *are* a barbarian, Rikard."

"Come now, Tante. You know the worst compliment you can pay a modern composer is to tell him he's written something pleasant and harmonious that we can understand."

The general laughed loudly and clapped his son's back. "Capital, Rik!" He did not know that Rik had heard Brun say that.

"Ssssh," hissed Irmgard. "The concert is beginning."

To the men's dismay, Karl-August von Helsing, their relative, a rather precious young man, sat fussily down at the pianoforte and after a prolonged arrangement of the tails of his coat burst into the performance of one of the most "modern" composers. They endured the dissonance manfully; Rik's sister Maria looked pained. The other women, crocheting and knitting placidly, seemed not to hear. But they nodded their high-dressed heads with approval, smiling.

When the racket was at an end, Rik said in a low tone to the general, "I'm going out for a smoke."

"All right. I guess I'll see what this Mark girl is like."

Rik paused in the act of rising and sat down again abruptly. "Mark girl," he repeated. He had not even glanced at the program. "Let me see," he said, taking his father's program.

"What's this?" the general asked humorously.

"I've...heard the name," Rik said. "Her father's the architect, isn't he?"

"Well, well, my son is acquiring *Kultur*," von Helsing commented. To his embarrassment, Rik noticed that his aunt and mother were listening.

"The Marks are too well known," said Irmgard von Helsing. "They say the man is every bit as good as Hubrist, but the wife! She is actually working with the men. It's a disgrace. And she comes of a good family in America, too!"

"Come now, Irmgard," said Emma Krupp good-naturedly,

"there's another lady architect right here in Berlin, **and** hundreds of girls are going to the universities these days."

"And a foolish idea it is!" the general declared. "Very foolish indeed." He gave Emma Krupp a reproachful glance; **her** "forward" views were too well-known to him.

Rik hardly listened to the controversy; the last thing in the world he cared about was the education of women. He was looking forward with great eagerness to the appearance of the Mark beauty. He studied the program. Iris, her name was. Iris. It had a foreign, perfumed sound that stirred his senses.

"The daughter of a woman like that is no better than she should be, I imagine," Frau General said severely.

"Don't say that, Irmgard," the general warned, laughing. "You will only recommend her the more to our son."

"The idea," Frau General said, scandalized. But nevertheless she studied her handsome son.

"I'm not at all attracted to intellectual ladies, Mother," he said easily, and she relaxed a trifle.

But his attention was riveted to the stage as Iris Mark walked on. And she was a hundred times more enticing, more beautiful, than when he had seen her in the sun of the parade ground the other day.

Tonight she wore a dress of utter simplicity and a fashion that was uncommon among the bedecked ladies of Berlin: to Rik von Helsing the gown looked almost like a nightdress, it seemed so plain and thin, and the thought titillated him, making him go hot and cold under the tight-fitting coat of his splendid uniform.

Iris's wonderful hair was revealed in all its glory; she wore it plain and dressed high in an almost Grecian manner, a new American style. The golden-bronze color of her gown fired the girl's hair to a bright, sunny auburn and emphasized the wonderful topaz color of her intense eyes.

She moved gracefully to the pianoforte and sat down with poise and calm, and a minimum rearrangement of her skirt. She bowed her shapely little head a moment above the keys; Rik noticed that its contours were very apparent in the sleek, plain arrangement of hair. Then Iris Mark began to play.

The audience was very quiet: even Rik, who was not "musical" at all, and who had spent most of his life like a healthy, unthinking young animal, was touched by the beauty and power of the sound. Soldiers were always encouraged to sing on the march outside of the cities; an officer with musical talent was especially appointed in each battalion, battery or regiment to teach the men patriotic marching songs. In the Hussars' 2nd it was Brun; Rik was used to that, and responded to the stirring battle music, and he was as fond as any young man of the popular love songs of the day.

But the music Iris Mark was playing was different from anything young von Helsing had ever known; whether it was because she was playing it, or because of the music itself, he could not have said. He only knew that it gave him feelings he had never had before—the vision of an exquisite place he might have dreamed of, an exaltation he might have associated with the heights of the moment of love with a woman. But this young woman before him, hardly more than a girl, gave him a feeling utterly unknown before; he almost imagined that making love to her would be a vast thing, that it would be an experience entirely new to him, for all the many women he had had. Rik listened—without knowing or caring what they were—to the Three Piano Pieces of Arnold Schönberg, performed for the first time the year before.

He glanced at his father and noticed that the hard-bitten general was uneasily attentive, with a strangely tender expression on his stern face. Rik thought, He feels it, too, that peculiar magnetism and that warm...yearning in her. As soon as he thought it, Rik was amazed at himself and his fanciful way of putting it. He was reacting like one of those lovesick poets who were always the butt of jokes in the regiment.

To his intense relief, the next piece the girl played was a more familiar one, a sonata by Brahms, but she gave the piece an especial sweetness and languor; Rik was surprised that the piece could sound so exciting. It reminded him somehow of a dim, curtained bed that smelled of roses; an afternoon retreat, something like Kiki's small, crowded flat. And yet it was more than that, much more; this flat had a window that opened on a fresh, sunny garden...or the sea, where wild winds blew.

Rik von Helsing shook his head; nothing, nothing except perhaps Kiki's body or a great deal of wine, had ever sent him off into a dream like that. He glanced aside and saw his mother looking at him; the girl had stopped playing and was standing before the audience, which was applauding loudly. Iris Mark made a graceful little bow and started to walk off the stage, but the audience called her back with their continuing applause.

190

Rik stood up and cried out, "Bravo!" just like one of the young aesthetes at the opera, whom he despised. He sat down again, embarrassed; his family was staring at him with great surprise; he never reacted in such a way to music, not even to the great Emmy Destinn.

Iris Mark was the last performer on the program. Rik said casually to his mother, "Shall we go back and speak to Karl-August?" He knew at once that he had made a tactical error; his scorn for Karl-August was too well known to his parents, and this display of enthusiasm was suspect.

His mother and aunt exchanged amused glances, but his mother's face looked more anxious than amused. The general said ironically, "This is something new for you, Rikard, this passion for...music, is it not?"

"It was a good concert," Rik replied stiffly, avoiding his father's eye.

The men rose and went to the aisle, standing aside for the women to pass. Rik felt his heart beating with excitement; surely, he thought, he would get a glimpse of the girl backstage.

Impatiently he followed the women and his father; their progress was impeded by a vast number of well-wishing relatives and friends, and the necessity to move slowly in order not to tread on the trains of the women's skirts. At last they reached the backstage area inhabited by the artists; Rik forced himself to greet his anemic cousin with cordiality, to say some civil words about his performance.

But his sharp blue eyes were scanning the other dressing rooms; the door of one nearby was ajar, and he heard the enthusiastic voices of a man and woman, speaking English.

Rik stepped into the corridor outside the dressing room his cousin shared with another young performer, and frankly stared in the direction of the American voices. He saw a tall, striking-looking man of about forty standing at the back of the opposite dressing room, leaning slightly against the jamb of the door, half in profile to von Helsing. In spite of the tall man's casual manner, Rik von Helsing saw at once that he was a man of power and determination. The stubborn set of his mouth, the hawklike nose and tanned, scored cheeks were those of a man to reckon with.

If that is her father, thought Rik, it will not be easy.

"What are you mooning about for, Rikard?" He heard his mother's jarring voice, which had always reminded him of a creaking gate.

"I am merely waiting," he said curtly. The general, just beyond his wife, frowned at Rik's short answer.

"Do not speak so to your mother, Rikard." The general's use of his full name told Rik that he must be more careful; it was generally the prelude to the old man's ire.

"I am sorry," he said formally, bowing in a rather ironic fashion to his mother.

From the dressing room across the corridor, he heard that young warm voice again call out, "Go on ahead of us, then; we'll meet at the Rheingold."

The Rheingold was Berlin's most famous restaurant, and Rik decided at once to invite his party there. He had to see more of Iris Mark. She was no peasant girl who could be approached in a light manner; yet there had been a great difference in the way she spoke to her friends. Young German girls of good family were kept almost as strictly as the young women of Spain, with their grim dueñas. And there had been a lightness and freedom in her voice that he envied.

He saw them emerge from the dressing room: first, the beautiful woman with black hair who, Rik now understood, must be the girl's mother, wearing a striking gown of deep blue. She was followed by the tall, lean man, who wore his evening clothes with a raffish air. An artist, a "bohemian," Rik judged. Then he saw Iris Mark again, and thought ceased.

He started to go forward, to congratulate her on her performance, but the forbidding look in her father's eye gave him pause. Rik was struck dumb by seeing her so close; her skin was like silk, and he could almost feel the warm magnetism of her catlike eyes. Once again, as she had at the parade ground, she looked straight into Rik's eyes, and he stood staring after her.

"Well, Rik?" The general was standing at his side. "Are you ready to accompany us home? Or are you on frivolity bound, elsewhere?"

Rik smiled with tolerance for the general's heavy lightness and returned, "No, I'm not ready for home at all. Why don't you be my guests at the Rheingold?"

The general raised his shaggy brows. "The Rheingold! We are flying high, aren't we? Has the regiment been given a general rise in pay? Of course, my boy. That is most generous. It will be something unusual for the women. But I won't let you pay the freight alone, no, sir. Come, come then."

The women were in a flutter at the unexpected invitation.

It was a rare evening when young Rikard von Helsing chose to spend time with his relatives.

The general shepherded them to the carriage; he had a motorcar but the women disliked it, so they had come in the older vehicle. In a short time they were ushered into the splendor of the famous Rheingold; the general was flattered and delighted to be recognized and given a prominent table near that of a duke and duchess of his acquaintance.

Rik looked impatiently about the great room; finally he saw the Marks entering, being seated; to his dismay their table was quite a distance from the von Helsings'. He was both glad and dismayed to see that the Marks' party numbered a very prominent sculptor, Fritz Klimpsch, and a daughter of one of the members of the Imperial Parliament. Such company meant the Marks were people of standing and substance, which might possibly recommend them to his parents. But such acquaintances also meant, perhaps, that Iris Mark was a carefully brought up young woman.

"There's Klimpsch over there with that lovely girl's family," Emma Krupp commented in her genial way.

"Who's Klimpsch?" the general asked.

Rik told him. When his aunt looked delighted at his knowledge, he admitted that he had met Klimpsch at a beer garden, where the sculptor's capacity for drink had been well demonstrated.

"I might have known," his aunt commented ruefully, and Frau General von Helsing looked disapproving.

Rik was grateful to his aunt for mentioning the Mark table, for it gave him an excuse to talk about them. "The Americans are an interesting-looking family," he hazarded.

"Interesting," his mother repeated with scorn. She proceeded to tell him of the scandal connected with the Marks; she knew for a fact, she said, that they had been married in Berlin after their son was conceived and when their daughter was already six years old.

Rik's handsome face stiffened at this evidence of his mother's spite, and yet some demon in him exulted at the knowledge that the beautiful young woman was déclassé, possibly even illegitimate. For that surely meant that she was likely to be more approachable, in the bohemian circle of her freethinking parents' friends. Yes, he was presuming a good deal, but all the same the knowledge gave him the nerve to plan the approach.

"Really, Irmgard," the kindly Emma protested. The general murmured, "That's too bad, I must say. Such a handsome family." His sensual lips parted as he stared at the girl and her mother.

"Indeed they are," Rik commented. Quite by accident at that moment the golden eyes of the girl, Iris, met Rik's steady blue ones. She looked away. But the young Hussar's blood was pounding in his veins.

His head swam with the vision of the Mark girl, her ripe-looking skin, the blooming quality of her small mouth and those unique eyes that burned into his. He had never seen such a woman before in his brief but varied career. Like most young men of his class, he had made a tour of Europe, but nowhere, even among the lustrous-eyed women of Spain or the chic, pert Parisiennes, had he encountered such charm. And the sheltered young women of his set seemed to Rik, at this moment, like so many identical dolls, the Dresden dolls with heads and hands of glass, perfect, white and lacquered without, hollow within. Even Kiki was dim in his mind.

As he smiled and joked with his relatives, Rik's mind was worrying at the problem: how would he get to meet Iris Mark?

Chapter 15

AT EIGHTEEN, IRIS MARK was an unusual combination of cool, hardheaded sense and tempestuous feelings that she kept sternly in control. Once her father had said to her with a smile, "Even if you didn't look so much like me, I'd still know you were a Mark. You're a lot like my father, stubborn and silent."

And he had told her the story of William Mark, his wild, unhappy love and his daring flight from Texas. All the places seemed quite unreal to the cosmopolitan Iris, who had lived most of her life in luxury, and in the midst of cities.

On another occasion, she had overheard her father telling her mother that he hoped Iris wouldn't "end her life like his father, married to the wrong one... or not at all." Iris hadn't known that her grandfather had not loved her grandmother; she wondered who the woman was he did love.

"She won't," her mother had replied, "if she finds someone like you. But that won't be easy."

The younger Iris had agreed silently with her mother: there would never be anyone else like Jonas Mark. In any case, love was something Iris Mark would not seek, now that she had found her own ambition.

Of course Anita Mark was a beautiful and talented woman, but Iris felt in her a lack of ambition; it seemed to Iris that her mother lived too much for her father, Jon and herself. And somehow it diminished Anita in her daughter's eyes. She knew all that her mother had been through, but was too young to realize her mother's contentment had made her willing to place ambition second to her family.

So, at thirteen Iris had decided, I will never fall in love. And she bent every energy toward the building of her musical career. At sixteen she had been judged far in advance of any other student her age; the next year, her teacher had told Jonas and Anita, she would be ready for the concert stage. Their pride in her fairly shone from their faces.

Her brother, Jon, was the odd one, Iris thought. He was a very quiet and private boy; his only friend was the son of the prominent Jewish poet Abraham Gold. Jon seemed to read everything he could get his hands on, and he was always, in Iris's words, "mooning about, thinking of things." She herself found that books were never enough to occupy her restless mind: her hands had to be constantly busy, and she practiced five or six hours every day.

At times in the last few months Iris had noticed that her mother studied her with a watchful expression, and she wondered what Anita was looking for. Iris saw almost with indifference the ripening of her body. In this year of 1912, she was as developed as a grown woman. And, afraid of becoming fat and matronly-looking like so many of the young German girls, Iris was extremely careful of her diet. She felt that it was all right to be pretty—it couldn't hurt her on the concert stage—but aside from that she gave the matter little thought.

There hadn't been any problems with boys: Iris found them either brutal or silly. The university students she had seen were either scarred and bloated from dueling and drinking or pale, bespectacled creatures who wrote die-away love poems or who were so engrossed in their specialized studies that they were like machines.

She had always thought the Hussars a handsome lot, however; some of them were almost as vital and good-looking as her father. But then Jonas Mark was a man apart. Her father was like a god to Iris; she had gone many times to the cathedral site while it was being erected, and the feeling she had looking at its vaulted heights and convoluted wonders produced feelings in her similar to those her music engendered—an exaltation, almost a dissolution of her self that was like turning into a powerful bird on great wings, and flying, flying above the rest of the ordinary and toiling world.

Until this last year music had been her life, vital, busy and content. But for some time now there had been nights when she woke from peculiar dreams and felt a warm stirring in her body, an unfamiliar ache, a lack of some kind that puzzled and dismayed her. Somehow she could not confide that feeling to Anita, but she noticed that her mother looked more watchful than ever and spoke to her with an especial tenderness.

I suppose it must be Sex, Iris reflected with distaste. In the freethinking climate of her parents' circle, these things were referred to freely. But in her cool and dualistic fashion Iris resolved not to let this thing interfere with her life. She resented the whole process—when most women loved men, they married and had children. Their bodies thickened and— she was convinced—their personalities disintegrated.

The annoying sensation of emptiness nevertheless continued to haunt her. Then, that morning on the bright parade ground, when the young Hussar had looked into her eyes, for one uncomfortable moment, Iris had not known who she was any more. She had a feeling of utter helplessness, that sensation of dissolution akin to the sensation of flying she had experienced at the cathedral, and in her music. It was disconcerting to see him again, first at the recital hall, and later at the Rheingold.

Therefore she was actually flustered at seeing him two nights after the concert at the home of the sculptor Klimpsch. At first she hardly knew him, because he was not in uniform but in a faultlessly tailored suit of blue-gray. The other men in the party, mostly artists and poets, were casually dressed. Her own father wore a disreputable-looking corduroy jacket of which he was very fond, and a loose, open collar.

The young Hussar looked quite at sea amid the unconventional gathering, and Iris wondered what he was doing there. He was hardly the type of companion to attract a man like Klimpsch or the poet Gold, who was an habitué of the house. As a matter of fact, Iris noticed that the Hussar was looking at Gold with distaste. She wondered why that was. It was all a puzzle.

But as soon as she entered with her parents, Iris saw the young soldier's attention turned at once to them. And she knew then why he had come: it had been to meet her. His steady, hard blue gaze remained fixed on her, and Iris felt an excited discomfort.

Klimpsch came forward with a genial smile for the Marks, holding out his hand. The Hussar moved deliberately forward so that he was almost in their path. "Good evening, my dear friends," Klimpsch said in his gentle voice. Stepping back to invite them in to the sitting room, the sculptor almost collided with the stiff young Hussar.

"Well, Rik," the sculptor said good-humoredly. "There you

are. May I present my friends, the Marks—Mr. and Mrs. Jonas Mark, Miss Iris Mark. Oberleutnant Rikard von Helsing." He pronounced the title and imposing name with a faint humorous irony, and Iris saw at once that the Hussar was the novelty of the evening.

The Marks acknowledged the introduction, and Rikard von Helsing said eagerly, "May I get you some wine?"

Jonas declined; Anita took his arm as if to move away. But Iris answered, "Yes, thank you. That would be very nice." She had a sudden, impish desire to make von Helsing uncomfortable; why this was, she could not say, but she had a vague wish to punish him for the confusion of feelings he had awakened in her. She was innocently unaware that her golden eyes, filled with mischief, were more than ever very like a cat's.

Rik von Helsing stared into the girl's strange topaz-colored eyes for a moment, and then recalled himself to his social duties. He hurried away to get the wine; when he was returning with both their glasses in his big, awkward hands— a glass of port for himself and a goblet of pale, mild Liebfraumilch for Iris Mark—he marveled at the freedom with which she greeted the people at the party. The whole affair was so unlike anything he had ever attended, the deportment of the women so ambiguous, that he was utterly out of his element.

Rik von Helsing had known only two kinds of women— the actresses and dancers with whom the regiment passed its freer hours, and the stiff young ladies of the respectable homes of Berlin. The women here fit into neither category: there was the woman Anita Mark, a married woman and mother of children, elegant as a princess, and yet there was something free about her; her daughter had the same quality.

But soon Rik knew what the difference was: Iris Mark's free and easy manners were born of an utter innocence, a total unawareness of how seductive, indeed dangerous, she was. He approached her and handed her the glass of wine.

"Thank you," she said, taking the glass and smiling at him. She looked at him with a directness that confirmed his earlier judgment of her—she was a complete innocent.

"I am honored," he replied formally, making her a little bow that he could see amused her, and he kicked himself for his stiff manners. "I have admired the work of your father," he said, and she looked at him with surprise.

"I wouldn't have thought you would," she said bluntly.

He was utterly confounded; her frankness amounted almost to rudeness, and he hardly knew how to proceed.

Matching her blunt tone, he asked, "Why is that?"

"I would have thought you admired war monuments, with generals and snorting horses." She grinned.

"I admire beautiful musicians more." He recouped.

"And not music?" She raised her tawny brows.

"I like music very much," he protested. "All Germans do. Especially Wagner and Johann Strauss."

"Tunes you can whistle," she said with a specious enthusiasm. When he realized what she was doing, he felt his face grow hot. I'll show the wench, he thought, and his look wandered from her silken, mischievous face downward to her shapely neck and the swelling bosom above the low-cut bodice of her gown. He was glad to see her cheeks color; for the first time she looked away from him.

"I'm sorry," she said in a low voice. "That was very rude indeed." His heartbeat thudded in his throat, and he was overcome with desire for this strange girl. After a time, she said in a gentle, sincere tone, "I admire fine riding. I saw you at the parade ground, when the Kaiser was reviewing your regiment."

Ah! he thought exultantly. She is enough like the others to admire a fine figure in the saddle. His spirits soared. "You are most kind, Miss Mark. I am proud of my regiment, it is true. But I would rather discuss your performance at the recital hall. It was magnificent."

Rik noticed with satisfaction that she was a little taken aback, and he wondered what she had expected. How peculiar these Americans are, he reflected. But then she was not wholly American, he recalled.

"You were brought to Germany as a small child?" he asked her suddenly. "I knew that you had lived here a long time; your German is excellent."

"Yes," she answered, and again he noticed that she was uncertain now, quite shy. It went to his heart. The combination of childlike innocence and ripe magnetism was one he had never met, and he felt his whole body responding to her. "Yes," she said. "I was only six years old." For some reason, then, she turned and looked around the room. She caught her mother's eye and smiled at her. Rik thought, The mother is very wise. I think she knows what I'm up to. But all of a sudden he himself was not sure what he was up to. It had seemed so simple before, even an hour before. Then he had thought of the girl as another conquest; a more interesting one, to be sure, than the usual run, but a conquest just the same. Her family and their friends were not *hoffähig*—that is, not received at court and not admitted socially to the houses of nobility. Therefore Rik had assumed the Mark girl would be an easy target; the women out of his *Kreis,* or circle, usually were.

But now he was not even sure any more of his very *Kreis,* or the sanctity of all his father had taught him—to meet or mix or marry outside one's *Kreis* was to invite chaos, a condition unthinkable to the orderly Prussian mind. Right now, in the midst of these incomprehensible but attractive and gifted people, that whole way of life seemed dull. Rik suddenly recalled that Brun had said this to him, but he had dismissed it as the pronouncement of a sorehead, a dog-in-the-manger attitude of one whose name was not ennobled by a *von* before it.

Yet looking at Iris Mark and her beautiful mother, at the varied and interesting wives and female artists at the gathering, who seemed to have no mark of disreputability, Rik was totally nonplussed. He was so deep in thought that Iris remarked, not unkindly, "You look quite profound, lieutenant."

Embarrassed, he realized how inattentive he had seemed, and said hastily, "I am all apologies, Fräulein. Only a boor or a fool...or indeed both...could think of anything else in your presence."

"I'm disappointed," she said, the last comment he had expected. "Your thoughts seemed so serious and interesting, from your expression, that I was hoping you might share them with me."

"You see, Fräulein Mark, these people...this place..." He smiled and gestured about them. "They are all new to my experience. As *you* are, Fräulein. Never have I known a...lady like you, one who talks so...freely and plainly. Tell me, are all Americans so?"

Iris smiled, and the wide smile lit up her glowing face. Rik wished she would smile more.

"My mother says not," Iris answered. "My parents and I, and my brother, too, I suppose, do not belong to any country, you see. At least that's what my parents have always told me."

He thought there was something wistful in her voice, as

well as proud, and he asked, "How can that be? I cannot imagine, for myself, being anything other than German."

She smiled at that in a different way, he noticed, amazed that he had become so sensitive to her different reactions. What was happening to him?

"I cannot imagine your being anything else, either." Her reply was so clever, he thought, that he did not know whether it was a compliment or the reverse. "You are a wonderful example of young German manhood."

Again Rik was taken off balance by her plain speaking; he wondered if she realized how provocative she was. Probably not, he concluded. She was as much a child as she was a woman. Then he realized something else: in all his life he had barely noticed, much less cared, what a woman said or how she reacted. Uneasily, he thought, I wonder if I am falling in love.

"You see," Iris continued earnestly, "my parents' work is more international than national. But I'm sure you already know that," she added politely.

Rik did not know, and he wished now he had paid more attention to his Aunt Emma and to Brun when they had discussed such things. He did not know what Iris meant at all.

"No, I don't," he admitted in a burst of honesty. "You were right when you suggested I prefer statues of warriors on horses." And he grinned at her, looking down into her eyes. He imagined he saw a warm softness in their golden depths; she looked away from him in apparent shyness, and he wanted more than ever to take her in his arms.

The opportunity presented itself sooner than he had hoped; one of the younger people had begun to work the phonograph, and a sensuous tango rhythm was filling their corner of the room.

"Will you dance, Fräulein?"

"Yes, of course." And she moved with graceful naturalness into his arms for the long, measured steps of the rather shocking dance which he had never danced with a member of his own class.

Her young body was supple and very soft; to Rik's excitement her flesh felt almost uncovered, and the silk material slid over her narrow waist and her young back as his big hand turned and guided her in the dance. Their bodies met again and again in the tango's measures, and Rik felt his excitement grow. How sweet she was, how satiny her body;

so different from the corseted and dowdy young women of his *Kreis*.

He wanted to go on dancing with her forever, wishing the sensuous beat of the dance would never end. But to his dismay, the next melody was a waltz. "It is warm," he said. "Would you like to go on dancing, or perhaps you would like to take a turn in the garden?"

"Yes," she answered, looking up at him steadily. "Let us take a walk in the garden."

He was elated; she took his arm and they moved toward the long French windows, ajar in the warm, fragrant night. As they were leaving the room, Rik heard a deep male voice proclaiming, "My studio overlooks the Tiergarten...all Hohenzollerns in helmets, in triumphant attitudes. I can draw the shutters, but it's a life sentence all the same." There was general laughter. Rik realized he was in the enemy camp. He could hardly credit that these people could make fun of the wonderful statues raised at the Kaiser's direction, the splendid Arch of Triumph at the Brandenburg Gate. Why, it was the most magnificent boulevard, the biggest, in all of Europe. He imagined that he had heard the Jew poet, Abraham Gold, laughing loudest of all. And his body heated with resentment.

"Lieutenant?" He started and looked down at Iris Mark. She was studying him. "You didn't like what you heard, did you?"

Rik was at once gratified and chagrined that this girl could read him with such ease. "No," he said bluntly.

But now she was smiling up at him, and he could not think of the insult to his Kaiser. All he could see in the bright moonlight was Iris Mark; her fiery golden hair was a glory in the moon's gentle glow, her wonderful eyes all at once had that ageless wisdom that he had sometimes seen in the seductive eyes of whores. He took her savagely in his arms and bent to her young, parted mouth to kiss her. There was no resistance in her, but the unpracticed way in which she submitted to his kiss told Rik that she had never been touched by another man. That certain knowledge made him burn to possess her; he was obsessed by the imagined loveliness of her untutored body.

However, in just another instant he felt her struggle to draw back from him; instinctively his hard arms tightened around that dazzling, novel prize, her body. Then he heard her saying, through the heated mist of his desire, "No, no."

At first he took it for the conventional protest to which he

202

was accustomed, and he ignored her, still holding her close, kissing her luxuriant hair. In truth, as he had imagined, the scent of her was like a sunny garden, profuse with wonderful and unknown flowers.

But she protested again with all her body to his embrace. He let her go, and stood looking down at her, breathing quickly, half angry, half intrigued by the swift change in her.

"It was wrong of me," she said in her serious way, "to come here with you. I have misled you. Forgive me, Lieutenant von Helsing."

Rik was speechless. Of all the things he had expected, that was the furthest from his mind. He had acted like a savage, he realized, almost leaping upon her as soon as they were out of the door. And she was apologizing to him.

"Fräulein, I don't know what to make of you." He blurted out the words like a confounded schoolboy.

"Please, Lieutenant von Helsing, let us sit down," she said quietly. She sat down on a marble bench.

"Of course, Fräulein." He sank down beside her, adding, "It is I who should apologize. I have offended you."

"Come now," she said, smiling, "you know quite well you haven't." There was justice in that, he thought; she had responded so willingly at first to his kiss. "Please don't say these formal things to me; I am not used to them, you see. In fact, I am not used to men. I have known only my father and brother, my parents' friends, the professors at the academy."

She kept smiling up at him in the moonlight, and he was so enchanted with her little mouth, the innocent slant of her shapely head, that he melted again. And exultantly the knowledge repeated itself: she had known no other man.

"How old are you?" he demanded suddenly. Such bluntness would have been unthinkable with any girl of his *Kreis,* but this girl violated all rules.

"Eighteen," she replied simply.

"I see." He felt an overwhelming warm tide of tender, protective feeling. "You understand, Fräulein, the young ladies of Germany at eighteen are..."

"Both younger and older?"

Rik marveled at her quality of understanding. She had said, succinctly, what he had been only searching for.

"Yes. Yes, exactly that." He sat with his hands on his knees, thinking, I have never had such a conversation with a woman. She makes my head swim.

"You see, Lieutenant von Helsing," she said softly, "I should never have . . . let you kiss me at all. I have no desire, no plan, to live as other women do."

"What on earth do you mean, Fräulein?"

"I will pursue my music. That is all."

"Of course," he said warmly. "You will play and sing for your husband and children."

"No, no," she said sharply. "You don't understand."

"No, Fräulein, I do not. I only understand that you were born for love and happiness; what this other ghost is you pursue is beyond my understanding." He heard his own lyrical speech with a start of amazement; Brun, he thought wryly, would be proud of me—if he survived the shock. And Rik von Helsing felt laughter bubbling up inside him.

"What is it, lieutenant?" she asked, looking at his lips, twitching with repressed humor.

"I am thinking," he said frankly, "that no lady has ever said such things to me, or I to her. I am talking like one of those poets who lie under a tree and die of love."

She laughed. "Not quite. They are awful, aren't they? I've often wondered why 'sensitive men' must look like mushrooms."

Rik's laughter rose over hers, hearty and loud, and he reached out to touch her arm.

"I'm sorry, Lieutenant von Helsing, but I had better go in now. My parents will wonder what happened to me," Iris said, smoothly moving away.

He rose at once, all courtesy and formal concern. "Of course, Fräulein." He bowed with the click of the heels he had learned as a young boy in the military academy. But his heart sank that the moment of peculiar intimacy was at an end. Perhaps it was just as well; nothing could ever come of it, this sweet and utterly hopeless feeling of his. He would strike it off as a pleasant interlude which he would long remember.

But in the very next moment, when Iris Mark looked up at him again and smiled, Rik fancied he saw a certain reluctance in her face, a wistfulness that stirred his heart, inevitably rekindled his hot yearning. And he asked, "Fräulein, would it not be possible for us to meet again . . . for me to call upon you?"

She hesitated, and he heard his own heart thudding in his ears. Then she answered, "No, Lieutenant von Helsing. I do not think it would."

Dejected, he offered her his arm, and they walked out of the garden.

In the shadows Anita Mark, who had heard only their last words, gave an intense sigh of relief. Jonas, standing behind her, put his hands on her shoulders.

"You see," he said softly, "she is a very sensible child."

They had debated quietly between themselves whether to follow Iris into the garden. Iris had never shown any interest in a young man before, and when Anita saw her leave the room with the hard-eyed young Hussar her anxiety had been great.

"Let's go back," Jonas said, and they returned through the long French windows to the animated party. To Anita's relief, the young Hussar had disappeared; Iris was talking calmly and with apparent pleasure to one of Klimpsch's daughters.

"We have lost our token Hussar," said Abraham Gold to Jonas. "What could have possessed our host, old man?"

"I can't imagine," Jonas said lightly.

Anita, glancing at Iris, thought she saw her stiffen, and wished Abraham would lower his voice. She remembered the respect and gentleness the young officer had shown to Iris, and remarked in a contrary manner, "I thought he was a very good-looking and mannerly young man."

Jonas was staring at her in surprise, and now, Anita was convinced, she had attracted Iris's attention. Glancing at her daughter, Anita saw that Iris's eyes were wandering in their direction, and that she seemed to be having a difficult time following her companion's conversation.

Shortly Iris excused herself and came to join her parents. She sat down on the arm of her mother's chair, and Anita patted her daughter's knee and looked up at her.

The girl had an expression that Anita had never seen before—wistful and distant, yet very alert, as if she were waiting for them to continue their friendly debate.

"Well, well, Anita, what is all this?" Gold demanded with good humor. "Aren't you the lady who misses Munich, that 'sentimental' and 'self-indulgent' town, as the Berliners put it?"

"No," she said with spirit. "I am a lady who likes cities, and you know it, Abe. Besides, Berlin is so ugly it makes me feel at home. Remember, I'm a native of Chicago."

"Impossible," he said gallantly, "to connect you with that city."

"We are a family without a city, or a country, Mr. Gold." Jonas and Anita looked at Iris, surprised. It was rare for her to interrupt an adult conversation. And there was something haunted, a little lonely, in her words that disturbed Anita.

"Germany is our country now, Iris."

"Is it, Mother?" Iris's reply was not contentious, only thoughtful, and her voice still had that wistful sadness that was so uncharacteristic of her.

"Good for the Marks," said Gold cheerfully. "None of us"— he waved expansively around the room—"is a citizen of anything but the world."

Anita did not reply, but she wondered if that was really true. In these last years she had had a sharp homesickness at times for the United States. She missed the sharp, thin air, the aura of hurry and excitement.

And if they were in America now, she could not help thinking, she would not have felt the anxiety she had when Iris went into the garden with that handsome young soldier; the young man from another world where women were judged to be the rightful denizens of *Kirche* and *Küche,* church and kitchen.

But all was well, Anita concluded serenely, glancing up again at her beautiful daughter. Iris had told the young soldier she would not see him again. There was nothing that could stand in the way of Iris and her music. And yet a faint nagging voice inside Anita asked why it was necessary to keep reassuring herself about her daughter.

Chapter 16

LIKE THE SCORNFUL PAINTER whose studio overlooked the Tiergarten, the Marks also lived in view of the "Hohenzollerns in helmets." The statues were so pompous they made Iris laugh; she was as sophisticated as her parents about art. And still Iris had a soft spot for them. By now the stiff heroes had become as familiar to her as the trees she had climbed in Chicago when she was a child.

On a late-December afternoon in 1913, more than a year after the Klimpsch party, Iris paused at one of the long front windows of the luxurious living room, staring out at the statues. Their heads were masked in snow. They looked like misshapen ghosts, but suddenly Iris was struck with an unaccountable pang. There was something in the warriors' bearing that reminded her of Rik von Helsing.

Rik von Helsing had called four times after the Klimpsch party; her father and mother had received him politely, but Jon had hated him on sight. Iris herself felt his strong attraction, yet she was distant as her parents. Something always held her back. He had not called since last autumn, and Iris wondered if he had forgotten her.

Christmas was only two days away and already the wonderful smell of Frau Benz's pastries wafted up from the big kitchen downstairs. Iris heard her uncertain and homey contralto: she was singing "O Tannenbaum."

Christmas was the Germans' greatest festivity and was celebrated with fervor, more so than in any other country. For weeks Frau Benz and the servants had been getting ready, and there was an air of mystery and joyousness in the house. It infected even Jon, who always tried to seem more blasé than he was. He had dropped broad hints and was constantly trying to find out what the others had gotten him for Christmas.

Iris turned and looked at the gleaming Christmas tree: it was more than six feet tall and laden with glittering decorations. Iris usually loved the tree, loved the singing of "Stille Nacht" and all the old carols. But somehow this season it all left her cold. She turned back to the window with a feeling of confusion and restlessness.

"What are you doing, Iris?"

She started at the quiet sound of her little brother's voice. He had come in so softly she hadn't heard him. She said, "Looking at the snow. Were you in the workshop?"

"Yes." He came toward her with the cats, as always, at his heels—the old black cat, Adler, and the two young ones, Vikky and Wil. Their full names were Viktoria and Wilhelm, for members of the Kaiser's royal family. The Marks had gotten Adler as soon as they came to Germany to compensate Iris for her lost puppy. It had amused Jonas to name him for the famous Chicago architect. Now all the cats attached themselves to Jon, who was as quiet as they and could sit still for an hour while they lay on and about him.

Iris thought, Jon's like a cat himself. Neither she nor Jon looked like Anita, except that Jon had their mother's night-black hair. Otherwise they were both the image of Jonas Mark. Iris felt that her mother loved Jon best, though she would have been hard put to offer tangible evidence. Still, it made a difference in the way Iris felt about her brother.

"What are you working on?" she asked casually. Everything had to be pried from Jon, and the only way to reach him was to pretend indifference.

"My study in perpetual motion." The matter-of-fact answer from an eleven-year-old amazed Iris. But at least he was talking to her. "That's very interesting. Has Dad seen it?"

"Oh, sure. He gave me some good advice. I think I can make it run for ten years. But Dad said, 'So what? Who needs a wheel that runs ten years?' I guess I'll have to work on it some more."

"That's good. Anyway, ten years is on the way to forever." Iris thought how well her father understood Jon. He was so stubborn that opposition only spurred him on. He was already showing them the way he would go; he would be an engineer, a builder. But he was only interested in the way things worked, not how they looked, as Jonas and Anita were.

"Maybe I'll come down and take a look some time," Iris said.

"All right," Jon answered indifferently. "But you won't like it much; it's not pretty." He picked up Adler and embraced the old cat, carrying him to a hassock near the screened hearth. An inviting fire was casting orange light.

"Music scores aren't pretty, either," Iris retorted, "but something very beautiful comes from them. In a way they're like your plans and formulas; it's all structure and mathematics."

"I hadn't thought of it that way," Jon remarked with interest. He lay down on the hearth rug with his head near the old reclining cat. "Are you going to practice?" he asked in a lazy but apprehensive tone. "You haven't practiced yet today."

"I know," Iris admitted, feeling guilty. She generally practiced at least five hours a day; Jon would always flee to his workshop, or outdoors, when she did. He had a peculiar distaste for music, even when she was not practicing scales, which, she admitted silently, could drive anyone mad.

Her glance strayed to the grand piano in an alcove at the room's other end. The piano's surface held none of the typical clutter that so irritated musicians—framed pictures, shawls, vases of flowers. It was a bare, workmanlike instrument.

"I'm not going to practice for a while yet," she said to Jon. He gave a sigh of patent relief.

"Where's David today?" Jon visited his friend David, the son of the poet Gold, every day, or he came to the Marks'.

"Skating with that dumb Heinrich Kuller."

"Didn't you want to go?"

"With that *shlemiel*?"

Iris laughed. Jon had picked up a number of Yiddish expressions from David. She thought, Jon is uneasy with all the boys except David. It was an unsettling thought, but she made no further comment.

Jon was relaxed before the fire, staring into the flames, with Adler, Vikky and Wil curled up around him.

She wandered around the room and to the bookshelves.

"Did I put *Winnetou* back?" Jon called to her.

She scanned the shelves. "Yes. Do you want it?"

"Please." She took down the Karl May novel and tossed it on the hassock.

"Thanks," Jon said. He took up the book and began to read; the cats stirred and then resettled around him.

Iris looked along the shelves. She saw nothing that interested her. The new Forster novel, *Howards End,* had had some good passages about music; otherwise it had seemed incomprehensible—the women especially; one was free and independent, then married an insensitive man, and her sister became impregnated by a rather useless one. Well, it made no difference; she really should practice anyhow.

She heard the doorbell and was going to answer when Frau Benz's heavy footsteps sounded on the stairs. She listened to the opening door, Frau Benz's respectful greeting and the murmur of a man's voice.

"Come in," Frau Benz said with unusual excitement, "I shall inquire."

She entered, and Iris noticed a pleased and conspiratorial expression on her broad face. Her small green eyes were very bright. "Leutnant von Helsing wishes to see you," she announced, and to Iris's amusement she gave the military title an impressive sound.

Iris felt her own excitement. But she answered calmly, "Very well. Ask him to join us."

"Gut." Frau Benz smiled. "I shall bring some tea and my new pastries. And some wine, you think?"

"Whatever you like." Iris assumed a cool indifference. But as soon as Frau Benz had left, she went to a mirror and glanced at her reflection, smoothing her tawny hair. Her amber eyes looked big and shining, and her warm russet dress made her skin look very white.

Frau Benz opened the doors again, announcing, "Leutnant von Helsing," like a footman at a royal reception.

He had removed his hat and greatcoat and was dressed very formally in a splendid, tight-fitting uniform that made his shoulders seem enormous and his booted legs very long; the jacket showed off his trim waist and magnificent torso. He looked as hard and trim as steel, but there was a warm light in his blue eyes when he looked at Iris. He bowed with great correctness, clicking his heels. "Fräulein Mark, Meister Mark," he added genially, with a smile for Jon.

"How are you?" Iris asked casually, smiling. To her consternation, Jon did not answer von Helsing's greeting, but got up and stalked out of the room, followed by the cats. "Won't you sit down?" Iris said, chagrined. She noticed that he had reddened with vexation. "I must apologize for my brother," she said. "He is at a...difficult age."

"Never mind." Rik von Helsing smiled at her and sat down

beside her on the sofa. "It is of no importance." He was staring at her intently, his sharp eyes taking in her face and dress and hair. His keen glance dropped to her hands; she was making a nervous, embarrassed gesture. "Truly, it doesn't matter. Nothing matters except to see you."

She was taken aback but was saved from replying by Frau Benz's bustling entrance. The housekeeper was carrying a heavy silver tray laden with tea things and a plate of cakes.

"Ah! How pleasant. All this is very festive. You are most kind." Frau Benz beamed, fluttering about them.

"Perhaps the Herr Leutnant would prefer wine?"

"No, no. Tea is fine. *Danke.*"

When the excited Frau Benz had poured their tea and left them, von Helsing set down his tea untouched and repeated, "Nothing matters except to see you."

Iris still did not answer, but she felt her warm excitement grow. His nearness made her forget all the reasons she had found for avoiding him—he had a crisp, clean smell of leather and fine wool, a tangy scent of lemon from his freshly barbered face, and one of his big hands rested lightly on the sofa near her hand. She glanced at it, and the other hand resting on his muscular, high-booted leg. His presence seemed to fill the big room, and she remembered his proud, easy posture in the mounted parade.

And she realized with amazement that she had missed him, that she was glad he was here, sitting beside her. She wanted to touch him.

He must have felt it, because he reached out and took her hand in his; the hand was very warm and felt as hard as his body looked. Iris did not withdraw her hand; his touch ignited her skin. She had never felt like that before, not even when he had kissed her in the Klimpsches' garden.

"Iris," he said softly. "Iris." She loved the strange way he pronounced her name; it touched her and made her feel a peculiar tenderness. "I have been thinking of nothing but you, nothing...all these months, ever since last summer. Have you thought of me at all?" He leaned toward her, and their faces were very close.

"Yes," she admitted. "Yes, I have."

"You have, you have!" he said, smiling, and suddenly his face looked very young to her, and gentle. He raised his hands to her face and turned it upward very slowly for his kiss.

It was not like the other time at all, she reflected dizzily, after he had taken his mouth from hers. No, this time it was

211

like floating, like flying. Quickly he bent to her and kissed her again, less gently, and Iris could not draw away. She was captured, wholly, boneless and compliant in the hard circle of his arms. The whole world centered on the feel of his mouth, and radiated outward from their embrace.

When it ended, it was, for Iris, like the silence after music; she was vibrant with it and exalted and could find no word beyond a helpless exhalation of the breath, and she clung to him, making a sound like one moaning word as she leaned against him, with her lips against his neck, tasting the clean acrid tang of his skin where the pulse beat drummed under his ear.

"Gott, Gott," she heard him whisper, at last, and felt the shaking of his body. "How I have waited for this, and waited," he said softly, his hand caressing her side.

She leaned against him, clinging to him, and her lips brushed the tanned skin of his neck above the high, stiff collar of his uniform. She said in a muffled voice, "I have never known anything like this, Rik. I've never felt such a thing for a man."

He held her close, kissing the top of her head. "I know."

"How?" She moved back and looked up at his face. He was looking down at her, smiling, and there were gentle lines around his mouth that surprised her. He seemed like another man, nothing like the proud, cool man she had seen on the shining horse in the parade.

"Oh, there are ways, my dear." He drew her head onto his shoulder, and went on, "It makes me feel like a king...a pasha, to know that I am the first. Oh, Iris." He gently lifted her head and turned up her chin to study her face. "You have big golden eyes like a little lioness," he said. "You are so warm, so warm, with all your golden color and your dress like the fire."

Iris looked into his eyes for a long moment. Then she said in a sudden and impulsive way, "Let's go out, Rik."

He raised his brows. "So suddenly, just like that?"

"Yes. Just like that. I want to walk in the snow with you."

"But my dear girl, I want to greet your parents in a proper fashion. If you are going to allow me to call on you—and you are, aren't you?" He looked at her earnestly.

"Yes," she said hesitantly. "Yes, of course."

"Well, then, it is only right that I present myself to them... *hein?*"

"Not today, Rik. Not just now."

"But what is the matter? Your parents...they disapprove of me? Is that it?"

She felt a deep chagrin. How could she tell him how they felt—that he was utterly alien, the product of an outdated and incomprehensible circle that both amused and horrified them? "Not really," Iris answered. "There are just so many...things that enter in..." She broke off vaguely, frowning. Then she repeated urgently, "Please, let us go out now and take a walk."

He stared at her a moment, then he smiled and stood up. "Very well, then, let us go out for a walk. But you must wrap up well; it is very cold."

"I will," she promised. They went into the hall. She took a fur cloak from the closet, and he helped her into it. Then he put on his greatcoat and cap.

Frau Benz came hurrying out of the pantry. "You are going out, my dear?" She studied Iris's face and then Rik von Helsing's; her expression was so eager and approving that Iris almost laughed.

"Just for a walk," she said. "Will you tell my mother and father *I* went for a walk?" She emphasized the pronoun a little, and Frau Benz understood.

"Of course, my dear child, I'll tell them *you* went for a walk." She, too, gave the pronoun emphasis, and a broad grin lit her face.

"I hope," she added in a timid way, as if she knew she was being presumptuous, "that the Herr Leutnant will come again soon."

"Perhaps for Christmas," Iris said impulsively.

He beamed. "I would be honored."

"Ah, that is delightful," Frau Benz said.

Iris looked back at her as they were leaving. The old lady was staring after them, and her smile was like a blessing. But already Iris regretted the invitation, for casual acquaintances were not invited to the Marks' on Christmas Day. But then, when Rik smiled at her, Iris forgot everything except the present moment.

"Merry Christmas, Mr. Klimpsch, Mr. Gold," Iris murmured politely to the guests coming in. She glanced behind them to see if Rik was coming in, and made a nervous gesture with her hand, fingering the brooch her parents had given her for Christmas.

It was a unique and striking piece, fashioned by the Bel-
213

gian architect Henri van de Velde, who was living in Germany. The brooch was gold designed in a graceful whorl, like a tongue of fire, and was set with a golden-orange honey topaz. Iris's dress matched the topaz; she had purposely worn the same one she had worn when she had first received Rik von Helsing.

"What's the matter?" Anita asked her in an undertone in the intervals of greeting guests. "You're very tense today."

"Nothing, Mother, nothing at all," Iris said sharply. Anita studied her briefly and remarked, "You're not wearing your green Christmas dress, I see." She herself was in a simple, vivid dress of scarlet; it was traditional for them to wear the festive colors on Christmas Day.

"This dress matches the topaz," Iris said.

"So it does; it looks beautiful." Anita's comment was gentle and calm, but Iris felt that her mother was still curious about her mood.

"Oh, there's Emma," Iris said quickly, and moved away to greet the new arrival. Soon her mother was caught up with other guests, and it was a relief to escape her scrutiny.

Her friend Emma Klimpsch was exclaiming over Iris's brooch when the voices of arriving guests were heard in the hall. Iris recognized the effusive greeting of Frau Benz; there was a flood of German, then the deep and measured voice of Rik von Helsing. Iris's heart began to beat so heavily that she felt a little dizzy; the drum and whirr of the beat was loud in her ears, like the wings of a giant moth.

She wished she had never invited him here: it could only mean disaster. Already she could imagine his reaction to the conversation of their circle. She remembered vividly what had happened at the Klimpsch party—the stiffness of his disapproval, his great discomfort.

But as soon as he entered the room, and she saw his face again, nothing else mattered except that he was there; the confusion and ambivalence of the last two days melted away.

Iris was near the door, so his eyes went to her at once: he looked bigger and taller than ever, and a gentle, happy smile was on his lips, softening the strong lines of his face. To Iris's relief, he was not in uniform, which would have been an additional affront to the antimilitary gathering.

For one fantasy moment Rik became an eligible young man welcome in her parents' house. But Iris saw Emma Klimpsch stiffen, and caught the look of dismay on Anita's face, across the room. Worst of all, Jon, who was wolfing down

214

pastries in the company of David Gold, paused in his eating and stared at Rik. Jon's face was hostile and angry.

All these things flashed on Iris's vision before she had time to greet Rik. His demeanor, the set of his shoulders and the straightness of his posture told the world that he was a soldier; nothing could disguise it. Iris smiled and held out her hand, welcoming him in German.

"Merry Christmas, Rik," she said in a clear and friendly voice. There was a sudden silence around them, then the well-bred guests all started talking again at once. Anita approached from across the long, brilliantly lit room.

"Merry Christmas," Anita said to Rik, holding out her own hand. Iris was proud of her mother's self-possession, ashamed that she had not told her he had been invited.

"Frau Mark," Rik said, kissing her hand, "it is kind of you to receive me on this particular day." The kiss was accompanied by a bow and the Prussian click of heels the Marks ridiculed but that Iris secretly liked. She noticed then that Rik was holding two square, flat packages under his arm. He handed one to Anita and one to Iris; the packages were obviously handkerchief boxes. It was so proper a gift that Anita could not be offended even if she were as correct as the Kaiserin.

Iris stifled a grin and thanked Rik warmly; she held the box in her hand, eager as a child to open it. Anita thanked Rik with a little less warmth and put the box down on a table.

Jonas came up to them, and Anita said politely, "I think you know my husband, Lieutenant...Jonas Mark?"

"I have had the honor," Rik said, and bowed again. "Your great artistry is much admired in Germany, Herr Mark."

Iris glanced at her father: his lean face was a study. There was a faint gleam of irony in his sharp hazel eyes, but he said easily, "It's good of you to say so, lieutenant. Will you have something—some refreshments, a drink?"

"Thank you, Herr Mark." Iris was relieved that Rik did not bow again; he seemed on the verge of it. She could feel a slight unease in the people surrounding them; they seemed less relaxed and festive, and their voices grew softer.

In a lull, Iris heard someone say irritably, "What about that Hamburg speech...and Germany's 'Place in the Sun.' You know damned well what that means."

They were talking about the Kaiser's speech, and she glanced at Rik, who was standing at the sideboard with her father, accepting a glass of brandy. Rik's expression was

215

pained: he was a member of the Kaiser's Honor Guard. She could imagine what it cost him to hear such a traitorous remark.

And suddenly she realized in full what it all meant: he cared enough for her to brave anything for her sake. The realization was so deep and sudden that the force of it stunned her.

When Rik turned from the sideboard, with a courteous word to her father, and came to join her by the fire, his blue gaze was fixed on her, and he looked open and young and beseeching. She realized she had never seen a man so beautiful—there was no other word for it—and never had any man so thrilled her, or touched her.

Iris thought fearfully, I must love him. I must love him, too. She wondered if he could read what was in her mind: he stared at her intently for a moment before he asked, "Can I get you some wine?"

"No, no, thank you," she answered shyly. She was still holding the flat package in her hands. And quite abruptly, like a child, she said, "May I open it?"

"Of course," he said, and he smiled at her way of asking it. "It is only a little remembrance...it is not what I wanted to give you, Iris. But I could not risk offending your mother."

She started to say that her mother's ideas were not as old-fashioned as that, but she didn't know how he would construe that, so she said nothing, but opened the flat box with careful fingers. Inside were a half-dozen gossamer handkerchiefs, bordered with fragile lace, delicately embroidered with the letter I.

"They are beautiful," she said softly. "Beautiful."

"The Belgian nuns make them," he said dismissively. "I want to be allowed to give you something that matters."

She did not know how to answer that, and was uneasily aware that her face was flushed, that her expression might reflect the seriousness of what he was saying. Almost as a reflex, she glanced at her mother, who was talking to Mrs. Gold, David's mother. At that moment Anita happened to glance at Iris, and then she turned back to Mrs. Gold and said something in a low voice.

"Do you understand me, Iris?"

She looked up at him; he was standing before her, looking down at her, and his face looked like a young god of the Teutons. Iris thought of Lohengrin and Parsifal when she studied his brief, shining hair, fresh, ruddy skin and clear blue eyes. His fine, heroic features were classically perfect—the thin, shapely mouth, the straight nose and well-shaped head. Iris continued to stare up at him, and she felt a new and alien emotion, an utter letting-go. She wanted to draw his face down to hers and kiss his mouth, feel his hard arms about her again, press her body to his fine and muscular young body, never to let him go.

"Yes," she said at last, "yes, I understand you. But I..."

He leaned down a little more, smiling, looking into her eyes, whispering in a meaning way, "But you are afraid. Afraid because our lives, our worlds, are so different. Is that it?"

She nodded, looking down.

"No, no, Iris, look at me. Look at me, please," he insisted softly. And she obeyed with reluctance, for to look at him was to fall under his spell; to look at him was to lose her reason. Yet she could not help doing so, for his eyes and his face pulled at her, the nearness of him dragged upon her senses. He continued in the same low, persuasive voice, "I know you could not have kissed me the way you did if you did not care. That is true, isn't it, Iris?"

She looked down and was silent, struggling to find words. Finally she looked up, feeling the magnet of his searching eyes, and said in a solemn voice, "That is true."

When she said that his eyes lit, and he said softly, "Iris, Iris, you must let me..." He reached out his hand toward her.

"Leutnant von Helsing, I believe." The slurred greeting crossed with Rik's earnest words, muffling them. It was Morris Gold, David's older brother. He and Iris were in several classes together at the conservatory; Morris's anti-Prussian feelings were all too well known. Iris felt apprehensive. Morris had had too much to drink, which did not often happen, and Iris particularly regretted that it had happened this evening.

The intonation of Morris's greeting had evidently not escaped Rik. He straightened with a cold, formal expression on his face and ignored Morris Gold's outstretched hand.

"You have the advantage of me, *mein Herr*," Rik said stiffly. "I don't believe we've been introduced."

"This is Morris Gold, Rik. I thought you might have met at the Klimpsches'." Iris made the introduction uneasily.

"I'm sorry, I did not remember." Rik's voice was still coldly polite, but the implication was all too clear: Morris Gold was

217

a nonentity. Everything in Rik von Helsing's manner said so.

The angry, sensitive Morris caught his meaning, and with renewed anxiety Iris saw an excited flush creep over his thin face.

"Iris, my dear, your guest is right out of the *Simplicissimus*." She made an indignant gesture; he referred to the German liberals' magazine that ran antimilitarist cartoons. "I'm surprised that we are not even safe here from the barbarians."

"You're drunk, Morris," Iris said in a low voice. "I'm tired of your parlor liberalism. If you are so interested in politics, why don't you engage in them?" She had not meant to say so much, but her anger got the better of her. She glanced up at Rik; he seemed to be holding himself in with great difficulty, and she was afraid of what might happen next. Dear God, she thought, don't let Morris touch him. They will go somewhere and fight, and then...

She saw Abraham Gold approaching. He said to his eldest son in a stern, disgusted voice, "We are leaving, Morris." Then to Rik he said, "I beg your pardon for this exhibition, Leutnant von Helsing. My son has had too much wine. This is most improper behavior in the home of a friend."

Rik bowed coldly to Abraham Gold, but did not answer. He was still glaring at Morris; his hard blue gaze had not left the younger man's face.

"What do you mean, Father?" Morris cried out indignantly. They had attracted everyone's attention now; the sculptor Klimpsch and Jonas Mark were moving to Abraham Gold's side. Jonas put his hand on Morris's arm and said something to him in a soft voice.

Morris shook off Jonas's arm and said, "I won't be quiet. And I won't go home until I tell this toy soldier what I think of the Kaiser. When he came to the university last year in all his regalia, he looked worse than his caricatures."

"You have insulted my monarch," Rik said in a dangerously quiet voice. "I shall not forget it, Herr Morris Gold."

Klimpsch took hold of Morris's arm, and he and Jonas steered him from the room. Iris was trembling with agitation and fear. She had never imagined such rage as the rage she saw now on Rik's handsome face.

"I'm sorry, I'm sorry," she told him in a whisper.

At first she thought he had not heard her, because his glare followed Morris from the room; he looked like a man

218

almost hypnotized by his own anger. But then he seemed to bring himself under control and he looked down at her, his eyes still blazing. But there was a slight smile on his mouth when he answered. "It is not your fault. It is in no way your fault. But I must go now; I must go before more is said, Iris. Don't you see, I cannot tolerate it?"

She nodded miserably.

He took her hand boldly, although he must have been aware that the others were staring at them, and he urged her in an almost inaudible voice, "My love, do not let these things come between us. This has nothing to do with us, nothing. Please, please say you will meet me tomorrow. You will, won't you?"

As she had before, Iris felt mesmerized by him; when those commanding, pale-blue eyes stared at her, she could not deny him. At last she said, "Yes. Yes, I will meet you, Rik."

"You make me so happy, my dear, so happy." He smiled broadly and added, "I know you are still on holiday from the school. At noon then, at the Rheingold. We will have luncheon together. *Ja?*"

"Jawohl." She smiled back at him, despite the stares of her parents' guests, totally indifferent to what her mother and father might be thinking.

"Gut. Noon, then. Now I must make my excuses to your mother and father."

With a quick bow to her, he strode across the room. Smiling and with perfect poise, he received the apologies of Jonas and Anita with a dismissive wave of his hand, and thanked them profusely for the evening. Iris watched in proud amazement to see his self-possession, his flawless courtesy in the face of Morris Gold's declaration and the surrounding hostility.

Without bothering to excuse herself, she went to the hall just in time to see his broad, straight back and shoulders as he disappeared through the front door. Frau Benz was standing there, staring after him. The great door was still ajar in spite of the freezing night. She turned when she heard Iris come into the hall and gave Iris a look of sad compassion.

Chapter 17

ONE MORNING IN FEBRUARY, as Rik was running down the stairs to go out, he heard his father on the telephone. In tones of deep respect the general was saying, "Yes, sir. Yes, Baron. I will see to it, be assured."

Good, Rik thought exultantly. I'll get away before he catches me. He knew that his father was going to question him about his activities; General Friedrich von Helsing was no fool, and the stories about Kiki the dancer had not taken him in, Rik was sure.

Just before Rik got to the front door, the general said, "Where are you off to at this hour? You're not due at the barracks—you're becoming a very early riser."

Rik paused impatiently with his hand on the doorknob. He had an early appointment with Iris before her class at the conservatory. He had not returned to the Marks' since the ill-fated Christmas party, but he and Iris had managed to see each other almost every day since then. Even at this moment, in his headlong haste and irritation, Rik's body grew warm at the thought of her.

They had still not become lovers; as painful as it was for him, Rik thought with amusement at his own perversity, the highly charged situation made her even more adorable to him. He went to each rendezvous with the perpetual hope that this would be the one, the occasion of his possessing her. He knew very well that she wanted him as much as he wanted her; still she was hesitant.

"I thought I'd go out early today; Dabih needs some exercise," Rik said. Dabih was Rik's magnificent gelding. Like most young men of his position, he rode his own horse, not the army's mount.

"Nonsense. Do you think I don't know that there are corporals and privates for that at the stables? Come in here. I want to talk to you, and I am not going to put it off any longer."

General von Helsing walked back and forth across the carpet with his hands behind his back; half apprehensive, half amused, Rik almost expected to see a riding crop emerge at any moment, held in the hidden hands. He smiled.

"What is so amusing to you?" the general demanded in an exasperated manner. "I have several matters to discuss with you, matters of import."

Rik made his face solemn and waited, silent.

"That was Baron von Lyncker, the adjutant, on the telephone." Rik nodded. "I assume," the general continued dryly, "that you are aware of the arrival of the Princess Viktoria Luise and Prince Ernst August in Berlin."

"I could hardly be unaware," Rik returned as dryly as the general, "when nothing else has been talked of for weeks."

Apparently he had not hidden his boredom, for the general frowned darkly and snapped, "It is a great honor to be consulted by the Baron. We will be part of the welcoming guard tomorrow at 0830 hours, at the Potsdam Station, when the royal party arrives in the city."

Rik made an involuntary gesture of annoyance, blurting, "Damnit."

"Do you have a more urgent appointment?" the general asked sarcastically.

Rik was silent; he longed to say that he did have a far more urgent appointment. He and Iris were in the habit of meeting at that very hour before she went to the conservatory each weekday morning.

Instead he said, "No."

"That is fortunate." The general's voice was heavy with sarcasm. "The royal princes, the cabinet, and HQ staff will be on hand, as well. Not to mention the lord mayor, the commandant and the state ministers. We will be on the platform with the regimental band when the party arrives. The Brandenburg Hussars will be in front of the depot to escort their majesties and the royal bridal pair. The other four squadrons will be at Lustgarten—mounted. You will be in parade uniform tomorrow morning at 0600 for my inspection."

God, Rik thought, six o'clock in the morning. That killed tonight, too. It annoyed him very much when his father talked

221

to him at home as if they were in the barracks or on the parade ground. Yet this manner of a general father with a lieutenant son had become an integral part of their days together; Rik had gotten used to it. But now, when there was Iris...

"And this matter of your mysterious 'appointments,'" the general said abruptly. "I had no idea that Kiki Schmidt kept such hours." The comment was almost a question; it was probing, suspicious; it demanded an answer.

"She doesn't," Rik said briefly.

"Who is it, then?" the general asked. "If you'd been exercising Dabih this much, the horse would be dead with exhaustion. I demand to know, Rik. There are rumors that you've been seen with that American girl...what's her name? Mark. Iris Mark. Is this true?"

Rik stood up and faced his father. "Yes, it is true. I love her and I intend to marry her."

The general stared at his tall son for a shocked instant; they stood eye to eye, looking at each other belligerently.

"You must be mad." The general turned away from Rik. Despite the early hour he strode to a sideboard and poured himself a dollop of brandy. He drank it down and, replacing the goblet, turned to his defiant son.

"Do you know what you're saying? You actually want to marry the daughter of this...wild bohemian artist?"

"Herr Mark is hardly a bohemian," Rik protested hotly. "He is one of the most respected architects in Germany...he is known throughout the world."

"Gott in Himmel, Rikard!" The general's face was plum-color with ire, and his voice was rising. "These people associate with anarchists, with liberals! They laugh at everything that is good and proper. Why, the Marks are actually friends with that traitor Georg Simmel!"

Rik did not know how to answer that attack: the professor of philosophy Simmel, who lectured at the university, was a well-known antimilitarist.

Rik shuddered to think of what the general would say about the statements of Morris Gold. But none of that, he thought stubbornly, had anything to do with Iris. He maintained a sullen quiet.

"Answer me!" the general bellowed. "How can you think of marrying a girl with such connections?"

"I love her," Rik answered defiantly.

"'Love'!" his father repeated with contempt. "You have the

itch that all young stallions have, that's all. And you call it 'love.' You are too young to know what the word means. Duty is more important than love. It will be years before you are responsible enough for marriage. Take her to bed, and get it out of your system."

Rik stiffened. "She is not a Kiki, to be taken to bed."

"Are you so sure?" Suddenly the general's anger seemed to evaporate; Rik thought, He is becoming a father again instead of a general. But the abrupt transition did not move Rik, as it sometimes had in the past.

"I am going to marry her," he repeated in a calm, quiet tone that renewed his father's anger.

"Not while I live," the general declared, his face reddening once more.

Rik did not answer. In stony silence he put on his cap and greatcoat, buttoning the coat with deliberation. He did not look again at his father, but strode from the parlor into the hall. Going out, he slammed the door.

Iris looked at her watch; Rik was very late. She peered out of the window of the coffeehouse. The glass was steamed over; it was freezing outside, warm within. She rubbed at the pane and looked down the snowy street. There he was, striding along toward her, so fast that the tails of his Hussar's coat flew behind him in the wind.

She felt the warmth, the wild exhilaration, she always felt when she saw him; how beautiful he was! He entered the warm coffeehouse, smiling at her, snatching his cap from his head.

"My love," he said, and bent to kiss her unashamedly before the curious students, the staring proprietor, the interested waiters. They always stare at us, Iris thought. She wondered if it was because of who they were, or merely that they were so in love that their presence drew the eye. It had always made her a little uneasy: it would do no good for either Jonas Mark or General von Helsing to hear about them.

But she thrust the unwelcome thoughts away, and gave herself up to the pleasure of the moment. Rik was sitting across from her, holding both her hands, staring into her eyes. And although he was smiling, she detected something else in his manner—an anxiety in his eyes, a tension, possibly anger.

"What is it?" she asked.

223

"I can never fool you, can I?" Rik grinned at her, and his hold on her fingers tightened. "I had it out with my father."

She took a deep, trembling breath, feeling great conflict within her. She wanted to know what had happened, yet she dreaded it. These last two months had been enchanted, days and nights from a fairy tale. And now the trouble and hate, the contention and anger would enter in. "What happened?"

"We . . . strongly disagreed about my choice," he began tactfully. "I told him that I intend to marry you."

His statement was so confident, so matter-of-fact, that she could not help smiling and asking in a teasing voice, "And I have nothing to say about that?"

Rik studied her, his expression chagrined and anxious. "But you will marry me, won't you? You will marry me, Iris." It was a declaration, not an inquiry.

"Nothing I have said to you for the last two months has made any impression at all," she said with mock irritation, but she could not hide the tenderness in her voice.

"That is precisely true," he answered, grinning. "We are meant to be together; anything else is nonsense, trivia. You have told me you love me. That is enough."

"Is it, Rik?" she asked him soberly. "Can you imagine me as a soldier's wife?"

"I imagine you as *my* wife, Iris. That is all I need to imagine. And I have told you time and again"—he lowered his voice after glancing at the students at the next table—"I cannot bear it much longer, the way things are with us."

She looked down, coloring. Every time they had met, it became harder and harder to say goodbye. She felt it as keenly as he. Now she said, "You know how I feel."

"Yes, I do know, my darling. So why should we wait any longer? Now it is out in the open. I will go and speak to your parents tonight."

"Tonight!" She looked away from him for a moment, in confusion. "Oh, Rik, tonight . . ."

"Look at me, Iris. Look at me."

It was always his command; he had learned that when she looked at him, he won. Reluctantly she turned her face from the window and looked at his eyes. They were commanding her, cajoling her, capturing her will. As she had done so many times before, she nodded and said, "Very well. Tonight."

He was elated. "That is wonderful. Wonderful."

Iris already regretted her promise. I can't do this to them,

224

she thought with rising panic; I can't tell them this so abruptly. I've got to have time.

"At what hour may I call?" he urged her.

"Rik...my dear, it cannot be tonight," she said slowly.

"Why not?" He reached out and grasped her hand. "What is it? Is it that you do not love me after all...that you don't want to marry me? Tell me, Iris." His anxiety was so great that she was deeply touched.

"Oh, Rik, you know it isn't that." She tried to put all her love for him, her tenderness, into her voice, and in the pressure of her fingers on his hand. He relaxed a little, but he still looked fearful and unhappy. "I must have a little time, that's all. Can it be...tomorrow night, at least?"

He let out a great sigh of relief. "Of course, my darling. Of course. And what hour can I come tomorrow night, then?" She laughed softly at his insistence, at his obdurate questions. He was exactly like a small child demanding to know exactly when he would be taken to the circus.

"At eight tomorrow night," she said firmly. "Now I really must go, and so must you."

"Yes," he said absently and with distaste. As he was signaling for the bill, he added, "And then there is this rotten nonsense tomorrow morning." He looked at the bill, threw some coins down on the table and rose to help Iris into her coat.

"What is that?" She watched him as he put on his greatcoat and cap.

Buttoning up his heavy military coat, he replied, "I have to be on hand at eight-thirty at Potsdam Station. The princess and her new husband are coming in. I won't be able to see you in the morning."

"It's all right, my dear. I understand." She marveled at how much his attitude had changed in the last two months—the arrival of royal visitors would never, in the past, have been "rotten nonsense." A few weeks ago he would have been aroused to patriotic fervor. Now it was only an onerous duty that kept him from seeing her; Iris's heart was light with the knowledge, and she felt a new hope and optimism for their future.

As they left the coffeehouse, he looked down and said admiringly, "You look so alive, so vibrant, all of a sudden. May I hope it is because of tomorrow night?"

She took his arm and squeezed it. "Of course it is that...and something else. It was the way you referred to

225

the duty you have tomorrow morning. You have changed so much, Rik. And it makes me very happy."

He looked thoughtful, then he smiled broadly and nodded quickly, several times. "*Ja, ja.* I have." He lifted up his face to the softly drifting snow and laughed with a sound of carefree happiness. "It is because you have become my Kaiserin."

She was so elated that when he left her at the entrance to the music school, she fairly floated in. And when the cacophony of instruments struck her ears—strident saws of violins, crying of horns and hammering of pianos at their maddening scales—it sounded like the most beautiful love song in the world.

The next afternoon she hurried home to prepare herself for the evening, but she found a telegram addressed to her on the hall table. It was from Rik. It said that he had been ordered to Königsberg and he had had to leave at noon. "Do not give me up, my love," the long message ended. "Nothing will part us, not even this."

Königsberg! It was an immeasurable distance away, near the Baltic Sea. Iris crushed the telegram in her hand and ran up the stairs to her room. She lay down on the bed, feeling the silent tears stream down her face. I cannot bear it, she thought, I cannot bear to be away from him for a single day. The general had arranged his transfer, she knew.

At least, she concluded with a kind of despairing relief, she had not told her parents yet. There had not been time the night before; she had planned to speak to her mother late this afternoon. It was just as well, for she knew now, no matter what Rik said, that they would never be married.

The next week was the most difficult one of Iris's life: she went about her daily routines like an automaton. She had received one long, impassioned letter from Rik, but for several days she had not had the heart to answer it. How could she tell him that she utterly despaired, in the face of his constant assurances that they would somehow be together again? She knew she would have to answer soon, but she postponed it for another day, and then another.

Her parents seemed to be studying her covertly, and her mother remarked on her lack of appetite and lifeless manner. Frau Benz attempted new culinary delights to try to arouse Iris's appetite, but she picked at her food. The smell and taste of food were abhorrent. Iris suspected that Frau Benz knew something of what had happened; her manner was gentler than ever, and she hinted more than once that Iris could confide in her. But miserably Iris kept silent.

Other letters arrived from Rik, and at last Iris felt obliged to answer him. His inquiries had been so desperate, his letters so urgent, that she tried to reply in kind, to put in the letters all of the tenderness and desire she had felt in his presence. But something prevented her from referring to the future, because she did not believe there was one for them.

In the second week a parcel came from Königsberg, a small velvet box that she opened with trembling fingers. It was an exquisite garnet ring, a bright blood-red stone set in an antique setting of gold filigree. She knew it was his birthstone; he had been born in January. With the ring Rik had sent a note that tore at her heart. "This ring is my heart's blood and the fire we have between us." She put the ring on her right hand, feeling a resurgence of hope. That night she wrote Rik a very different kind of letter, in which she spoke of the time they would be together. She hoped it would atone for the other letters and resolved that she would never take the ring from her hand. Her mother noticed it but said nothing.

He had told her he would not be granted leave until May. When she thought of the intervening months, Iris was almost overtaken by the old despair. Meanwhile her concert was scheduled for April, and she was obliged to practice long hours daily, to work harder than she ever had in her life. But she welcomed the grueling practice, for it left her too tired at night to do anything but fall quickly asleep, without brooding, to sleep so deeply she hardly even dreamed.

The snows of February melted in the quickening wind of March; she continued to receive long, regular letters from him, which she always answered the same day. Her life had become a succession of practice and letters; she was alive only in her music and in thoughts of Rik von Helsing. Her parents, her brother, even Frau Benz seemed like strangers to her. But fortunately her preoccupation passed without too much remark; Jonas and Anita assumed that she was bending all her energies toward the vital concert, and left her very much alone. She could feel their relief over the continued absence of Rik von Helsing.

One wild and windy morning, she noted absently that it was the ides of March. She put on a bright russet cape, with a great hood, to liven her spirits and to shelter herself from the biting wind, and set out for the coffeehouse near the conservatory. When she arrived at the café, she saw a tall young man approaching from the end of the street. He was also wearing a cape, but it was dark gray; the cape was whipped by the wind and its high, upturned collar, and a large-billed cap, nearly obscured the young man's face. But there was something very familiar about his bearing and his walk; he had the air of a soldier and a horseman. When the wind blew the cape back from his legs, and it fluttered like a dark banner in the gale, it revealed lean muscular legs in close-fitting breeches and black boots to the knee.

The man caught sight of her and began to hurry toward her, then he was running. She could see his face now, below the great dark cap. It was Rik.

She cried out and ran toward him. He held out his arms and she thrust herself against him, crying out wildly, weeping with happiness. The impact of their meeting bodies was so strong that it jarred him backward on his booted feet, and he said hoarsely, "Gott, Gott, Iris. Iris, Liebchen," and his voice sounded broken and strange, but his blue eyes were blazing with excitement.

She stayed against him, wrapped in his arms, for a still, long moment, finding no more words to say. Then in the sight of all the passersby, he lifted her face to his and kissed her with sweet ferocity. All the desperate loneliness of their days apart, all the starved wanting, was in the kiss, and she was weakened and dizzied by it.

Finally, when he let her go, she looked closely at his face for the first time, and exclaimed. "Oh, my God, you look so tired, my dear." His ordinarily fresh-looking skin had a muddy tinge and his bright eyes were dark-circled. There were fine new lines between his brows and around his mouth.

"I am, I am," he admitted. "I have not slept since the night before last. I could not sleep for thinking of you."

"Come in here," she urged him, indicating the coffeehouse, "and let us sit down."

"No, no, my love, not here. Let's get a cab. If I can't be alone with you, at once, I'll explode."

He took her by the arm and led her to the curb, where he hailed a passing vehicle.

When they were inside, and he had given an address to the driver, he took her in his arms and kissed her again, deeply and with a terrible hunger.

Breathless, he leaned back a moment, then said, "We are going to my friend Brun's flat. We can be alone there. I have managed to get a three-day pass. Think of it, three whole days."

Her heart hammered with excitement. She must think of a way, some way, to spend all of those days alone with him. Perhaps Clara would... but his nearness excited her so she could not complete the thought. She moved into the circle of his arm and leaned against him.

The cab drew up before a building Iris knew; she recognized it as an apartment building designed by her father, in 1902. But she was so preoccupied with Rik that the irony of this fact made only a fleeting impression.

Rik unlocked the front door and led her into a stark and beautiful room, the walls, ceiling and fireplace divided into simple geometric patterns. It was all quietness and peace and polished wood. A heavy blood-red drapery of velvet covered part of one wall.

"Sit down, my love," she said to Rik. Exhausted, he sank into a gray velvet armchair by the fire and, taking off his cap, threw it on the floor. He leaned back a moment, without even removing his heavy cape, and closed his eyes.

"Come here," he said. She obeyed, and he drew her down onto his lap. She relaxed against him, and he put his hand under her chin, turning her face to his. Then he kissed her repeatedly, again and again, making deep, urgent sounds in his throat. She could feel herself melting against him, and the total dissolution of her will.

There was nothing else now, nothing but his arms and his mouth, and she knew quite surely, without fear or hesitation, that they would now be wholly together, as they had never been before.

Boldly she rose and held out her hand to him. "Come," she said, knowing that he realized the implication of the one soft, simple word.

He stared at her with wonder, almost as if he could not believe his own ears, then with bright eyes he rose quickly from the deep chair and threw off his heavy cape. He fumbled at the fastening of her cape and, with a triumphant exclamation, watched it fall to the floor.

Without another word, he put one arm tightly around her and led her to the great red drapery, which he pulled aside, to reveal a dark wooden door. Beyond the door was yet another beautiful room, dimly lit; in the center was a wide scarlet-covered bed.

In the faint golden glow from the living room, Iris saw

him removing his clothes, and his muscular, tawny body was revealed to her. Again she thought, with a thickly beating heart, how beautiful he was; he looked like a heroic statue created by a sculptor of unimaginable skill; the definition of muscle and the play of movement almost took her breath away.

"Iris, Iris, my beloved, come to me." She went toward him timidly but with great delight and allowed him to undress her. He held her close to him for an instant, and she gloried in the feel of his hard, perfect body. He was making the same urgent noises he had made when he had held her in the chair; suddenly he knelt down before her and took her body in his arms. The touch of his warm, urgent mouth on her bare skin thrilled her every nerve: her body felt hollowed out, then flooded with a burning fullness. An indescribable sensation, part pleasure, part ache, gnawed at her, and in a moment she had lost whatever hesitance and shyness held her back before. She heard her own voice pleading with him to love her, felt as if she were melting, so much so that she did not believe she could stand.

She hardly knew what he was doing, she was so overwhelmed, but only that his motions and caresses aroused her to a wildness and a joy she had never envisioned. Fleetingly, in the midst of their mad, obsessive delight, Iris had a flashing knowledge: this, this was what her father and mother must have; this was the magic that held them close.

Feeling her sway, he rose and took her in his arms, holding her securely and tight. His mouth found hers again.

He picked her up in his arms and put her on the bed, standing over her, staring at her in the dim light, saying, "You are so lovely, so lovely, Iris."

In the golden light filtering in from the other room, Rik looked, to her heated fancy, like a young god of the Rhine, a heroic figure from one of the great musical dramas, capturing her senses, thrilling her with his power as the titanic music had done from the first moment she awakened to its sounds. His arms and torso were muscular, narrowing to a lean waist and long legs. He stood a moment longer looking down at her with an expression of triumphant happiness.

Then Iris saw him move to her, lowering his body to the wide scarlet bed, and she felt her whole self opening to his embrace. There was a feeling so bladed and narrow and warm that her untutored flesh took it for pain, but then the thing that had seemed to be pain softened and flowed and turned to a pleasure so perfect and pure that she could not help her wild and sudden outcry, and the pleasure widened and deepened, widened like circles of fire, lapping at all her senses until she felt she could bear no more; she felt as if she were drowning, drowning then in a warm wild sea, and there was nothing in the world or in her mind but that one great feeling; she heard another cry, and it was his.

And then there was a kind of ending, yet it was not done for her; a slower, softer delight, a drowsy pleasure still lingered in an ecstatic place that was neither sleep nor waking. She listened to his slackening breath, felt his relaxed body close to her, very close; his strong arms holding her tightly, his parted lips kissing, with quick, light kisses, her nose and cheeks and forehead and hair.

He moaned and whispered her name, exclaiming in his astonished pleasure, and began to caress her gently and slowly until once more their bodies were together, and this time they were closer than before. At last she lay back exhausted with his head near hers, and his hard hand stroking her vibrant skin.

"I cannot quite believe this is true," he said in his own tongue, and she thought, How wrong it is to say that the German language is harsh. His words sound soft and thick as fur.

She turned her face to hide it in the shelter of his arm and replied, "I cannot believe it, either. But it is true, Rik, it's true."

"Iris, Iris. We will never be apart again, never. No matter what happens I will see to that. I promise you."

"Please, yes, please make it so," she whispered, putting her arm across his lean body and stroking his hard, shapely back. They remained that way for an unmeasured time.

An opening in the velvet curtains revealed a thin shaft of lamplight. Iris realized the day had darkened and wondered idly how long they had been there. She gave a swift, uncaring thought to her stolen day, then put it out of mind. Nothing mattered, not this moment, except their being here, alone and close, encircled, undisturbed.

They were drowsing when suddenly she recalled what she had thought in the cab, the half-formed plan that involved her friend Clara Kreis. All through the winter Clara had been urging her to visit the Kreis home in the suburbs. That's it, Iris realized with triumph. I'll tell Mother I am visiting

231

Clara; I know I can depend on Clara to keep quiet. Then we can have the whole weekend.

She sat up abruptly in the bed. Rik made a sleepy sound of protest.

"Darling," she said softly, leaning over him, stroking his head. "I must go."

He was instantly awake: his blue eyes were full of consternation. "No. Oh, no." He raised himself and took her in his arms, holding her tightly.

"Yes," she said softly. And she explained her plan. "I'll be back soon. And then we will have the weekend together, all of it, alone. With nothing to interrupt and interfere."

"Oh, my dear, that is wonderful." His face was transfigured now and he was smiling. But she could see that his long exhaustion was already overpowering him, for his eyelids were getting heavy. "The key," he began drowsily, "on the table there."

"Yes, darling. Sleep now. Sleep. I will be back very soon. *Auf Wiedersehen.*" She kissed him gently.

"*...Wiedersehen,*" he answered, his tongue thick with fatigue. Even before she had finished dressing, he fell into a deep, exhausted slumber.

Iris was too overjoyed with the success of her plan to feel the slightest twinge of guilt about deceiving her mother. Fortunately she had no weekend classes; she would not be missed at the music school, and Clara was willing to help her.

Iris and Rik barely left the flat for the two days following, an interval so timeless and so strange that once he remarked, "I feel as if we have had years together," and in another instance that it seemed they had been together only an hour before it was time for him to go.

Rik was reluctant to leave, and it was Sunday evening, before he did. Iris watched him putting on his splendid jacket, buttoning the brass buttons from his waist to the high collar under his chin, settling the peaked cap at the proper angle on his proud, well-shaped head.

She almost cried out in her grief at their imminent parting; she felt the tears gather in her eyes, but was determined not to give way, not when he himself looked so abject and desperate. So she forced herself to be calm, and asked him quietly, "When will you be back?"

"I don't know, Iris. But you must know that I will come

232

to you as soon as I possibly can...you must believe that nothing will keep us apart again, for long."

He took her in his arms and kissed her with a savage urgency. "I must go now, my darling. God, it hurts to leave you. It hurts, Iris."

"I know, I know." She clung to him with the same desperate strength, wanting to prolong his nearness. But she knew he had missed the train he should have taken and would have to sneak into the garrison in the early morning.

"You'll be all right?"

"Of course. Of course I will." She kept her voice as even as she could. "I will go home. I will wait to hear from you."

"Bless you, my darling." He kissed her once more, and for an instant she thought his nerve would fail him; that he, too, could not bear to go.

But she urged him, "Go, Rik, please. You must not miss another train."

"You are right. *Auf Wiedersehen,* my darling." He held her close for an instant, then he went out the street door, not looking back. She parted the curtains over a window and watched him walk away. He turned back, then, suddenly, and saw her. But the smile he gave her was the saddest smile she had ever seen.

Chapter 18

THROUGH THE EARLY days of the following week, Iris went back to school with total indifference, almost deaf to the professors' voices. Numb even to the music, she practiced with fingers that hardly seemed her own. All she could think of was the sweet, brief days of the weekend; all she hoped for was word from Rik.

Then, late on Wednesday afternoon, as she was leaving the school, she was approached by a tall, lean young Hussar. Her heartbeat quickened: his uniform was the same as Rik's. But he did not wear it with a splendid air. This young man was thin and ironic, almost scholarly-looking, and his rather ugly face had a grim and sad expression.

"Fräulein Mark?" He addressed her with a gentle, respectful manner.

"Yes?"

"My name is Brun." Brun! Rik's friend. But what was he doing here ... and why did he look like that? She was seized with a sudden cold fear, and she felt her body tremble.

Brun must have noticed her reaction, for he put out his hand and said, "Will you come with me? I have ... something to tell you, Fräulein." Her heart began to pound.

At last, she replied, in a voice she barely recognized as hers, it was so weak and uncertain, "The park. Let us go to the park."

"Very well." The unsmiling Hussar took her arm and led her across the boulevard toward the great park that bordered the school. The snow was melting and the winds had calmed, but the air was still cold and the sky so threatening that the park was almost empty. They sought out a bench and sat down.

"Fräulein," Brun began slowly, "I have some very bad news."

She waited, breathless, then brokenly she repeated, hearing her voice go high, "Bad news?"

"There has been an ... accident." He held out his hand with a pleading gesture, for she was rising from the bench, crying out, "An accident?" and she was almost screaming. "What happened?"

Brun gently touched her arm. "Fräulein, I beg you to sit down. I think you should sit down."

"Sit down?" she shrieked. "Why? What's happened? I demand to know."

Brun rose from the bench and put his hands on her shoulders. "Please, please, Fräulein Mark, sit down."

She continued standing, and Brun shook his head, rubbing his eyes with his hand. "Fräulein, Rik is dead."

She was unable to speak. She could not repeat the dreaded word, the short, ugly word that was like a stone falling on her breast. He could not be dead. He was too alive, too beautiful.

At last she managed to say, "Oh, no, that could not be true."

Brun stood by her, keeping his hand on her shoulder. "Yes, I am afraid that it is true. He was late getting back to the encampment. He was shot by a ..." Brun hesitated; his expression was bitter, enraged. Then he continued, "... by an overzealous guard." Brun shook his head again and put his hand over his mouth. He cleared his throat with a loud, harsh sound. When he spoke again, his words sounded forced and hollow, as if they came from deep in his throat. He reached into his jacket and pulled out a letter. "This was found in his pocket. It was addressed to you. He must have written it on the train. I ... wanted to be quite sure it fell into the right hands."

Unexpressed between them was the name of General Friedrich von Helsing, and she felt a wave of hot, grieving anger.

She took the envelope from him with a trembling hand. And then she sank down onto the bench. Brun remained standing. He looked down at her with concern.

"Please, Fräulein. Shall we go somewhere and get you a restorative ... a glass of wine?"

At first she could not grasp what he was saying. She stared at the envelope in her hands. He repeated his question gently.

235

She shook her head. "No." Her voice sounded like a weak croaking. "No, *danke*." She felt so tired, so tired, that she could not rise from the bench.

"Let me get you a taxi," he said quietly. "I think you must lie down, at home."

She nodded indifferently. It was true that she could not be left alone; she felt as if she could hardly walk.

Vaguely she realized Brun was helping her to rise, that she was leaning against him as they crossed the boulevard again and he hailed a taxi.

Brun handed her in. She leaned back against the cushion of scratchy plush; when her face was abraded by it, she gave one low cry. It reminded her of Rik's short-cropped hair, and the slight stubble he had had on his face when they were together the first day in Brun's apartment.

In a state bordering on sleep, she felt the taxi stop at her house.

"Fräulein," Brun asked gently, "shall I see you to your door?"

She shook her head, and limply waited for him to open the door. He got out and carefully handed her down to the sidewalk.

"Th...thank you," she managed to say to Brun in that awful croak that her voice had become. He stood on the sidewalk and waited while she climbed the stairs, one step at a time, like an old and very weary woman.

Frau Benz opened the door and cried out, *"Gott in Himmel,* what is it, child?"

Iris threw herself into the old woman's arms for an instant. Then without another word she broke away and went as fast as she could up the stairs to the haven of her room. His letter was still in her hand, the last of him that she had.

She heard Frau Benz's voice, then her mother's. She lay on the bed with the letter held against her face. At last she opened it, with trembling fingers. She read it again and again, especially the last paragraph:

"All these long days to come, and every endless night, I will live with the memory of our time of love. In my heart we are together all the time. But that is not enough. I need your presence, I want to see your sweet face and hold you again. I will be counting the hours until I can see you."

She put the letter down and, feeling the weight of her ring on her right hand, struggled to take it from her finger. It came loose, and she put it on the third finger of her left hand.

She looked at it for a long time, then she picked up the letter and held it with both hands over her mouth. She had thought it had his scent, but that was foolish. It was scented now only with the cold March wind, the harsh wool of Brun's uniform. Rik was gone.

Iris opened her eyes to utter blackness, and the blackness of the room was like death, so hastily she turned on the lamp by her bed. She had dreamed that she saw Rik in a coffin. Dear God, she thought, a coffin! In her shock she had not even asked Brun where his body was. She had to see him, to see his face once more; even in death it would be a kind of meeting.

Iris looked at the clock on her bedside table, amazed to see that it was four o'clock in the morning. She could not believe that she could have slept so long.

I must go out, she thought. I must go out and get a newspaper; there will be something in it. There was no other way at this hour to find out anything.

As she got out of bed she saw a tray of cold food on her table. Someone, likely Frau Benz, must have stolen in and placed the tray there for her. The sight of the cold food made her queasy, but she was touched by this evidence of love.

She went to the window and looked out. It was very dark, still, and the thought of going out alone into the great city dismayed her. But she was determined to find out something: there was no other way. To wait any longer would be torture.

So she dressed hastily and threw on the heavy warm cape of russet-orange, thinking with a fresh stab of agony, I wore this when we were last together. But she stifled the idea—it would so upset her to dwell on that that she would be too weak to go out; already she felt the trembling in her arms and legs, the unpleasant nausea of long hunger—and went out into the hall. She crept down the stairs to the telephone in the foyer, hoping against hope that she would not awaken anyone.

Softly she ordered a taxi. Then quietly she let herself out and stood on the stoop to wait. The wind had risen, whipping the naked trees of the Unter den Linden; far off she saw the Hohenzollern statues, barely perceptible in the gray-black light, and she nearly cried out in her grief and pain, they reminded her so of Rik.

When the taxi arrived she told the driver to take her to the Potsdam Station. It would be the safest place to go, she

237

thought, with late travelers about. And she knew that there the newspapers were always available.

At the station, almost empty and echoing desolately with her footsteps, Iris went to the bookstall and bought both the *Lokal Anzeiger* and the *Tageblatt*. Her hands were trembling now from hunger, weariness and cold. She went into the restaurant adjoining the depot, blessing the nocturnal habits of cosmopolitan Berlin. If she did not have a cup of coffee soon she knew she would faint.

With the steaming cup of coffee before her, she warmed her hands over it and then took a cautious sip. It burned her tongue, and somehow this minute thing set off the long-frozen tears: she felt them gushing over her face. She was too overwhelmed even to feel shame at such a public display. She let the tears come freely and cried for an endless moment, without sound, without sobbing, feeling some of the awful pressure in her breast and throat easing ever so slightly.

She drank a little more of the coffee and then, taking a deep, shuddering breath, began to scan the *Anzeiger*. There was nothing in it, anywhere, but in the *Tageblatt* she found a discreetly worded announcement on the obituary page. Leutnant Rikard Erich Jurgen von Helsing, son of General Friedrich Georg von Helsing, had died an accidental death at the garrison. The body was in Königsberg, in East Prussia, the birthplace of Leutnant von Helsing, and a private funeral, with military honors, would be held on Monday. Only the immediate family would be in attendance.

Iris exclaimed and let the paper fall on the table. Even now, in death, the general was denying her, denying her the right to look for the last time on Rik's beloved face.

Iris let herself in with her key; the house was very quiet. But as she was going into her room again, her mother came out into the hall.

"Iris, Iris." Anita came to her and took her in her arms. Iris stood passively in her mother's embrace. "Please," Anita whispered, "let us talk. May I come in?" She indicated Iris's room.

Iris nodded. Anita opened the door to Iris's room and they went in together.

"Here," Anita said, unfastening Iris's cape as if she were a small child. She threw the cape over a chair and ordered gently, "Sit down." When Iris sank down on the bed, Anita knelt by her and took off her shoes. Iris submitted, feeling a warm gratitude to her mother. For the first time in many long hours she felt the slightest stir of warm life in her body. In an instant, however, the chill of loss and desolation overtook her again and she drew a deep, sobbing breath.

Her mother seemed to understand and urged her to lie down on the bed. She did so, closing her eyes.

Anita pulled a chair up beside the bed and sat down. "We saw it in the *Tageblatt* last night," she said softly. "You must have been seeing him since Christmas. Oh, darling, couldn't you have told us about it?" Anita's voice was so tender that there was no reproach in her question, only concern.

"We...were. We were going to tell you." And she revealed it all, in halting, painful words to her mother.

"Don't talk now if you're tired." Anita stroked Iris's hair.

"It helps," Iris said. "It helps, Mother. It's all I have now, except this"—she indicated the ring—"and this." She took the letter out from under her pillow.

She glanced at Anita's face, and saw her perfect understanding.

"I felt just like that once," Anita said, tears of remembrance in her eyes.

"Thank you, Mother, thank you for not saying all the false and stupid things that don't do any good." She felt her control slip away, and the tears flooded her eyes and streamed down her face.

Anita said no more, but took Iris's hand firmly in hers and held it.

Iris's exhaustion was so utter, her weariness so deep that suddenly her bones felt like water, and she began to drift away into the feathery, healing depths of sleep, aware that as the light crept through the curtains, her mother was still holding tightly to her hand.

One mild evening near the middle of April, Anita stood by an open window of the living room, looking out at the budding trees of the Unter den Linden. Her thoughts, as they had been for the last several weeks, were all of Iris. The perpetual, nagging anxiety which Anita had tried to hide from Jonas had returned.

A few days after the terrible night in Iris's room, the girl had returned to a kind of numb life. But although a little of her appetite was restored, Iris had grown so thin and listless that Anita feared for her health. When Anita timidly suggested that they shop for new spring clothes, Iris refused, saying that she was too busy. Anita did not comment on the fact that she had already missed a week of school, and spent most of the days and evenings alone in her room.

A few weeks ago she had gone back to the conservatory, and thrown herself into her music with a grim new doggedness. Anita was greatly relieved; at least in that Iris was still functioning, even if she looked like someone they didn't know—a plain, withdrawn new Iris who took no interest in her appearance or her friends. And Anita had noticed a peculiar quality in Iris's playing; it seemed technically brilliant but devoid of feeling.

Well, I must give her time, Anita reflected. She heard Jonas coming in the front door.

When he came into the room, he said, "Hello, darling. You're looking very thoughtful."

She turned from the window and smiled at him. She clung to him when he kissed her, and he said, "You look worried. It's Iris, isn't it?"

Anita nodded.

"There was something I wanted to talk to you about, Anita, but now I think it can wait."

"You look worried, too." She studied the lines of his lean, familiar face, thinking that they had deepened in these last few months. "I don't think it should wait," she added with a feeling of self-reproach. "Iris isn't the only one in this family, you know." She patted his face, and he gave her a tight half-smile, but she could feel his slight relaxing.

"Sit with me," she said, and took his hand, leading him to the sofa. "What is it, Jonas?" she asked as they sat down.

"It's Germany, Anita," he said bluntly, and she looked at him, realizing fully how tired and anxious he was.

"Germany?" she repeated.

"I think we've had our heads buried in the sand. We've both been so preoccupied with our own lives—with the children, our work—that neither of us has realized what's happening."

"That's true of me," she admitted. Guiltily she thought, I haven't cared at all, I haven't even been reading the papers.

Jonas seemed to read her thought, because he smiled and said, "Don't reproach yourself. It's not only you. I've been living in a kind of dream. But Hubrist and I had a long talk today. Germany's challenging Britain, more and more, and threatening France. She's never gotten over the loss of Alsace-Lorraine. Anita, I think there's going to be a war. Hubrist thinks it could happen at any time."

At her look of anxiety, he put his arm around her, and said bitterly, "I should not have brought this up now. Forgive me. With all you've got on your mind...with Iris, and..."

"Iris is better," she said. "Never mind that, now. I can see this has been worrying you, and you haven't said a word to me. Jonas, you've always got to talk to me about what's worrying you. Don't you know that?"

"I should by now." He grinned and kissed the top of her head. He sobered, and added, "You realize what it means...we've got to think of leaving Germany. Maybe it's time to go back to America. You know that I have commitments here. I was thinking that you and the children should—"

"The children can go," she broke in. "I will never leave you again. You promised me, Jonas, you promised me that we wouldn't be parted again."

"I know," he said gently, caressing her shoulder. "But this is another matter, my dear. Do you think I'm going to let you risk your life?"

She sat up and looked into his eyes. "I have no life apart from you."

He stared back into her eyes for a long moment, then he said, "I know that. And I know your determination. Let's not talk about it any more, tonight."

"Let's not talk ever again of my going anywhere without you," she retorted.

He caressed her but he did not answer, and Anita knew that the matter was not ended, that he was far from convinced.

But I will convince him, she thought. Remembering the deathlike time without him twenty years before, Anita could not imagine anything on earth that would induce her to part from him again.

Chapter 19

IRIS'S CONCERT WAS scheduled for Sunday, June 28, 1914;
Jonas and Anita were delighted that the mild, sunny weather
had arrived. A few days before there had been an unseason-
able dampness and cold. The concert hall at the conservatory
was well-filled.

Anita, seated between Jonas and Frau Benz, with Jon and
Hubrist on Jonas's other side, thought with pleasure, I have
not been aware of politics for three whole days. She smiled
at Frau Benz and said in a low voice, "Iris looked lovely in
her dressing room, didn't she?"

"Ja, it is like a miracle. Suddenly she is almost...glowing,
she is healthy. It is good, it is that life is coming back. And
how clever you were in the matter of the dress." The old
woman's green eyes twinkled at Anita.

"I learned to be sly in dealing with her father," Anita
remarked in an undertone during Jonas's conversation with
Jon and Hubrist on his left side. "They are both so stubborn."

Frau Benz laughed softly, a wheezy chuckle, and protested,
"Still, it was remarkable. She would have worn the old dress,
had you not given her the idea about the sleeves."

Anita grinned and looked at her watch, wishing the concert would begin. It was true, she reflected; her comment that
the sleeves of the old dress were too constricting to give Iris
full freedom in playing had reached her as nothing else could.
And while they were shopping for a new dress Anita had been
able to get Iris to the hairdresser's for a new coiffure suitable
to the dress.

Thinking back over the last weeks, Anita remembered
how grim and unfeeling Iris had been. She knew quite well
that Iris had no interest in the concert at all, that she was

preparing for it only as a duty to her parents, who had invested so much in her education. Then, only yesterday, Iris had gone out on an unspecified errand. When she returned, her eyes were bright and her color was high. She seemed like a new woman. Anita did not know the cause, but her spirits soared at the sight of her daughter's transfigured face. She knew her secretive child; Iris would tell her what it was when she was ready, but not a moment before.

But now it did not matter. Even the threat of the political situation was lifted, for the moment. All of Anita's concentration was centered on the empty stage, and the gleaming piano, where in a few moments her beautiful daughter would sit and play.

It was almost time: there was a hush over the audience now, with only the sibilant rustle of programs and random whispers.

Jonas reached over and took Anita's hand; his face was as excited and joyful as Anita's feelings.

Then Iris walked onto the stage, to rising applause. Anita, clapping her hands wildly, took a deep breath of utter wonder. Iris was transformed: she was wearing a soft, flowing dress of cream-colored silk with panels of warm, rich garnet, the color of the single ring on her left hand. Her simply coifed hair was a dark, gleaming gold; garnet earrings dangled from her ears, half hidden by the wealth of hair, and her strange, tawny eyes were bright and clear. She seemed so full of abundant life and vitality that her look and her smile sent out, to the audience, an exaltation.

Gracefully she sat down at the piano, and with a simple and expert arrangement of her skirt, and a minimum of preparatory gestures, began to play.

Anita was astounded at the force and zest she brought to the Scarlatti fugue she had chosen for her opening selection; it was a glimmering waterfall of sound, and there was joy and life, enormous loveliness in her interpretation. Anita stole a glance at Jonas; she could see that he was as overwhelmed as she.

This was another artist, performing here; there was none of the cold, unfeeling glitter they had heard on the Steinway in the living room. Here was the profoundest emotion, coupled with the technical proficiency Iris had attained so easily.

Enchanted, Anita sat with her hand in Jonas's, listening as if in a dream to each succeeding delight—a Chopin waltz that held the gaiety of childhood play and sunlight, a noc-

243

turne rendered without sentimentality, but with deep sentiment, the performance of a brilliant woman who had known the greatest sorrow and the greatest love, transforming them in this moment to a beauty indescribable that touched them all.

Suddenly to her dismay Anita heard a disturbance in the lobby; she turned to Jonas and saw him frown. Proudly she looked back at the stage; Iris was utterly poised, and the sureness of her touch did not falter.

There was quiet in the lobby now, but a faint whisper, like a gentle wind in leaves, was sweeping the audience. From behind her, Anita caught a whispered name: "the Archduke Ferdinand," and then, "...some strange place."

She glanced at Jonas; he made an almost imperceptible sign to Hubrist, and the old architect rose quietly and went up the aisle toward the lobby.

Anita noticed a few other men leaving: their civilian clothes could not disguise the fact that they were Prussian, and likely army officers, for their backs were very straight and stiff, their steps precise. Uneasily she wondered what the whispered news had been.

As Iris played her last selection, Anita concentrated on the stage, hoping fervently that nothing would mar this splendid afternoon. Iris played on, Anita saw with pride, in exquisite perfection. She had never been so proud of her daughter as she was at this moment. The audience had grown very still again.

The sonata ended and Iris sat for an instant with her head a little bowed and her hands folded on her lap. The audience burst into loud applause, as an usher walked down the aisle, carrying flowers, and presented them to Iris on the stage. Then another usher followed, with more flowers, and Iris stood on the stage, bowing, her arms full of flowers, her beautiful face alight.

Anita stood with the others, still applauding, and she thought, Thank God, thank God Iris has this to sustain her. Hubrist entered from the aisle, and she saw him whisper to Jonas. Jonas stiffened, and his face looked grim. Hubrist whispered something else to him; he shook his head and smiled at Anita. He was applauding with the others, but his mind seemed far away and his smile was forced.

"What is it, Jonas? Tell me," she urged him.

He hesitated, then he said, "The Archduke Ferdinand of Austria and his wife were assassinated in Sarajevo."

She stared at him. He took her arm and led her to the aisle. "What does it mean, Jonas?"

"It may not come to much. Don't worry about it now, darling."

Anita nodded and followed him down the aisle toward the backstage entrance. She knew from the look on his face that he was not so sure as he sounded.

As she stood in the long living room of the Mark house, receiving their guests, Anita's anxiety sharpened. She had a strong feeling that under the babble of congratulations, behind the festive manner of the celebrants, there was a great deal unspoken.

Anita was relieved that there had been no disturbances in the street; desperately she tried to convince herself that Jonas had been right, that "nothing much would come of it." After all, it was only a crazed peasant killing an obscure nobleman in a place she had never even heard of.

"Even the summer celebrates today with Iris." Otto Hubrist was standing by Anita's side, smiling at her. She took his arm, and they walked to the long windows open to the warm twilight; the fragrance of her carefully tended flowers, planted in the window boxes along the facade, drifted in to them.

"I am glad this ugly incident has not spoiled Iris's triumph," Hubrist said in a low voice. "The child was looking so peaked, but now she is radiant."

"Yes." Anita looked across the room at Iris, surrounded by friends from the conservatory. She did look radiant, and again Anita puzzled at the cause of her sudden change. She did not think it was the concert alone, and she longed for a private moment with her daughter, to talk with her.

"It would seem strange," Anita remarked to Hubrist, "for the poor archduke to be important enough to cause an international incident. You know, I danced with him more than twenty years ago in Chicago," she added with an ironic smile.

"Did you indeed? And what was he like?"

"Not a very pleasant man," she said frankly. "I remember he wouldn't even condescend to visit the Exposition. The social critics called him a tightwad and a boor. Oh, dear, I suppose that wasn't in the best of taste."

"Nonsense," Hubrist protested. "I've never thought death automatically conferred sainthood."

She laughed. "You are always so practical, Otto, you do

me good." Then she asked him abruptly, "Tell me the truth. Do you think this 'incident' will have serious repercussions?"

"I doubt it very much, my dear. These things are always happening in the Balkans. They are very dramatic people, worse than the Italians." He patted her hand.

Anita smiled at his jest, but again she had the feeling that Hubrist, like Jonas and the others, was making light of it all to spare her feelings on this happy day. While she was touched by the gesture, she was also annoyed at being treated like a child. It was to be expected of Hubrist, with his Old World ways, and Jonas, who knew what this occasion meant to Iris and to her. But the others—Gold, Klimpsch, Brütt and Breuer, artists who believed in the equality of women and their ability to face facts—were acting the same way. At least one of them could speak his mind to me, Anita thought.

All in all, it was one of the most uncomfortable evenings she had ever spent. Iris and her friends seemed untouched by any worry, but Anita found it more and more difficult to play the role of hostess as the time wore on. After the buffet supper was served, the guests began to drift away.

When they had all left, Jon disappeared into his basement workshop, and Anita was alone with Jonas and Iris in the great living room, already restored to order by Frau Benz and the servants.

"Thank you for the wonderful day," Iris said to them, and Jonas hugged her, replying, "You were splendid today. But you know that. I heard nothing all evening but praise for you. They tell me I have a very talented daughter."

Anita caught the same forced cheerfulness in his voice she had noticed at the concert, but she resolved not to think of it until she had talked with Iris.

"Excuse me," Jonas said, "I've got to look over some plans." He kissed Iris and Anita and went upstairs to the small office he had installed next to their bedroom.

"Mother." Iris came to Anita and took her hand. "Please sit down. There's something I've got to tell you."

"I'd like that," Anita said. "Something has changed, hasn't it?"

"Everything has changed." She still had that look of almost unearthly exaltation, Anita thought.

Anita sat beside Iris on the sofa, and Iris, still holding tightly to her mother's hand, said abruptly, "I'm pregnant, Mother. I am going to have Rik's child."

"It can't be true. It can't be. You are so young, you are at the beginning of your life and your career...Iris."

For the first time that day the glow, the look of exaltation, left her daughter's face, and she asked Anita sadly, "Is that what you thought when you were pregnant with me?"

As if she had been slapped, Anita started. "No," she answered strongly. "I am a fool. What you are feeling is just what I felt when I thought Jonas was dead. And you were the greatest consolation of my life, because you were not only a joy in yourself, but you were also all of him that was left to me."

Iris smiled, and the happiness shone again on her face. "You see?" she asked softly. "Now you see, don't you, Mother? I was afraid you were going to ask me to...do something about this. Not have it."

Anita was silent for an instant; she had thought of that, yes, when Iris had first told her. But looking at her child's face, she knew that would be impossible. Impossible to put out that light in the happy young eyes. No matter how hard it was for an unmarried woman with a child. But she need not be an "unmarried woman," Anita realized. No, in America, she could...America.

"What is it, Mother? What are you thinking about?"

"A number of things." Anita made herself smile. Going to America meant going without Jonas, and she was not sure she could bear it. Yet it might have to be borne. Briskly, she asked, "It was the doctor you saw yesterday, then?"

"Yes." Iris nodded, and she smiled widely. "He said that I am fine, that the baby should come about the middle of December." She paused, then added, "Don't worry, I did not use my own name."

"Iris," Anita said softly and took her daughter in her arms, "I'm glad. I'm very glad for you. It will be a very beautiful baby."

Leaning against her mother, Iris said dreamily, "Yes, yes, I hope he'll look like Rik. And Mother, by the time he grows up, the whole world may be different. There may be no more fears and conflict, no more wars."

"You're thinking about what happened in Sarajevo."

"Yes. I'm not as unaware as all that." Iris smiled. "I just didn't want anything to spoil your day, yours and my father's."

Our day," Anita repeated, marveling, How sweet she is,

how different she has become already. "Our day," she said again, and kissed Iris's head.

"Iris, I'm not going to tell your father, not for a little while. He has...a great deal on his mind."

"There may be a war, you mean." Iris's answer was calm and matter-of-fact, and once again Anita wondered at her sudden maturity. Just knowing about the child, she thought, has made a woman of her overnight. And she felt a great protective tenderness for her daughter, resolving that whatever came she would be with Iris in this wonderful and very frightening time.

Less than a month later, on July 24, Austria delivered an ultimatum to Serbia. Perhaps, Anita desperately told herself, this would be another Agadir, another Balkan War, full of sound and fury, ending in nothing. She waited with the world in agonized hope. But on July 31 Germany made its declaration of *Kriegsgefahr,* preliminary mobilization.

When Anita finally told Jonas the "secret" about Iris which, in spite of her camouflaged dresses, he had already perceived, he insisted, "There is no choice now; you must go to America with the children, Anita. It will not be safe in Europe now. And in her condition..."

"I cannot bear it," Anita cried. "How can I bear to be away from you again? How can I live through that a second time?"

"But you survived that other time, and when we came together again, it seemed as if only a week had passed. Nothing can destroy what we have, Anita. Nothing. I'll be all right, you'll see. And in a few months we'll be together again."

Crying, she leaned against him, holding him with desperate longing. This time, she thought darkly, it is different. This time there is a war. And worst of all, the love she felt for him now was a thousand times deeper and stronger than it had been those twenty-one long years ago.

With a speed that dizzied her, Jonas made arrangements for their voyage to New York.

On August 2, 1914, before France and Germany fully mobilized, Anita, Iris and Jon were aboard the *Kronprinzessin Cecilie* from Bremen.

Only the actual time of the war's coming was any surprise to Berlin: the event itself had been long expected and a good deal of preparation had been carried out. Plans for such a war had affected the design and construction of both British and German liner fleets. Already the *Cecilie*'s yellow funnel tops had been painted black in the hope that she might pass for the British White Star's *Olympic*.

I hope to God we didn't wait too long, Jonas thought, his heart like stone inside him as he stood on the landing pier beside a weeping Frau Benz, waving at the three small figures on the deck of the parting *Cecilie* until the massive ship was out of sight.

With the aid of Hubrist and Frau Benz, Jonas closed the house and moved with a few possessions into a small modern flat near his office in a building he had designed ten years before. Frau Benz insisted she would come in daily to take care of him, although he protested there was little to take care of.

He had brought nothing with him but a few books and some clothes; he had taken the apartment furnished. Somehow he had not been able to face the idea of a hotel with its lonely anonymity and daily contact with hotel employees. Yet his new surroundings had the same transient look in spite of its luxurious furniture and beautiful interior design. Jonas ached for Anita.

He lay awake most of the first night; the bed seemed cold as a hospital bed without the warm body and sweet scent of Anita. Once he thought he heard her footstep outside the bedroom door and even imagined the faint click of the cats' claws on the burnished floor, a sound so familiar over the years.

Jonas woke after an hour of fitful sleep. His head ached: he had had a terrrifying dream. Their ship had been bombed. It was sinking. He was drenched with cold sweat. Exhausted, he slept another hour.

He got up wearily, bathed and dressed, took something for his head and went out into the street. Outside the Reichstag a military band was playing a lively march. From the wet pavements, in the cold rain, came the unbroken rhythm of clopping hoofs. The cavalry regiments were pulling out in endless ranks.

Jonas stopped and watched them: squadron followed squadron. The horses were shining, perfectly groomed, the men's lances decorated with flowers. But he saw no enthusiasm on the soldiers' faces; they seemed as grim as he, and the stirring march contrasted grotesquely with the expression of the riders, and the blackness in Jonas's mind.

He walked on through the pouring rain, suddenly recalling

249

that he had not eaten at all the night before. He went into a small café and ordered some breakfast. A passing newsboy was offering the first morning paper.

Jonas searched it eagerly, but there was no significant news. A systematic spy hunt was being called for; a frantic search was raging throughout the country for French gold bars which, the War Ministry announced, were being sent to Russia to finance the war. Jonas saw an item that chilled his blood. A number of law-abiding foreign travelers had been shot. Feelings were more and more aroused.

Jonas ate some of the food and went out again into the rain. There was a great crowd in front of the British Embassy on the Wilhelm Strasse. Some in the mob were throwing pieces of paving stones; Jonas saw one of the embassy windows break, then another.

"Gott!" An old woman near him exclaimed to her companion.

"From the Unter den Linden and the Wilhelm Platz, I heard someone say. They brought them here."

"Let us go," the first old woman cried. "I am frightened."

The two women scurried away. Jonas walked around to the Unter den Linden; there was also a large crowd in front of the Hotel Aldon.

"I advise you not to go in there, *mein Herr,*" a man said to Jonas. "They are looking for British newspaper correspondents. You are British, are you not?"

"American," Jonas said briefly, and thanked the man. He walked on past the crowd, assailed by that strange hissing word that the Germans used when they were especially angry, conveying the utmost contempt—*"Pfui, pfui"* was hissed out from many Teutonic throats.

As he left the outskirts of the crowd, a respectable-looking man spat at Jonas, and struck him across the face with his hat. Then ran. Jonas chased the man down the street and caught him. He was seething with rage: he had lifted his fist, about to smash it into the man's jaw, when he heard a familiar voice. "He is an American!"

Jonas let go of the man and turned to see Otto Hubrist.

"I am sorry, *mein Herr,*" the respectable-looking man said to Jonas. "I am very sorry indeed." To Jonas's surprise the man bowed and, taking an engraved card from his breast pocket, presented it to Jonas. He was a Berlin lawyer of some repute.

"So am I." Jonas nodded to the chagrined attorney.

"Come," Hubrist said, taking Jonas by the arm. He was wearing a raincoat and a battered hat. He shook his head, observing Jonas's dripping hair.

"What are you doing uncovered in the rain?" he demanded. "Come, let us go to Johannes."

"They can't work in this today," Jonas protested.

"I know that, but I think you ought to get away from all this madness for a while, and so should I." Hubrist grinned. "Besides, the sun will shine again. We can discuss what work we will do when that happens."

"I was going there myself," Jonas admitted, and they walked in the direction of the still-unfinished Cathedral of St. Johannes. Suddenly Jonas felt a new excitement; for an instant he was able even to forget the gnawing worry about Anita and the children.

They walked into the vestibule of the towering structure and looked up at its gleaming arches; even in the gloom they shone. The structure was only a month away from completion; already it had taken on a mysterious stateliness, an air of miracle.

More than a decade ago both Jonas and Hubrist had come under the influence of the great Bruno Taut, who was obsessed with crystalline forms. The crystal, to the Expressionists, represented the ultimate, the supreme. The purely aesthetic properties of crystalline structures had always fascinated Jonas, and in the Cathedral of St. Johannes elements drawn from the mineral world were legion. Jonas had united cubes and hexahedrons, octahedrons and other prismatic shapes into a dazzling and coherent whole of unique domes and towers.

For one happy moment, he was lost in the contemplation of the prismatic world he had made. Then he glanced at Hubrist.

The old man said softly, "The city was pure gold, clear as glass...the river of the water of life, bright as crystal."

"What are you quoting from?"

Hubrist smiled. "You are the most religious irreligious man I know." Jonas had often remarked to him that the only gods he had ever known were work and love. "It's from the Song of Songs, about the new Jerusalem."

His sharp old gaze swept the vaulted forms and returned to Jonas. "I hope they let you finish."

"I'll finish, Otto. The archdiocese will intervene with the Kaiser in the event building is halted."

251

"And if your workmen become afflicted with patriotism, and rush off in a fever to enlist?" Hubrist inquired sadly.

"I'll finish it myself."

Hubrist stared at him, and said, "That is impossible."

Jonas retorted, "You know that the impossible intrigues me, Otto. Besides, there's no work here I don't know how to do. You forget I've worked at almost everything in the building trades. You see that the major building is completed; all that remains are minor pieces of carpentry, a few touches in stone. I've worked in glass, too. You know that."

"I know all that." Hubrist sighed. "This is the ultimate expression of your bravery and stubbornness."

"I have a commitment," Jonas said calmly. "In America we would go right on, war or no war. And I'll do it here. Besides, the war is not being fought in Berlin."

"Not yet." They were silent for a time, then Jonas put his head in his hands. Hubrist patted him on the shoulders. "They will be all right. Please believe that. I pray for them constantly. I know you are not a praying man, but I am praying for them every moment."

"I'm a praying man now," Jonas said grimly. He stood up and squared his shoulders. "I've got to get the men together. There are tasks we can do inside today."

"I wish you well," Hubrist said and, after another look at the vaulted forms, slowly walked out of the cathedral.

The following day, Great Britain declared war on Germany. Jonas heard of it about midnight, when he left his apartment, unable to sleep, and began to walk with the crowds. Outside a café where there was always some kind of stir, the war was being played up to the crowds. As Jonas passed by, a Turk with a red fez jumped up on a chair. He was apparently finishing an impassioned speech.

"Germany has one loyal friend...Turkey!" he shouted. There were cheers from the crowd. And someone began singing, *"Ich hatt' einen Kameraden,"* "I had a comrade." Someone else took up the song, and soon many people were singing.

Then in the square Jonas heard a newsboy crying, "Latest extra! England has declared war on Germany!"

Jonas stood stricken, thinking, The world is in flames, and they are singing patriotic songs.

During the next few days there was a mighty exodus of British and Americans. The British correspondents left on an embassy train. British subjects, regardless of age or sex, were being seized and sent to the fortress of Spandau. There was great spy excitement in Germany. People were seized by mobs in the streets and in some instances were shot. Foreigners were in great danger in Berlin, and many Americans were subjected to arrest and indignities.

Jonas was in the anomalous position of having lived for years in Germany without abandoning his American citizenship. But he hardly thought of the danger; all he could think of, at every moment the work was not preoccupying him, was the safety of Anita and the children.

Finally, eight days after the departure of the *Cecilie,* Jonas received a cable through the American Embassy; it was delivered to Hubrist's office. It was from New York, signed by Anita with all her love, saying that they were safe on American soil.

Jonas sat down in a chair by Hubrist's desk and wept with relief, openly and without shame, although he had never done so before in his whole life.

"My prayers were answered." Hubrist put his arm around Jonas's shoulders. "Soon, now, you too will go back to America, my dear friend."

Chapter 20

RELIEVED OF HIS GNAWING anxiety about his family, Jonas was able to throw himself into the work with a new and obsessive energy; all that mattered now was to be finished, so that he might rejoin Anita. Four days after the cable, he received six letters that she had written on the ship, all mailed from New York. The American Embassy, apparently, was seeing to all American interests. Otherwise, he had no doubt, the letters would never have reached him so quickly.

He devoured them all, rapidly, like a ravenous man who wolfs down food. Then he read them more slowly, and after that again, each one with great leisure in the late nights, savoring every word. Even this brief time away from Anita seemed like an eternity to him, and it was almost like being with her again to read the letters. After he had had his fill of reading, he sat down and wrote a long letter addressed to her in care of Byrne Associates, the firm she had sold her interests in so long ago. But he was confident the letter would reach her, and he had no idea of what other address he could use.

As Hubrist had predicted, Jonas's crew had dwindled; in the last weeks he worked sometimes with as few as four or five loyal men. He thought, They probably think I'm crazy. But if they did, they still stood by him. And at last, at the end of September, the cathedral was finished.

He was free to go home. Late one evening Otto Hubrist stood him to a "last supper," as he put it, and the two men lingered over their wine in a favorite café. Jonas would leave Berlin in the morning; all that remained was to pick up his passport at the Foreign Office. The American Embassy had already sent it through. He would board a train at the Char-

254

lottenburg Station, in a quiet part of the city; it was the same station that had been used for the departure of special trains arranged by the embassy.

"I wish," Hubrist said when they parted at Jonas's flat, "that you had been on one of those special trains. Traveling by train these days is a risky business, you know. The army can commandeer your space if it's needed by the troops."

"I know, my friend. But it's a risk I've got to take."

Hubrist nodded, but he looked at Jonas with anxiety.

"General von Helsing is in Berlin," Hubrist remarked.

"Well?"

"I don't know, Jonas. I just have a feeling. He's never forgotten what happened to his son."

"Neither have I, Otto. But what has that to do with me?"

"Nothing, I hope. I sincerely hope." Hubrist grasped Jonas's hand, then they embraced. "Godspeed, my dear friend."

"I wish you were coming."

Hubrist shook his head. "This is my country, whatever happens." His voice seemed about to break. Abruptly he said, "Goodbye, Jonas," and walked away into the dark.

Jonas was at the Foreign Office the next morning before its doors opened. His train would leave within the hour, and he was tense and impatient.

Instead of the routine he expected, he was dismayed to see the clerk's manner grow stiff and cautious. "If you will wait a moment, Herr Mark," the man said, and he rose and went into an inner office. Jonas strode up and down the room, growing almost mad with irritation.

After about a quarter of an hour the man returned, looking uneasy. "I am sorry, but there will be a slight delay," he said to Jonas. "Won't you sit down?"

"I don't think you understand," Jonas said angrily. "My train leaves within the hour."

"I am sorry," the man said again. "There will be a slight delay."

In another ten minutes, a stiff-looking official, apparently of higher rank than the clerk, came into the reception room. "If you will please step in my office, Herr Mark."

Jonas controlled his rising ire and followed the official into another room. The man told Jonas his name, which Jonas utterly ignored.

"Won't you please sit down?"

255

Jonas asked abruptly, still standing, "What is the problem about my passport?"

The official replied, looking at a point just past Jonas's ear, "It appears your passport has been...misplaced."

"That's impossible. The American Embassy assured me—"

"The fact remains that your passport has been misplaced. There will be a slight delay in your departure from Berlin."

"I'll be damned if there'll be a delay," Jonas retorted angrily. "I'll see the American ambassador."

"That is entirely up to you, of course." The man looked at his watch, and he seemed suddenly to relax. He was almost smiling. Jonas wondered why.

He was to find out when he stormed out of the Foreign Office. On the stairs, he was approached by two young army officers who had just gotten out of an automobile and rushed to detain him.

"I regret to advise," one said, "that you are under arrest. By order of General Friedrich von Helsing."

"On what charge?"

"Sabotage, Herr Mark."

"This is insane. I am an American."

"Could I see your passport, please?"

Jonas understood at once: the whole absurd conspiracy was the doing of von Helsing. The "loss" of his passport, the sudden relaxation of the pompous official when he looked at his watch and realized that he had detained Jonas long enough for the soldiers to arrive.

He repeated stubbornly, "I am an American. I demand to see the American ambassador."

The young officer said, "You are British, Herr Mark. And we are now at war with that nation. If you will come with us, please."

Jonas weighed his chances of escape: both of the officers had their hands upon their guns.

Jonas got into the car.

During the first months of the war, the Germans had established prison or work camps for military captives as well as civilians who were subjects of enemy nations.

One of the civilian camps was at Ruhleben; it was to that camp Jonas Mark was sent. He was enraged at his captivity, but nevertheless he felt an undercurrent of confidence: his nationality would be discovered, and he would be released.

His feeling of unreality was emphasized by the physical layout of the camp site; it was a former track where trotting races had been held. The barracks were built behind the oval spectator stand, and the men took their exercise around the track in front of the stand.

On his first day of detention Jonas set out to discover the best means of escape. The prisoners had organized themselves in their various barracks, each barrack having a captain. The captains in turn elected one of their number as camp captain or *Obmann*.

The *Obmann* of Ruhleben was a Britisher named Parsloe who in civilian life had been the proprietor of a cinematograph. Parsloe conducted the affairs of the camp as well as possible, considering the difficulties of dealing with the prisoners on the one hand and the authorities on the other. Some of the British prisoners, members of the upper class, strenuously objected to taking orders from someone so beneath them. There were others who envied Parsloe and wanted his place. The authorities allowed him to visit the British Embassy at least once weekly under heavy guard; in that way the ambassador was able to keep in touch with the camp.

Jonas was swift to befriend Parsloe, who was amazed that an American had been detained. What's more, he liked Jonas's "cut," as he put it, noticing the American had none of the snobbish attitudes of the British prisoners. Parsloe assured Jonas that the British ambassador would hear of his plight on the next visit. He was "not to worry."

But to Jonas's and Parsloe's dismay, Parsloe was replaced by one of the aristocratic prisoners who hated Parsloe and disliked Jonas even more. Jonas was desperate; a chance was gone.

It was another week before he discovered that there might be another way. The Ruhleben hospital was in very poor shape. The British ambassador, Jonas learned through the grapevine, was arranging with camp authorities for permission to draw up a contract with a doctor who had a sanatorium in the west of Berlin. Under that contract the doctor would receive patients from Ruhleben. The ones who could afford it paid for themselves, the others were paid for by the British Embassy. At the time of his arrest, Jonas had been carrying a good deal of German paper money, which he had kept concealed from the guards ever since his internment. By day he kept it in his shoes, by night he strapped it to his body. He thought wryly how fortunate it was that the German money was thinner than American greenbacks, or he certainly would have aroused suspicion.

He knew then what he had to do: it was an act he faced with distaste but with cool determination. Waiting his chance, he stole a knife from one of the prisoners. He hated knives, he always had, but he looked on this one almost with affection. He gave himself a brutal cut on the arm.

He was taken to the camp hospital. As he had expected, the cut developed a nasty infection. By bribing one of the attendants Jonas arranged to be taken to the villa of the Berlin doctor, where he knew escape would be possible.

Jonas was sent by ambulance, under guard, to the west of Berlin. Miraculously he still had all his money; he had seen to that, with the craftiness that all prisoners soon learn. He had made places for it in his heavy boots; now it was folded and hidden in the hollowed heels and some of it lay flat and snug below the inner linings of the boots' calves, which he had slit open and then laboriously resewn.

When the doctor examined his wound and saw the extent of the infection, he said bluntly to Jonas, "I am not sure what I can do. We can only hope for the best."

For the next few days Jonas lay in a terrible stupor, alternating with delirium. At last his fever began to abate, and the doctor declared him well enough to be returned to Ruhleben. He would go back in the morning.

That night Jonas waited until the household was asleep. The only attendant was a middle-aged woman nurse who slept in a chair in the hall.

Stealthily Jonas got up and struggled weakly into his trousers, shoes and jacket. He put his money in his trouser pockets and stole into the corridor. The woman was asleep, snoring loudly in the late silence. He took off his shoes and tiptoed past her, his heart in his mouth. Once she stirred, and he thought his heart would stop beating. He had no desire to hurt a woman, but at this point he would have killed her to get away.

He crept barefooted down the stairs. Hearing a footstep, he hid in a closet. The footsteps faded. Cautiously he looked out. It seemed clear. He let himself out of the house and ran through the cold, silent streets all the way to his flat. In desperate haste he put on warmer clothes, took his supply of gold from a locked cabinet and put it in a small bag. Quietly he let himself out of the flat and, with his hat pulled low over

258

his eyes, took the small side streets on foot to the Charlottenburg Station.

He had some bad times on the way; twice he saw patrolling police, and ducked into dark passageways until they had passed. And once he almost collided head on with some soldiers. When they came near him, he began to stagger along, singing, in a drunken voice, "Deutschland, Deutschland, über Alles." The soldiers laughed good-naturedly, and one remarked, "He has the right spirit."

"That's very good, Hans, very good indeed. He has too much of the right spirit." The soldiers laughed uproariously at the pun, and one of them clapped Jonas on the shoulder. He swayed and hiccupped.

"Go home, my friend, and sleep it off," the first soldier said to Jonas.

"Yes, sir," Jonas answered drunkenly and swayed off down the street. He kept up his act until he was sure the soldiers were out of sight.

When they had gone, he began to run and ran almost the whole way to the station. About two blocks from his destination, he slowed to a walk. A running man was a suspicious sight these days in Berlin. And he did not want to appear breathless when he spoke to the ticket seller at the station. He stepped into an alley near the station, straightening his hat and tie, brushing his jacket. Then with all the calm he could muster, he strolled up to the barred window and asked in German for the next train to Zurich.

It was the long way, the very long way; he wished fervently he could go to Holland and from there to London. But he would have to get to Italy, somehow. From Italy he would make his way back to America.

His luck was holding: the next train would be leaving in a half hour. With magnificent calm he bought a ticket and went out again to the street. He was exhausted, and yearned for at least a cup of coffee, but he dared not sit in the brightly lit café. His arm throbbed painfully.

He timed his reentry so that he boarded the train just as it was pulling out. He blessed his continuing luck. No one had so much as given him a glance. Most of the passengers were bone-weary, half of them asleep.

He was terrified, for he realized how helpless he was without a passport in a country at war. He prayed that the trainman would not ask him for his passport or that if he did, he would take a bribe. At least his passport would not be required until he reached the Swiss border. He slept a little, fitfully.

When the train reached Zurich, he stumbled wearily from the car. "Please show your passport in the office," the Swiss guard directed, gesturing toward a glass-enclosed room in the middle of the station.

Jonas's heart sank. This was the end, then. He wondered where they would send him.

He followed the other grumbling passengers into the glass-enclosed room. When his turn came, he said to the inspector, "If I could speak with you privately."

Heartened, he noticed that the man had bright, merry eyes and a kindly face. The eyes of a man, Jonas thought with rising hope, who might let him pass for a consideration.

"Of course, *mein Herr.*" The inspector gestured courteously at an inner room and led Jonas in.

"There were some . . . difficulties about my passport," Jonas began, explaining who he was.

"It is understandable," the man murmured, giving Jonas a wily look. "These are difficult times . . . for all of us. *Mein Herr* is an American? The country of Switzerland has never taken sides," the inspector commented.

Jonas reached into his small leather bag and brought out several pieces of gold.

"Particularly," the inspector added, grinning, "when someone is so helpful. I will have an identity card issued to you which will take care of the people on the Italian border. There you can contact the American ambassador."

Jonas was so overcome with relief he felt the tears gather in his eyes. Embarrassed, he covered them for a moment with his hand and said in a voice he could barely control, "Thank you. Thank you very much."

That evening he ate his first full meal in two days, and soon after, in a clean little inn, collapsed into sleep.

Early the next morning he was on a train for Genoa, where a sympathetic official allowed him to telephone the American ambassador in Rome. The ambassador, after a protracted conversation with the official in Genoa, who assured him of Jonas's identity after a careful examination of his professional documents, decreed that a passport could be arranged in Genoa. That took most of the day, but soon Jonas was moving again.

He took a boat to Spain, and there a train across the country to Portugal. In Lisbon he cabled Anita. It was November 1 when the ship left the port of Lisbon, bound for New York.

The first day out, Jonas barely considered the danger; it was such a blessed relief, he reflected, to have this breathing space, this time without running. His arm was healing rapidly. There was no sign of fever or infection and he suffered no more spells of dizziness.

But on the second day he realized that his childlike euphoria had blinded him to his surroundings: the ship was not that far south of British waters, which had long ago been declared a war zone. They would be in danger until the ship passed the Azores, and the Azores were two days away.

Jonas began to count every hour of the journey. Finally the islands hove into view. He stood on the deck of the small merchant ship, sure that nothing would stop them. Not now, he said to himself in silence, not so near!

But then he was almost deafened by the piercing sound of the ship's alarm. He was rocked by the brutal suddenness of the horrendous wail that nearly knocked him off his feet.

He heard someone shouting, "German U-24 off the port bow! All passengers below!"

Jonas scrambled down the bulkhead to a lower deck. Quite suddenly, with the swiftness of a bolt of lightning, there was an earsplitting explosion and the ship rocked back and forth like a fragile seashell in the waves. They had been hit.

He clung to the rail, waiting for the cry to abandon ship. It did not come. The members of the crew, wild-eyed, rushed past him and about him; he felt he dared not ask any of them anything, so desperately intent were they on the tasks at hand. After a moment he concluded that the captain was going to try to make it into port. He knew that only a few hundred yards remained until they reached the neutral zone.

Jonas felt the stricken ship, in its agony of effort, labor forward. If only they made it across the line! Jonas waited, cold sweat drenching his body, listening to the shouts of men and the screams of women.

The gallant merchantman struggled on. Finally a great cheer rose from the throats of the passengers and crew as the ship limped into port. Jonas realized with a feeling of disbelief that they had made it, after all.

After they had disembarked, he found that his legs were trembling so he could hardly stand. The ship, he was advised, would not be seaworthy again for months, until extensive repairs had been made. But another ship would arrive within two days for the rest of the journey to New York.

In contrast to the months of loneliness and terror, the moment Jonas first saw the slender distant towers of New York, and the lady of the harbor holding high her lamp, he felt a happiness so overwhelming the scene blurred before him. And as the ship drew nearer Manhattan, he blinked away the moisture in his eyes: his builder's instinct was already alert, comparing this skyline with the one of 1900 when he had last sailed home to Anita. After the gray streets of Berlin with their ponderous structures, the buildings looked as insubstantial as the watercolor castles of a fairy tale.

He saw a new, immensely tall Gothic spire; it must be Gilbert's Woolworth Building. Jonas studied it with fascination.

Then, as the ship slid into its resting place, he forgot everything else, pressing against the rail among the other passengers, scanning eagerly the figures waiting at the pier.

At last he saw her, a slender form in blazing royal blue; her vivid eyes were gazing upward and her face was transfigured. She was crying; even from the ship, Jonas could see the tears gushing down her face. His own eyes filled again.

The gangplank went down: he was the first to step upon it, and he rushed down, his whole body trembling with excitement, carrying his one small leather bag in his hand.

Elbowing his way through the crowds, Jonas at last reached Anita, and he flung down his bag at his feet and grabbed her in his arms as if he could never bear, again, to let her go.

He could not tell what either of them said, or if they spoke at all; but he thought she was crying out his name, again and again. He kissed her savagely, indifferent to the people milling about them; he could see nothing, nothing now but her lovely face, inhaling the sweet white scent, the perfume of some mysterious white flower, that she always had about her skin and hair.

And twenty years fell away. There was no longer any war, and the place they were standing in together was a place of enchantment.

They did not leave the suite at the Plaza that night, or the next morning. Anita, studying Jonas as he slept, was filled with tender concern for his thinness, the deep lines etched upon his face.

When he awoke, the meal she had ordered was already waiting. After a leisurely breakfast, they dressed and went out together into the bright, crisp air. Jonas looked at the hansom cabs drawn up together at Fifth Avenue, and then at the green expanse of Central Park. He said in a wondering voice, "I can't believe all this. There is a world at peace."

She put her arm through his, and said, "Let's walk awhile in the park."

He willingly agreed, and they crossed the small triangle in front of the hotel, walking north into the urban forest bordering the avenue.

After they had walked a distance, they sat down on a bench and he looked up at the sun filtering through the ancient trees. He moved closer to her and put his arm around her shoulders. "Now," he said, "You must tell me everything ... everything that has happened since I've been away."

Slowly she began to tell him. "First of all, you have a grandson now." She smiled. "He was born on November fourth."

That was his own birthday. He exclaimed with joy, and said, "So soon? I had hoped to be here for his arrival."

"He came before he was due."

"And how are Iris ... Jon?"

"They are fine." She colored and asked in an embarrassed way, "Was it selfish of me to come alone? Iris did not want to leave the baby, but Jon ..."

"Selfish?" he repeated. He bent and kissed her. "This has been a perfect night and day. No, my darling, it was not selfish at all. I needed this as much ... more than you, if anything. This brief time together, after being gone from you so long."

"It was awful ... so awful, Jonas. I cannot bear the thought of being away from you again."

"You will never have to, I swear that, Anita. No matter what happens, no matter what." He drew her close to him, glad of their aloneness in the green place. He kissed her once more, lingeringly and with enormous tenderness.

In a moment, she asked, "Was it very ... bad in Berlin, and after? It must have been."

"Pretty bad." He began to tell her some of the things that had happened, trying to make light of the hardship and horror. Purposely he omitted any reference to General von Hels-

263

ing. Somehow he could not tell her that, yet, not in the light of the birth of the little boy. It might mar her happiness in the child, and she had spoken of him with such delight, such pride.

When he had finished speaking, she said gently, "It's all over now. All that is over. Now there will be nothing any more but peace and happiness. Many people doubt that we will ever go to war."

"I hope not." He was silent, remembering. She must have realized what he was thinking about, because she said brightly, as if to distract him, "We have a great many things to do before we go back to Chicago."

"Oh?"

"Yes. I thought we would stay a few days ... see Cass Gilbert's new building, go to some of our favorite places. And get you some clothes." She grinned.

"I do look like a bit of a beggar," he admitted, looking ruefully down at his shabby suit, the same one he had worn all across Europe.

"Let's do that today," she said gaily. "But first we should telephone the children."

He laughed with pleasure at her enthusiasm. "We will go back to the hotel and do that at once. You made me forget I *had* children, for these few hours."

"That is a very high compliment." She walked close to him, squeezing his arm.

"And then," he said, "we will outfit the ragamuffin."

"And you missed a birthday—we should celebrate it now," she reminded him.

Jonas looked down at her, delighting in her happiness. It seemed to him that when they crossed the little triangle again, neither of them walked; they floated.

He felt that the twentieth century had really begun that year in New York. They had experienced the final lingering moments of the nineteenth century on their last visit here. Then, both the airplane and the motorcar were still toys for the rich. Now, Jonas was astounded by the number of motors on the streets.

In their brief stay, he and Anita got their first close look at the Gothic skyscraper called the Woolworth Building. It was modeled on the style of the British Houses of Parliament, but it was modern and daring, looming sixty stories high, just under eight hundred feet of stone lace. It had cost thirteen and a half million dollars, with no mortgage or building loans; Frank W. Woolworth had paid in cash, just the way his customers did in his 684 five-and-ten-cent stores.

They walked across Broadway and looked at the new Municipal Building, an imposing structure of unusual design that spanned busy Chambers Street like a great bridge; a constant stream of traffic rushed through its archways. The new forces that would affect the future were surging up strongly in America. Jonas was dazzled at the air of plenty, which he had all but forgotten in Germany.

They had lunch downtown at the famous old Fraunces Tavern, where Washington had dined with his troops more than a hundred years before. From there they went to Brooks Brothers, where Jonas was outfitted.

When they emerged again into the Babel of the street, Jonas asked suddenly, "What are they building in Chicago? You know, all of a sudden, I can't wait to get back."

"Then we'll go, as soon as your things are altered." Anita smiled up at him. "As for what they're building, Frank Wright's designing something called the Midway Gardens—it's an outdoor restaurant and cabaret. And Mark-Byrne Associates has entered a city planning competition," she added casually.

"Mark-Byrne Associates!" He stopped in the middle of the busy sidewalk, staring at Anita, colliding with hurrying passersby.

"Yes," she said calmly. "It's a new firm that I hope you'll approve of."

"Approve of!" He took her in his arms, much to the surprise of the pedestrians along the crowded street. "Anita, we are going to build such wonderful things together."

"Yes, yes, we are," she said joyfully. "And this time there won't be anything to stop us."

On the westbound train a few days later, Jonas looked back at the towers of the city growing smaller and smaller until they were lost to sight.

They were in a private compartment on the sleek speeding streamliner. He leaned back, glancing now and then contentedly at Anita, whose eyes were closed.

He remembered the dusty, terror-filled trains of Germany, and the rickety boat to Spain, and his heart overflowed with thanksgiving.

And he recalled the Cathedral of St. Johannes. There

would be many other churches, and other houses and office buildings, he reflected happily, before they both were done.

Suddenly an even happier thought came to him, and he touched Anita on the arm, softly saying her name.

She opened her eyes and smiled at him.

"Anita, before I do anything else, I will build us the most wonderful house," he rushed into speech, and her eyes warmed at his exuberance.

"You know," he added in a dreamy voice, "we have reached a kind of pinnacle in our lives, at this very moment. Let's call the house that, the Pinnacle."

"Yes, oh yes," she answered, and he heard the same joy in her voice that he felt in his heart. "We will build the Pinnacle," she said, looking into his eyes.

Already his busy mind was at work; already he could visualize how beautiful the house, and all their years, would be.

PART III

THE PINNACLE:
1933–1941

Chapter 21

"WE'RE COMING IN," he called to her in a friendly way across the aisle of the twin-engined plane, raising his voice to make himself heard over the racket.

Rachel answered Rick's smile, but her heart sank. For the first time, she was sorry to see the spires of Chicago under the gray, snow-threatened sky. Last year, she had come home from Wellesley for the winter holidays by train, and was delighted to be home.

Rachel Levitt's family lived in a magnificent house on Lake Shore Drive designed by Roderick Byrne, where they had lived as long as she could remember; the house was filled with love and comfort. Last year, coming back to Lake Shore Drive from the relative austerity of college life at Wellesley had been wonderful, and she could hardly wait to get home.

But now, quite suddenly, it had all changed for her. It had changed in Boston, only seven hours before, when Rick von Helsing had boarded the plane. He was the handsomest boy she had ever seen in her life, lean, straight and tall, with short-cropped, very blond hair, uncovered by a hat despite the freezing cold; his features were classically even, with a perfectly straight nose and narrow yet generous lips. He looked a little like a Prussian, she reflected with a blend of excitement and dismay; the thought thrilled her perversely, although she could imagine what her brother would have said about a face like that.

Rick's eyes were his most striking feature; he was some-what tanned—so at first Rachel had almost dismissed him as a typical nonintellectual athlete—and his eyes, a peculiar golden-hazel, stood out in his face in a startling and romantic way.

Rachel had taken off her beaver coat and tossed it over the seat ahead—there were only five other people traveling on their flight, instead of the capacity twelve; the weather looked bad, and this particular type of airplane had come into service only last year. She sat down and pretended to interest herself in the new Rosamond Lehmann novel, *Invitation to the Waltz*.

She had begun it at the airport in Boston, and had loved it, identifying closely with the thrilling emotions of the young heroine. But now she was sitting right across from a young man who looked like a hero in a novel, and she couldn't concentrate at all. Rachel had glanced at his fine leather suitcase stamped with gold initials R. M. von H. She herself had an enormous amount of luggage in the baggage compartment of the plane, and was carrying a purse and traveling case with her.

But the handsome blond boy apparently had only the one case, which he had slung carelessly on the rack overhead before he immersed himself in his own book, Ruskin's *Stones of Venice*. Excited, she thought, Maybe he is an English major like me. She had been advised to study Ruskin for style. Then she decided he was probably studying architecture, at M.I.T. Her brother Daniel, who was taking engineering there, had said the architecture students read Ruskin, too.

Her brother Daniel, she reflected dryly, seemed to know everything about everything; he could be obnoxiously superior on occasion. But he was always nice to her, and as a matter of fact, was the main reason she had been sent to Wellesley and not Barnard. At Wellesley Daniel could keep an eye on her, her mother said; even if they weren't in the same city, at least they weren't that far away from each other.

Rachel wondered if the young man across the aisle knew her brother, and she stole another glance at him. Catching him looking at her, she put her head down and pretended to be reading her book.

Rick von Helsing realized he was staring and, embarrassed, went back to his reading, thinking what a pretty girl she was.

His distracting thoughts conflicted with the syrupy phrases of Ruskin: she looked a little like Greta Garbo, with that brown hat dipping down over her eye. Except Greta Garbo was skinny, and looked so remote and sad, like his own mother.

There was nothing remote about the girl across the aisle; her big brown eyes were warm and shining, and her figure, under the bright jacket, was slender but round. He flicked his glance at her slim legs, half concealed by the brown dress reaching to the middle of her calves. She was definitely someone he would like to know.

Rick's thoughts drifted into more interesting channels as he recalled the way she had smiled at him. It was cold on the plane—and he shifted his shoulders slightly under his well-tailored blazer. He felt something lumpy under him and realized he had been sitting, like an absent-minded fool, on his camel's-hair coat. Impatiently he leaned forward and jerked the coat out from under him. Swinging the coat around, he accidentally brushed her book with it.

"Oh, sorry," he said, feeling more awkward than ever. "Did I...hurt you?"

"A polo coat's not a lethal weapon," she answered brightly, grinning at him.

"No, I guess not." He stood in the aisle, looking down at her. "So you're going to Chicago, too," he said, wishing he had thought of something a little less stupid.

But she smiled up at him and answered easily, "Oh, yes. Home for the holidays."

He sat down again, facing her across the aisle. "Where do you go?"

"Wellesley. And you?"

"M.I.T."

"Ohhh, my brother goes there." She sounded very pleased; she leaned forward a little in her seat and the turquoise jacket fell back, revealing the full, mature line of her breasts under the clinging brown fabric. It excited Rick very much.

But he managed to maintain the air of coolness required of college sophomores. "What's your brother's name?"

"Daniel Levitt. He's in engineering."

Oh, no, he thought. Of all the people in the world I had to travel with Dan Levitt's sister. Dan was one of the biggest pains in the neck at M.I.T., and it didn't help that he was the fairhaired student of Rick's Uncle Jon.

"I'm Rachel Levitt," she added, laughing a little.

"I'm Rick von Helsing." He held out his strong, capable-looking hand and shook hers. When her soft palm touched his, he felt a kind of tingling in his hand. "You live on Lake Shore Drive?"

"How did you know that?"

"Well, I know your brother, sort of. And my great-grand-father designed your house." He grinned.

"Isn't that a coincidence? It...gives us something in common, doesn't it?" She smiled at him, her eyes even warmer, and shiny. "My goodness, it just occurred to me—Jonas and Anita Mark are your grandparents. That's wonderful."

"I think they're wonderful," Rick admitted, afraid he sounded his age. Consciously he deepened his voice, and added, "As a matter of fact, I'm going to work with my grandfather this next term, instead of going back to school. On the Century of Progress." He blushed. "I'm sorry. I guess that sounds like I'm bragging."

"Why shouldn't you?" she asked enthusiastically. "You must be awfully good at your work...getting an assignment like that when you're still an undergraduate. Even if Jonas Mark *is* your grandfather."

"It's not just because of that," he protested. "He's tough, let me tell you. And so are my profs. I had to...prove myself, you see."

"I'm sure you did." She was staring at him with open admiration.

"Oh, gee, I've been talking too much, kind of blowing my horn."

"Well, you know what George Bernard Shaw said...'Blow your horn, young man, for assuredly no one else will.'"

There was something about the way she said it that made Rick laugh. He hadn't laughed like that for a long time. He was always so serious that Dean and Eve kidded him about it. But his stepfather liked it, he thought. His stepfather, Donald Brewster, was a stuffed shirt, though. He would dislike Rachel, Rick knew.

Rick put down the Ruskin and stared out of the small window at the gray clouds beyond the glass, thinking how different all his relatives were. His mother, who was so pretty and sad, pushed Eve, his ten-year-old half sister, to play the piano the way she had herself in Germany. Dean, his half brother, was growing up fast. A good kid, spoiled by his father and ignored by his mother. Rick's grandparents were ...wonderful, there was no other word for it. Jonas Mark was famous now throughout America and all over the world; his grandmother, an unusually understanding and intelligent person, was still so beautiful.

Then there was his Uncle Jon, who didn't seem to belong anywhere. Uncle Jon was a "prodigy," they said, a full professor at M.I.T. at the age of thirty-two and involved in all kinds of weird research into physics and atomic theory.

271

His father, Rikard von Helsing, had died before Rick was born. Rick looked a lot like his father—he had a picture of him—except for his eyes, which his grandmother said were a "mirror" of his mother's. Rick wished fervently he had known his father. He was well aware that his mother was still in love with Rikard von Helsing; it was evident in so many ways. When his stepfather had offered to adopt him and name him Richard Brewster, Rick's mother had hit the ceiling. Sometimes Rick felt awkward with Dean and Eve, because it was so obvious that he was his mother's favorite.

When he was getting ready to go away to M.I.T., she had presented him with the very costly suitcase, and it embarrassed him a little, with its gold-stamped initials for Richard Mark von Helsing, making him sound like a German baron or something. Guys at school didn't go for that kind of thing, so when they asked his name, he quickly said "Rick," not "Richard."

He glanced across the aisle at Rachel Levitt; she looked a little subdued, and he hoped he hadn't seemed rude and abrupt. There was the Chicago Municipal Airport; he leaned forward, excited, and called across the aisle to Rachel, to be friendly, "We're coming in."

It was the winter of 1933, and the nation's economic health was slightly on the mend. Several million of the unemployed had gotten jobs; industrial production was slowly rising. President Franklin Delano Roosevelt had put into effect fifteen major pieces of legislation to remedy the country's many problems. A thirsty nation saw the unpopular Prohibition amendment begin to be reversed. It seemed that a "new deal" would indeed come to all Americans.

Jonas and Anita Mark had fervently supported Roosevelt. Their son-in-law, Donald Brewster, favored Herbert Hoover and ridiculed the promises made by the man from Hyde Park, called a traitor to his class.

The effects of the Depression fell as heavily on Chicago as on other cities, yet, as it had done in 1893 in the face of a financial panic, the feisty city went ahead with its plans to celebrate a Century of Progress—the one hundredth year since Chicago's incorporation as a village.

And the contract for most of the building at the fair was awarded to Anita Byrne Mark and her husband, Jonas, who were partners in the firm of Mark-Byrne Associates. Hardly anyone recalled the scandal of more than thirty years ago;

the woman whose father had been responsible for the splendors of the 1893 fair was highly respected now, and the worldwide fame of Jonas Mark would lend a new glamour to the exposition.

Chicago, the pioneer city, admired survivors, and though some were uneasy over Jonas Mark's close connection with Germany, his detractors had to admit that Jonas and Anita had survived the Depression better than most. There had been a rocky time in 1930, when the municipal government was bankrupt, but the firm surmounted the panic; now, in 1933, with healthier economic outlook returning, Chicago was reassured and full of hope.

If Jonas and Anita had survived the Crash, the family of Donald Brewster had actually triumphed. When the Chicago titan Samuel Insull had gone bankrupt in 1931, he was bested by the Cleveland financier Cyrus Eaton. Eaton had learned that Insull was borrowing and buying heavily to keep up the values of his stocks. Eaton knew the stock-market game and Insull did not.

And Cyrus Eaton was an old family friend of the Brewsters of Cleveland. Donald Brewster, whose family still lived in that city, heeded Eaton's advice, and passed it on to Jonas Mark.

Slowly they accumulated a large holding of Insull stocks. When he saw that Insull was committed to keeping their price up, Eaton showed his hand: unless Insull took over his holdings far above market price, Eaton would dump them. That would force the price down and place Insull in bankruptcy. Insull was trapped: he had to pay Cyrus Eaton forty million dollars for the stocks to keep them off the market. Insull was desperately playing for time, waiting for "normal conditions" to return. Normal conditions did not.

Meanwhile Cyrus Eaton, and Donald Brewster—who also had a large portion of Insull stocks—came out on top.

Jonas Mark, who shared in the Brewsters' prosperity, was slightly uneasy about the transaction, but he did not protest. He had no love for Samuel Insull, who had made their working lives difficult during the building of the opera house. Anita was glad of their security, she said, but would not go about in furs while people were starving.

Iris von Helsing Brewster was not restrained by such considerations: that afternoon, at the airport waiting for Rick's plane to land, she was dressed sumptuously in a black afternoon dress by Lanvin. Over it was tossed, with magnificent casualness, a long coat of red fox fur. The coat accented the tawny shade of her golden-red hair almost hidden under a small black skullcap; her hair was feathered short a few inches below her ears. And the strange lion-colored eyes now had a habitually sad and disillusioned look. She was carrying in her black-gloved hands a neat, costly lizard clutch bag, handmade for her. The bag had a small disc of eighteen-karat gold on its side with her initials inscribed on it.

Her other children, Eve and Dean, were standing a little apart in the glass-enclosed waiting room. Fifteen-year-old Dean, who looked exactly like his father, stood close to his uncle, Jon Mark.

Eve was waiting between Jonas and Anita. The child idolized her grandmother, Iris thought, studying her daughter. Eve had Donald Brewster's even, rather insignificant features, and his dull-brown hair, but her eyes were identical to Iris's own.

"Where the hell is the plane?" Eve demanded. Iris responded sharply, "Don't use that language, Eve Brewster," and Anita looked shocked and pained.

The lion-colored eyes glared at Iris. She is going to give us all trouble, I know it, Iris reflected wearily. She has the very devil in those eyes.

But Iris was determined not to spoil the pleasure of Rick's homecoming, and she turned away, eagerly scanning the gray horizon for the plane.

It appeared, finally, and as it was coming in for a landing, Iris went forward eagerly, ahead of them all. She wanted to be standing in front when he came out of the plane, so hers would be the first face he saw, that wonderful boy of hers, the only one in the world who still meant anything. It was going to be the best year of her life: Rick would be with her until next September. Iris's heart was thudding in her throat as she waited impatiently for the door of the plane to open.

Rick was the last to disembark from the plane. Iris's indifferent glance flicked over a couple of students and three middle-aged men, lingered for an instant longer on a rather attractive young girl wearing a Schiaparelli dress under a fur coat, then she saw Rick.

The first sight of his close-cropped golden head and proud bearing—so like his father that she felt a momentary pain—distracted her from the other passengers.

But almost immediately she noticed that he was walking beside the girl in the Schiaparelli, carrying two suitcases instead of his usual one. Iris had an unpleasant sensation very like jealousy.

"Darling, darling!" Iris cried out. Running to him, she took his head between her hands, kissing his face.

"Hello, Mother, I'm glad to see you." It was awkward; he was still holding the cases, and could not embrace her. He put his own case down and put one arm around her, kissing her lightly on the cheek while she clung to him.

When he released her and retrieved the case, Iris noticed that the girl was studying her with wide, dark eyes in which there was curiosity and a peculiar amusement.

"Mother, this is Rachel Levitt," Rick said. "My mother, Mrs. Brewster."

Disliking the girl on sight, Iris said coldly, "How do you do, Miss Levitt," and turned her back on Rachel.

Then Jonas and Anita were there, embracing Rick. Jonas took Rick's bag and Jon Mark relieved him of Rachel Levitt's.

Iris thought irritably, Why did Jon ever come? He hates me and he has never been fond of Rick. Surprised, she saw her brother's eyes light up when he recognized the girl.

"Why, Rachel!" Jon took both her hands in his, and added, "What a pleasant surprise. Is Dan home yet?"

"No, Professor Mark, he's coming tomorrow or the next day. There were things he had to finish up, he told me."

Jon said to Jonas and Anita, "Rachel's brother Daniel is one of my most brilliant students."

"How nice," Anita said warmly. "Is anyone meeting you, Rachel? Can we drop you off?"

"As a matter of fact, no one is. I came a day early. But I wouldn't think of troubling you. I'll get a taxi."

"Nonsense," Jonas said gruffly. "We'll take you home. Where do you live?"

She gave him the address on Lake Shore Drive. "Why, that's one of my father's houses," Anita remarked. Belatedly Jon introduced Rachel to Jonas and Anita.

Iris was very annoyed. She had wanted Rick to herself and now he would be paying attention to this girl; furthermore, she would crowd them, even in the ugly Lincoln limousine that Jonas and Anita drove.

But Iris had forgotten Jon's snappy red Wolseley Hornet, which was parked next to the sedate gray Lincoln.

"Why don't I drop Rachel off?" Jon asked. "I'm afraid I've only got room for one passenger, but there's space for your luggage behind," he said to Rachel, "Besides, I'd like to get

275

to know Dan's sister better." He grinned. "Dan's talked about you a lot."

"That's very kind of you, Professor Mark," the girl said primly.

She doesn't fool me, Iris thought cynically. She's quite a coquette, that one. But she's obviously after Rick. At least Jon will keep her away from him for a while.

"What a good idea," Iris said warmly to Jon. Her brother looked at her with puzzlement and suspicion; his sister never bothered to be warm to him.

Iris's annoyance returned all too soon; she heard Rick say to the girl in a low voice, just before they parted, "I'll call you, Rachel." And when she saw the girl's face light up, Iris started to form a little plan of her own.

On the long drive from the airport to the house, Anita Mark was content to gaze at the landscape speeding by; she was assailed by memories. Jonas, intent on driving, was silent. It was a companionable silence they often fell into, a happy custom for the last three decades.

From behind Anita, in the back seat, Iris's chatter and questions, Rick's brief answers, could be heard. There was a quiet comment now and then from Dean or Eve. On the edge of her reverie Anita wished that Iris could let the boy be, a little; but that was not possible, Anita reflected, in Iris's obsessive love. Listening more carefully, she heard Rick talking to Eve and Dean, trying to bring them into the conversation with his mother. But Iris always turned the talk back to Rick.

Anita felt sorry for them—the two forgotten children. She turned and smiled at them both. "Are you looking forward to a big Christmas?"

"We've gotten too old for that, Grandma," Dean replied with patient scorn. Somehow it was always like that with Donald Brewster's children. Eve adored her and Jonas, but was tongue-tied with them. Dean cared only for Jon, merely tolerating his mother, awarding a grudging respect to his father, Donald Brewster. His grandparents didn't count much.

Eve said nothing, but smiled at her grandmother with affection. Anita added, "I'm sorry your father couldn't be with us today."

"He had an important board meeting, or something," Dean announced.

To stem Iris's questions, Rick started talking to Dean and Eve, and Anita turned back to her contemplation of the road.

She could not believe how quickly the years had gone since that glorious Christmas of Jonas's return from Germany. Nineteen years, this last November, had passed since Rick was born. That had been a worrying time, she reflected; Rick had arrived prematurely and for three horrible days they thought that he would not survive. She and Iris had faced it alone, without Jonas, Jon a brooding presence in the background.

Perhaps I was wrong, Anita thought with guilt, to neglect Jon the way I did, those years after we came back. But Iris had needed her so much, right after the baby came. When finally Iris was well enough to need less attention, the constant concern had become a habit with Anita, and Jon already felt left out, had developed an independent aloofness.

She sighed, thinking of her son, and his alienation from them. He had become violently anti-German, although the climate of opinion in Chicago was on the whole neutral about the international scene. So many Chicagoans were German-born that even the last war had not aroused the kind of patriotic fervor common in other cities. But now...Anita sighed again, deeply, and Jonas asked, without turning his eyes from the road, "What's the matter, darling?"

"Nothing, my dear," Anita said. "A little tired, I guess."

"You should have an early night," he remarked, and she heard concern in his voice.

"I'm fine, really I am. It'll be nice to get home."

"It's always good to get home," he said, and he slowed the car, taking one hand from the wheel to touch her briefly on the knee. Then he replaced his hand on the steering wheel and sped on.

"Yes, yes, always," she agreed, peering ahead for the familiar outlines of the Pinnacle.

"The Pinnacle" was the Marks' private name for their house, used only by members of the family. The name referred to the house's location on the crest of a high, flowing hill; the building consisted of only two stories and was long and sprawling.

To Jonas and Anita the name had a much deeper meaning: the house was the pinnacle of Jonas's creative power, the realization of his own true style. Although the house's lines were stark and clean, Jonas had managed to retain some of the fantasy of their long-ago idol, Gaudí. With the use of mass, structure and equilibrated tension, Jonas had attained through garden elevations and consummate skill the illusion that the structure "floated" above its site. The sense of lift was so remarkable that the viewer was not conscious of the compressive forces that held the house to the ground. Yet the house related perfectly to the plane of earth on which it stood.

As the family piled out of the car and straggled into the entrance hall, Rick looked around with shining eyes and said, as he always did, "I love this house. Every time I come back, it's more beautiful than I remembered."

"I know. And it's so good to have you home." Anita put her arm around her tall grandson and hugged him.

"Well, we are not home yet," Iris remarked with a little laugh, but her tone was an emphatic reminder that her house, not this one, was Rick's home.

"Of course not, my dear," Anita said quickly, but some of the pleasure was gone from her eyes. "But you know this is Rick's second home." She smiled uncertainly at her daughter.

"Lord, it's great to be here," Rick said again.

"You must be very tired and hungry, darling." Iris came to Rick and put her arm around his waist.

"Not now, Ma. I want to look around for a while." Rick's impatience had surfaced; there was an edge to his voice that the sensitive Iris did not miss. She detested being called "Ma"; it was grotesquely inappropriate to her enameled chic, and her impatient manner seemed to imply that all this fuss about a mere house was ridiculous.

But Rick continued to look around fondly at the striking entrance hall. Its features were prophetic of developments of the future, and had been especially in 1916, when the house was completed. It contained the kind of innovation that had made Jonas one of the foremost architects of his time.

"Believe it or not, Granddad, I've finally got a glimmer of how you did this." Rick grinned at Jonas. He caressed with his hand the flush walls of mahogany, free of both baseboard and picture molding. The stair enclosure was a sheer slab, open only for inset spindles of square cross section. The ceiling was white, the walls a slightly grayed white that was achieved by mixing white with three primary colors, so that the walls would reflect the changing colors outdoors. There was a subtle iridescence that was almost like mother-of-pearl.

"Rick, we mustn't keep everyone standing here," Jonas said. "Let's go in and have something to eat."

"Oh, of course, I'm sorry. I'll just take my bag up." Rick started up the stairs.

"Where on earth are you going?" Iris demanded. "We're only going to have a drink and then your granddad will run us home."

"Oh, dear, didn't Rick...?" Anita paused, embarrassed.

Rick stood on the stairs and looked at his mother. "Gee, Ma, I thought I'd written you. I want to stay a few days. Granddad and I have an awful lot to talk over—about the exposition."

"But your father's expecting us all for dinner!" Iris's voice was rising and there was a note of hysteria. "Anyway, you belong at home. I won't have it!"

Anita felt deeply chagrined. She looked at their faces: Rick was looking stubborn and impatient, Eve and Dean bored. Then Anita gave Jonas a meaningful glance.

Jonas said, "Rick, you should have told your mother about this; that was inconsiderate, son. Why don't you leave your case in the hall, and go on home this evening. We can always get together later. After all, the exposition's five months away."

To Iris, Jonas said, "Can't you at least stay for dinner? We're prepared for the whole bunch, Anita tells me. Call Donald and ask him to join us."

"Oh, very well," Iris answered ungraciously. "I'll call. Maybe I can catch him." Her tone implied that it was all very inconvenient. She stalked to the phone concealed in a cabinet below a round, pewter-framed mirror.

"Goodie," Eve said, and clapped her hands together. "It's fun to have dinner here."

Anita was thankful Iris was engrossed with her call and had not seemed to hear what Eve said. She hugged Eve to her. "Let's all hang up our coats and go in the living room. We'll get some hot chocolate for you and Dean, and some drinks for us."

The massive living room had one glass wall that seemed to bring the outdoors into the house. But for the winter Anita had designed a wonderful space for an indoor garden; indoors were masses of crimson, orange and yellow flowers. Behind it the great pines and evergreens loomed, masked now with snow. The contrast was dramatic, yet it gave one a feeling of coziness and security: there, the arrangement seemed to say, is the lonely cold, and here within are color and warmth and love.

279

Anita spoke to the maid, and in a little while they were settled around the room near the heavy tile fireplace, which was crackling with a huge fire. The fireplace, like the round-arched entrance to the room, was one of the glories of the past that Jonas had kept in the strikingly modern house.

Iris came in sulkily and accepted a glass of sherry from Jonas. "Don will be along soon," she said.

"I'm glad he can come." Anita smiled at Iris.

The phone rang in the hall; Jonas went to answer. When he came back he said, "We'll go on with dinner when Donald comes, Anita. That was Jon. He's staying at the Levitts for dinner."

Iris smiled a catlike smile, fitting a cigarette into her long onyx holder. She remarked, "I think there's a little romance going there. Miss Levitt seemed very smitten with Jon."

Anita glanced at Rick. He liked the girl, she knew; his face revealed hurt. Anita thought sadly, Iris is plotting something. And Rick's feelings don't matter at all.

Chapter 22

"SO YOU CAN THANK Miss Sally Rand for our project," Jonas said to Rick, early Sunday morning, as they inspected the fairgrounds. He made a sweeping gesture down the Midway of the Century of Progress, turning up his coat collar against the cold wind from the lakefront.

Rick laughed. "'The pendulum is swinging to finer things,'" he quoted Lenox Lohr, the manager of the fair.

The Midway of the 1933 fair had been as provocative as that of the exposition of 1893, when Little Egypt had scandalized Chicago. Last year when Sally Rand had done her dance, wearing only two big ostrich-feather fans, she all but pushed into obscurity the scientific theme of the fair. An injunction failed to stop her dancing, but the arguments over the morality of the Midway's attractions had started a movement toward the "finer things" predicted by Mr. Lohr. He announced that a concentration of villages—Swiss, Black Forest, English, Early American, Venetian, Spanish, Irish and Tunisian—would replace much of the 1933 Midway.

Rick von Helsing would be working closely with Jonas Mark on several of the villages; the Black Forest village in particular was close to their hearts.

"You can see," Jonas said, "why this is a very special project." He smiled at his grandson, who stood hatless in the freezing wind, the sun bright on his brief golden hair. "This will require attention to matters you may not have run into before—ground contouring, earth retention, the pattern of tree planting and, of course, a hundred different aspects of lighting and electricity."

Seeing Rick's intimidated expression, Jonas laughed. "No, we're not directly responsible for all that. But I work differ-

281

ently from the way we did in the old days. In 1893, Anita's father designed buildings, period. He left the other matters to the specialists; they conformed to his buildings. But I get involved with all of it, and work very closely with the electricians, the landscape artists, the whole crew. We're more of a unit. I really feel this makes for greater harmony."

"I like that idea," Rick said.

"Good. Come on, let's walk down a ways. I'll show you where the Black Forest village will be."

They walked on down the Midway, and Jonas remarked, "You'll never believe how much I learned from Gaudí about light. We're going to need twice as much light in the Black Forest village because of the dark, shadowy surfaces. And we've got quite a corrosion factor here. I don't have to tell you that."

"You don't," Rick said with feeling. "I know about this swamp we're building on."

"What kind of lamps would you choose?" Jonas asked, feeling him out.

"Halide," Rick said promptly. "I know it's sixty percent more efficient than fluorescents, and I hate those as much as you do."

"Not bad," Jonas answered, "but halogen quartz gives you twice the life of a GLS and you get good color rendering instead of 'reasonable.' And remember 'reasonable' is all they guarantee with halide."

"I've got some homework to do." Rick sounded chastened.

"Not that much." Jonas clapped him on the shoulder. "You're doing fine. Most students at your level never heard of halide."

"I think I've learned more from you than anyone at M.I.T."

"Don't be too sure, son. I learned plenty there myself. They teach you how to draw, for one thing, and draw well. They turn out engineers, which is what we've got to be. Remember, the first M.I.T. student thesis was a waterworks design." He glanced at Rick and asked, "Think you've gotten the lay of the land now? Ready to visit your grandmother for a while?"

"Sure." Rick nodded.

As they got into his car, Jonas said, "The main thing to remember is not to step on toes." He smiled at Rick. "We've got to tread that thin line between interference and cooperation, with the electrical men, the landscape bunch, the lot. You'll have to be a better diplomat than I am." Jonas grinned.

"I'll try, Granddad. I think I can handle it." Rick's young face was serious and unsmiling.

I think he can, Jonas reflected as they turned off the lakefront and took the road to the Pinnacle. He could always handle things. Jonas's memory drifted back to when Rick was only nine years old, when already he had begun to manage his life.

Even at that age, Richard Mark von Helsing had taken on the secretive air that Jonas himself had had as a child. And one fine midmorning in March, Jonas and Anita were driving Rick home, wondering what the boy was thinking about the latest change in his life.

Rick was sitting behind, and Anita was beside Jonas in the front seat. Jonas said to Anita in a low voice, as he pulled into the great circular drive before the Brewster mansion, "You know, I just remembered what that old lady—what was her name?—said to me in Spain all those years ago."

"Señora Eusebia?" Anita smiled, and her smile was suddenly wistful, almost childlike. "What was it she said?"

"She instructed me on the natures of people born in November—stubborn, passionate, relentless and secretive."

"How right she was," Anita retorted. "You and your grandson are cut from the same cloth." Purposely she raised her voice and turned a little, glancing over her shoulder at Rick. He smiled at her, a wide, affectionate smile, but his blue eyes were still veiled and blank.

"But I look like my father, *hein*?"

Jonas heard the German word with a blend of nostalgia and dismay. Iris had taught the child German at a very early age, and he was almost bilingual. Iris spoke German to Rick very frequently, which seemed to shut them off together in a world of their own. Iris's husband, Donald Brewster, spoke no German, and apart from Jonas's letters to Otto Hubrist, neither Jonas nor Anita used the language any more at all.

"Yes," Anita said to Rick. "You look just like your father, but you think like your grandfather."

"I'm glad of that."

"So am I," Anita replied warmly and put her gloved hand on Jonas's knee. Jonas glanced at her and thought admiringly, She doesn't look like a woman who's been a grandmother twice...no, three times now. She had just turned fifty-three, but today under her blue cloche hat, Anita's skin was as fresh and smooth as that of a woman of thirty, and her wonderful eyes of bright blue had lost none of their magic.

In her slim, long-waisted coat her body, too, looked very young.

"I can't believe we're grandparents again," he said to Anita.

"But we are, and this time Rick has a sister. What do you think of all that?" Anita asked the boy.

Jonas had pulled to a stop, and Donald Brewster was coming down the stairs of the great house to welcome them.

"I can't go," Rick said abruptly.

Jonas paused in the act of opening the door, a habit of his which always disconcerted the Brewster servants, and repeated, "Can't go?"

"I don't want to go back...here," Rick said in a low voice. Jonas could not help noticing that he did not say "home." He had a suspicion that Rick was more at home with him and Anita at the Pinnacle; there, he was a lighthearted, natural little boy, who played with the animals and listened with them to funny radio programs. But here, at the Brewster house, he had immediately become the solemn little prince of Iris's making.

"Come on, Rick," Jonas said firmly. "We'll talk about this again before we leave. You want to see your sister, don't you? And your mother?"

Donald Brewster was helping Anita from the car; their greetings had covered the voices of Jonas and Rick. But now Donald Brewster was looking at them in a puzzled fashion, and with some disapproval.

"Come along, Richard," Brewster said in his slow, careful speech. It irritated Jonas that Iris forbade Donald to call Rick by his nickname.

"Hello, Don," Rick said deliberately. Nothing, Jonas knew, could induce Rick to call Donald Brewster Dad or Father.

Jonas saw the impeccable Brewster wince and felt a little sorry for him.

To atone for Rick's cold greeting, Jonas said heartily, "How are you, Don? It's good to see you. How are the beautiful women?"

Brewster's tight face relaxed into a delighted smile, and he answered, "Fine, just fine. Iris is dying to see...you all." Jonas noticed the hesitation and knew at once that the thing they had hoped for had not yet happened—Iris's obsession with Rick was unchanged, despite the birth of her third child, and a girl child at that, in a household of males. Jonas and

284

Anita had hoped that it would make a difference. But the well-bred discomfort in Donald Brewster told Jonas the story.

Another one of the perfect servants opened the great front door, and they stepped into the rather comical magnificence of the entrance hall. It was a Tudor mansion very much like the one Anita had grown up in, one of the more lavish productions of the late Roderick Byrne. Jonas had the uneasy feeling that Rick disliked the house as much as he and Anita did, although they had never given the boy a hint of their true feelings.

"You haven't ridden in our elevator yet, have you, Mrs. Mark?" Donald Brewster would have found it most improper to address Anita and Jonas by their first names.

"Why, no," Anita answered in a warm and friendly fashion. Like Jonas, she felt a little sorry for Donald Brewster. "How delightful. Let's give it a try."

"We'll walk up," Jonas said lightly. "I need the exercise, and I'm sure it won't hurt this one." He nodded toward Rick, who grinned up at him.

"Let's go," Rick said, and Jonas could hear the gratitude in his voice.

"We'll meet you upstairs," Anita said, as Donald handed her into the small gilded cage.

Jonas walked up the curved stairs slowly with his hand on Rick's shoulder.

"Now what is this," he demanded, "about your not wanting to come home?"

"I'd rather stay with you." Rick's voice was flat and matter-of-fact, and Jonas admired his proud posture, the strange maturity of his bearing, while it pained him, in a child.

"Why?" Jonas asked bluntly.

"My mother ... watches me all the time." There was a deep uneasiness in the boy that pained Jonas as much as his unnatural solemnity.

They had reached the upper landing. Jonas could hear the voices of Donald and Anita in Iris's room, and then he heard Iris demanding in a strong, sharp voice, "Where's Richard?"

Jonas looked at Rick, and saw him stiffen at the sound of his mother's voice. In spite of the perfectly controlled temperature of the magnificent house, Jonas felt a chill on his body, as if goose pimples were breaking out on his arms.

"Watches you?" he repeated softly.

Rick nodded. "Yes. Granddad, it's not the way it is at your

285

house. You let me...do things on my own. Mother calls me Rikard, and..."

Jonas's feeling of dismay deepened. Was Iris trying to make the boy into Rik von Helsing? It was eerie, unhealthy.

"Look, Rick, things may be different now," Jonas said in a reassuring tone. "You have a new sister, and your mother will be very busy with her, you know." He tried to smile at the solemn boy.

Rick shook his head and looked back at Jonas with wise eyes, eyes too old for his nine years.

"Richard!" Donald Brewster was standing outside Iris's door, staring at them. His face was disapproving and severe.

"Come on, son." Jonas took Rick by the hand and led him into Iris's room.

When they walked in, Iris held up her arms to Rick. Without greeting her father, Iris called out in an emotional, almost desperate way, "Richard, Richard, my darling!"

Everyone else in the room, including the small baby in her pink blanket, held in the arms of a nurse, was utterly ignored. Iris's beautiful, tawny eyes were blazing with happiness at the sight of her son.

Reluctantly he went to the bed and submitted to her smothering embrace.

When at last Iris released Rick, Jonas looked at the boy's strong, calm face and thought, Rick will manage somehow, in spite of everything. He's not my grandson for nothing.

The memory was still sharp and clear in Jonas's mind as he walked with Rick into the welcoming hallway of the Pinnacle.

"Sounds as if we have company," Jonas remarked. The voices of two people, a young woman's and a man's, mingled with Anita's, drifting out to them through the archway that connected the hall and living room.

"It's Jon," Rick said in that neutral voice that Jonas had come to know so well, the voice the boy used when he was hiding something. "It's Jon and..." Rick paused, and his face lit up. "Rachel."

"Oh, yes," Jonas said, with a glance at Rick, "that pretty young lady at the plane." He saw that the boy's eyes were bright and an expectant smile was on his mouth.

His blue gaze went to the girl's face as soon as they stepped into the room. "Rachel!" Rick went to her with his hand outstretched, and she extended hers. He took it and held it for a rather long time before he recalled himself and said to Anita, "Hello, Grandma." He went to Anita and, bending, kissed her on the cheek.

Then he nodded and said briefly, "Jon." His uncle was standing by the fireplace with a glass of sherry in his hand. "Rick, Dad." Jon bent his head in a curt fashion, an amused expression on his face. The expression did not escape Rick: Jon always looked at him like that, as if he were a bumbling young dog and Jon was waiting to see what he would do next.

"Hello, Mr. Mark." The girl spoke to Jonas shyly, and he noticed again how pretty she was; she had large, lustrous dark eyes and her brief bobbed hair was very black, so shining that it fairly glittered in the orange firelight, like Anita's hair when she was young, Jonas thought.

"It's nice to see you again, Rachel," he answered, smiling. In spite of her shyness she had a good deal of grace and poise, Jonas reflected. She sat down comfortably on the big cream-colored couch, her slender black wool skirt swirling about her shapely legs. Her ensemble was attractive and very expensive-looking, with a long fitted blouse of scarlet, gray and black stripes that enhanced her dark beauty.

Jonas wondered about Rachel and Jon; it was all too clear that Rick was smitten with her. He glanced at Jon, whose face was expressionless. Then he looked at Rachel: it seemed to him she was as glad to see Rick as he was to see her. He hoped so.

Boldly, Rick sat down beside her and said, "It's been a long time."

A deeper color came into her cheeks, and she said lightly, "Not so long, Rick. Only three days."

"But we've accomplished a lot in three days, haven't we, Rachel?" Jon's voice was deliberately intimate, and Rick shot him an annoyed glance. "We've been doing the town," Jon added in a lazy voice.

"You've been out every time I called," Rick said to Rachel in a low voice. She stared at him for an instant, and answered, "Yes."

To fill the awkward silence, Jonas moved toward Jon and held out his hand. "Let me get you a refill."

"Thanks. I'm glad to know that prohibition hasn't touched the Pinnacle." Jon smiled. "This is the wonderful Amontillado."

"We still have wine from Father's cellar," Anita said. She came to stand beside them, and Jonas had the feeling that she was joining him in the conspiracy, to give Rick a little time with Rachel. "Jon's been telling me about his latest project," she added quickly. "Come, my dear, let's sit down while you tell your father about it."

Anita led them to the couch at the other side of the hearth, leaving Rick and Rachel sitting apart, talking in quiet tones.

Jon knew what Anita was doing, and he said, "Of course. Rick can entertain my guest."

They sat down, and Jonas asked his son about his new project.

"I'm working with Rachel's brother," Jon said, "and another very promising graduate student. His name is Van de Graaff, a Rhodes scholar. Actually we're all working under Harrison, on the use of spectroscopy to study the action of electrons and atoms."

"That's an exciting field," Jonas said. "I've been hearing a good bit about Harrison. That ruling engine of his has amazing accuracy. No one's ever mastered it quite like that before."

"You're getting too technical for me," Anita said, smiling. "What excites me most is that this power could be used to treat disease, even malignant disease. Isn't that so, Jon?"

"Well, roughly, Mother," Jon said consideringly but with a little condescension. "I'm afraid such a high-flown purpose will be lost in its more urgent uses, though."

"What do you mean by that?" Jonas asked.

"I have a strong feeling we're going to be making bombs first, Dad. The Nazi party is getting very strong in Germany, and Austria will go this year, I have no doubt about it. We'll have to fight them before it's over."

"No," Anita said. "Oh, no. Not that, Jon." She had turned white. Jonas frowned and started to speak.

It seemed to him that Jon raised his voice deliberately to pull Rick into the discussion. Jon said, "Come now, we've lived in Germany. You know the Germans, Mother. It's the Prussian madness all over again; that's a tradition that will never die."

Jonas looked across the room at Rick. He had turned and was listening intently. For the moment he seemed to have forgotten the beautiful Rachel Levitt.

Jonas cursed silently, recalling the heated arguments of the past. Germany was a subject they usually tried to avoid. Jonas glanced at Anita; her eyes were anxious. They both knew too well what could happen when Jon and Rick got started.

"'Prussian madness,'" Rick repeated in a soft, dangerous voice. "You're calling that insane rabble-rouser a 'Prussian,' Jon?" Rick got up and walked slowly toward his uncle.

"Rick..." Anita said. Looking at Rachel Levitt's uneasy expression, she added, "You are embarrassing our guest."

"I am not the one who said the embarrassing thing, Grandma." Jonas was amazed at how much Rick looked like his father at that moment; it was as if the young Hussar had returned. Rick's stiff, proud posture, his blond hair and fine face were the image of Rikard von Helsing. Jonas looked at the sensitive Rachel and saw a new expression on her face, one of conflicted, almost fearful emotions. "I will not have the memory of my father insulted. He was a great soldier; the Prussians have always been soldiers, not Communists and rabble-rousers."

"Communists!" Jon exclaimed. "That's absurd. Your ignorance is appalling, boy."

Rick glared at Jon, clenching his fists in anger.

"Rick is right, you know." Anita's calm words surprised them all. They stared at her. "The Prussians have nothing whatsoever to do with this awful little Hitler."

"This 'awful little Hitler,' Mother, will rule the world if he is not stopped. Do you know what is already happening to the Jews?"

"That's enough, both of you," Jonas said abruptly.

But Rick broke into his stern order, the younger voice drowning the older man's, and he said loudly, "You have always hated the Germans. Ever since I was a little kid I remember the awful things you said about my father, about the Germans. My mother told me that when you were just a child your playmates all had fathers who were anarchists or Communists. You don't fool me, Jon. They're still your playmates, and they're going to get you into a lot of trouble. Furthermore..." Rick's handsome face was suffused with anger.

"Shut up," Jon said.

Rachel Levitt got up and left the room.

"That is quite enough from both of you. Jon, I think you'd better go see to your guest." Jonas's anger was rising to a dangerous level, and he knew that Anita could feel it, for she put a detaining hand on his arm.

"I'll go myself," she said, looking embarrassed and pained.

289

"All of you sit down and behave yourselves. Really, I don't know what's gotten into you."

Chagrined into obedience, all of the men sat down, and avoided looking at one another.

They heard Anita's voice in the hall, soft and apologetic, and Rachel Levitt's almost inaudible answer.

Anita came back looking exasperated. "Jon, Miss Levitt wants you to take her home, and I'm not surprised," she commented in a low voice. "Both of you have spoiled a perfectly nice evening. I really wonder if she will ever come back again. I don't know what I'm going to do with the pair of you." She looked at Rick and Jon and she sounded near tears.

"Sorry, Mother. Dad. I'll be glad to take her home." Jon stood up and left the room.

Anita went to Rick and put her hand on his head. "Rick, my dear..."

He got up abruptly, and his grandmother's consoling hand slipped off his brief golden hair. Jonas saw the look of pain on his face. He wanted desperately to say something to the boy, but he didn't know what it could be.

"I'm going for a walk," Rick said curtly, and walked to the door that opened into the bare, desolate garden, before Anita could call out to him to put on a coat.

They watched him through the great glass window-wall as he made his way down the gloomy aisle of evergreens, hunched against the freezing winds, his jacket collar turned up around his ears and his fists jammed into his pockets. He was the picture of loneliness and confusion.

When he was out of sight, Jonas took Anita in his arms and held her for a long moment.

She sighed against his chest, and said in a muffled voice, "He will get pneumonia out there."

"I doubt it," Jonas said easily, stroking her hair. "He's a very strong young man."

Anita remained in his arms and burrowed into his chest. "It's all too much for me," she commented. Suddenly she raised her head, and Jonas was touched at the young, wistful, frightened look on her wonderful, unchanging face. "What did Rick mean by Jon's 'playmates,' Jonas?"

"Nothing, I'm sure," Jonas reassured her, patting her shoulder. "Just boy's bravado, probably. Remember," he said and smiled, "Rick's awfully jealous, too."

"I know. Poor boy." Anita gently released herself from Jonas's arms and asked, "Would you like some more wine?"

290

"I could do with some. We've got a very complicated situation here, it seems." He took the proffered glass of Amontillado and waited for Anita to pour her own glass.

When Anita's glass was filled, Jonas raised his own in a toasting gesture, and said, "Don't worry, darling. Jon and Rachel will be going back east next week, and all this will be over. Rick's young; he'll get over it. Besides, he's already taking hold of the project at the fair. Sit down," he invited, seating himself on the big couch and patting the seat beside him. "Let me tell you what he said today."

But even as Jonas enthusiastically described Rick's ideas for Anita, another part of his mind was worrying at the problem of Rick and Rachel and Jon, and Rick's mysterious comments about the companions who would get Jon into "a lot of trouble."

Rachel Levitt leaned back against the leather seat of Jon's swift Hornet and examined him out of the corner of her eye. He had a peculiar smile on his lips, and was staring straight ahead, all of his attention on the road. He drove with pleasure and with ease, and the touch of his hands on the steering wheel and gears was almost a caressing one, as if the car were a lovely woman. Jon Mark had a sensual quality that made her feel close to him, yet in a way they were so much alike that she did not find him very exciting. He was the exact opposite of Rick.

"What was his father like?" she asked abruptly.

The firm grasp of Jon's hands on the wheel did not loosen, nor did he turn his eyes from the road, but the suddenness of her question made him start a little.

"Whose?"

"Rick's." Rachel realized with embarrassment that Rick had already become "he" in her mind, that the implication of that might not escape Jon.

He raised his brows, and his lips twisted in a not very pleasant smile. "Like a Prussian cartoon."

"I take it you didn't like him much."

"Not a bit."

"What do you mean, a Prussian cartoon?"

"Oh, very handsome, straight as a ramrod in that Hussar uniform up to his ears. A heel-clicker, no less. With a dueling scar, like something from an operetta. Rick is the image of him."

Rachel felt a keen excitement. She knew it; she had known

that there was something tragic, romantic, in Rick's blood. "He's not a Nazi, Jon. He was absolutely right. The Nazis and the Prussians are two different kinds."

"Rachel Levitt, I don't understand you at all. Rick upset you so much you had to leave... now you're defending him. What's up?"

Rachel studied Jon. It was amazing how friendly they had become in just these few days, even with the difference in their ages. She supposed it was partly because of Dan, her brother, who hero-worshiped Jon Mark in such a patent way; partly because of her parents, who had welcomed Jon into their home, and her father, who said admiringly that Jon had a "Jewish head." Also, she couldn't fool herself, it was very flattering to be taken about by an M.I.T. professor when she was only a student. But all the time she had thought longingly of Rick von Helsing.

"I wasn't upset by the Prussian business," she retorted calmly. "I was upset by what Rick said about your 'playmates.' I have a feeling they're Dan's playmates, too. And my family's not too thrilled about them."

"What are you talking about?" he demanded, with a swift look at her before his sharp eyes returned to the highway.

"I'm talking about these trouble-making groups in Chicago—and back at school—who are spreading anit-German feelings. And trying to get us into a war."

He did not answer, but she could tell the shot had gone home, because his lips tightened and he looked extremely annoyed.

"How about some dinner?" he asked abruptly.

"All right." She nodded, still studying the handsome profile of the man who looked so much like Jonas Mark.

They had reached downtown Chicago. She wondered where he would take her tonight; the last few days of the holiday had been marked by a great variety of entertainment, from the opera and theater to the plainest of workmen's cafés. Rachel had been very interested in those. They were a total contrast to the magnificence of the Levitt mansion and the order of her sheltered life.

Once she had made a light, joking remark about how colorful the patrons of the café were, saying they looked like "bomb-throwing anarchists," her father's favorite expression.

Jon Mark had not responded in kind, and now, as they approached another such place in a gloomy section near the waterfront, Rachel Levitt wondered how much of her speculation had been fantasy, after all.

Jon opened the door of smudged glass for Rachel to enter and she looked around the café's steamy interior. It seemed to be composed mostly of workmen, eating in a dogged and serious way, but there were also several tables of people who looked like students. In a far corner she saw her brother, Daniel, with three young men she did not know. Dan was not wearing his usual natty clothes; he looked downright seedy to Rachel, like his oddly assorted companions. Some were Jews, some were obviously not, and most of them did not look like students, but workingmen. They did not have that rather unworldly look of college men who had never had to support themselves; these men looked tough and experienced and self-reliant. All of them huddled over the table talking in low voices, glancing up now and then. When Dan Levitt saw Rachel and Jon his face was a blend of pleasure and dismay.

"Well, well," Jon said, smiling. "Look who's here."

Rachel was glad there was no room for her and Jon at the table. She didn't like the looks of her brother's companions. But she smiled in a social way.

"There's a table for two right over there. Why don't you take it? I'll just say hello to Dan," Jon said.

"All right." She waved at her brother and went to the table Jon had pointed out, wondering why he had suggested that. It was almost as if he didn't want her to meet the others. But then she told herself it was only because the small café was so crowded and it was practical to claim the table before somebody else did.

Nevertheless she sat down facing her brother's table and listened to Jon speaking to the young men in a quiet voice. She thought she heard him say, "Not until the spring." But she couldn't really get much of the conversation.

Jon soon concluded his conversation and joined her. While he was ordering, Rachel glanced at her brother again. He returned her look and smiled. He made a gesture of pleasure and approval at Jon Mark's back, as if to say, *"Mazel tov. I admire your taste."*

She returned his smile uncertainly. The waiter left them, and Jon Mark looked at her eyes across the table. Somehow tonight it was not quite so thrilling to be escorted by a professor from M.I.T. Jon raised his coffee cup, which contained chianti, in a kind of amiable salute.

Rachel raised her cup, too, and they drank. But all during

the pleasant meal, while she and Jon talked of many things, Rachel Levitt thought of Rick von Helsing, of how his face had lit up when they had met again. And she knew, for certain, that she had accepted all of Jon Mark's invitations because she had really hoped to see Rick.

She would find a way to see him alone, even if he didn't call. She knew what her father would think of Rick, but she no longer cared. Her heartbeat quickened as she planned for tomorrow.

the pleasant meal, while she and Jeh talked of many thi
Rachel Levell thought of Hick von Helsing, of how his
had lit up when they had met again. And she knew, for
tain, that she had accepted all of Jon Mark's invitatio
cause she had really hoped to see Hick

She smiled, and Jon gave her —no

Chapter 23

IRIS BREWSTER LOOKED at the contents of her bed tray with
distaste. "Take this away, Céleste," she called out sharply to
the small, thin woman who was going through the clothes in
the closet across the room. It was an immense closet extended
along an entire wall, with compartments for furs and other
coats, day and evening dresses and sports things, and drawers
for hats and shoes and gloves and lingerie. The maid, Céleste,
was dwarfed by the closet's vastness.

"Oui, madame," she said with cold patience and came to
take the tray.

"Would you ask my son to come here, please?"

Céleste stood with the tray in her hands and looked at Iris
with unreadable black eyes. I never know what the damned
woman is thinking, Iris reflected sourly. If she weren't such
a good maid...

"Dean has gone to school, madame," Céleste said respectfully.

"I'm talking about Richard." The woman was purposely
trying to irritate her this morning.

"Surely madame remembers," Céleste said smoothly, a
trace of a smile at the corners of her thin mouth, "he spent
the night with his grandparents."

Iris bit her lip with vexation. Yes, she remembered now.
Last night, when Richard had called, she had had a good deal
to drink, and forgotten a good deal more. The circumstances
of her forgetting were reflected now in the nasty smile of
Céleste. I wish to God I had the nerve to do without her, Iris
thought. But she is so perfect she has me at her mercy.

Iris imagined she could see that realization in the woman's
black gaze. "Of course," she said quickly and laughed a little.

295

She could feel the embarrassed heat in her cheeks. "It must have slipped my mind."

"Shall I get you more coffee?" Céleste asked in a meaning way. "And perhaps a little remedy?" The remedy usually consisted of tomato juice with a dash of Tabasco; on very bad mornings Iris had a suspicion that Céleste laced the drink with bathtub gin, for at times the remedy seemed to improve her spirits more than at others.

"No remedy," she said curtly, "just more coffee. Then you can let the dresses go until later. I have some phone calls to make."

Céleste performed her mysterious trick of seeming to raise her brows without actually doing so, a mannerism that particularly annoyed Iris, but she answered, "Very well." And left.

Iris lay back on her pillows, feeling the unpleasant pounding between her eyebrows and the accustomed nausea of an unfed hangover. She took some aspirin from a little glass box on her bed table—the box was amber Lalique and the cover was in the shape of a tiny woman sitting on a swan—and swallowed the aspirin without water. She fitted a cigarette into an amber holder and lit it, inhaling deeply. The feeling of nausea worsened but she smoked on; she felt too shattered not to smoke this morning.

After Céleste had returned with a fresh pot of coffee, poured a Spode cup full and set it on the bed table, Iris murmured, "Thank you. That will be all." The woman nodded once and left the room, moving like a small poised cat.

Iris sighed and took a sip of the coffee. Then she opened a drawer in the bed table and took out a narrow book bound in russet silk brocade. Her long enameled fingernail slid down the alphabetical notched pages to the M's.

She smiled a little. "Never thought I'd live to see the day." She had called her brother, Jon, so rarely that she could not remember his number. Finding it, she picked up the receiver of the gilded phone and dialed.

*"Hell*o." His answer was fractious and sleepy.

"My *dear*," she said softly into the phone, "I *hope* I didn't wake you."

"You did, Iris. I'm on holiday, remember?"

"Jon, my dear, I *am* sorry."

"What's all this dear-ing, Iris?" He sounded more awake, suspicious. "What do you want?"

Iris smiled and knew the smile was transmitting itself into

her voice. "You are a gruff old bear in the mornings, Jon. I feel sorry for Rachel Levitt."

"What the hell do you mean by that?" He sounded really angry now, and Iris regretted her remark.

"I'm sorry, Jon. I was only joking." She listened to his silence and then said softly, "I wanted to invite you and Rachel to dinner...here...Thursday night."

"Why?" he asked abruptly. "You've never liked me, Iris, and I don't think you like Rachel any better. What are you plotting?"

Her head was pounding again. Damn the clever devil. Iris took another aspirin, swallowed it so fast that there was not a break before she answered earnestly, "I want us to be friends, Jon. You're my brother." There was a puzzled silence on the line again.

At last he said, sounding chagrined, "Well, that's...decent of you, Iris. I'm sorry. And you want me to bring Rachel?"

"Yes, darling. I understand you've been 'rushing' her, as they call it." She knew no such thing but was dying to find out.

"I've been seeing a bit of her, yes," Jon admitted.

Then the little bitch hasn't been seeing Richard! Iris thought with triumph. She would be able to see Jon and Rachel together, to see how far it had gone, with Richard safely out of the way. He had made it clear he wouldn't be home on Thursday.

"That's delightful, Jon. The Levitts are very...nice people." Again there was a silence. Jon knew quite well that the Brewsters were not friendly with Jews. To stem Jon's possible comment, Iris rushed on, "At eight, then, Thursday? I look forward to it."

"So do I. It'll be...an interesting evening."

Iris mistrusted his tone but was determined not to take him up on it. Not for a while, not until she had seen for herself how that girl felt about Jon.

"We'll see you then." She hung up and lay back on her pillows. Her headache was going; she was hungry. She rang for breakfast.

Later, Iris was beginning to feel human again, and had made plans to meet a friend at a gallery. She was about to leave the house when the phone rang.

"Mother?"

"Richard, my love! I'm so glad to hear from you!"

"Good to talk to you," he rushed on. "About Thursday dinner..Would you still have room for me?"

Damn, she thought with annoyance, he must have talked to Jon already. But she answered quickly, "For my own son? I should hope so." She tried to keep the dismay out of her voice. Now the whole thing was a mess; unwittingly she had brought him and that girl together again.

"Great. See you then. I've got to run. 'Bye, Mother."

Well, Iris thought, with a pettish frown, now I've got an awkward evening on my hands. My hands and Donald's, she amended. But then, she reflected, Donald had always been the least of her problems. Even when they had first met, thirteen years ago....

In the five years after Rick's birth, Iris Mark went through immeasurable changes. She was no less beautiful; if anything, even more attractive. Maturity had given her slender body a new richness; the droop of her mouth and her eyes' weary look did not detract from her appeal. On the contrary, they gave her the air of a sleepy and arrogant young lioness. Several young men had learned to their cost that the look about her mouth and eyes was deceptive. What they had misread as sensuousness was a habitual sullenness.

With the death of Rikard von Helsing, most of Iris had died, never to be revived. She did not touch the piano again, after Richard's birth. He was the only thing in her life that meant anything at all—the tiny premature baby who miraculously survived his untimely arrival and grew into a handsome, sturdy toddler who already had his father's upright bearing and handsome features in miniature.

For the first year or two of the baby's life it was easy and consoling to live with Jonas and Anita; Iris was possessed of a terrible lassitude that made it impossible to consider the slightest change. But as the little boy grew, and her parents moved them into the Pinnacle, Iris began to sense a subtle change in her son. He already adored his grandparents, and it soon developed that little Rick ran to his grandparents before he came to her.

He is all my life, she thought with burning resentment, and I will not let them take him from me. The first time Iris thought it through, she was horrified at her own bizarre notion. She reproached herself for feeling such hostility toward her mother, who had made such an enormous sacrifice, leaving Jonas alone in Germany, so that she might look after Iris.

298

But whenever she called out to the small boy, "Come to Mother, darling," and he shook his head in that stubborn way of his and said, "Grandma," the sore feeling returned to Iris's heart. Her resentment burned hotter than ever.

And she noticed that her mother and father often studied her in an anxious way. Iris had developed such solitary habits that they were overjoyed when she consented to join them at the theater or the opera, or at one of the numerous evening parties and dinners to which they were invited. She often excused herself on the grounds that there was no one to look after the baby; several times Anita insisted that Iris go somewhere with Jonas while she stayed at home with Rick. They had hired a nurse who was gentle and responsible, an utterly reliable woman on whom they could depend, but Iris always found some fault in the woman's care. And she was unwilling to leave Rick with her mother; jealously she felt they were already too close. She wanted to take her son and move away. Then he would be hers and hers alone.

Iris was haunted by that idea the autumn night in 1919 when she went to see *Parsifal* with Anita and Jonas. Listening to the heroic sounds of the music, Iris felt that for the first time in years she was alive to it again, surrounded by it. Her absent glance touched an opposite box where a young man was sitting behind a dignified gray-haired couple. The young man looked a little like Rik, she thought. He was handsome in a stiff way. He might have posed for an advertisement of the Right Young Man, with his aristocratic features and faultless attire. But Iris looked away and forgot him in the imposing strains of *Parsifal*.

However, at the interval, he appeared in the Marks' box and Jonas introduced him as Donald Brewster. Brewster was so patently bewitched by Iris that it amused her. He continued to amuse her in the weeks to follow. First he called at the Marks' house several times; eventually Iris consented to be escorted by him to various functions—a play, a concert, a dance.

He was always perfectly respectful and correct; his manner was so perfect that sometimes, Iris noticed with a kind of bleak amusement, she would forget he was there. And yet he was not displeasing, with that faint resemblance to Rik that once or twice made her feel almost warm to him. And he persisted.

Finally, after repeated proposals from him, Iris decided at the end of a six-month courtship that Donald was the right one to take her and the baby away from the Pinnacle. There would be no one between them, then, and she would be free to raise Rick in the perfect image of his father.

And I was right, the older Iris thought with satisfaction, as she shrugged into her fur coat. Donald has always been very useful.

Yes, she would be sure to remind him to be home for Thursday's dinner. It would be amusing to see the effect of Donald's cold politeness on Rachel Levitt.

"It was so kind of you to come to my little dinner."

They were saying their goodnights in the gloomy splendor of the Tudor entrance hall.

Rachel smiled at Iris Brewster and said calmly, "It was good of you to have me." She was surprised to find how sorry she felt for the woman. In the bright light of the hall, Iris looked older than her years, and her perfunctory warmth contrasted horribly with the anger in her eyes and the lines extending from the corners of her nose to the edges of her painted mouth. Rachel wondered what had gone wrong for Iris Brewster; something had, that was certain.

"Why don't we drop Rick off?" Rachel asked Jon. Jon Mark looked annoyed, and Iris blurted, "Richard, you're not staying there *tonight*?"

Mr. Brewster, Rachel noticed, was embarrassed. But he hid it pretty well. He just seemed to get stiffer and more correct.

"The Pinnacle is closer to the site, Iris," Donald said smoothly to his wife.

"Well, come on," Jon said gruffly. "We'll give you a lift."

Rachel looked at Rick von Helsing and felt a warm elation. The whole boring, uncomfortable evening he had spent staring at her, across the formal table, across that awful music room, where they had sat so stiffly.

"Thank you again, Mrs. Brewster, Mr. Brewster," Rachel said politely, as the three moved toward the massive entrance door.

"Richard!" Iris Brewster called out sharply to her son.

He retraced his steps and went to her, bending to kiss her cheek. "Goodnight, Mother." She clung to him. Donald Brewster shifted his shoulders in his faultless evening jacket.

At last the three were out on the graveled drive. "We're a little tight for space," Jon Mark said to no one in particular, but Rachel knew the remark was a reproach to Rick for coming with them, to her for inviting Rick.

Well, that's too bad, she thought, with a mischievous delight in Jon's annoyance. She was a little ashamed of using him to see Rick, but it was worth it. Dammit, it was worth it.

Rachel's heart was beating fast when she got into the narrow seat of the Hornet, and Rick got in beside her. The space was very close indeed, and she thrilled to the touch of Rick's hard flank, pressed so close to her own. She took a rather shuddery little breath, chagrined at how loud it sounded in the enclosed space of the small car before Jon started the engine.

"May I?" Rick asked, and put his arm over the back of the seat. "I think we'll all fit in better this way."

"Of course," she said, and her voice sounded breathless in her own ears. His arm just grazed the upturned collar of her fur, but even that slight touch had set her pulse racing.

Jon Mark maintained a sullen silence as they turned onto the main road and raced away. He was driving very fast; Rachel realized from that how angry he was, but she didn't care, because at that speed she was thrown against Rick with every turn. She could feel the perilous warmth of her body increasing; her blood seemed to be fairly boiling, making an uncomfortable heat inside the long fur coat.

Suddenly she had an inspiration and, raising her voice to make herself heard over the Hornet's roar, she said, "Why don't you both come to my house instead, for a little while? Dan's having some friends in, and maybe you'd like to meet them."

"I'd like that," Rick said at once. She glanced quickly at him and saw that his face was turned toward her, his blue eyes shining.

"Afraid I can't," Jon answered tersely. "I've got an early appointment."

"On vacation?" Rick asked lightly, and Rachel could feel the tension between them.

"Yes, on vacation. I'd better take you on to the Pinnacle, Rick." Jon's voice was cool but tightly controlled.

"Don't worry, Jon. I can call a taxi. That's OK." Rick's tone was calm and stubborn, and Rachel's pulse beat quickened. He did want to be alone with her, he did. She almost held her breath for Jon's reply. She hoped fervently he wouldn't change his mind.

301

She was in luck, for Jon growled, "All right. Suit yourself." They raced down Lake Shore Drive and soon Jon pulled up before the Levitt mansion to let them out.

Rick was out of the car in a moment, holding out his hand to help Rachel. "Thanks, Jon," he said.

Rachel added her polite thanks, and Jon answered coldly, "You're very welcome." He did not mention calling her tomorrow, as he always did, and Rachel was both delighted and a little ashamed.

But then she forgot Jon Mark completely, forgot everything but Rick's hand on her elbow, guiding her up the stairs. Even through the thickness of the heavy fur, she could feel the touch of his hard fingers, and again her breath grew short.

She opened the door with her key, remarking in a high, nervous voice, "We don't stand much on formality here. I don't know where the boys are—I guess they're playing pool downstairs."

"That's great," Rick said, looking around him. The place was splendid, but warm. "I'm pretty tired of formal things."

Rachel thought of Iris Brewster's "little dinner," and recalled her own mother's informal gatherings, the buffet suppers where everybody had such a good time. And she felt a tender pity for Rick that made her physical excitement a hundred times more poignant.

Rick took off his coat and handed it to her; their fingers brushed and she felt the crackle of electricity.

She laughed. "From the cold, and my fur."

His look held hers. "Not from the cold. Not from your fur." His voice had deepened and sounded rather shaky.

She turned away, feeling her face grow hot, and hung his coat and hers in the closet. Then she turned back to him and forced herself to ask casually, "Shall we look for Dan and the others?"

"No," he answered quietly, still looking into her eyes. His eyes were like blue water, and Rachel thought she might drown in them. It was a dizzying emotion; Rachel imagined it would be like that to be hypnotized, just to let oneself go, drifting and drifting into a kind of heightened sleep, utterly in another's power. "No," he repeated, smiling, "not tonight. I came here to be with you."

Rachel stood quite still, looking up at him, examining with a kind of hunger his strong, beautiful face with its proud, high-bridged nose, the straight golden brows over the brilliant eyes, the mouth that was so firm and kind at the same time, and the strong, shapely jaw. She wanted to reach up and touch his face with her hands, but instead she invited, "Come to the library, then, and I'll give you a drink."

She was buoyed by such elation that she seemed to be floating, not walking, as she led him through a double doorway to the left of the high, curving stair.

He closed the doors and stood with his back to them, still staring at her, with that glazed, bright-eyed look of intoxicated happiness.

Suddenly she felt her heart flutter in her throat; it was painful, the feeling was so strong, and she thought she could not breathe. She said, "I think my parents are still out. I..."

He shook his head and smiled. "Rachel, Rachel," he said softly, almost with reproach, and he came to her and took her in his arms, holding her so close that she could feel all of his hard, vital body through the fine wool of his clothes, and she could not speak or think any longer.

"Rachel," he said again, and his hands moved from her pliant back and caressed her sides, learning the shape of her hips and waist. His hands felt so hot upon her that she imagined wildly for an instant that they would burn through her dress.

"Oh, Rachel, you don't know what you do to me. When I looked at you that very first day, all of you was so... lovely." He raised her face in both his hands and kissed her deeply. She moved closer and closer to him, giving herself utterly to his kiss. Abruptly, he released her.

"What is it? What's the matter, Rick?"

He smiled and gazed at her. She thought how different he looked now, gentle and vulnerable, not at all like the proud, distant young man on the plane. "I just think I'd better stop kissing you, for a while." He grinned. "You make me too..."

"There's no 'too,'" she protested, and she was amazed at the sound of her own voice. It was deeper, and almost throbbing with her own excitement. "There's no 'too' with us," she repeated. "Please, please kiss me, go on kissing me."

She tightened her arms around his neck and pressed her body nearer to his, hearing him make strange, excited, almost pained sounds as he kissed her, never raising his mouth from hers, and there was nothing left for her in the world but his scent and closeness and the feel of his body and his mouth. She could hear nothing but the pounding of her heart, and his, he was so near to her, and the tidelike pull and sigh of their long-held breaths. There had never been anything, in all her days, so whole or quite so beautiful.

"Well, well!"

The sarcastic male voice broke in, shattering their spell. They moved apart quickly, dismayed, and stared at the library door.

Rachel's brother, Daniel, was standing in the doorway, glaring at them with an expression of distaste, his long, sensitive hands holding the great doors open on either side of him. It was an accusing stance.

Rick straightened his jacket. He looked levelly at Daniel Levitt and said calmly, "Hello, Dan."

Daniel nodded coldly and asked, "What does this mean, von Helsing?"

Rachel brushed back her shining hair and snapped, "Don't talk to Rick like that!"

Daniel Levitt closed the doors and came into the room. Rachel could see that he was trembling with anger; his lips were tight and his eyes were narrowed. He strode to a sideboard against the wall and poured himself a short glass of whiskey. He drained the glass and set it down on the sideboard with a curt gesture, and Rachel winced at the angry snick of glass on wood.

Daniel turned and faced Rick, who was still standing.

"I won't have my sister cheapened, von Helsing, in her own house."

"Cheapened!" Rachel repeated with indignation. She glanced at Rick and saw his hands tighten into fists. "You are the cheap one," Rachel said to her brother. "To come in here, intruding—"

"Intruding on my sister's seduction," Daniel sneered, glaring at Rick.

"Be careful, Levitt," Rick said in a low voice. "I'm about to knock you down, but I can't do it here. Nothing would please me more, in another place."

"Please," Rachel said to both of them. She got up and went toward her brother.

"Look at you," he said, his glance lingering contemptuously on her tumbled hair, her smeared lips and the neck of her gown pulled awry. "You look like a whore."

Rick exclaimed angrily and moved toward Daniel Levitt. "No, Rick, no!"

Rachel's voice made him pause, but he stood glaring at

er brother and said, "Never use that word again in Rachel's resence, I warn you."

Something in Rick's manner daunted her brother; to Rachel's amazement and relief, he said, "I apologize. But you ave no business being here alone with her in my parents' bsence."

"I was not aware that they were absent when I came," Rick said coldly.

"I think you'd better leave, von Helsing."

"I will leave when Rachel asks me to." Rachel looked at he two young men, facing each other and taking each other's measure like gladiators. They were of a height, but Rick was ar stronger then the reedy Daniel, and Rachel had the feeling hat Rick's academic career had included a great deal of sports. He was muscular and lithe and moved with a lethal race.

"Perhaps you will leave us while we say goodnight," achel said at last in a shaky voice. She was on the verge of ears but was determined not to give her brother the satisaction of seeing her cry.

Instinctively Rick heard her pain and came to stand by er. He put his arm around her.

"You are not welcome in this house, von Helsing." Daniel evitt turned on his heel and strode out of the room, slamming the big double doors to behind him.

As the doors crashed shut, Rachel burst into tears and eaned sobbing on Rick's chest.

"Oh, my God, I'm sorry, I'm sorry," she said over and over. How horrible, how..."

"Hush, hush, Rachel darling." Rick held her as if she were child, and kept murmuring until she was quiet again. Then e fumbled in his jacket pocket and took out a handkerchief. e moved back from her and wiped her eyes very gently. He miled at her, and kissed her reddened nose, both of her eeks, and then her mouth, with a tender lightness.

"It'll be better if I go now," he said.

"No, no!" She clutched at him and held him close to her. Don't you see? I'm leaving tomorrow. Tomorrow," she reated tragically.

"Oh, Rachel, dear Rachel." He kissed her again, and she lt as if it were the last time in their lives. "You'll be coming ack. And I'll come to see you, I promise."

"Will you? Will you?" She looked at him, and she felt a reat anxiety.

305

"Of course I will." He met her look solemnly. "I swear it. Do you think I could bear to be away from you for very long?"

She was reassured by his eager face, his pleading tone.

"Oh, Rick, I hope not."

"I couldn't. I couldn't, Rachel. I love you."

She was too overwhelmed to speak. She went into his arms again. Finally she whispered, "I love you, too."

"I'd better go now. What time does your flight leave tomorrow?"

She shook her head. "Dan will be flying with me."

"Never mind. We can meet somewhere before. Think about it, and I'll call you as soon as I get home."

"I have a private phone in my rooms," she said. She gave him the number. "Don't you want to write it down?"

He shook his head, smiling. "I don't need to. I'll never forget it." And he repeated it for her.

He took her urgently in his arms once more. "I'll call you as soon as I get home."

They went into the hall. Rachel was relieved that her parents had still not returned and there was no sign of Daniel anywhere. The house was very quiet. Apparently his friend had left too.

Rachel got Rick's coat from the guest closet and helped him to put it on. He gave her one last fervent kiss before he said goodnight, and she walked him to the door. Then she went to one of the long front windows and watched as he disappeared into the night.

At last, when he was out of sight, she went upstairs to her suite. Dan's door opened down the hall and he came out. "What's the matter with you?" he demanded. "You have one of the smartest men in America running after you, and you have to get mixed up with that Nazi kid."

She started to make an angry reply, but instead looked at him with contempt and went into her suite.

She sat down by the phone and waited. It was a long time before the phone rang, but when she heard Rick's voice, everything was beautiful again. Everything would be all right.

Chapter 24

DURING THE BLEAK MONTH of January, Rick threw himself into the exposition project with such obsessive concentration that even the compulsive Jonas warned him now and then to back off and take it easier. Even so the work was no longer the center of his life.

Jonas suspected the cause of his obsessive work, Rick thought, though his grandfather had not asked him why he decided so abruptly to move in with them at the end of January. It had all begun with Rachel's letters, and with Iris.

Rick and Rachel wrote each other every day. Twice Iris saw Rick with a lilac-colored envelope in his hand, and she must have guessed from his expression who had sent the letters. He made some awkward remark about friends at school. Iris raised her graceful brows and drawled, "The members of your rowing team must be very peculiar, my dear, to use that color stationery."

Rick mentioned it to Rachel in his next letter. From that time on her letters arrived in square white envelopes, but Iris was still not fooled. She had taken to coming downstairs for breakfast, a departure for her, and riffling casually through the mail on the hall table before it was separated by the butler and distributed to the various family members through their servants. Rachel could use a white envelope but she could not disguise the obvious femininity of her hand-writing.

It was after another confrontation with his mother about the letters and his privacy that Rick packed up, stormed out of the Brewster house and went to stay with Jonas and Anita. Rick called Rachel and warned her not to address any more letters to the Brewster house.

There were a few rough days, with Iris making tipsy phone calls to the Pinnacle, accusing her parents of alienating her child from her. Only the intervention of the exasperated Donald put a stop to the calls. Thereafter Rachel's letters came to the Pinnacle, in lilac envelopes once again. The kindly butler at the Brewsters' rescued one that arrived after Rick left and forwarded it to him.

Jonas and Anita guessed what was going on, but never commented to Rick.

Early in February, however, Jonas told Anita that he was worried about the boy. Rick had lost weight and had dark circles under his eyes. He ate little for days at a time, then suddenly was so ravenous he would eat gluttonously and get indigestion. He spent all of his evenings alone in his room, evidently writing letters and listening to music. The warm companionable times the three had spent in the past were at an end.

Rick and Jonas were at the site six days a week, checking and overseeing. On some occasions Rick visited the site on Sundays. At last, in early February, Jonas decided to talk to him.

They were preparing to leave the site on a snowy evening when Rick asked Jonas to drop him off in town before the stores closed. "I've got to get something in the mail soon," Rick said.

"Before Valentine's Day," Jonas said casually. He always remembered to have a gift for Anita that day. He glanced aside at Rick and saw the boy's lean cheeks color.

"Yes."

"All right, son. Why don't I wait for you? Where do you want to go... Carson's?"

"I guess so." Rick's color deepened. "How's their jewelry department? All right?"

"One of the best, Anita tells me." Jonas drove Rick downtown and parked. After a while Rick emerged from the great store with a square bulge in the pocket of his trim overcoat.

"All set?" Jonas asked in a carefully casual tone.

"Yes. Thanks."

"Don't mention it." Jonas started the car, and they drove for a time in silence. When he turned in to the road leading to the Pinnacle, Jonas asked Rick quietly, "Why don't you deliver the present?"

His eyes were on the road, but he could sense Rick's surprise. "Take it? But how can I...how can I leave the project at this point?"

Jonas smiled. "We're way ahead, Rick. Besides, I think my men and I could handle things for a couple of days. We took care of a few things before you came along." Jonas's chuckle took any sting from the remark.

Rick cleared his throat. Carefully Jonas did not look at him, but out of the corner of his eye he thought he saw the boy's hand make a pass at his own face. Rick cleared his throat again, and said, "Thanks, Granddad. Thanks."

Jonas took his hand from the wheel for an instant and touched his grandson's arm. "It's all right. I felt the same way about Anita." He was quiet for an instant, remembering. Then he added, "I'll tell your mother I sent you back, for some research or something. Keep the peace."

"I don't know what to say."

"Don't say anything, Rick. Just go home and pack. Take a week back east."

"A week?" Rick sounded stunned.

"A week," Jonas said firmly. When they got home, Jonas did not have to tell Anita what had been decided. She took one look at them and smiled. Rick, she said later, looked like a small boy on Christmas morning.

The landing was a rocky one, because of a strong wind sweeping in from Boston Harbor, but Rick was on his feet before the plane touched down. The attendant said sharply, "Keep your seat, sir, until we have landed."

Impatiently he obeyed, leaning to the small round window of the plane, trying vainly to see through the faint mist of snow the people waiting behind the glass barrier. It was still a blur. He flexed his hands tensely, waiting for what seemed an hour while the plane taxied to a stop.

The attendant nodded at him, smiling, and said, "It's all right now. I've never seen anyone so anxious to arrive."

"You bet you haven't," he retorted, grinning. He had already hoisted down his bag, and now he stood with it in his hand, almost pushing those ahead of him in his eagerness to disembark. His heart was beating so hard it felt painful and scratchy, high up in his throat, and his knees were weak.

Somehow they were all out, then, and he was striding across the slippery runway, his long legs leaving the others behind. He saw her.

She was bright and warm and smiling, and she was all

scarlet and fur, a long, slender cocoon of dark shining fur, a high red collar of wool under her chin and a red woolen cap concealing her brief dark hair, making her look more vivid than ever, wholly vibrant and alive, unbelievably beautiful. Her great dark eyes were shining.

He dropped his suitcase and strode to her, crying out, "Rachel, Rachel."

Unconscious of everything and everyone, they swayed a little in each other's desperate grasp, and he bent his head to kiss her warm, parted mouth.

After a long, breathless moment he let her go and stood back to look down into her face. She is so beautiful, he thought with wonder, and so glad. Her eyes were huge and blazing with her excited happiness; her red lips trembled, and when she tried to speak, at first all she could say was, "Rick, oh, Rick. You're here, you're here."

"I'm here," he repeated with wonder. "Oh, yes. My God, it seems so long." He took her in his arms again. Then he said, "Let's get out of here."

"Yes, yes." They began to walk away, and she said, "Good Lord, Rick. Your bag. My bag."

"*Your* bag?" For the first time he saw the handsome leather case. It was standing a few feet from his own. "Rachel, what...?" He was almost afraid to ask what it meant; it seemed too good to be true. He had pictured checking into a hotel and then taking her out somewhere.

"I have a weekend pass." She looked at him steadily, her eyes still bright and blazing, and she was open and vulnerable, utterly full of trust. It was as if she had said, "I am in your hands now, I have surrendered everything to you."

A wide, delighted smile broke out on his face, and he stammered, "Rachel, you mean we...we will. Jesus, Rachel."

"I've arranged it all," she said. "There's a place..." She stopped and looked into his eyes. "That is, if you want to go there with me."

"*Want* to! Oh, my God, Rachel." He put his arm around her and held her with a viselike grip about her waist. "Just tell me how, where. Let's go!"

"It's wonderful," Rick said, smiling down at Rachel, "it's as if there were no one else in all creation."

They were walking by the ocean on the following Sunday afternoon, the first time they had been out of the house since Friday evening. The day was milder and the snow had ceased to fall, but the wind from Pleasure Bay was very cold, and Rick hugged Rachel close to him. She was wearing one of his sweaters and a pair of his thick wool trousers under her long fur coat; the trousers were tucked into sturdy boots. Rick had smiled at the sight of her slender, rounded body in the masculine clothes, her small head emerging from the huge turtleneck of the sweater.

"We are the only ones," she said, "except the gulls." They looked up at the gray expanse of sky above the rolling gray fields of water; the gulls wheeled around with thin, creaking cries, then in the distance a small fishing boat appeared. "And the fishermen."

"Are you warm enough?" he asked with concern, drawing her closer to his body.

She fell into step with him, and said, "Oh, yes. I love it. Remember, we got our training in Chicago."

She grinned up at him, and her face looked like a happy elf's under the rakish cap pulled down over her brow.

"I love you, I love you," he said, and stopped to kiss her. Then suddenly he began to run down the wet gray sand, waving his arms at the sky and shouting, "I love her, I love her! I love her, gulls! Do you understand?"

She ran after him, laughing and skipping, and he caught her in his arms. They overbalanced, and fell on the sand.

"Good God, woman, you are insatiable," he said in mock dismay.

"And you are mad."

"We both are. There's a warmer place than this to make love." He stood up and held out his hand. She rose as lightly as a little cat and grinned at him.

"Your face is full of sand. And you're beautiful. Let's go inside."

They were shivering when they went into the house and hurried to sit before the fire. He took off her gloves and rubbed her hands with his. "You're cold as a little frog," he said. "Put your hands in here." He pulled her hands under his heavy Irish sweater.

"No, no! How cruel! I wouldn't do that to an enemy."

"You may do it to me." He held her hands firmly under his sweater until he felt her stop shivering. "There, isn't that better? Do you want a glass of wine?"

"No, I don't want anything but you." He heard the words he had said to her their first night being repeated to him. He thought again of the sweetness and shyness of her first attempts at love, and his own eagerness. Now he watched her joyfully as she stood up, and with a more practiced motion, pulled his heavy sweater over her head. Her own soft cashmere swiftly followed; then she unfastened her boots, and, wordless, he pulled them from her feet.

He could hear the loud, fast beating of his own heart, feel the shortening of his excited breath as he stared at her, naked in the orange glow of the fire. Slowly she knelt down, and then with a catlike grace, all of it like one lovely motion, lay down on the giant pillows before the hearth. The pillows were scarlet and orange and gold, and glorying in the sight of her shining eyes and hair, her red parted mouth, and her soft, bare body, he thought, She is like fire.

"You make me warm just to look at you," he whispered, and she propelled herself upward like a dancer, looking at him with great yearning and tenderness, and began to draw his sweater over his head. She unbuttoned his shirt and kissed his stomach and his chest with many small, quick kisses as he felt the vast throbbing begin in the depths of his loins.

They were quickly together, and he said in a low, shaken voice, "It's so good, oh, it's so good, my love, my Rachel."

And it was different from the times before, deeper and more satisfying than he had ever known.

Afterward he told her so, as she lay in the hollow of his arm. "It's because I have to go back tonight."

"Oh, Rachel, you can't."

"I know, I can't, Rick." She turned and lay closer to him with her head on his chest, and he felt a warm wetness on his skin.

"You're crying." He hugged her to him and said, "Oh, don't Don't."

"How can I help it?" she protested, sobbing. "How can I ever go away from you again? How can I live away from you?"

"I don't know. I don't know how I can, either, Rachel." They were silent for a moment; he stroked her hair until her sobbing quietened, and then he said, "Listen, darling. Maybe there's a way. Maybe you can be with me this whole week; why not? Tell them . . . someone's sick at home, something like that. That you have to fly back."

He could feel her excited attention. Her body was alert, listening, to his touch. "Maybe I can," she said slowly with rising hope. "Yes, I can. I will." She sat up so abruptly that she surprised him.

"Where are you going?"

"To phone."

"To *phone?*" he repeated in astonishment.

"There's one here," she said, laughing at his expression. "It's the last thing I would have thought of before, or wanted."

"That's great. Phone then. What will you tell them?"

"That my mother's sick, and I'm flying home tonight from Boston."

He lay back on the pillows and listened as she called.

When she returned, triumphantly smiling, he said, "Now it's all right."

"Yes, yes, my darling, now it's fine." She lay down beside him again and put her head on his shoulder. "If only Dan doesn't take it into his head to come see me, or call."

He stiffened. "Does he do that often?"

"Not lately. Not since I was home last." For a moment the ugliness of that encounter lay over them both like a pall.

"Never mind," she said softly, stroking his chest, and kissing him. "Never mind that now. We have this whole long week together, this little lifetime of days."

There was something so poignant in the expression that he cried out and drew her closer and closer, kissing her with a deeper hunger than he had known before. A little lifetime, and it was theirs, for this one week, at least.

Later, she asked him in a wondering voice, "How can it be so easy, so right with us? You know there was never ... anyone for me before."

"Of course I know. It was because we already knew each other, from our letters."

And that was true, he reflected happily, as they drowsed before the fire. In their letters they had told each other everything about themselves and their whole lives. So by the time their bodies came together, it was a meeting also of two minds that had known each other deeply.

They were stunned at the swiftness of the passing week. It was almost time for The Taxi, as Rachel called the rattletrap driven by the dour man, to come for them. The driver would be the first person they had seen for eight days, except for the man who had come on one occasion to deliver some supplies of food and firewood.

Rachel had been almost unwilling even to allow that; on Monday and Tuesday they had even dragged in some soggy driftwood, hoping to dry it enough to use for a fire, but they had not succeeded. Now she stood in front of the dark hearth, looking around the room. They had left the house neat and in perfect order; it was the same lovely room that had welcomed them on the first night.

But to Rachel it seemed that the joy had gone from it, just as the joy would go from her with Rick's departure. She shivered and turned up the high collar of her fur, huddling down into it as if she wished to hide.

Rick was putting on his city overcoat; there was a square bulge in the trim right pocket, obvious with the coat's lean line. "My God!" he exclaimed and put a hand to his head.

"What's the matter?" Quickly she walked toward him.

"The matter is, I completely forgot this," he said, exasperated. He took a square white box from his pocket. "Completely forgot Valentine's Day." He handed her the box.

"What's Valentine's Day?" she asked lightly. "I forgot it myself. You are totally absolved for forgetting anything this week." She grinned. In spite of herself, she was eager to see what was in the box.

She sat down and opened it. Inside was another box of russet velvet. She opened it and found an exquisite ring; it was gold and set with two perfectly formed hearts of golden-orange topaz. He sat down beside her and took the ring from its slot of padded satin and slipped it on the third finger of Rachel's left hand.

"Rick, oh, Rick, it's beautiful. A honey topaz." She gazed at it, holding her hand up in the dim light to admire the brightness and fire of the stones.

"A honey topaz," he repeated. He lifted her hand and kissed the fingers one by one. "I didn't know. That's perfect, because you are the sweetest thing of my whole life."

"And it's your birthstone." She kissed him and touched his face. "The birthstone of my 'fate,' a Scorpio."

"I didn't know that either." She told him what it meant—they were opposites, and wildly drawn to each other. He was determined and relentless and strong, born under the influence of Mars; she was equally strong, but her strength was softer, of the earth, and she came under the influence of Venus.

"I knew when you were born," she said softly, "the first time I ever saw you."

"That's amazing." He smiled at her with tender indulgence, and she felt an overwhelming flood of love. "I always

314

thought that stuff was silly, before. But when you describe it... I can understand."

They sat for a moment in happy silence. He looked at his watch. "It's almost time." He picked up her left hand again and kissed it. "Rachel, you saw what finger I put the ring on."

He was looking at her very earnestly, and once more she felt that almost painful tenderness, looking at his relaxed mouth and the lean lines of his handsome face. It was a different face now; the dark circles under his eyes had gone and his face had already filled out a little.

"Yes, yes, Rick, I did."

"I want us to get married, as soon as we can."

"Rick, are you sure?"

His blue gaze was answer enough—he looked at her with steady, sober eyes. Unsmiling, he said, "You know I am. Rachel, this is the first time in my life I've ever been really happy... the first time I can remember, since I was a little kid at my grandparents' house, that I haven't been lonely. You've changed the whole world for me; you're more important to me than anything I'll ever build, or know, or do."

She was too overwhelmed to say a word. She came into his arms and leaned against him.

"You will marry me, won't you?" Her face was hidden against his chest, but she could hear the urgency in his voice.

She raised her head. "Have you ever doubted that, for a moment?"

"No, I guess I haven't. I just couldn't doubt it. I couldn't have stood it."

She took his face between her hands and kissed him, wishing that they could stay in this one place forever.

"Oh," she said, "I wish... how I wish that we never had to say goodbye."

Like a symbolic answer, they heard the chugging sound of The Taxi approaching the house.

"Oh, Rachel, Rachel, what are we going to do until the spring?"

She clung to him, answering, "Write each other every night, think of each other all the time."

"Yes, that is exactly what we'll have to do."

They heard The Taxi's raucous horn, like an enormous hoarse bullfrog at the end of the path.

"Well, my lady, it is time." Rick stood up and buttoned his

315

coat. He hoisted their bags and went to the door. "Goodbye, house. It's been a lovely honeymoon."

Rachel's throat hurt with unshed tears. She made herself smile at him but could not speak. He held the door open for her and waited while she locked it. Then they got into The Taxi and Rick directed the driver to take them to the ferry.

They hardly spoke at all while the ferry lumbered across the Inner Harbor, and were still silent at the landing on the other side. The weather had cleared and grown very mild: the sun was bright, and Rachel almost resented its happy brightness on a day when her whole self felt dark and pained.

When it was time for Rick to board the plane, she gave a little cry and went into his arms, burying her face in his chest, indifferent to the staring people around them, indifferent to everything but the clean musky scent of his skin and his clothes, and the last sweet touch of his arms so tightly around her.

"Darling, darling," he said in her ear, "don't cry. We'll be together in the spring, at Eastertime. At Passover," he amended, smiling.

"At Eastertime," she repeated, and the pain welled up higher in her throat.

"There will not be one moment of the day or night when I'm not thinking of you, I swear it," he said. He kissed her one more time and turned away quickly, striding toward the plane. She stood and watched him climb the boarding stairs. The sky was bright blue, the air so clear that she could see his face vividly, even at the distance between the barrier and the plane. When he reached the mouth of the plane's door, he turned and waved.

She kept watching. At last his face appeared again, at one of the small round windows, and they looked at each other steadily until the door closed and the engines started, until the plane began to taxi down the field. She saw that he was looking back, still straining to see her until the last moment.

"Where in the hell have you been?" Startled, Rachel turned around and encountered the angry face of her brother, Daniel. She was sure now that Rick must have seen him, too, in the bright visibility of the cold blue day; the loud world closed in on her and her heart sank, as she prepared an answer for her brother.

Chapter 25

"IT'S WONDERFUL," SAID Anita Mark, looking with pleasure at
the shadowy trees and winding streams, the fairytale huts
nestling in the depths of the Black Forest village. "It is like
a scene from the Brothers Grimm." She smiled at Rick and
Jonas. "And the things you've done with floodlights, Rick.
Remarkable."

Rick glowed with her praise; he was quite pleased with
the lighting himself. It gave the illusion of sunlight through
the heavy trees of a dark forest, exactly as he had planned.

"Don't you wish Hubrist...and Frau Benz were alive to
see it?" Anita asked Jonas softly. She took his arm, and he
nodded, a look of nostalgia on his face. Otto Hubrist had died
in 1926, Frau Benz a few years later, and Rick knew that for
both his grandparents an era had ended with those deaths.

He looked at them with affection, feeling the pleasant
weight of Rachel's letter in his breast pocket. He hadn't read
it yet; it had been a hectic day, but soon, he thought with
anticipation, he would go away somewhere alone and read
it. And she would be back tomorrow.

Rick heard Jonas say in a low voice, "What does it remind
you of? Do you remember that holiday we took?"

Anita looked up at him and answered in the same low
tone, "Do you think I could forget?"

"Come on, let us show you the interiors."

"You go ahead, Granddad. You do the honors. I'll
just...wander around."

Jonas looked pointedly at the edge of the lilac envelope
protruding from Rick's pocket and grinned. "Maybe you can
find something to read while I show your grandmother the
317

house." Anita laughed, and they went together up the stairs to the wooden cottage.

Rick wandered off to a secluded spot and sat down on the thick, spongy grass to read Rachel's letter.

My darling,

I can hardly believe that the day after you get this letter we will be in each other's arms again, after all these empty weeks without each other. I couldn't have stood it without your calls and letters; knowing I could hear your voice, now and then, sustained me all the way. And your wonderful letters—I read them over and over and carry each day's letter with me everywhere.

I'm sorry I was so evasive about your question about Dan. I just didn't want you to brood about it all this time, because there was nothing we could do until the time came, anyway. But now that I've learned he's coming back for the holiday—he usually doesn't—I thought I'd better tell you what happened the afternoon you left.

What I dreaded that week did happen; he came to see me, for some strange reason, at school, and of course they were very puzzled, since my mother was supposedly ill. I have to give him credit, he didn't give me away, but made up some cock-and-bull story about being away and not getting the message from home himself. That, in itself, frightened me; he has always been so open about everything. It was almost as if he's plotting something. I will not go into what he said to me, but he was furious, and he saw you get on the plane. I don't know what he's up to, Rick, but I'm convinced that whatever it is, it's the thing that's bringing him home for Passover. He may even be traveling on the same plane. In that case, please don't meet me, my darling. I can't bear to have our first few moments marred by his being there. I will call you after I arrive.

Oh, Rick, I've missed you, missed you so desperately much.

As always, Rick imagined he could hear her voice as he read her letter.

"Rick." He could swear that he had heard Rachel say his name. He shook his head, preparing to read on. "Rick." There it was again. He looked up and saw her, standing at the edge of the Black Forest site. For an instant, he thought he must

318

be hallucinating, and he shook his head again like a bewildered animal. But she was still there.

He threw down the letter, scrambling to his feet, and sprinted across the green expanse of spongy grass, holding his arms out to take her in them.

Their bodies met with such a force that it nearly unbalanced her; firmly he held her, saying again and again against her hair, "Rachel, Rachel, you're here, you're here."

He kissed her then, and their bodies slowly moved against each other with that sweet, accustomed motion he had dreamed of for so many weeks and hungered for. He felt her trembling softness under the fragile, downy-feeling slide of her garment, and his hands explored the loveliness that was familiar again, and real.

When he could say anything, he asked her, still holding her tight, "What happened? You're here a day early, and it's wonderful."

She answered with her face against his chest, "I couldn't wait another day. And I didn't want to come back with Dan. I missed my last class, but it doesn't matter...nothing matters, Rick, now that I'm with you again."

Dimly he realized she must have been wearing a hat—he simply couldn't see much of anything before, except her lovely face—but he saw a hat lying on the grass at their feet.

He stooped down and picked it up, handing it to her. "Sorry—I didn't realize I was so rough.".

She tossed the hat away again and came into his arms. "You've read my letter."

"Yes." He caressed her arms, covered by long, soft sleeves. He was beginning to notice things again. The sleeves were a golden-orange, the color of the ring he had given her. "You don't know what it meant to me, Rachel, to have one every day. It was almost like being with you."

"I know. It was the same for me."

"Let's get out of here," he said abruptly.

"Yes. I have my car."

"Where can we go?" he asked her soberly, looking down into her shining black eyes, thinking how wonderful, how lustrous those eyes were. He could see himself in them.

"To a hotel."

He was staggered at the coolness, the simplicity of her answer.

"I still have my luggage. Isn't that convenient?" She added with a grin.

319

He laughed. "You're incredible. Come on, let's go."

They walked across the thick grass to the edge of the Black Forest village. He saw a little Rolls sporting coupe, a light six of the kind he had often admired. It was jet black except for its graceful sides, which were a bright golden yellow.

"Here's my Bee," she said gaily. "Do you want to drive?"

"Sure." He took the keys from her and got into the driver's seat. She slid in the other side before he could open the door for her. He sat for a moment, studying her from head to toe, and he said, "You look beautiful, so beautiful."

She had retrieved the saucy little gray hat and put it on again. It was like a man's fedora and made her look impudent and charming. Now he had the leisure to enjoy her appearance, he admired her golden-orange shirt, tailored also like a man's, with a fresh white collar and gray necktie that matched the slender, gracefully moving gray skirt. With the motion of sitting, the skirt had slid up a trifle, revealing her long, beautiful legs.

Rick felt a sudden stirring of urgent desire. He put his hand on her silk-covered knee and leaned over to kiss her.

She made a moaning sound and leaned back against the black leather seat of the little car, submitting wholly to his caress.

Finally, he moved away from her and started the car. Soon they were speeding toward the center of Chicago.

"I've never stayed in a hotel here in my life," he admitted ruefully as they sighted the Palmer House.

"Neither have I. But I've gone to a thousand things at the Palmer House. Shall we go there?"

"This is a very conspicuous car to park there, darling."

"Oh, they made at least three thousand of them," she remarked, and he was touched by her effort to hide the nervousness in her voice.

"But I'll bet yours is the only one in Chicago." He glanced at her; she looked anxious and jumpy, and he added, "I don't want to do anything that will hurt you."

"*Hurt* me?" she repeated in a wondering voice. "Nothing can hurt me, since we've been with each other. I love you, Rick, you are my whole life. I don't care about anything else any more. Anyway, my parents think my car is still getting a tune-up. My cousin Helene arranged that for me."

He laughed and said, "If I don't kiss you soon, I'll explode."

"Then park the car," she said. "Just turn it right over to

the doorman, and then let's walk into the Palmer House and not come out until the day after tomorrow."

He jammed on the brakes and stared at her. "Day after tomorrow? It sounds too good to be true."

"Well, I'll have to 'arrive' a day late, so my family won't know. I've already taken care of that; I wrote them that I'd be coming back on a later plane than Dan's."

"You think of everything," he said admiringly. Then he leaned over and in view of all the passersby, kissed her hard and long.

"I'll get your bags," he said, getting out of the car.

"Only the small case." Coolly she waited while the hotel doorman opened the door on her side, and stood waiting for Rick with a poise and dignity that made him swell with pride to be seen with her.

They walked calmly to the desk, where he registered them as Mr. and Mrs. Richard von Helsing.

In the elevator to their suite, they stood close together, silent, and did not speak again until the bellboy had put down Rachel's bag and made a careful inspection of the luxurious rooms to see that all was in order.

The door closed at last, and Rick said, "This is the last time in our lives, Rachel, that those names will be a lie."

"Those names?"

"Mr. and Mrs. von Helsing. Next time it will be true, I swear it to you. I don't ever want you to have to go through this again...all the lies and deceptions. I owe you more than that. I owe you everything."

She came to him and took his hand. "We will talk about it, Rick. We will talk about it later. Right now, I want to show you something." She pulled at his hand, urging him to the windows.

"Look out there," she said softly, indicating the panorama of the city spread out before them. "Don't you see? We're as alone here as we were before. This is our new Pleasure Bay." She moved closer to him and he tightened his arm around her waist.

"Yes. Yes, it is, Rachel. You have made it so."

And he drew the curtains closed over the picture of the city in the April sunlight.

They did not leave the hotel that night, or the day and night after. Rick blessed the circumstance of the finished work at the fair that made his absence possible. He had called

Jonas on the first evening to tell his grandfather that he was staying for a day or two with friends. If Jonas knew the truth, his calm, amiable answer had given no hint at all.

On the last morning, Rick awoke early to a bright slant of April sun through an opening in the heavy drapery. He felt a not unpleasant tingling in his arm, from the sweet weight of Rachel's head. He shifted gently to free it, and kissed her sleeping face. Her face was as silky-smooth as a rose petal, the scent she always had about her, and her long dark lashes were gleaming crescents on her flushed cheeks. A lock of glowing black hair had curled itself around her nose.

Rick smiled and gently moved the lock of hair. Her eyes fluttered open, and in her waking eyes there was a look of such love that he exclaimed and drew her close to him.

"Wake up, wake up," he whispered. "There's something very important we have to do today."

Her smile disappeared. She retorted, "We have to say good-bye to this."

"Oh, no. I have another idea altogether." He got up and dialed room service, ordering their breakfast.

"What?" She sat up in the bed and rubbed her eyes, looking so childlike that he was overwhelmed with tenderness. He put down the phone and came to her, sitting down on the edge of the bed and taking both her hands in his. He kissed each hand in turn, and said, "Get married."

She stared at him, speechless, then a wide smile creased her elfin face. "I thought you'd never ask."

"You will, then?" He had never felt such delight.

"Of course I will." Her eyes were big and glowing, and they looked a little wet. "But we're not old enough."

"It doesn't matter. We can drive up the lake to Wisconsin. It's only about fifty miles. I've checked into it and there's a place right over the state line. You only have to be seventeen, and they don't even ask for birth certificates, or anything. For a price we can get out of all the red tape. Speaking of that..."

He grinned and stood up, gathering his clothes and starting to dress. "I've got to get to the bank," he continued. "I don't want my wife to pick up all the bills."

"Your wife." She repeated the words with pleasure and, getting up, came running to him and took him around the waist.

He kissed her lightly. "This is not getting me dressed."

"Nor me!" She hurried to the bureau and took stockings and underthings from a drawer, then went to the closet to choose a dress. She took out a dress the color of yellow-green leaves, and from the shelf above picked up a small, soft hat the same color. "How's this?"

"Perfect. It looks like spring." She was so excited, so happy, that he could not resist taking her in his arms one more time. "Now go," he said, patting her. She went into the bathroom to dress, a modest aspect of her that both delighted and amused him in one so open and free in the actual times of love.

When she emerged, he thought he had never seen her look so beautiful, and he said so. The pale bright shade made her eyes and hair glow darker, and gave a vivid color to her face.

Their breakfast came, but both were too excited to eat much. They drank a great deal of coffee. Suddenly she said, "Oh, Rick, a ring! We have to get a ring."

"Ah," he said slyly, "But we already have a ring." He laughed at her surprise and went to the closet, reaching in his jacket pocket. "I've been carrying it with me everywhere." He handed her the box. She opened it and took out a golden circlet set with emeralds and honey topaz.

"Oh," she breathed. "Our birthstones."

"Yes. I found out what the birthstone was for May and I had this made, weeks ago. I know things like that mean a lot to you."

"Oh, yes, yes. Oh, Rick." She put the ring back in its box and got up to come around the table. She stood beside him, holding his head against her breast. He could feel the excited swift beat of her heart, the glorious softness of her.

"I've got to get out of here, while I still can," he said humorously. He stood up, giving her a quick, violent hug. "I'm going to the bank and then come back and pay the bill. You get packed. All right?"

"*Jawohl.* At once." She saluted him. He put on his jacket, saying, "I'll see you soon."

She kissed him once again before he went out the door.

When he returned to the hotel, she was waiting in the lobby. He picked up her bag, declining the services of a bellboy, and they hurried out to the street. The Bee was waiting in front of the hotel. Rick tipped the doorman, who had put the suitcase in the rumble and was helping Rachel into the car.

In another moment they had left the center of town, and

323

were speeding north through Wilmette and Highwood, passing the turnoff to the Pinnacle, heading for the border of Wisconsin.

That afternoon, heading south again from Lake Forest, and the Pinnacle, they smiled at each other for a moment before Rick turned his full attention to the road. "I'm glad we had the best part first," Rachel said, and held up her hand, admiring the circlet of topaz and emeralds, designed to fit the companion ring of topaz hearts.

"I knew they'd be happy about us." Rick smiled more broadly, thinking of the reception Jonas and Anita had given them.

"Now for the hard part," Rachel commented, and sighed. They were both silent, and he knew they were thinking the same thing—she was dreading the interview with her parents, and he was not looking forward to seeing his mother.

"Where shall we go first?" Rick asked.

"Let's take them as they come," she said. "And your house comes first, darling."

"Right." He knew he sounded more casual than he felt; his mother was not going to make it easy. Anita had told them they were welcome back at the Pinnacle that evening, if they chose. Rick was very grateful; it was no ordinary invitation. It was a symbolic declaration of her and Jonas's support. Anita had fortified them with a magnificent lunch, made festive with their oldest wine. "To keep up your strength," she had commented lightly, but both Rick and Rachel were aware of what faced them.

Rick felt a shamed relief when they were told at the Tudor mansion that Mrs. Brewster was out, and would not return until dinnertime.

"Tomorrow, then," Rachel sighed with a relief as great as Rick's as they drove away. "One more to go," she added lightly, and Rick reached out and squeezed her hand.

"I love you," he said. "Mrs. von Helsing."

"And I love you."

Rick's heart was light in that moment, and he thought, It will be all right. But his feeling of optimism deserted him when they pulled up in front of the Levitt mansion on Lake Shore Drive. Dan Levitt was standing on the broad front stairs. When he sighted the Rolls, he hurried down to them. The annoyance on his thin face deepened to rage at his recognition of the driver of the car.

Rick stopped the engine and got out of the car at once, preparing to go around and open the door for Rachel, but Daniel Levitt was already opening it, pulling Rachel out of the Bee.

"Where in hell have you been? What have you been doing?" Dan demanded savagely. "Irv Stein saw you coming out of the Palmer House with this . . . this Hun."

Rachel gasped, and Rick moved toward them, ordering coldly, "Take your hands off my wife."

"Your *wife*?" Dan Levitt turned pale with shock for an instant, stepping back involuntarily. Then his black eyes burned darker in his white face, and he said, "Do you mean to tell me you're married?" He confronted Rachel.

She answered calmly, "This morning. In Wisconsin."

"Well, you're not married in Illinois. It's illegal without your parents' consent. You're underage . . . and so is von Helsing."

"Don't try to pull that, Levitt," Rick retorted in a cool voice; his calm surprised even himself, but he would be damned if he would let the bastard know how mad he was. "We have my grandparents' consent."

"That has nothing to do with Rachel." Daniel Levitt looked at Rick with naked hate.

"Where are Mother and Father, Dan?" Rachel asked quietly.

"Father's at the bank, where he always is. And Mother went to a tea. She was going to go to the airport to meet you."

"Didn't she get my message?"

"Yes, of course. She's on the way back home now."

"Then we will go in and wait for my mother," Rachel said.

"*You* will come in with me." Daniel Levitt reached out and took her arm. "I told you before, von Helsing is not welcome in this house."

"And I've told you before, Levitt," Rick answered, feeling his rage boil near the surface, "not to manhandle my wife. I will not tell you again."

"Please, Rick." Rachel shook off Daniel's grasp and got into the car. "We'll go now. Please, let's go."

Rick stood undecided for a moment, then when she repeated, "Please," he got into the driver's seat.

"You can tell Mother, Dan," Rachel said through the window, "that I do not go anywhere my husband is not welcome. And that you barred us from this house."

"Rachel, wait," Dan began.

325

"Let's go, Rick."

He started the car, and they drove around the circular drive and headed back toward the river road.

Rachel was weeping, and Rick put out one hand and stroked her arm. "Don't cry, darling, please don't cry. God, I'm sorry."

"*Sorry*?" she repeated. "For what, Rick?"

"For putting you in this unpleasant position...for exposing you to all this."

"Oh, my dear, it's not your fault. It's my brother. Marrying you has been the greatest happiness I ever knew in all my life."

"Thank you for that." They drove in silence for a moment, then he asked, "Where shall we go?"

"Let's go back to the Pinnacle."

"Yes, yes. I'd like that." He turned the car and they headed north again; in a little while he felt his rage and indignation dying, and when he touched Rachel's hand, it felt soft and calm again in his. The thought of the Pinnacle had soothed them both, he reflected. It had always been the place he longed for, in the hard times, the place he knew he would find acceptance and peace. And now Rachel, he thought joyfully, can share in all that with me.

He felt that Rachel's spirits were rising, too, when they sighted the flowing grace of the house on the hill. But as they drove up they saw Jonas come out of the house toward them, and his face, while welcoming, looked sad and grim.

"What is it, Granddad? What's happened?" Rick called out before he even stopped the car.

Jonas opened the door for Rachel and smiled at her, handing her out before he answered, "I'm sorry to spoil your wedding day. Did you see the papers yet? Of course you haven't."

"What happened?" Rick repeated.

"We've got a hell of a job facing us tomorrow, Rick." Jonas looked weary and depressed. "Some vandals have torn up the Black Forest village. They think there's some connection with an anti-German group."

Rachel went to Rick and took his arm. She looked devastated, he thought. "It's all right, darling," he said. But her expression did not change, and he wondered why she looked so angry, exactly what she was thinking of.

He put his arm around her, and slowly they walked toward the house. Perhaps she was only thinking of the inconvenience for him, the work involved. And yet it seemed deeper than that.

Rick was still puzzling about it when Anita came to meet them at the door, trying to hide her consternation in a smile of welcome as she held out her arms to both of them and said, "Welcome to the Pinnacle."

Chapter 26

ANITA HEARD RACHEL say into the phone, "Yes, Mother, this afternoon at two. I have something very important to tell you." Anita thought, They are very formal together. Then she realized, too, that Daniel Levitt must not have told his mother the news.

But the situation was complicated enough; they had another problem right now, with Iris. Anita looked out the window again and saw the chauffeur opening the back door, handing Iris from the gloomy Lincoln. She was dressed with great formality for a visit to her own mother's house, Anita thought, but as usual in the height of fashion. She seems to hide in her own elegance, Anita reflected, glancing at her daughter's suit of soft ivory wool; it had faint flecks of scarlet and ocean green, matching her green blouse and tiny green skullcap framing her short bronze hair.

The face below the skullcap looked angry and haggard, and even from that distance Anita noticed that Iris's tawny eyes were bloodshot. Iris caught sight of her at the window. She did not smile, but marched up the stairs and banged the great brass knocker on the door.

Anita opened the door at once. "Iris," she began apologetically. Anita felt shamed and sad. Her daughter's anger was justifiable; Rick should have visited her last night, she reflected. "Iris, my dear, I'm glad you've come. I assume you know what's happened."

"Why wasn't I told?" Iris demanded with ire. Her white-gloved hands were trembling, and she was very pale.

"Please, Iris, come in. Come in and sit down. Here's Rachel," she said pointedly.

Iris brushed past Anita into the long living room without

a word to Rachel. Vexed, Anita took Rachel by the arm and gently urged her into the room. Anita was deeply dismayed at Iris's patent hostility, appalled by her rudeness.

"Where is my son?" Iris demanded, facing them accusingly.

"He is at the site, Iris. Surely you know what happened yesterday afternoon." Anita was finding it difficult to control her temper.

"Oh, that nonsense," Iris said dismissively, waving her gloved hand in an impatient fashion. She sat down on the long ivory-colored couch and took a cigarette case from her small green bag and fitted it into a long jade holder. Then with deliberation she took a minute silver lighter from the bag and lit her cigarette. When she had finished, she put the items back into her bag and snapped it shut with a belligerent motion.

"What I want to know is—why are you hiding these runaways from their parents? They have broken the law; they are underage. And I for one intend to take legal steps to see that this so-called marriage is dissolved."

"Iris, please listen to me." Anita glanced at Rachel and was stricken by the look of despair on her face. "I agree that Jonas and I were remiss. We should all have come to see you last night. But you see, a great deal has happened; surely you can understand that. Jonas and Rick went to the site early this morning. Rick and Rachel came to see you yesterday afternoon, but you were out. And then last night, we were all so distracted by what had happened...Rachel and I would have come to you this afternoon after we went to see her mother."

"*Rachel* and you!" Iris cried. "I want to talk to my *son*. I have nothing to say to this girl." It was the first time she had acknowledged Rachel's presence, and Anita was almost ready to weep with embarrassment. At the same time, she felt her anger rising.

"Please try to be calm." Anita went to Iris and sat down beside her. She took her daughter's hand. Rachel was still standing miserably under the archway between the living room and the hall.

Horrified, Anita caught the strong aroma of gin on Iris's breath. My God, at ten o'clock in the morning.

"Iris, are you...all right?"

"What do you mean by that?" Iris was immediately on the defensive, drawing back from Anita. She looked down, and her tawny lashes hid her reddened eyes for a moment. She said sullenly, "How can I be all right, when this little . . . tramp has taken my son away from me?"

Anita heard Rachel's quick intake of breath, saw her run through the entrance hall and up the stairs.

"Rachel!" Anita half rose from the couch.

"No, let her go. At least now we can talk."

Anita sat down and looked at Iris; her face had hardened and she was smiling a very unpleasant smile. For a moment Anita felt that she hardly knew her own daughter.

"You're drunk, aren't you, Iris?" Anita asked curtly.

Iris recoiled as if she had been struck.

"I don't know what you mean."

"Don't fence with me, Iris. How long have you been drinking like this? Donald has hinted of it more than once, but I just didn't want to believe . . ."

"Donald!" Iris's voice was contemptuous. "That goddam fool has never been anything but a nuisance. And now he is lying about me to my own mother."

"Iris, please let's not quarrel," Anita placated. "But I can't have you say such things to Rick's wife. She is a guest in my house."

"Rick's *wife*!" Iris shrieked. "Why not call her what she is—Rick's whore?"

"Stop it, Iris. She'll hear you."

"I want her to hear me!" Iris's voice had risen almost to a scream. "First she seduces my brother, then she runs off with my son. I want to know what you and my father are going to do about this alleged marriage . . . the marriage I had to learn about from Jon," she added with reproach.

"Jon's in town?" Anita was very surprised. "He hardly ever comes back at this time of year."

"Apparently he had come back to continue his pursuit of Rick's . . . wife," Iris commented. "He was as dismayed as I was to hear of it from Daniel Levitt. Jon is disgusted with Rick."

"But I don't understand how he could be 'disgusted.' If he was interested in Rachel himself . . ."

"Jon's interest, apparently, was more appropriate. He never had any notion of *marrying* the girl." Iris smiled unpleasantly again, and Anita's temper broke.

"I told you I will not have you talk like that. She is a lovely girl and she and Rick are very much in love with each other."

"Really, Mother! You sound absolutely senile. Rick is merely blinded by sex, and he's too young to know better. I,

330

for one, intend to pursue this legally. And I'm sure Rachel's mother will agree. I can still cut off Richard's funds. I'll see to that."

Iris's face was flushed and her slender neck was mottled with redness. Her eyes were full of hate, and she looked like someone Anita had never met, much less her own daughter.

"Oh, Iris, Iris, how can you talk like this? What's happened to you? Don't you remember how you felt about Rik von Helsing? How do you know that Rachel and your son don't love each other the same way?"

But Anita saw that her appeal had not touched Iris at all; if anything, it made her even more angry. Coldly she retorted, in a low, flat tone that was worse than her sharp shrieking, "Now you are comparing me to this déclassé little Jew. You're worse than Jon, with his fanatic attachment to those people. To think that anyone with the pure blood of my son..."

"'Pure'!" Anita cried. "Why, you sound like a Nazi...you sound like that maniac Hitler!"

"Donald says Hitler has the right idea...and I agree with him. Well, you'll all wake up someday, the lot of you—you and Father and Jon, with his destructive little friends. Why, they're like a lot of infants, rushing about, tearing up things..."

Iris paused, and her face turned an uglier, deeper red.

"What on earth do you mean?" Anita got up and stood before her. "Tell me what you mean, Iris. At once. Did Jon have something to do with what happened at the site? You *knew* about it and said nothing to anyone?"

"Of course I knew. I overheard Jon say something to Dan Levitt about it, and then I put two and two together for myself."

Anita sat down beside Iris and took her by the arm. She shook it, demanding, "Why haven't you told someone? Are you out of your mind with drinking? What's wrong with you, Iris?"

Iris shook off her mother's grasp. "Why in hell should I tell anyone? I'm delighted that they've torn up that goddam village! It kept Richard away from home every minute since he's returned—that village and that little trollop!"

"Iris, don't you realize what it means?" Anita cried. "They could get hurt—Rick and Jonas could be hurt if the vandals return. Are you too drunk and too mad to realize that?"

Iris stared at her, and a terror shone in her bloodshot eyes.

Her lips fell open slackly. "Oh, my God, no," she said in a low, shaky voice. "No, it can't be. If anything happened to Richard, I would die, Mother. I would die."

Iris stood up, swaying on her feet. "I am going there now. I am going to warn them."

Anita stood up and put out her hand. "No, Iris, you can't go there like this. I think you should go home now. They are aware that it was more than ordinary vandals...they will be careful, I'm sure." Anita wished she felt as confident as she sounded.

"I'm going there," Iris insisted stubbornly, and walked unsteadily out of the room and through the entrance hall without looking back. Anita followed her, but she saw that it was useless to protest.

When Anita and Rachel were ready to leave the house, a little later, the phone rang.

Anita said, "We're running late, but I'd better answer. It might be Jonas or Rick."

But when she picked up the receiver, it was the voice of a stranger. She listened to what he said, at first, without comprehension. She heard the word "explosion," then others too terrible to grasp. The sympathetic caller had to repeat the message twice before Anita could make herself understand.

When Anita hung up the phone, she leaned for an instant against the table.

"What is it?" Rachel cried out. "Tell me, tell me!" Hysterical, she took Anita by the arms and shook her. "Tell me!"

"Please, Rachel. Please." Anita's firm voice brought the girl to her senses. She dropped her arms and stood waiting helplessly. Anita took Rachel in her arms and said gently, "There was an explosion at the site. They were knocked down—hurt. They're both alive. But Rick...something has happened to his hand."

"His hand. Dear God." Rachel leaned against Anita for an instant, then she looked up and asked, "What was it?"

"We...don't know yet," she lied.

"You do know, don't you?" Rachel asked in a dead, hollow voice.

Anita hesitated, then she said briefly, "His hand was blown off, Rachel."

Rachel stared at Anita, shaking her head over and over, like a pathetic broken doll.

* * *

Rachel was not allowed to see Rick until the next afternoon. She was trembling all over and her heart was thudding in her throat when she went quietly into his hospital room. He seemed to be asleep. He was lying so stiffly on his back, breathing evenly, his left hand concealed under the sheet. A huge bandage swathed the end of his right arm. Where his hand had been, Rachel thought, and she was overcome with a terrible nausea, a panic that weakened her arms and legs, making her tremble so she was not sure she could even stand.

But she took a deep breath and moved softly toward the bed. She leaned over and kissed his face. "Rick," she whispered.

At once he opened his eyes. He did not smile. The look in his eyes struck her like a blow. It was empty, despairing and cold. He lifted his left arm and covered the great bandage with the sheet.

"Oh, Rick, my love, my darling." Rachel continued to lean over him, kissing his cheeks and his forehead, stroking his head with her trembling hands. If only he would touch me, she thought. He must touch me. And she felt the tears begin to form in her eyes.

But still he did not respond. He did not touch her. She put her hands on his face and realized that a trickle of moisture was running between her fingers. He turned his head away and said, "I wish you hadn't come. I don't want you to see me like this."

Sadly she sat down in a chair by the bed and folded her hands in her lap, waiting.

"If I couldn't see you," she said at last, "I might as well be blind."

She knew then that he was crying, and still trying to hide it from her. His face was still turned away, but his breath was coming in labored, convulsive gasps.

"I love you, Rick. I need you. Don't...go away from me like this."

"You don't need a cripple!" he answered bitterly, still not turning his head. "An architect without a right hand?"

"I need you to have any life at all. You must know that by now." She leaned forward and took his left hand in hers; she raised the hand to her face and rubbed her cheek against it. She could feel him tremble. She kissed his hand, again and again.

Slowly he turned his head and looked at her. "Sweet Rachel, beautiful Rachel." She had never seen such a despairing look in anyone's eyes. "Don't you know it's over for us now? I'm nothing, like this. Nothing, Rachel."

"That's not true!" she cried out passionately. "You are everything to me. I would die without you, Rick, I'd just...die. What would happen to me without you?"

"What will happen to you *with* me?" he retorted.

"Everything good and happy, Rick. I've been thinking about all this...thinking about it almost every moment since this happened. Everything can be just the way it was before." She stopped, appalled. The look on his face told her what an awful thing she had said; he would never again be the way he was before. She nearly cried out, knowing that she had caused him pain, but she controlled herself and went stubbornly on, "Things can be...good again. For both of us. You see, *I* can be your hand."

"What do you mean?"

"You remember we planned to go back east together...that you would—" She stopped abruptly, and amended, "That I'd be going back to Wellesley. I'm not going back. I'm going to M.I.T."

He was staring at her, and it seemed to her that his look of despairing sadness had lightened, ever so little.

Encouraged, she went on, "I'm going to study architecture. We'll both take up where you left off."

"'We'?" he repeated, and the grim lines returned to his mouth.

"Oh, my love, don't you see?" she urged, stroking his face with her hand. "We can work together. I can be the hand that executes your inspirations."

He lay back, staring at the ceiling, shaking his head. "Rachel, I don't know. I don't..."

"But I *do* know, and I will make you see. I promise, Rick. You must believe that this is not the end of...everything. There can never be an end to us. You do know that, don't you? Oh, my God, Rick, don't you love me any more?"

She began to cry and hid her face in her hands.

"Rachel, Rachel. *Love* you...I worship you, Rachel." She took her hands away from her face and looked at him. He was holding out his left hand to her, and as she took it between both of hers and caressed it, she saw an entirely new look in his eyes, the look of a man who has begun to hope a little.

* * *

"I'm afraid I can't allow any visits yet," the doctor said in an evasive manner.

Donald Brewster tightened his grip on Iris's hand. It was not a wholly tender gesture; he had been holding his breath, dreading an outburst from his wife before all the people in the waiting room.

To his relief she merely nodded her head, sitting bowed and still on the couch beside him. He put his arm around her waist. She felt no more substantial than a shadow, she had grown so thin in these few days.

Donald's vast pity was swallowed up now in his apprehension: Iris raised her veil, indifferent to her ravaged face, and was glaring at the door to her son's room. "They're doing this purposely," she said in a low, savage tone as the doctor walked away. "They let that little bitch go in, but not his own mother."

In her agitation she swayed toward him, and Donald caught an overpowering whiff of gin on her breath. It seemed almost to pervade her skin and clothes. Where in hell had she hidden it? Donald wondered. He had been watching her like a hawk.

"You know you can't drink, with the pills," he said sharply.

Instead of the counterattack he expected, Donald was surprised when she answered in a slurred, whining voice, "I don't have your strength. I can't stand the pain." She smiled at him crookedly. "This is my little-girl voice, the doctor said." Her sudden switch to coquetry made his stomach turn.

"It's your little *drunk's* voice. Rachel and Anita stand the pain. And Rachel is his *wife*."

He heard himself and stopped, appalled. After all, she was the boy's mother. He'd been a fool to say these things, now, when he needed to hold her together.

"I'm sorry. But you know it's very dangerous to drink on top of those pills." He felt a deep weariness and disgust. And he reflected with horror that she had drunk no more when her son lost his hand than she did over the late delivery of an evening dress, a broken nail or a run in her stocking.

Suddenly Iris cried out, in a mad, piercing voice that chilled his blood, "I've got to see my son!"

She tore herself from her husband's grasp and stumbled to the hall, screaming, "I'm coming, Richard!"

The other visitors in the waiting room, and a passing nurse, stood transfixed for an instant, then the nurse moved toward Iris Brewster at the same moment that Donald

335

reached her and took her firmly in his grip. "I'm sorry," he said to the nurse, feeling his face heat with shame. "She's ... very overwrought."

The nurse looked back at him with cynical, compassionate eyes. Then Donald Brewster saw that Rick's doctor had heard the commotion and was coming toward them.

"I think," the doctor said calmly, "that I had better give Mrs. Brewster something for her nerves."

His eyes met Donald's with perfect understanding.

"After we find a place for Mrs. Brewster to lie down," the doctor said, "perhaps you and I could have a little talk, Mr. Brewster."

"Yes," Donald replied. "I think it's time we did."

Jon Mark stared with unseeing eyes at the fading skyline of Chicago. Finally, he leaned back against the seat of the westbound plane and shut his eyes, but he could not shut out the horrible pictures that flashed again and again in his mind's sight, below the closed lids.

His father hurt and Rick maimed, the shattered site. And Daniel Levitt shrinking back before Jon's shouted questions, his accusations. Dan Levitt unable to meet his eyes.

What a fool I was, Jon reflected, what a goddam misguided fool. It was never supposed to be like this; he had never received a hint, a whisper of what they really planned. From the first he had been opposed to any violent means of gaining their ends or drawing attention to their cause.

But I should have known, Jon thought. I should have known that the organization always lies. This time, he had been sure it would be different. But he hadn't realized how much Dan hated Rick, or how little he controlled his own group.

Jon Mark felt a painful constriction in his throat. With horror he realized he was about to cry, in front of the other passengers. He clenched his fists and felt the hot waves of remorse and shame sweep over him.

He had not been able to face his parents; he couldn't even go to the hospital. What they would think of him he couldn't even imagine. But it didn't matter: he could not have brought himself to look into his mother's or his father's eyes. And most of all, into Rachel's.

I began it all, he thought. I was the one who influenced Dan, drew him into the group. I was able to control the situation at first, but when the others took the reins from me because I was too "intellectual," too "detached," I refused to look at where the organization was going.

The tears flooded Jon's eyes at last, and he turned his face toward the small round window of the plane to shield it from the curious stares of the stewardess and passengers. He could never go back now; he could never go back to Chicago again.

None of the Marks or Brewsters attended the opening of the new exposition called the Century of Progress, which took place while Rick was still confined to the hospital. Jonas, who had fully recovered from his minor injuries, said bitterly to Anita that he would never set foot on the site again. The explosion that had maimed Rick forever had knocked Jonas unconscious but he had been hurt only slightly; he walked with a faint limp for a week or two. When Anita examined his cuts and abrasions, Jonas said, "It should have been *my* hand, Anita. I have done so much and he is just beginning."

The local police and the FBI still had not apprehended the ones responsible for the bombing.

Jonas threw himself with fanatic energy into new projects, and Anita made the Pinnacle ready for Rick's homecoming. It was already May; by the time Rick's wound had healed enough, the spring term at M.I.T. would be over. Anita felt a great relief, thankful for that minor blessing. At least the matter of Rick's return to school would be postponed until the autumn.

She looked forward to his release with both dread and joy: seeing him bandaged in the hospital was one thing, she reflected, but to watch him meet the outside world again—that was another. However, she was heartened by what his doctor had said to them: "I have never had a patient of this kind with fewer adjustment problems, and so soon... all in a matter of weeks. Let's hope and pray it lasts."

It was all because of Rachel, Anita told Jonas. She was awed by the girl's courage, and tried to follow her example of matter-of-fact acceptance. Even if she cried and paced her room—and Anita had heard her, almost every night—to Rick, Rachel presented another face.

"I hope to God," Anita said, "I can be half as good as Rachel."

"You will," Jonas assured her. "You've got to be, my dear. We've both got to be, for Rick's sake. Just be as natural as you can. If we can neither overemphasize or avoid the matter..." But even Jonas sounded uncertain, and Anita was full of apprehension when Rachel brought Rick home.

Anita was glad of one thing, at least: Iris had been sent away to a sanitarium for an indefinite stay. Jonas shared Anita's relief; Iris's hysterical presence would have been unbearable to them all. She would have undone all that Rachel had begun to build so painfully but so well.

Anita went outside to meet them, and she was relieved by the look on Rick's face. He had grown much thinner, and there were new hollows under his cheekbones, sharp planes to the young face that made him look much older, but there was an air of life renewed in him. His eyes were bright and he smiled broadly when he put his left arm around Anita and drew her close for his kiss.

His eyes had lost that dead, drugged look they had had at first; he seemed more animated than Anita had thought possible.

"It's good, it's so good to be home," he said. Anita noticed that he had his right arm, the maimed one, around Rachel. It seemed miraculous that already the girl had given him such confidence; he felt no self-consciousness, it was clear, in touching his wife with that arm.

"You're mighty welcome, boy," Jonas said gruffly to hide his deep emotion. And as they went into the house together, Anita thought again of Rachel's intention—she would be the boy's "hand," and somehow, someday, they would all work it out together.

It was a healing summer. In the early weeks of Rick's homecoming, Jonas occasionally brought up his current projects in an offhand manner. To their surprise and pleasure, Rick took the bait and once or twice ventured a suggestion. And then one evening Rick mentioned with splendid casualness that he was going back to M.I.T. in the fall to take a slightly revised course, concentrating on aesthetics and theory. Rachel would begin as a freshman in architecture and receive his additional tutoring.

In June, Rachel announced she was pregnant. The baby was due to arrive the following December. "If it's a boy," she said, smiling, "we'll name him Richard Jonas von Helsing."

They were all delighted, but their happiness was overshadowed by Jon's silence. Anita never mentioned his name in front of Rick and Rachel; the horrible suspicion that he had been connected with the bombing still haunted her.

She had phoned his office at the school twice. The first

time she was told he was away, and on the second occasion she learned he was on sabbatical leave in California. And once Jonas brought her a scientific journal with news of Jon's work, which now centered around the development of nuclear fission.

Then in August, after Rick and Rachel had left for Boston to find a house, a letter came.

Anita saw Jon's familiar handwriting on the envelope—solid and legible, so different from hers and Jonas's—and opened the letter with trembling hands.

"My dearest mother," she read eagerly, "I have at last come to the place where I can write you again and tell you why I had to go away."

She took a trembling breath and closed her eyes for a moment. She almost feared to read on. Dear God, she thought, it cannot be that he shared in that monstrous thing.

Anita made herself open her eyes and continue reading.

"I had no role in the horror at the site."

Anita's eyes filled and she felt an overwhelming relief; her whole body felt lighter, as if an unbearable weight had lifted from her breast.

"My role was a subtler and, in the long run, perhaps even a more dangerous one. I was a prime mover in the organization of the Save America party, in Boston and Cambridge as well as in Chicago. I was the one who influenced younger and more impressionable minds, such as Dan Levitt's, and failed to stop the fanatics who later joined the group and used it as a vehicle for their violent actions."

Carefully the letter explained that the Save America movement had originally begun to encourage the election of more interventionist representatives throughout America, to urge the country into a war to defeat the German threat of world domination.

More than a year after he had become involved, Jon wrote, he began to suspect that terrorists had infiltrated the organization. But so much progress was being made, particularly in New York, where anti-Nazi feelings ran high, that he was reluctant to abandon the project, foolishly assuming that the more responsible elements would prevail.

The Chicago wing had planned to picket the Black Forest village, he said, and he had come back to the city at Easter to assure himself that the younger members would behave. And then he had learned of Rachel's marriage, and realized the depth of Dan Levitt's hatred for Rick. When the site was vandalized and the explosion occurred, Jon went on, he realized what a fool he had been. He had played them all into the hands of ignorant, violent rabble-rousers. Dan Levitt had not had an actual hand in the bombing; he had, however, encouraged the others to vandalize the site, the supreme act of vengeance, Dan thought, against Rick von Helsing.

The bombing had sickened Dan as much as it had horrified Jon.

"Technically," Jon went on, "Dan and I were not guilty. And yet morally we share in the guilt. Dan's hatred of Rick was a dreadful thing, and for too long I hated him, too, both for his Prussian blood and for his having won Rachel, for whom I cared more than I let anyone know. My sublime arrogance! It seemed inconceivable to me that she could love that 'callow boy' when she could have had the great Jon Mark of M.I.T."

Anita was astonished and touched by the last remark, almost more than by anything else in the letter. Jon's ridicule of himself was a mark of wisdom and maturity, the qualities she had always known were latent in him, but which he had never allowed to develop and grow.

"I could not face any of you," the letter went on, "and I know you will understand that now. But I have had a great deal of time to think this over. My life in California has been one of work and, aside from that, much aloneness. I have purposely made no friends, kept myself apart so that I might have the solitude I needed to get to know myself, to understand this terrible thing that I caused obliquely.

"I have been keeping tabs on Rick and Rachel, through friends at M.I.T. I've found out that Rick is planning to return to school, and that Rachel is going to study architecture. I applaud them and bless them. It is a miracle. My hope for their success is also a selfish one; I feel that in it, I will find a kind of atonement."

The tears ran down Anita's cheeks. She brushed them away and read the conclusion of the letter, which promised that Jon would be coming for a visit soon, and she thought how courageous he was, to face the prospect of seeing Rick and Rachel again.

When Jonas came home that evening, Anita met him at the door with the letter in her hand. He took it from her and without a word went into the living room, sat down and read it intently.

340

When he finished, he looked up at her. "Then he was not guilty, thank God." Anita sat down beside him; he took her hand.

"Are we going to tell Rick and Rachel about this? What do you think?" he asked.

She stared into space for a long moment, then she said, "Yes. Yes, I think we should. Think what a relief it will be to Rachel, to know that Dan had no real part in setting off the explosion. It has been an agony for her, not knowing."

Later that night Anita wrote to Rachel in Cambridge.

In September a banner headline in a Chicago paper told them that the exposition bombers had been arrested, through an anonymous tip to the FBI. And Anita and Jonas received letters from Jon with regularity throughout the fall. It was almost, Anita thought, the way it was before, but in one way, at least, even better. This was a new and more loving Jon than she had ever known.

Richard Jonas von Helsing was born on December 7, 1934.

The four years that followed flew with an astonishing speed. Jonas and Anita received almost daily letters from Rachel. She was proud of her progress in school; however, she mentioned that Rick was becoming increasingly withdrawn; he would shut himself up in the study for hours at a time, emerging with a strangely satisfied but secretive air.

Then about six months later Rachel wrote Anita with pride and delight: "All this time Rick has been learning to draw with his left hand, and didn't want me to know until he became proficient."

Jon remained in California at his work, and seemed heartened by the news of the couple's progress that Anita passed along.

Jon wrote to his mother, "My atonement, then, may be almost over." But Anita still had the feeling that it was more than geographical distance and circumstance that kept Jon from visiting when he thought Rick and Rachel might be there. He still could not quite face the meeting, she knew. And yet the time was drawing nearer, she felt, when he would return—an event she anticipated with the same joy and dread she had experienced before Rick came home from the hospital.

Once, after reading a letter of Jon's, Jonas remarked, "Soon, perhaps, things will be really mended. And it will be

341

like the old days...well, almost." There was a hint of nostalgia in his tone.

Anita went into his arms. "How long ago it was," she said dreamily.

"I don't know where it went," Jonas said, and they looked at each other with a strange new sadness. It would soon be time to fly east for Rachel's graduation.

Not only the last four years, but more than two decades had flown past since they returned to Chicago. The thirties were nearly at an end. During that decade Jonas and Anita realized with wonder that they were growing old. Jonas was sixty-five in November, Anita would soon be sixty-four.

Iris had returned from the sanitarium subdued and marked with a new maturity. Anita noticed with interest that the change reflected itself even in her clothes, which were no longer aggressively chic, but softer and more understated. "She's finally grown up," Jonas said, "about twenty years behind schedule."

Slowly and painfully Iris had returned to her music. After years of absence from it, it had been grueling, but she was succeeding, day by day.

Anita was struck by the similarity in Iris and Rick; they were both stubbornly determined to succeed. "They come from good stock," Jonas said lightly, but Anita could hear the love and pride in his words.

They noticed with amazement that all the photos and portraits of Rick, which for years had overshadowed the pictures of the other children in the Brewster mansion, had been put away or given to Rachel. There was only one portrait of Rick in Iris's bedroom, next to portraits of Donald, Eve and Dean.

Anita's world was almost perfect in those years, except for the monstrous shadow that was creeping over Europe once more and threatened to darken the rest of the globe. During the thirties, events abroad had presented dilemmas to America. Most Americans abhorred the dictatorships that had risen overseas, and sympathized with China in its unequal struggle against Japanese aggression. At the same time America was strongly isolationist; she had been greatly disillusioned by the World War and had no desire to become involved abroad again.

Then, in the closing months of the thirties, Hitler's blitzkrieg tore through Europe. Soon America's neutrality would be eroded, little by little.

Chapter 27

LIKE THE REKNOWNED ARCHITECT Walter Gropius, whom he greatly admired, Jonas Mark applied the principles of the Bauhaus, a tradition of his German years, to the internal organization of Mark-Byrne. In 1940 he set an unusual example of collaborative decision-making that resulted in all the partners' participation in a weekly review of the projects on the drawing boards.

Everyone looked over everyone else's shoulder and shared his experience and expertise. That made for a higher degree of excellence and more consistency in the firm's design and allowed for significant time and cost savings.

It was also significant to Rick and Rachel von Helsing that such sharing removed from them the onus of relatives accepting a sinecure. Rachel was a woman, and several of the partners had not yet accepted women on an equal basis. Rick's physical disability was another sensitive point.

But Jonas told Anita privately that he was flabbergasted by the boy's adjustment; Rick's co-workers had learned at once that Rick treated his own physical condition almost as an irrelevance. Once he said casually to a staff member, in Jonas's hearing, "It's not a tragedy, really, more of an inconvenience."

Furthermore, Rick's creative imagination had bloomed, even beyond what Jonas had seen in him seven years before. And it was common knowledge that Rachel's scholastic record and original work had been so outstanding at M.I.T. that when she had graduated she had had invitations to join three other Chicago firms. She had proudly shown the letters to Jonas and Anita.

Jonas said, laughing, "Are you sure we can afford you? I'll

343

have to throw in some fringe benefits to make it worth your while." He spoke lightly to Rachel and Rick, but every night he came home to Anita with another report of their triumphs and he fairly burst with pride. Their first assignment was a lakefront beach house, unique and startling, which they executed with a brilliant economy that astounded even Jonas.

He told Anita that working with them "took him back." In the first few months of their employment, both worked with the dedicated seriousness and professionalism that Anita herself had shown in 1893 when she worked under Jonas's supervision.

Late one night as they talked drowsily before going to sleep, Jonas said, "Do you remember those facade designs you did that reminded me of Gaudí? Well, I came across a design of Rachel's today that knocked me for a loop. You know what's happened to stairs." Anita nodded at his reference to the "sad ascendancy of the elevator," his favorite pun. "I sometimes think there haven't been decent stairs for forty years," he went on.

Anita settled her head on his shoulder, murmuring in agreement with his long-standing obsession, one which she shared.

"It's odd," Jonas said, his arm tightening around Anita, "but Rachel, who is not a great admirer of Gaudí or the Expressionists, designed a spiral staircase with an overview that is exactly like the whorls of a seashell. My God, it took me back. The watery, oceanic symbols, the feeling of the old fantasies. Gaudiesque as hell."

Anita smiled at his enthusiasm and, drawing near him, kissed him under the ear. He made a sound of pleasure, and continued, "She's preoccupied with watery symbols. Now isn't that strange?"

"Not in the least," Anita retorted calmly. "She's preoccupied with watery symbols because Rick is a Scorpio, like you, associated with the sea, the element of water."

Jonas drew back and looked down at her with surprise. "You know, you always amaze me," he said. "We've been married for forty-eight years, and you still come up with things I never knew about you."

"Forty," Anita corrected, "the last time."

"Forty-eight, as far as I'm concerned, madam. Why didn't you ever mention this?"

"Because you laughed at Señora Eusebia when she said

that to you in Spain. Remember? I know how to keep things to myself."

"Oh, Anita." He hugged her close to him. "You are a delightful lady." She nestled in his arms and sighed with contentment.

"God," he remarked sleepily, "it's 1940."

"Isn't it unbelievable?"

"It is. And you still make me feel as if I were twenty-three. I think I love you more now than I did then. I know it, as a matter of fact."

"I know it, too." She felt sleep steal over her as they lay close together, thinking, It's 1940. And despite her content she felt that long, relentless shadow creep over her, the shadow of the stunning, dreadful events of the far-off world beyond the water, the world that was growing ever closer to their own serene and happy lives.

During the first months of the 1940s the foreign scene became more grim and shocking. Little Finland had been beaten into submission by Russia. Hitler had seized Denmark and Norway. Ten of Rachel's relatives had already fled Germany and Poland in terror, and were on the way to America. The Low Countries were shattered by the Nazi blitzkrieg; France collapsed before the end of June. Only Great Britain was left to oppose Hitler's conquest of the entire west of Europe.

In August 1940, Dean Brewster ran away and joined the Royal Canadian Air Force. Donald and Iris were sick at heart, yet Donald was very proud of him.

In Asia, Japanese armies continued to ravage China.

Jonas and Anita, like all Americans, were stunned and confused. The spirit of isolationism was still strong throughout the country, especially in Chicago, where the German population was so large, but with each terrible new development the feeling grew that something would have to be done. England and Europe would have to be helped.

There was wide disagreement on how deeply America should get involved. A great debate went on, frequently with violence. The Committee to Defend America by Aiding the Allies was the loudest spokesman for intervention short of declaring war; the America First Committee, strong in Germanic Chicago, was the defender of cautious isolation. America started to build defenses, nevertheless, and initiated a peacetime draft. Then as public opinion gradually shifted in favor of aid to the Allies, America began sending help to Britain in greater and greater quantities.

And on young Rick's seventh birthday, the debate ended once and for all.

"It's monstrous...it's glorious!" Iris von Helsing clapped her hands when she saw the cake Rachel had had made for the boy. It was an enormous dachshund, at least five feet long, iced in caramel, an exact replica of his dog Fritz, who even now was milling among the guests and threatening his own image on the table.

Today was a double celebration: Rick had reached, as Rachel said with wry affection, "The age of reason, thank God," and tomorrow, December 8, she and her husband would be made junior partners in the firm of Mark-Byrne Associates. Anita thought it might be friendlier to have the festivities at the Pinnacle, and had converted the gigantic living room and foyer into two party rooms so that neither celebration would intrude on or outshine the other.

The children's party had begun early; a little later, the partnership celebration would begin. Anita planned to surprise Rick and Rachel with their own cake—a towering vanilla building that was a replica of one of their designs. Small candy figures of Jonas and Anita, Rick and Rachel and other staff members were placed at various windows. The cake, covered now, would be unveiled about four o'clock.

Anita was standing next to Iris and Eve, and she thought, I've never been happier in my life. They were enjoying the sight of young Rick; he was having a wonderful time, surrounded by friends from school and some of the staff members' children.

Anita glanced at Iris. This new woman bore no resemblance to the sullen, frivolous woman of a few years ago; something of the spirit and beauty of the very young Iris still remained. This afternoon she was wearing a most flattering crepe dress from Lanvin. Its billowing sleeves, snug waist and draped skirt, of a cheerful ginger color, pointed up her still-youthful body. The dress had three big matching buttons in the shape of flowers down the waist, and two more at either end of the wide snug belt. A tight brown turban covered most of her hair, and the face beneath was smooth and serene.

"You look about twenty in that dress," Anita remarked.

"You look wonderful yourself," Iris said warmly, and studied Anita's gown approvingly. It was a simple V-necked after-

346

noon dress of crepe with long, tight sleeves, the color of a hyacinth, trimmed with silver-gray cord at the waist and over the shoulders.

"Jonas calls this my Gaudí dress," Anita said, smiling, "because of the whorls." She touched the cord trimming on her slender waist, shaped like flowing waves of water.

"I think you're beautiful," Eve said. Anita put her arms around the girl; since Iris had changed so much, Eve had become much livelier. And she looked more like her mother every day.

"So are you," Anita said. "I imagine there are a lot of boys running in and out of your house these days."

Eve blushed and Iris commented, "How did you guess, Mother?"

"I think it's nice that someone still blushes in 1941." Jonas had come up to them, and he lightly ruffled Eve's long golden-brown hair. "Do you know what time it is?"

Anita looked at her platinum watch. "I can't believe it. It's almost time for the unveiling. Let's go."

She walked through the arch with Iris and Eve. "Come on, Jonas."

"I'll be right with you." Donald Brewster was whispering to Jonas, and the men laughed. "You go ahead." They moved off together into Jonas's den.

"I've got to see what's happening to the Giants," Donald said. "I've got fifty dollars on this game. It'll only take a minute."

"Help yourself. Like a drink?" Donald shook his head, and Jonas poured himself a bourbon.

"I can use one," Jonas said. "There's too much going on here for an old man." He sat down, stretched out his legs and took a contented sip of the bourbon. Donald was fiddling with the radio, and Jonas said, "You might have a little trouble with it today; it's been drifting a bit. I hope you can get New York clearly."

Jonas heard snatches of popular music—the clapping of hands, then an enthusiastic chorus of voices singing about Texas; the sound of a train, and the words about Chattanooga, which always amused him—then the mellifluous voice of a symphony concert announcer.

"In one moment the New York Philharmonic will present Shostakovich's Symphony Number One..."

"Damn!" Donald said. "That's not it."

"Wait a minute, Don." Jonas's voice was sharp. Another voice, a higher, more urgent voice, had cut in on the deep, elegant one. "Be quiet."

"We interrupt this broadcast," the penetrating voice said, "for a special news bulletin. Japanese forces have attacked the United States naval base at Pearl Harbor."

The two men were transfixed. Donald Brewster slowly straightened from his stooping position; Jonas sat stunned, his legs still stretched out, holding the empty whiskey glass stiffly in his hand.

They listened numbly as the voice went on: At seven fifty-five that morning, bombs had begun to fall on the sleeping installation at Pearl Harbor. It was the worst defeat in American history. The Army's Schofield Barracks and other bases were wrecked and burning; the Air Corps' Hickam, Bellows and Wheeler fields were rubble. One hundred and eighty-eight American planes had been destroyed, most on the ground, and another sixty-three severely damaged. Worst of all, more than one thousand American men were dead, another two thousand wounded.

"My God." Donald Brewster sat down. "What does it mean?" He looked with glazed eyes at Jonas.

"War," Jonas answered briefly. They heard Anita calling. She opened the door.

"Really, you men are..." Her smile died on her face and her words faded to silence when she saw their expressions.

Anita heard the announcer's voice going on to describe the scene of the disaster. Bewildered, she looked at Jonas.

"The Japanese bombed Pearl Harbor," he said tersely.

She made a helpless, wordless sound, and leaned against the wall.

Jonas went to the radio and snapped it off. His face was grim and his eyes looked tortured. "That's enough for now. This is only the beginning. We'd better go and tell the others."

Anita nodded. Reluctantly she followed the two men from the room; they walked through the room of boisterous children, into the foyer where Rick and Rachel stood, waiting expectantly, amid Eve and Iris and all their friends, beside the table with the tall cake, still veiled, in the center.

By eight o'clock that night Anita was exhausted. The adult party had broken up at once and the children's party a few minutes later.

Iris and Rachel had been wonderful, Anita thought, laying

348

er head back against the cushions of the big ivory couch. A
resh fire was blazing and the rooms had been restored to
ristine order under Rachel's and Iris's supervision. Jonas
as taking a nap upstairs. Rick and Rachel, who had decided
o spend the night, were in their suite, listening to their radio.
heir son, tired out from the festivities, was already asleep.

By common consent Anita and Jonas had stopped listening
o the radio for the night. There would be time enough for
hat tomorrow, Jonas said grimly.

Suddenly the doorbell rang. Anita was startled; she had
ot even heard a car drive up, she had been so deep in her
reamy fatigue. She hurried to the door. Jon stood there,
oking down at her and smiling.

"Oh, my dear," she cried, "come in, come in."

He stepped across the threshold and took her in his arms,
ending from his great height to kiss her cheek. Then he
eleased her and said quietly, "I had to come home, Mother.
have something to tell you and Dad."

He looked gentler and sadder than she had ever known
im, and somehow the change in him increased his resem-
lance to Jonas. He might have been Jonas himself, long ago,
he thought, except for the deep black hair that was like her
wn.

She held out her hand to him and, without another word,
d the way to the living room. A faint stirring in the upper
all caught her ear, the opening of a door. Then she heard
ft footsteps coming down the carpeted stairs, the footsteps
f more than one.

The moment she had longed for, and dreaded, was at hand.
But she said calmly, "Sit down, my darling, and let me
ive you a drink. Did you come here straight from the plane?"

Jon nodded. He looked around the gracious room with an
lmost wistful expression. "God, it seems so long," he said.

She was handing him a glass of sherry when she heard
onas call out Jon's name, and turned to see him coming
rough the archway. Behind him were Rick and Rachel.
achel's eyes were wide with apprehension and her lips were
arted, in a kind of waiting. Quickly Anita looked at her
randson. Rick seemed to have caught Rachel's attitude; his
ce was solemn, but his eyes were bright with anticipation,
lmost as if this were a challenge he welcomed.

Then to Anita's joy Rick came forward, holding out his
ndamaged left hand, saying calmly, "Welcome home, Jon.
's been a long, long time."

349

Jon hesitated, then he too held out his hand and clasped his nephew's.

"Thanks, Rick. It has been a long time. Too long." He went to Rachel and kissed her on the cheek.

Rachel did not speak, but the waiting attitude of her body had relaxed, and she was able to smile at him. She moved closer to Rick, and he put his damaged arm around her waist.

"America's in trouble, it seems," Rick said to break the sudden silence. "And dammit, I won't be able to go."

"I'm going for you," Jon said.

They all looked at him.

"I've enlisted."

Anita exclaimed with concern, and started to protest. But then she saw Jonas's face. His pride in his son was overwhelming; it shone from him.

"Congratulations, Jon." Jonas touched his tall son on the shoulder.

Observing them all, Anita was overcome with a new emotion: she felt a renewal of the old hopes, the old determination and confidence.

No matter what dangers faced her son, whatever the perilous horrors the war would bring, they would triumph over the future as they had over the past.

And she suddenly remembered the phoenix, the mythical bird of renascence and healing, a sign of Scorpio, the symbol of the birth of Jonas Mark and Rick von Helsing. She knew in full then the splendor of their hope.

Someday the war would end, and all of them would be building again together, with horror and hate behind, finding peace in the reconstruction. Perhaps the world of cities, then, would soar from its very ashes, like the phoenix arising from the fire.

GREAT ADVENTURES IN READING

FREE FALL IN CRIMSON   14441 $2.95
by John D. MacDonald
*Travis McGee comes close to losing his status as a living legend
when he agrees to track down the killers who brutally murdered an
ailing millionaire.*

THE PAGAN LAND   14446 $2.95
by Thomas Marriott
*The story of a bold journey through the wilderness of nineteenth
century South Africa in search of a homeland and of love.*

CAPTIVE OF DESIRE   14448 $2.75
by Becky Lee Weyrich
*Even in the arms of the king, young Zephromae's cries are for her
childhood sweetheart, Alexander. But Alexander can no longer
protect her from the sly priest, the lust-mad prince, or the bitter
queen.*

MARRAKESH   14443 $2.50
by Graham Diamond
*Magic and miracles, satanic evil and everlasting love. This is an
exotic adventure even more enchanting than the Arabian Nights.*

BRAGG #1: BRAGG'S HUNCH   14449 $2.25
by Jack Lynch
*The first book in a new action series. Bragg finds himself in the
middle of a deadly crossfire when he is hired to investigate who's
been threatening the life of an ex-hood.*

Buy them at your local bookstore or use this handy coupon for ordering.

COLUMBIA BOOK SERVICE, CBS Inc.
275 Mally Road, P.O. Box FB, Madison Heights, MI 48071

Please send me the books I have checked above. Orders for less than 5 books
must include 75¢ for the first book and 25¢ for each additional book to cover
postage and handling. Orders for 5 books or more postage is FREE. Send check
or money order only. Allow 3-4 weeks for delivery.

Cost $_____   Name_____

Sales tax*_____   Address_____

Postage _____   City_____

Total $_____   State_____ Zip_____

*The government requires us to collect sales tax in all states except AK, DE,
MT, NH and OR.*

Prices and availability subject to change without notice.   **8239**

CURRENT CREST BESTSELLERS

☐ **THE MASK OF THE ENCHANTRESS** 24418 $3.2
by Victoria Holt
Suewellyn knew she wanted to possess the Mateland family castle
but having been illegitimate and cloistered as a young woman, onl
a perilous deception could possibly make her dream come true.

☐ **THE HIDDEN TARGET** 24443 $3.5
by Helen MacInnes
A beautiful young woman on a European tour meets a handsom
American army major. All is not simple romance however when sh
finds that her tour leaders are active terrorists and her young arm
major is the chief of NATO's antiterrorist section.

☐ **BORN WITH THE CENTURY** 24295 $3.5
by William Kinsolving
A gripping chronicle of a man who creates an empire for his family
and how they engineer its destruction.

☐ **SINS OF THE FATHERS** 24417 $3.9
by Susan Howatch
The tale of a family divided from generation to generation by grea
wealth and the consequences of a terrible secret.

☐ **THE NINJA** 24367 $3.5
by Eric Van Lustbader
They were merciless assassins, skilled in the ways of love and th
deadliest of martial arts. An exotic thriller spanning postwar Japa
and present-day New York.

Buy them at your local bookstore or use this handy coupon for ordering.

COLUMBIA BOOK SERVICE, CBS Inc.
32275 Mally Road, P.O. Box FB, Madison Heights, MI 48071

Please send me the books I have checked above. Orders for less than 5 book
must include 75¢ for the first book and 25¢ for each additional book to cov
postage and handling. Orders for 5 books or more postage is FREE. Send che
or money order only. Allow 3-4 weeks for delivery.

Cost $_____ Name_____

Sales tax*_____ Address_____

Postage _____ City_____

Total $_____ State_____ Zip_____

*The government requires us to collect sales tax in all states except AK, D
MT, NH and OR.

Prices and availability subject to change without notice.

822